"I'LL NEVER GET MARRIED."

"You'll change your mind someday," Chris told Callie.

"What makes you say that?"

He laughed lightly, surprising her with his apparent and rare good mood. "Because you're young and pretty and resourceful and strong. Those are powerful attractions to a man. Young men will be calling on you plenty, and someday one will come along who makes your toes curl."

"My toes curl?"

"That's how—" He hesitated. "Somebody I knew a long time ago described it to me that way once."

Callie frowned. Was it his wife? She was afraid to ask. "That's a funny way to put it. How can a man make your toes curl?"

"It's just a figure of speech."

Callie thought a moment. "This person—you made *her* toes curl?"

He took a long time to reply. "Seems so," he answered quietly.

A tiny tremor of something Callie could not quite name softly rushed through her, and she found herself squeezing her toes. *"Good Lord!"* she thought. *"Is that what he's talking about?"*

BOOK YOUR PLACE ON OUR WEBSITE AND MAKE THE READING CONNECTION!

We've created a customized website just for our very special readers, where you can get the inside scoop on everything that's going on with Zebra, Pinnacle and Kensington books.

When you come online, you'll have the exciting opportunity to:

- View covers of upcoming books
- Read sample chapters
- Learn about our future publishing schedule (listed by publication month *and author*)
- Find out when your favorite authors will be visiting a city near you
- Search for and order backlist books from our online catalog
- Check out author bios and background information
- Send e-mail to your favorite authors
- Meet the Kensington staff online
- Join us in weekly chats with authors, readers and other guests
- Get writing guidelines
- AND MUCH MORE!

**Visit our website at
http://www.zebrabooks.com**

LOVE'S
BOUNTY

Rosanne Bittner

Zebra Books
Kensington Publishing Corp.

http://www.zebrabooks.com

ZEBRA BOOKS are published by

Kensington Publishing Corp.
850 Third Avenue
New York, NY 10022

First Printing: May, 2000
10 9 8 7 6 5 4 3 2 1

Printed in the United States of America

There is no greater wonder than the way the face of a young woman fits into a man's mind, and stays there, and he could never tell you why; it just seems it was the thing he wanted.

"Catriona"
—Robert Louis Stevenson

Chapter One

Late May, 1884

Callie walked slowly around the hanging platform, hardly aware of the bustle of people around her, the clatter of wagons, dogs barking, children laughing and screaming, playing tag. The hanging planned for tomorrow had turned the streets of Rawlins, Wyoming, into a virtual circus, with people coming in from as far away as Cheyenne to watch the gruesome event.

A train whistle wailed in the distance, and she did not doubt the train's passenger cars were stuffed with more gawkers. A hanging was big news. Whole families were coming in to watch. After all, seeing men justly punished was a good lesson to children, showing what could happen if you make the wrong choices in life.

Callie was herself curious. The newspaper said a good hangman fixed things so a man's neck would break instantly once the noose whipped tightly around his throat. Otherwise he'd kick for a while. She hoped that if she ever found her mother's murderers, their necks wouldn't break right away. She *wanted* to see them kick.

The smell of fresh lumber permeated her nostrils as she studied the sturdy crossbar, which displayed three drops of heavy rope, each with a beckoning noose at its end. A sudden gust of wind swirled particles of sawdust into her face then, forcing her to look away and cough. She blinked and rubbed at her eyes as she walked around where she could be out of the wind.

With the sun behind her, she could better see the professional hangman who stood atop the platform looking like the grim reaper. According to the town newspaper, his name was Jack Krebbs. A tall and bony man, with a cracked and weathered face, his attire fit his profession. The black frock coat and tall black hat reminded her more of a mortician than a hangman, but then, she supposed there wasn't much difference. Men of each profession relied on death for their income, but someone had to do this.

The men to be hung were train robbers, men bent on getting rich quickly and easily. The railroad had presented a new way to do just that. These men had killed innocent people during their robbery. She could not tolerate thieves, especially those who would kill to get what they wanted. How could a man enjoy his money when he got it that way?

She pulled a hand-knitted shawl closer around her narrow shoulders. In spite of a week of abnormally hot weather, there was a chill in the air today, maybe because of the gray clouds that spoke of death. Whatever the reason, her simple calico dress suddenly felt too thin. A person couldn't depend on the weather this time of year, not in Wyoming. Heck, many times she'd hung out wash in warm sunshine in February, only to huddle inside against a May snowstorm. The mountains liked to fool a person that way. Sometimes she pictured them talking to each other, planning their next surprise.

That was when she was little, when she could tell her stories to her mother. God, she missed her. Ellie Hobbs's passing wouldn't be so unbearable if she could have helped the woman . . . if her death had not been the horror that haunted her sleep every night.

The platform's trapdoors suddenly banged open, interrupting her thoughts and making Callie gasp and jump back. Her gaze darted toward the hangman, whose hand was still on the lever that controlled the doors, and she realized he was testing the door springs one last time.

"Come away from there, Callie!" Sheriff Taylor told her. "It isn't good for you to watch these things."

Callie turned to scowl at the man, whose gray hair and potbelly reminded her of her father. They'd been good friends before her father got himself kicked in the head by Buster, a big, sometimes ornery plow horse. Her mother had shot that horse, but Callie never really blamed the animal. Clayton Hobbs and Buster just plain never did get along, and sometimes her pa was kind of mean to the horse.

After her father's death, her mother managed to keep the farm going, even raised a few horses and cattle . . . until the day the outlaws came.

"I'm eighteen years old now, Sheriff Taylor. I might still have freckles and I know I'm not much for size, but I'm old enough to *be* anyplace I want and *watch* anything I want."

She thought how Rawlins could use a new sheriff, especially since the arrival of the railroad had brought so many new settlers. Court Taylor spent most of his time sitting on the front porch of the jailhouse, drinking coffee and eating biscuits and cookies townspeople brought to him, or having a smoke with one of the business owners. He could handle the common drunk who might get riled and start a fight in one of the town taverns, but if any big trouble rose, Court usually telegraphed for help from soldiers or a U.S. marshal.

Rawlins was growing in size, and so was Court Taylor, physically. His big belly made it hard for him to chase anyone down, and his two deputies weren't much help. Sam Tate and Johnny Corbin were both family men who were not eager to put their lives on the line for any cause.

"Besides," she added, "it does my heart good to watch bad men die." She walked closer to the sheriff so she didn't have to shout above the crowd.

Taylor looked down at her with a frown, putting his hands on his hips authoritatively. Callie thought how his sunburned nose looked extra red against his white mustache. It was almost comical.

"A hanging is just more violence, Callie Hobbs," he told her. "You've seen enough death and violence to last a lifetime. Besides, I let you come to the jail and look at these men, and you said they aren't the ones you're looking for, so why don't you just go home? Watching these three hang won't erase what happened to your mother. Get out of here and try to forget. Find some peace, Callie. Let it go for once and for all."

Callie raised her chin. "I will *never* find peace, Sheriff Taylor, until I see the men who killed my ma hanging from nooses just like these men," she answered. "Or dead some other way; don't matter to me *how* they die. And I didn't come here just to watch the hanging, Sheriff. I came to talk to the man who brought those murderers in. The paper said he'd be back to watch, that he gets another five hundred dollars once the deed is done. Besides that, he supposedly watches the men he captures hang, whenever possible. I expect that for some reason he takes pleasure in it. I reckon that's his business, but it means he must be ruthless, and that's the kind of man I need. I want you to point him out for me. I intend to hire him."

Taylor frowned, folding his arms in front of him, looking big as a bear to Callie, with his huge belly and his big arms and shoulders, a mixture of muscle and fat. He stood a good six feet, big, like her pa was. "Hire him for what?"

"What do you think? To help me find my ma's killers."

Taylor sighed and shook his head, his hands again moving to his hips. "Callie, it's been over a year, and there's been no trace of them. I couldn't find them, soldiers couldn't find them, and the U.S. marshal couldn't find them. How do you think a bounty hunter totally unfamiliar with the matter will find them, especially after over a year since the crime. Where in heck would he even begin to look?"

"I have some ideas."

"Like what?"

"That's between me and the bounty hunter."

He shook his head. "Callie, your pa and I were good friends. I feel responsible for you, especially now that your ma's dead too. I've asked you time and again to just sell that farm and move into town, where you'll be safe, meet yourself some nice young man who can take care of you, and—"

"I can take care of myself, thank you. And I'm not ready to let go of the farm yet. There's too many memories there. And Pa was good at paying his bills, so I don't owe any money. I even have a little saved, enough to maybe pay that bounty hunter."

Taylor drew in his breath in a long sigh. "Christian Mercy comes high."

"Christian Mercy?" Callie frowned. "His name is *Christian Mercy?*"

"Yes, ma'am."

Callie shook her head. "What kind of a name is that for a *bounty* hunter?"

Taylor shrugged. "A name is a name. He's damn good, so they say. I doubt he'll help you out, since we don't even know the names of the men who killed your mother, so technically there is no bounty on them—no reason for the man to go after them."

"Sure there is! They raped and killed my *mother!*"

The sheriff pushed back his hat. "Callie, bounty hunters hunt men for the *money,* not because of what they did."

"Well, I don't believe you. I think most of them must have more reason than that—something burning in their insides that makes them want to go after bad men."

Taylor watched her sadly. "And you're an innocent who doesn't understand a damn thing about men like Christian Mercy. You've got no business trying to hire the likes of him. Men like that don't have hearts. He won't care about your mother, or your own little broken heart, or the fact that you're alone now."

A wagon clattered by, stirring up a cloud of dust. Callie

moved up onto the boardwalk. "Well, now, I expect all of that is for me to find out, isn't it?"

"Callie, you've got to let this go. I've got U.S. marshals all over asking questions, talking to other men they bring in, seeing if they can find somebody who knows somebody who knows anything about what happened at your ranch. That's the best we can do. Hiring a bounty hunter to look for men who don't even have a bounty on their heads, men who don't fit the descriptions of wanted men we're aware of . . . it just won't do you any good at all."

Callie fought tears, absolutely hating it when anger and frustration made her want to cry. "Sheriff, I have to do *something* myself or go crazy. Every one of those men's faces is carved into my memory as clear as seeing my own face in the mirror. The least I can do for my mother is find the men who killed her and see that they *pay* for it! Are you going to introduce me to the man who brought in these train robbers, or do I have to march into every tavern, hotel room, and rooming house in town, looking for him?"

Taylor rubbed the back of his neck, shaking his head again. "I'll see if I can find him."

"Have him meet me out back of Chet Willis's stables."

Taylor looked around, pressing his lips together in frustration. "You don't even know what kind of man he is. Lord, girl, he kills men for money. Maybe it's not *safe* for you to meet with him alone."

Callie shrugged. "He goes after men who break the law. I doubt he'd turn around and break the law himself. Besides, there's enough people in town right now that a man couldn't get away with much without being noticed or without people hearing someone scream. And I can scream darn loud, had plenty of practice calling Pa in from the fields."

Taylor grinned resignedly. "You're too damn stubborn for your own good."

"Thank you for looking. I'll be at the stables." Callie marched off, dodging her way through the unusually crowded boardwalk. She passed a vendor selling medicine, another selling hats. Yet another was trying to sell small wooden carvings of hanging platforms, little pieces of rope and all.

"Something to remind the children of the wages of sin," he told parents.

In the distance the train whistle blew again, and Callie thought how convenient trains would have been for her parents when they first came out here in 1860 by covered wagon, six years before she was born. Her father had dreams of going all the way to California to look for gold, but he'd come across a family returning from there who told him finding that gold was not nearly as easy as some made it out to be, told him he'd be better off picking up a good piece of free land and staking it out for himself. Clayton Hobbs had done just that.

Callie remembered how unhappy her mother seemed when she was growing up, silently putting up with the hardships of settling in this harsh land, often talking wistfully about what life had been like back East. Callie knew Ellie Hobbs stayed only because of Callie's pa. The ranch became his dream, and a woman's place was with her husband. For her poor mother to die the way she did . . . it just wasn't fair.

She reached the stables, where her own horse was being held for her. She nodded to Chet Willis. "I'll be picking up my horse soon," she told him. "I'm meeting someone here first."

Willis nodded in reply, and Callie walked around behind the stables and climbed up on a fence to sit and wait for the man who'd caused all this commotion by bringing in three wanted train robbers. She tried to picture what he'd be like, imagining a burly, mean-looking, mean-spirited gunslinger who smelled bad and needed a shave. Oh, well. Who cared, as long as he was good at finding outlaws?

Chapter Two

An hour passed before Callie noticed someone walking toward her from around the front of the stables. He looked too young and too clean to be the bounty hunter she was expecting. He wore guns on both sides of his slender hips, and the gun belt that held them was slung low and packed with bullets.

Just in case he *was* the man she was supposed to meet, she took a close inventory as he approached. He looked strong, his upper torso obviously muscular from the way his shirt fit. The shirt was a simple white cotton front-button shirt, and he wore the same denim pants most men wore now. They were good, rugged pants, well suited for the rough life of a rancher or miner.

This man's pants fit him snugly. The brown leather boots that showed at the bottom of his pant legs looked worn but in good condition.

He was watching her now as he came closer. He wore a common wide-brimmed hat, and from under it she saw a few straight shocks of sand-colored hair that became wavy where it touched his shirt collar at the back of his neck. She thought how although he looked clean shaven, he needed a haircut. He stopped to light a cigarette before finally coming close enough that she could see his face better.

Lordy, he's maybe thirty, she thought. Thirty seemed old to her but still too young for what she expected. An emotion she couldn't even describe shot through her chest when she first met his eyes. They were the most amazing blue! His nose was straight, his chin square, his build just about right, with broad shoulders and powerful-looking forearms that showed from his rolled-up shirtsleeves.

He was just about the best-looking man she'd ever seen. The thought surprised her, since after witnessing what happened to her mother she felt no appreciation for any man in a womanly sense. Such feelings had left her. She acknowledged that he was simply quite handsome, and that was that.

When he reached to take the cigarette from his mouth, she noticed his hands also looked strong. They weren't soft and well manicured like Eddy Lewis's. Eddie was the young banker who'd shown an interest in her. They were tanned and weathered, and showed a dusty look, like when a man had been grooming his horse.

"You Callie Hobbs?" he asked, unsmiling.

Callie climbed down from the fence, realizing then that he stood perhaps not quite six feet tall. He wasn't huge all over like Sheriff Taylor, just a good, strong-looking man. "I am," she answered. "You the bounty hunter?"

He put the cigarette to his lips and took another draw from it before answering with a nod. Callie saw something there, a coldness. Yes, there was at least one little thing she'd expected. He was capable of no feelings at all when necessary.

"You don't *look* like a bounty hunter."

He kept the cigarette between his lips as he answered. "What the hell is a bounty hunter *supposed* to look like?"

Still that coldness there . . . no hint of a smile.

Callie shrugged, folding her arms. "I don't know. I just figured you'd be older, meaner-looking."

Now he showed a little smirk. "Sorry to disappoint you."

Those cold blue eyes showed no particular emotion as he

raked her body with a discerning gaze that made her stiffen. Were all men rapists at heart? Was she taking a chance in planning to travel alone with this man in search of her mother's killers? Maybe he was just as bad as some of the men he searched for after all. Sheriff Taylor could be right about her being wrong to trust this one just because he tracked down outlaws and brought them to justice.

Lordy! Here came the urge to cry again. She turned away. "Maybe we should just forget this."

There was a pause before he answered. "I don't even know what it is I'm supposed to forget. Sheriff Taylor just said there was a young lady waiting here back of the stables with a job for me. He didn't explain. He just seemed kind of peeved about it and said to let you explain."

Callie walked a few feet away. "He's peeved because he thinks he has to watch out for me on account of he was good friends with my folks and kind of watched me grow up." She turned to face him, squinting from the sunlight. "You called me a young lady. Does that mean you have respect for women? I mean, could a woman travel alone with the likes of you and trust you to be a gentleman?"

Now he snickered, making her feel embarrassed and angry. He took the cigarette from his lips before answering. "Well, now, I don't know about a woman, but you don't exactly look like one to me. How old are you? Sixteen, maybe? And you look like you weigh all of a hundred pounds with your clothes on."

Callie placed her hands on her hips and glared at him. "I am *eighteen* years old, mister. I don't even know what I weigh, but I guarantee I'm a lot stronger than you know! Besides that, I've helped work a ranch and helped farm most all my life. I can wield a pitchfork, herd cattle, slop hogs, haul feed, drive oxen, harness a team of plow horses and walk behind them, ride good as any man, and I'm not bad with a rifle or even a six-gun! I'm not afraid of anything, and I'm no stranger to violence! I seen my pa get his head kicked in by a horse, and I seen my ma raped and beat up and then murdered! Don't be calling me a kid, because I'm *not!* You can wipe that grin right off your pretty face and get serious. You're a bounty hunter, and I'm in need of one. Plain and simple. You want a job or not?''

His eyebrows shot up in obvious surprise at her response. ''You still haven't told me what the job is.''

''Can't you figure it out? I just told you I saw my mother raped and murdered. The men who did it rode off with some of our prize horses. I intend to find them and watch them all hang, unless you shoot them instead. It doesn't make much difference to me, long as they're dead and can't do the same thing to some other defenseless, innocent woman, if they haven't already.''

He took one more drag on his cigarette, then threw it down and stepped it out. He walked a few feet away, pushing back his hat and staring at the horizon as though lost in thought for the moment. ''Is there a bounty on them?''

''No.''

''Then how do you expect to pay me?''

''I own a ranch. Ma and I worked it after Pa was killed. When she died, it became mine alone. It's worth good money now that the railroad's come. I'll sign it over to you. Whatever you get for it is yours.''

He looked back at her without turning fully around. ''Where does that leave you? How would you fend for yourself after that?''

''I'd find a way. I'm not afraid of hard work. Ten gets you one that I'll manage on my own. I don't intend to depend on a man for survival, that's for sure. Not after—'' She hesitated, again feeling the stabbing pain that always came to her insides at the memory of her mother's murder. ''Never mind. Will you take the job or not?''

He shook his head before finally facing her. ''And you intend to go with me on this search?''

''That's the only way to find them. I know their faces like the back of my hand. I'll never forget them.''

''When did this happen?''

"A year ago. Nobody has been successful in finding anybody who might know the men who did it. They just seemed to disappear off the face of the earth, only I know they *are* out there somewhere."

"And where do you intend to look for them?"

She folded her arms, hoping that he just might take the job. "The one place where the soldiers wouldn't go, and neither would the U.S. marshal, on account of it's too dangerous for lawmen."

He rolled his eyes. "Not the Outlaw Trail."

"Yes, sir. The Outlaw Trail."

"You intend to go there?"

"I told you, I'm not afraid. And I *can* handle a gun. I trust you're pretty decent with them two you wear."

"Those two. Have you had any schooling?"

"Who cares?" She pouted.

"Not me. Just curious. Your use of the English language could stand some correcting."

"What?" Callie could not resist light laughter. "You're a bounty hunter, not an English teacher!"

He sighed, straightening his shoulders. "It just so happens I *did* used to teach."

Callie's eyes widened in surprise. "Lordy! Are you telling the honest truth?"

"I never lie."

She sobered, dumbfounded by the admission. "How in heck does an English teacher become a bounty hunter?"

"That's *my* business." Now the blue eyes that had shown a small hint of friendliness and humor turned cold again. "And I don't like the idea of a pretty little thing like you venturing out along the Outlaw Trail. You said you saw your mother raped and murdered. Something goes wrong out there, the same thing could happen to you."

Pretty little thing? He thought she was pretty? "I'll take the chance. And if you're any good with them . . . those guns, I won't have to worry about it."

"A man has only one set of eyes, and they can't see backward, which is where most murderers like to stand, *behind* a man instead of in front of him.''

"Yeah? Well, I have a feeling you can sense when somebody is behind you. You've searched out plenty of outlaws, and you're still alive.''

He gave out another long sigh and turned away again, throwing back his head for a quiet moment, then pacing for another few minutes. "I need to think about this,'' he finally told her. "And I want to see the deed to that ranch.''

"I'll show it to you. I'll take you out there tomorrow, in fact, after the hanging. You'll see that it's a nice place. Five hundred acres of good grazing land. It can be ranched, or it can be sold off to settlers for homes. Rawlins is growing pretty good now.''

"Sounds like it's worth a lot more than the men we're after.''

" 'Course it is. But to me, finding them is worth *ten* ranches like mine. I just want them found and hanged, mister, no matter what the cost.''

His gaze moved over her appreciatively again, making her fold her arms a little tighter around herself defensively.

"And if you get any ideas while we are out at the ranch alone, or any other time, I'll shoot you dead,'' she added. "That's a fact.''

For some reason, she suddenly could not look away from those intense blue eyes as he adjusted his hat. "Well, now, little girl, I don't think you have to worry about that. Consequently, *I* don't have to worry about getting shot.''

The remark made her feel like shooting him then and there. She didn't *want* him to get any wrong ideas, but for him to say that was next to impossible made her angry. The obvious insult made her boil inside. She squinted in anger as she answered, "Are you saying you'll help me?''

After another long gaze he turned. "I'm saying I'll think about it. Where's your ranch?''

"North of town. We'll take the Old Mountain Trail about a mile west of Rawlins and then go north. After about three more miles there's a gate with a sign on it—two C's cutting through each other. My pa named the ranch after me and him. His name was Clayton Hobbs. I know he always wished I was a boy, but I'm what he got, and I've worked just as good as a son would have.''

"No siblings?"

Callie frowned. "What are siblings?" Again she felt embarrassed when she sensed he wanted to laugh at the question. He was forcing himself to stay serious, she just knew it.

"Siblings are brothers or sisters," he answered.

She looked down to hide her embarrassment at not knowing the meaning of the word. "No. Just me."

"Well, it appears you turned out just as good as a son."

Callie shrugged. "I tried." She looked away. "That's why I didn't have much schooling, except what my ma taught me. Farming and ranching take hard work. That doesn't leave time for what Pa called fancy schooling." She looked straight at him again, holding her chin higher. "But I can read and write and spell pretty decent. And I know my numbers." Why on earth was she explaining this to a complete stranger who killed men or brought them in for hanging—for money? She still could not quite believe that was the man she looked at now.

"Seems like you've done well, considering. And your pa was wrong to think you didn't need schooling."

"Well, that doesn't much matter now. You coming out to the ranch, then, for sure?"

He nodded. "I'll come after the hanging."

"Fine. I intend to watch it myself."

He was already walking away. "See you then, Miss Hobbs."

Callie watched him leave without another word. She had more questions, but apparently he'd said all he meant to say for then. She shook her head. Christian Mercy sure wasn't anything like she'd imagined he would be. What the heck was she getting herself into?

Chapter Three

Callie was glad she took a room in town the night before. That way she could be one of the first ones at the hanging platform and assure herself a front-row view. She sat on the boardwalk in front of Hank's Supply watching the town come alive as peddlers rolled up the canvas flaps of their wagons and again displayed their various wares. Whole families began to gradually gather, taking their places around the platform area. Most women dressed as though going to church, their children cleaned up the same way, many men wearing suits.

Callie again wore a simple, short-sleeved calico dress. She really didn't have anything fancier. She was aware that some women thought short sleeves on a dress were too revealing, but those were mostly women who'd come to the area from the East. Anybody born and raised out here, or at least here since a baby, didn't worry much about what was proper and what wasn't. The only thing you worried about was being comfortable, and sometimes that even meant wearing pants instead of dresses when you were running a ranch. She'd done that too, and she didn't care what anybody thought about it. She'd led more a boy's life than a girl's anyway. This calico dress was about as fancy as she'd ever dressed, and there were no ruffles or frills about it.

She never did learn how to put her hair up fancy. Today she had simply brushed it out, pulling the sides back with combs. Nothing more. She didn't even own a frilly hat, not even a straw one. Her only hats were regular wide-brimmed hats for riding the range. She'd tried on one of her mother's fancy straw bonnets once and felt silly in it.

"Callie dear, what on earth are you doing here?"

Callie stood up to greet Betty Sooner, who helped her husband run Hank's Supply. Betty and Hank had both been good to Callie since her mother's death, giving her wholesale prices on supplies whenever possible and always buying any eggs and potatoes she brought to them.

"I came to watch the hanging," Callie answered, "just like everybody else." She noticed that Betty, too, was dressed up for the occasion. She wore a lovely brown taffeta dress trimmed with white lace at the shoulders, the bodice, and at the ends of the sleeves. A flowered hat was perched on her head, hiding most of the woman's graying hair, which Callie knew was twisted into a knot on top of her head. Betty always wore her hair that way. She noticed that today the woman even wore white lace gloves.

Betty put her hands on Callie's shoulders before she spoke again. "Honey, you shouldn't do this. You've been through so much. And when are you going to sell that ranch and come live with us, where you'll be safe?"

Callie reached up and took hold of the woman's hands. "I might do just that. And I thank you for always offering, Betty. Fact is, I might be giving up the ranch in a couple of months. I'll explain after the hanging. We'll have more time to talk then."

Betty squeezed her hands. "I'm glad you're finally considering it. We worry about you out there all by yourself, especially after—"

"I know." Callie let go of her hands. "I just couldn't bring myself to leave right away. That ranch meant so much to my folks, and they're both buried there. It wasn't fair to neither one of them, how they died. And Pa always meant for me to go on living there, except he thought it would be with a husband, someday in the future. He never thought he'd die so young. Ma neither." She turned to watch the building crowd. "I guess life just doesn't turn out like anybody plans it."

Betty patted her shoulder. "Well, I don't know what *your* plans are now, but you be sure to talk to us before you make any big decisions. Promise me that."

Callie knew Betty and Hank would both disagree passionately with what she really planned to do, but she also knew she'd have to tell them so they wouldn't wonder what had happened to her once she left with Christian Mercy. "I promise," she replied.

"And do come with us after the hanging," Betty added. "We're going to have a picnic with the Reeses—fried chicken, biscuits, and lots more."

Callie faced her again. "I'd like that, ma'am, but I have other plans after the hanging. I have to go back to the ranch."

"Oh, my dear, can't it wait?"

"No, ma'am, it can't. I do thank you though." Callie turned away again, not wanting to have to explain at the moment. Preacher Holliday came through the crowd then, leading a robed choir from the Methodist church, who all sang "Rock of Ages." She looked around for Christian Mercy, still hardly able to get over the irony of his name. He was nowhere to be seen, and she wondered if he would really keep his promise to come with her after the hanging to look at her ranch. A young girl and boy ran past her then, up the steps, around behind her, then jumped off the boardwalk. A woman darted past, chasing them. She scolded them soundly when she caught them and herded them back toward where their father waited. She apologized to Callie as she hurried by.

"It's all right," Callie answered. She watched the woman rejoin her husband, who lifted the boy to his shoulders. The sight made her wonder if she would ever be a wife and a mother. Just then she couldn't imagine being intimate with any man, even if she thought she loved him.

The crowd quieted as Preacher Holliday began a sermon about the price of sin. He went on for a good hour and a half. Children grew restless. A few cried. Some ran off to play, and this time their mothers did not bother chasing after them. Finally the preacher finished, and the choir began more hymns. Most joined in, singing "Shall We Gather at the River," "Love Divine," then "Abide with Me."

The crowd parted again, and Callie stretched her neck to see that this time it was the three robbers and murderers who were making their way toward the hanging platform, their hands tied behind their backs. Behind them walked Sheriff Taylor and his deputies, as well as a U.S. marshal . . . and Christian Mercy. Callie was relieved to see him, fearing he'd changed his mind and planned to leave without helping her. The man wore a clean shirt, blue calico, a dark blue bandanna tied at his neck. He looked clean shaven, and from what she could tell, he'd gotten a haircut. The curls at his neck didn't show. He carried a repeating rifle, and he wore both his six-guns. The sheriff, his men, and the marshal also carried rifles.

Apparently they considered the men they herded toward the platform as very dangerous, and Callie couldn't help wondering at the fact that Christian Mercy had brought all three of them in on his own. *He must be pretty darn good,* she thought. It made her more confident that she'd picked the right man to help her find her mother's killers. She just wished these were the men, so her search would be done and over with. But none of them fit the faces burned into her memory.

The condemned men reached the steps going up to the platform, and the first man, the biggest, meanest-looking one, went to his knees and began sobbing. Callie could not feel sorry for him. He'd helped rob and kill innocent people. A little boy had been shot, and Callie did not doubt that was the one thing that had caused the jury who'd condemned them to ask for the death penalty for all three men. The three killers had been brought to Rawlins from Cheyenne because the parents of the dead little boy lived here. Willa and Tom Truan had insisted the men be executed right here in their hometown. They stood right in front of the hanging platform now, their faces as unmoving as stone. Beside them stood the little boy's older brother and sister, looking more awestruck than upset by the occasion.

Sheriff Taylor told the first man to get up and face just punishment. Callie knew from newspaper descriptions that he was the one called Conner Hayes. Remaining bent over, Hayes got to his feet; but then he suddenly rammed his head into Taylor's middle, sending the sheriff sprawling. Women screamed as he ran into the crowd. In a split second Christian Mercy was on him, ramming the butt end of his rifle into the middle of the man's back. Hayes cried out with pain and fell, landing with his face in mud left from a light rain during the night.

Mercy jerked the man to his feet as though he weighed nothing, even though Hayes was taller and heavier. "Get back where you belong!" Mercy growled, kicking the man's rear as he herded him back to where the deputies and the marshal held guns on the other two, forcing them up the steps.

"Why don't you just shoot me now, you goddamn son of a bitch!" Hayes yelled at Mercy.

Women gasped and covered their children's ears.

"Christian Mercy is just as bad as *we* are!" Hayes yelled at the crowd then. "He's a stinking, no-good killer who goes after men for money even if they're innocent! He should hang *with* us!"

Good, Callie thought. That was just the kind of man she needed. Still, what would it be like traveling with him?

People stared at Mercy as he kept poking Hayes with his rifle barrel, forcing him up the steps toward imminent death.

"Shooting is too good for you," Mercy growled at him. "Too quick and easy. I hope your neck doesn't break, Hayes. It will take you longer to die that way."

Yes! That was exactly Callie's desire for her mother's killers. Now Mercy was close enough that she could see that cold, deadly look in his blue eyes. Here was a man who could be as ruthless as necessary when the occasion called for it.

"Christian Mercy! You hear that, folks?" Hayes yelled. "His name is Christian Mercy! How's that for a name for a *bounty* hunter! It's almost sacriligous, like taking the Lord's name in vain!"

"Shut up!" Mercy told him.

Hayes faced him. "Why? I'm gonna die anyway, Mercy, thanks to you! What are you gonna do to me now?"

Mercy started to turn away, then suddenly he whirled and slammed his rifle butt across Hayes's mouth. The man stumbled backward, and women screamed and gasped. Even a few men looked away, and one woman fainted when blood instantly began pouring from Hayes's split cheek. Callie did not doubt that several of his teeth had been knocked loose.

Well, well, she thought, folding her arms and watching Mercy shove Hayes to his spot under a noose. While the man still reeled from the blow, the hangman slipped the noose around his neck. Mercy stepped back, standing to the side but remaining on the platform. Callie almost felt like shouting with joy at how he'd handled Conner Hayes, but curiosity overwhelmed her. What on earth had caused a young, handsome, educated man like Christian Mercy to turn into a ruthless, cold-blooded bounty hunter? He surely had good parents. Otherwise they would not have given their son such a name, and they would not have seen that he got enough education to actually teach English to others.

The sheriff read the charges and the sentence, and all the while Hayes shouted obscenities at the crowd and at Christian Mercy. The preacher then led everyone in another hymn, obviously trying to ease their emotions after witnessing Mercy's violence and listening to Hayes's foul mouth. When the hymn was finished, Preacher Holliday asked each man about to die if he had any last words. Hayes could not speak. He simply spit blood at Mercy, hitting the man's clean calico shirt. The second man, much younger, just shook his head.

"I'm sorry," he said quietly. "That's all I can say."

The third man glared at Christian Mercy. "All I want to say is that I hope Mr. Christian Mercy burns in hell *with* us once he dies," he announced. "And I hope he, too, dies a violent death!"

Mercy showed no particular emotion at the words. He simply stood there watching, an ugly spot of bloody spittle on the front of his shirt.

The hangman placed a black cloth over the head of each man then, and Preacher Holliday prayed for them. After one more hymn, "Amazing Grace," the preacher stepped down. Sheriff Taylor held a stopwatch and announced that sixty seconds were left before the hangman pulled the lever that would send all three men to their death.

The crowd grew so still that Callie was sure she could hear the outlaws breathing as the black cloth over their faces moved in and out against their mouths. Hayes let out an odd, gurgling sound, and the younger man in the middle began crying.

"Burn in hell, Mercy!" the third man shouted. "Burn! Burn! Burn!"

With that the sheriff nodded his head, and the hangman pulled the lever. Gasps of "Oh!" moved through the crowd almost in unison. Another woman fainted, and most had looks of horror on their faces. Children just stared in wonder.

Conner Hayes wiggled, obviously still not dead, and for the first time Callie saw a true smile come across Christian Mercy's face, the most evil smile she'd ever seen. She swallowed in trepidation, thinking how there was nothing Christian or merciful about the man.

Chapter Four

Chris was not sure what to make of the woman/child riding ahead of him, straddled on the back of her horse like a man but wearing a calico dress. She'd thrown a blanket over her legs to cover them, but that didn't help much when it came to a man's imagination. Still, half of him wouldn't be interested anyway, considering she looked barely sixteen and in some ways acted even younger. The other half of him argued she was old enough to be considered a woman, one who'd said she would "shoot him dead" if he tried anything. The statement made him smile, but he suspected she meant every word.

He had no idea why he agreed to go see her ranch. Now she probably figured he meant to help her with her crazy idea of traveling the Outlaw Trail in search of her mother's killers. That was about the dumbest, riskiest thing he'd ever heard of, and the only reason he even considered it was because he had a feeling the damn fool of a girl would try it by herself if she couldn't find anyone to go with her.

She was a stubborn, determined young lady. She was also pretty. He had not failed to notice she had a pleasantly full bosom in spite of the fact that the rest of her seemed too small to be filled out that way. Her freckles gave her the look of a lingering child inside a woman's body. He figured she probably had a pretty smile, but so far he had not seen it. Lord knew she didn't have much to smile about.

Her brown eyes held a look of innocence in so many ways; but if she'd witnessed her mother being raped and killed, there was a part of her that had been forced to grow up real quick. The fact that she had watched the hanging without so much as a wince told him that.

She sat a horse damn well, knew what she was about when it came to that. This young lady had led a rugged life and would probably be just fine camping outside most of the time. It was difficult not to laugh at how she looked right then, in that dress, sitting the back of a horse, and wearing a plain old cowboy hat that looked too big for her. A man couldn't help feeling sorry for her. The main thing that made him unsure about helping her was having to take her along on his search. Not only was that dangerous for her, but it made things more dangerous for him. It only gave him double reason to have to watch his back when he took her to places like Robber's Roost and Brown's Park. If it weren't for those lovely breasts, he could maybe at least pass her off as a boy . . . maybe.

Her reddish-brown hair hung in wispy strings now, beat up by wind and dust since leaving town. The rhythmic way she rode her roan gelding was disturbing to a man. He decided to ride up beside her so he wouldn't have to watch her bouncing bottom; but when he did get beside her and glanced her way, her breasts also bounced rhythmically.

"Damn," he muttered under his breath.

"What?" she asked.

Chris turned to look straight ahead. "Much farther?" he asked.

"About a mile."

"You stay out here all alone?"

"Yes, sir. Me and my ma ran the place after Pa died, and then after she was—" She stopped midsentence and waited a moment before continuing. "After she was gone I just stayed on, hoping to take care of the place myself. I don't like admitting I can't do something, but it's all just too much for one person, man or woman. If you don't accept the ranch as payment, I'll just have to sell it to somebody and use the money to find me someone else to go after those outlaws. I'll find them one way or another, Mr. Mercy.''

"Call me Chris. Sir or Mr. Mercy both feel too formal to me.''

"They shouldn't. Heck, you were a schoolteacher once, right? I expect most everybody called you sir or Mr. Mercy.''

"Well, my teaching days are over, and what I do for a living now doesn't exactly compare.''

"I think it's just fine what you do. You go after men some others are too afraid to go after. And they are men who deserve what they get, whether you shoot them or they hang. I respect your courage and determination, Mr. Mercy. And for right now I don't feel right calling you by your first name. It's not proper.''

He glanced at her, but she stared straight ahead, a determined, hard line to her lips . . . lips that could be soft and inviting if she'd allow the woman in her to fly free. He tried to imagine how she'd look all done up with a fancy hairdo and a little color on her cheeks and lips, a pretty dress. . . .

"Weren't you afraid to stay out here alone, after what happened to your mother?''

She shrugged. "Sure I was, but I figured what happened to my ma was something that would probably never happen again. Besides, all the good horses and livestock got stole, so what was left for anybody to be interested in?''

Chris decided not to answer that one.

"This is a pretty good area around here,'' she continued. "We never had trouble like that before. I buried my ma, and I just . . . stayed. I didn't have any place else to go, and the ranch meant everything to my folks. I wanted to keep it alive— for them. But now I guess I'll have to give it up, one way or another.''

They rode on silently for a few minutes. "You buried your mother all by yourself?''

"Yes, sir."

Chris shook his head. "You're quite something, Miss Hobbs."

"You can call me Callie. You addressing me is different from me addressing you. You're older."

Chris frowned with irritation. "You make it sound like I'm old enough to be your father."

"Well? How old *are* you?"

Chris took a cigarette from his shirt pocket, along with a match. He struck the match with his thumbnail and lit the smoke before answering. "Thirty-two."

"That does sound *kind* of old to me."

"Well, it isn't."

"You ever been married, Mr. Mercy?"

The question struck a nerve. "I have. And I don't want to talk about it, just like I don't want to talk about why I quit teaching to go after wanted men. Got that straight?"

"Yes, sir." Callie kicked her horse into a faster lope and rode ahead of him. "Here we are!"

Chris watched her ride through the gate of the Double C. He followed, taking inventory along the way. The fences needed mending, but that was understandable. The land he saw on the way in looked damn good, green, good for grazing or farming, either one. And she was right about land like this being worth a lot now that the railroad had come to town.

After several minutes of riding, they approached a sturdy-looking log house. North of that was a huge corral and a large barn that looked in good shape. A few chickens scurried about, but other than that he saw no sign of livestock of any kind. Behind the house he could see a dried-up, weedy garden. Callie must have made up her mind that this year she would just let it all go, since she was determined to go find her mother's killers instead of running the ranch.

"Looks nice, doesn't it?" she asked.

"It does."

She waved her arm. "All the land beyond is just as good as what you saw coming in. And there's a waterfall against the mountains way at the back of the property that feeds a little creek where livestock can go and drink. Pa even dug us a well.'' She dismounted, apparently so intent on impressing him about the property that she forgot she wore a dress. She swung her leg over the back of the saddle as she got down, and Chris caught sight of white drawers. She walked her horse over to the well and cranked up a bucket of water, then carried it over to a trough in front of the house and poured the water into it.

''Come water your horse,'' she told him. ''You can come see the house inside. I can make you some coffee, something to eat, if you want.''

''Maybe just the coffee,'' he said, dismounting. He led his own horse to the trough, tying it and following her inside. He removed his hat and hung it over one post of a wooden chair that sat at what looked like a home-made table.

The house was pleasant and clean, with lace curtains at the windows and braided rugs on the pine plank floor. He could see that all of this was the product of two hardworking people ... actually three. Callie's folks had obviously worked hard to build a lovely and most likely profitable working ranch and farm ... only to have all of it cruelly taken from them through death. Now their only child was set to lose everything they had worked for. It made him feel guilty for even thinking about accepting it in return for finding her mother's killers, but without a bounty on their heads, a man had to see *some* kind of compensation. He wasn't going to go out there and risk his life for nothing.

''This is a real nice house,'' he told her.

''Thank you, Mr. Mercy.''

Callie lit some wood under a burner plate, then set the plate over it. She set an iron coffeepot on the plate, and from the way she hoisted it, Chris could tell it was already full of water. He watched her pry the lid off a can of coffee.

''I already ground some coffee so I could do this quicker. I like to have some ready for company so they don't wait so long.'' She scooped some of the grounds out and poured them into a strainer inside the coffeepot. ''There. It shouldn't take too long.'' She set the can of coffee aside. ''I have some fresh biscuits in the bread bin, or fresh bread. Some cookies too. Would you like any?''

He couldn't help a light smile at her eagerness to impress him with her proficiency. ''Maybe a biscuit with the coffee.''

''Fine.'' She opened the bread bin in the pantry and took out a basket of biscuits. She carried them to the table and sat down. ''Well, what do you think? I can even leave most of the furniture. I'll probably go live with Hank Sooner and his wife behind the supply store in town after we get back. I won't have any place else to go. You would be all set up here, either ready to ranch the place yourself or sell it for good money. I'll sign the deed over to you when we get back, and it's yours to do with what you want.''

Chris sighed, rubbing at his eyes. ''I don't like taking the only thing you have left, something your own parents built with blood, sweat, and tears. I don't feel right about it.''

''You don't have any choice if you intend to help me. If you don't take the ranch, I'll sell it outright and use the money to pay you. Same thing both ways. I just figured you'd rather have the ranch yourself. Then you'd have time to figure what you'd like to do with it. You could maybe lease it out to a neighboring farmer or rancher. It would be good, steady income for you. Or maybe by then you'd like to settle for a while, ranch it yourself instead of selling it. Rawlins is a nice place to live. It'll grow now that we have the railroad.''

Chris shook his head in wonder. ''That mind of yours never stops, does it? Always thinking ahead.''

''My pa taught me that. He was tough on me sometimes, but it was just because he wanted the best for me and wanted me to be able to take care of myself. He always said a person had to look out for his own self, because nobody else was going to do it for him ... or her. He also taught me to be practical about things. That's what I'm doing now. He'd want me to find Ma's killers, and I need help. Help takes money. I don't have any. All I have is this place.''

He ran a hand through his hair. ''And what if we don't find

the men you're looking for? What do I get for all my trouble and time?''

"I thought about that too. I'll still give you the ranch for your efforts. But you have to really try, give it a good three-month effort.''

"What will you live on during those three months? I've got money and can take care of myself, but I don't intend to put you up the whole time. You'll need coach fare. We'd take a stage up through Muddy Gap and into Lander, where we'd buy some good horses for the trip. I intend to leave my own horse boarded here until I can come back for him. We'd head up to Hole-in-the-Wall first, then proceed south. It's a long, long way. We could end up all the way down in El Paso, Texas. You're talking months of travel. Sometimes we'll stay in a rooming house or a hotel. We'll need supplies, meals—''

"I've got my and Ma's savings. I've got enough for that.''

"Got a good rifle?''

"Yes, sir. A good Winchester-Bonehill twelve-gauge double-barrel shotgun. Pa got it brand new just a couple of years before he died. I keep it oiled. It's in real good shape. I've shot several rabbits with it.''

"Good, because on the coach ride you might be using it to shoot at stage robbers.''

"What about Indians?''

"I don't think they'll be much of a problem. The Sioux and Cheyenne are more concerned with the Black Hills right now.'' Chris shifted in his chair. "Trouble is, once we get where we're going, you might have need of something with a longer range than a shotgun. I have two Winchester repeaters. One is a .44-caliber slide-action carbine. The other is a .45-caliber Hotchkiss magazine rifle. They're both pretty reliable, with true sites. Ever use rifles like that?''

"No, sir, but I expect I can handle pretty much any kind of firearm.''

Chris admired her confidence. "What about clothes? Dresses won't do.''

"I know that. I told you I usually wear pants. I've got plenty that fit me good. I'll dress real plain and practical so's I won't cause problems for you.''

Chris couldn't help a snicker. "Where we're going, it won't matter how you dress. Men are men, and having you along is going to be a headache." He almost regretted the words when he saw how she looked away, some of the excitement going out of her.

"I've learned a good lesson about how men can be," she answered. "I'll try real hard to cover up that I'm a woman."

A girl, he thought.

"And I don't mind sleeping under the stars or riding under the sun. I can ride all day without aching all over, and dirt and sweat don't bother me. I won't be a problem. I can hold my own, Mr. Mercy. You don't have to baby me."

"I can see that." What the hell was he doing, actually agreeing to this? "You'd have to follow every damn thing I tell you."

"I would."

"And if you did spot one of them, you wouldn't dare say a word in front of him. You'd have to wait and tell me later. Might save us getting our heads shot off."

"Yes, sir."

Chris frowned. "Wait a minute. Wouldn't they recognize you? And if they did, that means—" The coffeepot began to boil. "If you saw those men, then they saw you. And they don't sound like the kind of men who would leave you alone just because you look a little young. Why didn't they turn on you when they finished with your mother?"

She hung her head, and he saw a tear drip from her cheek. She quickly wiped angrily at her eyes and jumped up to grab the coffeepot. "They didn't see me." She poured him some coffee and set the pot back on the stove, away from the hot burner. "Better let this cool or it will get too strong," she said rather absently.

"How could they not see you?" Chris pressed her.

She swallowed, lowering her eyelids. "My ma saw them coming, and there were a lot of them, five, in fact. She'd left the rifle in the barn, so she couldn't shoot at them. She told me to . . . to get inside the wood box and not to come out no matter *what* happened. She begged me, made me promise on God's honor, said if anything went wrong, she couldn't stand going to her grave knowing the same thing might happen to me. I didn't want to do it, but I no sooner got into the wood box before one of them snuck in through a back window we'd left open. At the same time, the others kicked their way right through the front door. In no time at all they had hold of ma, and—''

Her shoulders jerked in a sob as she covered her face. "It was . . . awful! They took turns . . . shaming her . . . brutalizing her. I never felt such terror in my life . . . nor such awful, awful guilt! I'll never forgive myself! It just seems like . . . if I could find them . . . get them hanged . . . I'd have done something to help. But even that . . . won't erase my guilt.''

Chris had never felt more sorry for anyone in his life— except for his own dead wife . . . and little girl. If ever there was good cause to go after someone, this was it, even if she couldn't pay him. "Five men?''

She nodded, still sniffling.

"Did you catch any of their names?''

She raised her head and jerked in another sob, wiping at more tears. "Just one. Terrence, I think it was. I could see through a crack in the wood box. I remember all their faces . . . every last . . . one of them!'' She took a handkerchief from a pocket in the skirt of her dress and wiped her nose with it.

Chris rose and walked to the still-open door, listening to her pour more coffee, probably for herself. He heard the pot grate against the stove, and moments later she told him to come drink his. He turned to see she'd stopped crying, but her eyes were red and puffy.

"I hate crying,'' she told him. "I promise not to be a crybaby while we're traveling together. I won't cry if I get hurt. Pain doesn't make me cry, not physical pain anyway. It's the pain . . . inside . . . that makes me cry.''

He felt a stab at his own heart. How well he understood that statement. "You shouldn't feel guilty for watching from the wood box," he told her. "It's natural to feel guilty when someone we love gets hurt or killed. We all—" He sighed. "Folks look for ways to blame themselves. Your ma told you not to come out no matter what, and she left this life knowing you'd be okay. That's better than seeing the same thing happening to you in her last moments, don't you think?"

She glanced at her lap. "I suppose."

He walked over and sat down. "Okay. We've got a deal."

Her gaze shot back over at him, some of the agony leaving her face. "We do?"

He sipped some of the coffee. "Long as you agree to always make the coffee. This is damn good."

At last she smiled, and it was just as pretty as he'd figured it would be.

"Yes, sir! I'll make the coffee. I'll do *all* the cooking!"

He couldn't help a smile of his own. "That's pretty good payment right there." *Damn,* he thought all the while. *I have to be the craziest son of a bitch who ever walked.*

Chapter Five

"Oh, no! No! No! No! I can't let you do this, child!"

"Betty, I am not a child. I know what I'm doing." Callie sat on a love seat in Betty Sooner's parlor, still wearing her calico dress. She'd come back to town with Christian Mercy, this time driving a wagon. Tomorrow she intended to stock up on the supplies she would need, then go home and take care of closing up the house and barns. The two horses she kept for pulling her wagon would be sold to Chet Willis at the stables when she returned to town.

"You're being irrational." Hank tried to reason with Callie. "This is all because of what you've been through. You're looking for a way to relieve the grief you still suffer."

"I am looking for a way to keep these men from hurting or killing someone else," Callie told him. "From what I've heard about Mr. Mercy, and what I've seen, I think he's the man who can do the job."

"You don't know anything about him except that he's a bounty hunter," Betty answered. "How do you know you'll be safe traveling alone with him?"

"Because I just know. You get feelings about people. I

already know he taught English once, so he's an educated man. And he's also been married. When I ask him about either one, he gets real edgy, won't talk about it. I think it's all got something to do with why he does what he does. Maybe his wife was murdered or something. Anyways, anybody can see he's a good man at heart, a good man turned bounty hunter because of some kind of bad thing that happened to him. I can sure understand that. And he's clean and mannerly. I'll be just fine.''

"But ... the Outlaw Trail!" Hank Sooner threw up his hands. "Good Lord, girl, you'll run into some of the worst of them. What if something happens to Christian Mercy? There you'd be, all alone amid thieves and murderers.''

"They might be thieves and murderers, but they're not all rapists.'' Callie looked at her lap, feeling her cheeks going red. "Mr. Mercy says that most of those men live by a certain code when it comes to women. He knows it will be dangerous, but he said if he sets them straight about me, most of them won't be any bother that way.''

"Except if they steal your horses and leave you stranded. And the fact remains you won't know which ones to trust and which ones not to trust.''

"Then I will just have to take my chances.''

Betty closed her eyes and sighed. "You are such a stubborn young woman,'' she told her. "I know we can't legally stop you. We are your friends, not your guardians, and you are eighteen years old. But we so liked your parents, and I know they would want us to look out for you, Callie.''

The woman sat next to her, and Callie took hold of her hand. "You've been real good to me, Betty. But you have to stop worrying. You and Hank have your business to run, and you have two grown children of your own, your son in school back East, your daughter married and expecting. Pretty soon you'll have a grandchild to fuss over. I've made this decision all on my own, and you shouldn't feel bad if it does turn out to be a disaster. Me and Mr. Mercy will take a stagecoach through Muddy Gap and on up to Lander.''

"Oh, Callie, that's so dangerous! The precarious mountain roads, stage robbers, or maybe Indians."

"Mostly it's the Sioux who make trouble, Mr. Mercy says. They've been concentrating on the Black Hills to the east. I'm good with Pa's shotgun, and I *know* Mr. Mercy is good with six-guns *and* rifle. I'm not worried, and the coach ride can't be all that bad. We'll buy some good riding horses and more supplies when we reach Lander. Then we'll head on up to a place called Hole-in-the-Wall, where a lot of horse thieves graze their stolen horses. We might be able to get a lead there on the men who killed my mother."

Betty just rolled her eyes and shook her head.

"I promise to try to write to you once in a while," Callie told her, "if I can find a way to get mail back to you. But if you ... if you never hear from me again, you ought to just rest easy that I was happy inside trying to find those men. I just know in my heart it's the right thing to do. I'll never be truly happy again if I don't try this. All I want from you is your promise to go out once in a while and check on the house, make sure there's no squatters in it messing things up. And if me or Mr. Mercy never come back, you're free to sell it and keep the money."

She reached into a pocket of her dress. "I wrote this up for you to put away and keep. It says that if I don't return in a year, and if Mr. Mercy doesn't come to claim the ranch, it's yours to do with what you want. Mr. Mercy agreed to that. He signed the note, too, so he can't come along after you've claimed it and try to say it's his."

Betty's eyes teared as she took the note. "Oh, Callie." She sniffed. "I don't know what to say."

"Just wish me luck and pray for me."

Betty shook her head, reaching into a skirt pocket for a handkerchief. "It just isn't fair, what you've been through. I've never been able to understand why God let your mother suffer like that."

Callie felt a lump rise in her throat. "I guess we just aren't meant to understand some things. Life can be pretty mean to folks sometimes, but we know there's a better place to go to, and we'll all be there someday. My folks are already there, and they don't have to work so hard anymore.''

Hank walked over to a desk and pulled out a drawer, from which he took a metal box. ''Callie, I want to give you some money to help with expenses.''

''Oh, no, Hank. That's not necessary. I'm a good saver. I've got money.''

''You don't know how long this will take or what more you will need. You could end up stranded somewhere and need money to get back to Rawlins. If you're going to do this, the least you can do to make me feel better about it is let me help you out financially.''

Callie sighed in resignation. ''If it makes you feel better. But I'll pay back every cent when I return. In fact, I'll try hard not to use it at all.''

''You use it any way you need, and don't worry about paying it back.'' Hank walked over to where she sat, handing her several bills. ''There's fifty dollars there.''

''Fifty! Oh, that's too much, Hank. I can't take it all.''

''You can and you will, young lady. Just keep it to yourself until you know for sure you can trust Mercy.''

''Yes, sir.'' Callie rose. ''I thank you both for everything you've done for me, especially this past year. And I *will* see you again. I just know it.''

Betty also stood up, and she embraced Callie. ''I do hope you're right, Callie.'' She pulled away, and Hank reached out to shake Callie's hand.

''I'll keep an eye on the ranch. When are you leaving?''

''Day after tomorrow. Tomorrow I'll be packing and closing everything up. Then I'll ride back to town.'' She looked at Betty. ''You won't think less of me, traveling alone with him, will you?''

Betty shook her head. ''I know what a good, sweet young lady you are. We understand why you have to be along. You're the only one who can identify those men.''

Callie felt the piercing pain in her chest again. ''I sure can.''

She stuffed Hank's money into the drawstring handbag she carried. "Thanks again, both of you. I think I'll go to my hotel room and get some sleep. Got a couple of big days ahead of me."

Betty walked her to the door, and after more good-byes, Callie left, walking across the street and along the boardwalk to the two-story hotel where she would stay for the night. She walked inside, greeting the man at the desk, then went upstairs to her room, closing and locking the door. She walked to a window, watching the street below, wanting to cry at how kind the Sooners had been to her and at the thought that she just might never see them again after tomorrow.

The streets were quieter now. The vendors had closed up and gone their way, and farther up the street she could see the gallows were partially torn down. Everyone hoped they would not be needed again, but her own fondest wish was that they *would* be needed again . . . for the men who'd killed her mother.

She started to turn away, when she noticed him, Christian Mercy. He rode right past her window and halted his horse in front of the Boot 'N Saddle Saloon. A fancy-dressed saloon girl met him at the swinging doors at the front of the building. She saw Mercy put an arm around the girl and lead her farther inside, and a jealousy that surprised her burned at her. For the first time in her life she wondered how she would look if she was dressed like that saloon girl . . . and if so, would Christian Mercy notice?

"What a stupid thought!" she grumbled, turning away from the window. She had better things to think about.

Chapter Six

Callie felt nauseated from the swaying and jolting of the mud wagon, as their coach was called. For some reason, the smaller wheels in front and bigger wheels in back made the thing go through mud and soft riverbeds better than the standard stagecoach, and because the top was made of nothing more than light wood covered with canvas that could be rolled up to allow air in, or left down to help keep dust from rolling inside, it was lighter than the standard coach.

Callie struggled to keep from vomiting, clinging to a strap that hung from the side of the coach and watching the passing scenery, mostly quite pretty, as they made their way along a winding, rutted road that followed all the flattest spots possible.

"I'll be glad to travel by horseback if we ever reach Lander," she told Chris, whom she noticed did not seem terribly affected by the rough ride.

"You aren't the only one," he answered.

The wagon hit a hole so hard that Callie nearly came off her seat. She winced and clung more tightly to the strap, and without warning the vomit came up. She managed to get her head out the opening beside her just quick enough to disgorge the biscuits she'd eaten for lunch, hard as they were. They were the quickest and easiest thing to eat among the items she'd packed for sustenance along the way. There were no regular stage stops until Muddy Gap, a good thirty more miles.

"Oh, I'm so sorry," she moaned as she pulled her head back into the car. "It just came on me so quick." She glanced at the man who sat beside Chris, both men sitting opposite her. Her embarrassment knew no bounds, but the stranger with them just laughed.

"I've seen it happen before," he told her. "They advertise these things as a great way to travel. Great for your horses, maybe, since it saves a workout for them, but as far as I'm concerned, I'd take ten days on a horse to one day in one of these coaches."

Chris grinned as he maneuvered himself to reach into a front pocket on his denim pants. He pulled out a round peppermint and handed it to Callie. "Here. I had a feeling this could happen. This will make your stomach feel a little better."

Callie took the candy gladly. "Thank you so much."

The other passenger frowned. "Say, aren't you Callie Hobbs?"

Callie put the candy into her mouth and nodded, guessing the man to be perhaps forty years in age. He had a beanpole build, with bony cheeks and friendly brown eyes. He displayed a wide smile that made it look as though he had more teeth than the normal amount.

"Sure. I know you . . . knew your pa. He used to buy and sell livestock from my boss, Hurley Getz." He turned to Chris. "I'm on my way to Lander to look at some livestock for Mr. Getz. Name's Cal Becker."

He put out his hand, and Chris shook it. "Nice to know you."

"You too," Becker answered affably. "And your name?"

Chris glanced at Callie before answering. "Christian Mercy."

"Christian—" The man's eyebrows arched in remembrance.

"You're the bounty hunter who brought those men in for hanging!"

Chris sobered. "I am."

"I'll be damned." Becker snickered. "I'm sorry, but Christian Mercy sure is a strange name for a bounty hunter. The two just don't quite go together, if you get my meaning."

They all bounced on their seats as they passed over another hole in the road. "Nothing I can do about it. It's my given name."

Becker frowned and looked from Chris to Callie. "You traveling with *him?*" he asked Callie.

"Yes, sir. We're going to find the men who killed my mother, and Mr. Mercy is going to make sure they are brought in and hanged, just like those men who were hanged the other day."

"Why don't you let Mr. Mercy here go after those men alone?" he asked her.

"Because I'm the only one who can identify them."

Becker chuckled. "Whooeee! You've got your work cut out for you. Sounds like you're taking on a lot for such a young woman."

Callie enjoyed the peppermint, realizing it did make her stomach feel a little better. "I might be, but it will be worth it if I find those men."

Becker grinned and nodded. "Well, now, I expect it will. I always felt real sorry for you, the way you lost *both* your folks. What about your pa's ranch and farm?"

"I've got Mr. Sooner watching it for me. I'll decide what to do about that when I get back." She glanced at Chris, who looked away and took a silver cigarette box from his shirt pocket. He opened it and took out a pre-rolled cigarette, quickly closing the box before another bump could cause all the cigarettes to fall out. He took a match from the same pocket before putting back the slender box, then struck the match. His hands wavered as the coach hit yet another rut in the road, but he finally managed to light his smoke.

"You two going all the way to Lander?" Becker asked.

"Yes, sir."

"I think we've told Mr. Becker enough," Chris put in, giving Callie a warning look. He turned to Becker then. "I appreciate your interest, but it's best not too many people know where we're going and why," he told the man. "I think you can appreciate that. I'd appreciate it if you wouldn't say anything about us to anybody once we reach Lander."

"Yeah?" The man thought a moment. "Oh! Sure enough! I'll keep quiet." He smiled at Callie. "I wish you luck, Miss Hobbs. God knows you deserve some."

"Thank you very much, Mr. Becker."

Becker turned to Chris. "You must be pretty good with those guns."

Chris shrugged. "Some think so. That doesn't mean there aren't some who are better. I don't dwell on it much." He took a long drag on the cigarette and turned away to pull the cord that rolled up the canvas at the opening nearest his end of the seat. "Looks like storm clouds to the west."

Callie suspected he was trying to change the subject.

"Storms can hit hard, fast, and wild in these parts," Becker told him.

He no sooner spoke than they heard a rumble of thunder loud enough to be heard above the beating hooves of the team of horses pulling the coach, as well as the general clatter and squeaking of the coach itself.

"Well, now, I expect we'll get wet," Becker said. "The canvas flapped over the sides of this thing aren't much good keeping out rain. I've been through storms in these things before. I hope your gear is wrapped in slickers or something."

"It's all covered good," Callie told him, wishing he weren't so talkative. She felt too sick to talk. She felt some relief at the smell of rain in the air, glad a storm was coming. The day had been miserably hot, which was part of the reason she'd vomited. Already she felt cooler air from the storm.

"Storm's comin' on fast!" the driver shouted. "Tryin' to make it to an overhang of rock up ahead."

Callie hung on to her strap and lowered her head, fighting renewed nausea. She prayed she wouldn't throw up all the way to Lander. She so wanted to make a good impression on Chris Mercy. The last thing she wanted was to be a burden.

The coach clattered on for several more minutes as the claps of thunder grew closer and louder. Suddenly rain came down in torrents, blowing into Chris's side of the coach. He threw out what was left of his cigarette and pulled down the canvas, but just as Becker had warned, it did little to keep out the rain, which blew right in with the wind.

Finally the coach reached a rock overhang barely wide enough to protect it from the downpour. The driver, known only as Stumpy, and the man riding shotgun, who used only Taggert as his name, both climbed down from their seats and began holding and talking to the four horses pulling the wagon, trying to keep them calm. Chris and Becker climbed out to help, but Callie remained inside, folding her arms over her stomach. The effects of the peppermint were quickly wearing off.

"Lord, don't let it be like this all the way to Lander," she groaned. Just then there came another loud clap of thunder, and one of the horses whinnied loudly. Callie felt the coach rock, then suddenly bolt away as the horses charged off from fright. She hung on as the steeds took a sudden turn. The coach careened, tossed like a toy. The next thing Callie knew, the coach tumbled sideways, and rock and gravel slammed into the side of her head when it landed through the windowless opening of her side of the wagon.

Chapter Seven

Callie opened her eyes to darkness and the sound of a yipping coyote somewhere in the distant hills. At first she felt confused, unable to figure out just where she might be. She lay still for a moment, letting her eyes adjust to the sights and sounds of night—bright stars in the black sky, the whinny of a horse, a small campfire nearby . . . Christian Mercy sitting on the other side of it, watching her.

Now she remembered. A storm. A restless team of horses. Her nausea. The coach tumbling to its side. She was surprised to see true concern in Mercy's eyes. "What . . . happened?" she asked.

He stirred the fire slightly with a stick. "Damn team balked and ran, then tried to turn back. Made the wagon tip over. You took a pretty good blow to the head. We've since righted the wagon, and Becker and the driver and shotgun went after the horses. I stayed here to watch over you."

Callie winced as she put a hand to her sore head, realizing then that she had a bump above her temple and scrapes on the right side of her face. "You didn't have to do that."

"Sure I did. You're worth some money to me."

She had a deep suspicion he didn't really mean that. Did he really care about her as a person? Hell no. He was a bounty hunter. There she went again, thinking the best of a complete stranger. "Everybody back and okay now?"

"Yes. By the time we got everything back together, it was getting dark. Stumpy says it's too dangerous through here to travel after dark, and we didn't have time to reach the little stage stop farther ahead, so we made camp right here. Stumpy and the other two made their own little fire down by the road. I carried you up here, where there is some softer grass. How do you feel?"

He'd *carried* her? "I don't know yet, except at least I don't feel sick to my stomach. I'm ... real sorry about that. I've never traveled like this before. I didn't know that the way these coaches sway around would do that to me."

"It happens." He moved off the flat rock where he'd been sitting and laid his rifle down beside a bedroll spread out near hers. He stretched out on it, pulling his hat down over his eyes. "Seems pretty safe here. I think I'll get a little shut-eye of my own."

She wondered at the fact that he'd apparently waited up all this time just wanting to see if she'd come around. "Thanks for looking out for me. I promise I can take care of myself once we're on the trail."

"Accidents happen. Wasn't your fault."

She turned her head slightly, again feeling pain. "You know something? I've never been out of Rawlins since I was born. It's the only place I've ever known."

"Well, you'll soon learn this is a big country," he answered from under the hat. "Your folks must be from someplace else though. Most people out here are."

"They came out from Illinois."

"What town?"

"Rockford."

"I've been there."

"Really? You from Illinois?"

"Chicago."

"Chicago! *Really?*"

"Really."

"I'll be danged. We're both from Illinois. My folks were never in Chicago though. That's one big city now, they say." She lightly touched her cheek, wondering how terrible she must look all scraped up. "My pa came west in 1860, thinking to look for gold, but he never made it all the way to California. He decided to settle in Wyoming instead. He heard stories about how hard it was to find gold and that it wasn't worth the time and expense."

Chris sighed. "A wise decision."

"Have you ever been to California?"

"Sure. It's pretty."

"You've been a lot of places, I guess."

"You'd be surprised how far a wanted man will run. At any rate, I've seen enough of this country to be able to judge where I might want to settle someday . . . if I ever do settle again."

Callie heard pain in his voice. She thought what a waste it was, him being so educated and so downright handsome, to be such a lost and lonely man. He seemed like a good man at heart. He'd probably make a good husband, not that she was interested herself. It just seemed a shame that a man could be so hurt that he changed his life completely because of it. She knew full well there *were* good men, ones like Hank Sooner, and her own pa, strict as he was. Christian Mercy had probably been a good man like that, but now he wore guns and hunted outlaws. When he landed his rifle butt into Conner Hayes's back, he'd shown no emotion whatsoever. Same as when he watched the man hang, still kicking.

"I don't know if I'll ever settle either," she told him. "I'm not sure *what* I'll do after we find those men. The Sooners want me to come back to Rawlins and let young men court me and all that hogwash. I'm not interested. I might just get me some schooling and work for the newspaper. Newspapers fascinate me. I'd like to report for one someday, something like that. Maybe just get me a job in town. I'll find a way to support myself, that's sure. I won't depend on some man for it, because I'll never get married.''

He didn't answer right away, and Callie wondered if he was falling asleep. ''That's a pretty big decision for someone only eighteen years old,'' he finally said.

''Well, that's the decision I've made.'' Callie managed to shift a little, realizing everything ached. Lord, she never dreamed traveling by coach could be so physically taxing.

''You'll change your mind someday,'' Chris told her.

''What makes you say that?''

He laughed lightly, surprising her with his apparent and rare good mood. ''Because you're young and pretty and resourceful and strong. Those are powerful attractions to a man. Young men will be calling on you plenty, and someday one will come along who makes your toes curl.''

''My toes curl?''

''That's how—'' He hesitated. ''Somebody I knew a long time ago described it to me that way once.''

Callie frowned. Was it his wife? She was afraid to ask. ''That's a funny way to put it. How can a man make your toes curl?''

''It's just a figure of speech.''

Callie thought a moment. ''This person . . . you made *her* toes curl?''

He took a long time to reply. ''Seems so,'' he answered quietly.

A tiny tremor of something Callie could not quite name softly rushed through her, and she found herself squeezing her toes together. *Good Lord!* she thought. *Is that what he's talking about?*

She was glad he couldn't see her eyes at that moment. They might give away the thought. ''Right now I can't imagine *any* man making my toes curl, as you put it,'' she told him emphatically.

He took another deep sigh, as though very tired. ''Mark my words. It will happen.''

Callie lay there thinking, wondering if her father ever made her mother's toes curl. Maybe, when they first met, before he dragged her west. She didn't mind it out here herself, but that was because this land was all she'd ever known. Maybe if she'd lived in the East, became accustomed to bricked streets and theaters and easy supplies, had lots of relatives and all, she'd be as unhappy out here as her mother was.

"What's Chicago like?" she asked, trying to imagine a real city.

Chris pulled a blanket over himself. "Big. Busy. Railroads, horse-drawn streetcars, tall buildings, five, six stories high, some of them. Factories, goods coming in by ship. It's right on Lake Michigan. Between that and the railroad, it's pretty much a hub for travel. That's why it's growing so fast."

"I can't imagine such things. Are there big stores where you can buy fancy things?"

"Sure."

"Is Lake Michigan really so big, a person çan't get to the other side in a day? That's what my ma told me once. She said you can't see the other side. They never lived there, but she said folks told her that."

"Well, it's true. It's like looking at the ocean."

"I've never seen an ocean either." Callie sighed, trying to imagine a body of water that big. "You sure have been a lot of places."

"Oh, there are plenty I've missed."

"You *have* been along the Outlaw Trail, haven't you?"

"Of course I have."

"What's it like?"

"Dangerous. I'm not thrilled about going back."

"You won't change your mind on me, will you?"

"A promise is a promise." He adjusted his hat and pulled the blanket over his shoulders. "You sure do ask a lot of questions. It won't be like this the whole trip, will it?"

Callie felt embarrassed. "No, sir. If you don't want me to talk, I won't talk."

He said nothing in reply. She had no doubt the man was used to traveling alone and probably hated her blabber. She wished he wasn't so moody. Seemed like he wanted to talk, then all of a sudden he seemed angry with her for all her questions. Trouble was, they were going to spend a lot of nights like this, sharing a campfire. Would it always be this awkward? What the hell was she doing, going off with this complete stranger? For a quick moment she wanted to buck and run, but her head hurt too much.

Chapter Eight

Callie was not sure which was worse, the pain in her head, the pain in her stomach . . . or the near terror of looking down canyons hundreds of feet deep while the mud wagon careened around narrow switchbacks that made a person pray for mercy. All that was topped off by heat and dust and the constant swaying and jolting and creaking of the wagon, the rhythmic clatter of the wheels, and the flapping of the canvas shades.

It was like that for days on end. The only things that got better were her cuts and bruises. By the time they reached Muddy Gap, where Stumpy changed horses, the bump on her head had vanished and the swelling around the scrapes was gone. Muddy Gap fit its name and consisted of nothing more than a crude building where a person could get a meal of wormy biscuits and overdone beef, use an outhouse, and then sleep on the floor or outside. All chose outside, since they noticed roaches skittering across the floor, as well as mice.

All other nights were also spent under the stars. Callie loved the nights, because they were a wonderful relief from the constant movement and noise of the day. Christian Mercy spent most evenings sitting quietly while the other three men told

tall tales. Once Cal Becker tried to get Chris to show how fast
he could draw his guns, but he refused. Then Stumpy asked
him to show how good his aim was, daring him to shoot a
pinecone off a tree in the distance. Again he refused. Taggert
asked him how many men he had killed, and Chris told him
it was none of his business.

One good thing Callie saw in Christian Mercy was that he
was not full of himself. Most men who were pretty good with
a gun liked to brag about it and show off. And most men as
good-looking as he was would be all puffed up with conceit,
pretty sold on themselves, like young Ted Laughlin back in
Rawlins, who thought he was quite something because he had
a college education and worked for a lawyer. He wore his hair
all slicked back and dressed in fancy suits. He truly was good-
looking; but he was so sure of himself that it took away from
his looks. Mercy didn't even seem to realize how handsome
he was.

She closed her eyes and put a hand to her forehead, wondering
why the thought had even come to her. It was a damn ugly
thing men did to women. There was a time when she thought
about boys, dreamed about someday being married and all.
Now she couldn't imagine wanting to be with a man even as
a wife. Down deep inside she knew there must be something
pleasurable about it, but she couldn't wake up that feeling and
curiosity anymore.

More winding trails brought them closer to Lander, and
Callie couldn't wait to get out of the coach for the last time.
At least her body did seem to be adjusting to the constant sway.
Each day the nausea lessened, and finally she didn't have a
problem with it anymore. The only physical problem left was
the fact that she could barely walk at first each night when she
stepped from the wagon. It was as though her body wanted to
keep swaying, and she likened the way she felt to the way it
must feel to be drunk, since she literally stumbled around at
first. Even the men had a bit of a problem when first climbing
off the wagon. Lord, what a miserable way to travel, she

thought. She swore she'd never get back in a coach once this trip was over.

"Whoa!" Stumpy yelled, startling Callie out of her thoughts. It was midmorning, a bright, cool day, excellent for making good time through country that had become flatter although was splattered with large rock formations. Why would Stumpy stop the horses here?

"What's wrong?" Becker shouted, sticking his head out to look up at the drivers.

"Big tree, right across the road," Stumpy shouted in reply.

They sat between two rock walls. There was no way to go around the tree.

"Looks like it fell ... hell! The damn thing's been cut! I can see it from here!"

A shot rang out, and someone grunted. The coach rocked as a body fell off it. Callie watched through a slit in her canvas shade as Taggert hit the ground with a thud. Her mouth dropped open. "Somebody shot Taggert!" she whispered to Chris.

"Get down on the floor!" Chris told her, his six-gun already out of its holster.

Callie obeyed. Cal Becker, who wore no gun, bent low himself.

"Get your hands high in the air, old man," someone ordered Stumpy. "Don't make me put another notch in my gun."

"What the hell do you want?" Stumpy asked. "We're not carryin' anything special."

"No? Why don't you let *us* decide that? Get on down off of there so we can have a look under the driver's seat."

The coach rocked again as Stumpy climbed down.

"Check inside, Frank," the voice spoke again.

Callie waited with heart pounding. The door on the side of the coach where Chris sat opened, and immediately Chris pointed his six-gun straight between the eyes of the man who leaned to look inside. He froze in place, his eyes widening, even though he held a six-gun of his own.

"Drop it!" Chris told him. "And tell your friends out there to do the same."

The man slowly released his gun, and Callie grabbed it away.

"Mason!" the one called Frank shouted. "Drop your guns. There's a man in here with a gun between my eyes."

There was a moment of silence.

"Mason?" Frank yelled again. "Do like he says. I think he means business!"

"So do I," the one called Mason answered. "He shoots you, he's a dead man." Callie heard a horse ride a little closer. "Mister, whoever you are, we're here just to relieve you of anything worth something—a watch, your money, your guns, maybe a saddle—"

Callie jumped when suddenly Chris's gun fired. She screamed when blood splattered on the floor in front of her. Some even sprayed over her hair and left shoulder. At nearly the same moment, Chris shoved the canvas shade at the door aside and fired five more shots in rapid succession. He quickly climbed out, and Callie prayed he wouldn't get killed before he even had a chance to help her.

All was quiet.

"Come on out," Chris told her and Cal.

"Jesus, mister, that was some shootin'," Stumpy was saying.

Callie looked at Cal Becker, whose eyes were wide with surprise. She cocked the six-gun she'd grabbed and slowly peeked through the canvas to see the one called Frank lying on his back with a hole in his forehead. Another man hung from his horse, his foot caught in the stirrup. He, too, was obviously dead. A third man lay hanging over a rock several feet above them. "Take a look at all three of them," Chris told her. "See if any of them is someone you're looking for." He put his gun back in its holster and turned to Stumpy. "Sorry about Taggert."

"Nothin' you can do about it."

"We'll take their identification off them soon as Callie has a look," Chris told the man. "We can't take their bodies in this hot weather, so we'll just have to dump them over the ravine we passed just a few minutes ago. We'll try burying Taggert, but the rest don't deserve it."

So cold and indifferent, Callie thought. He'd shot them all so fast! Her stomach feeling a little sick again, she walked up to each body to look at each man's face. Then she turned to Chris. "No. None of them fit what I remember."

"Fine." Chris turned toward the coach. "Becker, get out here and help me and Stumpy drag these bodies to the ravine. Then we'll take turns helping dig a hole to bury Taggert."

A shaken Cal Becker emerged from the coach, looking around at the bodies as though in a daze. "Lord, did any of them get a chance to shoot back?" he asked.

"I prefer not to give them the chance," Chris told him. He looked at Callie. "Remember that."

"Yes, sir," she answered meekly. She'd picked the right man for the job, all right.

Chapter Nine

Callie gawked at the first real town she'd ever seen besides Rawlins. Lander was as big as Rawlins, even though there was no railroad leading to it, but it was more rugged, some buildings nothing more than tents with wooden fronts on them. Yet two buildings down was a two story brick building called the Golden Rule Store. She supposed that was where she and Chris would get more supplies for their trip, since the awning on the store read DRY GOODS, MILLINERY, CLOTHING, SHOES, FURNISHINGS, NOTIONS, ETC. Apparently the Golden Rule sold just about anything a person needed.

Due to another hard rain just before they arrived, the street was a mixture of churned mud and horse dung. Their coach passed two wagons piled high with large pine logs, the wagons hitched together and drawn by the biggest team of mules Callie had ever seen. She counted eighteen, shaking her head in wonder at how a man drove so many mules at once.

The mud wagon pulled up in front of a building that simply read HOTEL and came to a halt, and Callie gladly disembarked, never happier to leave something in her life. She vowed that if something happened where she needed transportation for a long distance again, she'd walk before she'd ride in a mud wagon. Maybe the fancier stagecoaches were better, but they were more expensive, and right now she didn't like the thought of being in *any*thing on wheels.

"We'll get a room, then go see about some horses and supplies," Chris told her matter-of-factly when he climbed out of the wagon. "You can clean up and get some rest. I want to leave early morning." He reached up to grab his saddle as Stumpy handed it down. He set it on the ground, then took down Callie's saddle. Then Stumpy handed him Callie's carpetbag, all the while relating the stage holdup to a group of men already gathered around the wagon. Cal Becker joined in the story, both men carrying on about how fast Chris was with a gun.

Chris didn't look at any of them or say a thing, and Callie could tell he was a little embarrassed by the attention, as Stumpy went on to tell about him bringing three murderers to Rawlins for a hanging.

Chris handed Callie her carpetbag, then reached for his repeating rifle as Stumpy handed that down. He handed that to Callie too.

"Hold that a minute."

"A *bounty* hunter," someone said. "I'll be damned."

Chris made no acknowledgment of the man or his remark. He took down his own carpetbag and another smaller bag Callie had brought along. He placed that under his arm and grabbed his bedroll, placing that, too, under his arm. He picked up his saddle with his other hand.

"Leave your saddle for a minute and bring my rifle and your carpetbag," he ordered her. He headed through the crowd, still refusing to acknowledge any of them.

Callie hurried after him, following him into the hotel, where he was already seeing about a room.

"One room?" she asked warily.

"I'll be staying someplace else."

"Oh? Where?"

"I thought you weren't going to ask so many questions."

Callie frowned, waiting while he set down his gear and went

back out to get her saddle. He came back in and paid the clerk for a room.

"I can pay for it," she objected.

"I'll get this one." He grabbed the key after signing the clerk's guest book, then left his bedroll, carpetbag, and saddle, as well as her saddle, on the floor and laid his rifle on the counter. "Watch this stuff for me," he told the clerk.

The older man, whose balding head looked pink against his white hair, glanced down through his spectacles at the gun. He cleared his throat. "Yes, sir, Mr. Mercy. You staying long this time?"

"Just tonight." Chris headed upstairs.

"He knows you?"

"I've been in Lander before."

"Lordy, is there anyplace you *haven't* been?"

"A few."

Callie followed him up a stairway to Room Five. He opened the door, and she moved inside the small room, which consisted of a bed, a table, and a washbowl. That was it. A picture of flowers hung crooked on a wall covered with wallpaper that showed even more flowers. She threw her two bags on the bed and faced Chris.

"I think I have a right to know where you're staying, seeing as how I've never been here before and don't know another soul in town. Besides, what if you go disappearing on me? I wouldn't know where to start looking for you."

Chris rubbed at his eyes. "I won't go disappearing on you, as you put it. Just get some sleep and plan on hearing me knock at your door in the morning. Right now you can follow me over to the livery and we'll look at some horses."

"You going to go around asking questions about the men who killed my mother? Maybe see if you can get some kind of lead?"

He left the room, and Callie again had to hurry to keep up.

"When you need to know something, I'll tell you," he told her on the way down the stairs. "We'll ask ol' Luke at the livery. If anybody has seen them, he would, since every man ends up taking his horse there to put up. Luke has a good memory." He told the clerk to keep watching his things, and that he'd return soon. He hurried out the door, where a crowd still lingered, listening to Stumpy. Callie felt their stares as she practically ran to keep up with Chris.

"Why are you in such an all-fired hurry?" Callie asked.

"Because I want to buy some horses *and* supplies and have time left to play some cards and still get a good night's sleep. We have a damn long trip ahead of us and no time to waste."

They kept mostly to the boardwalk as Callie followed him down the street to a stable, where Chris greeted a crusty old man named Luke. "Need some horses, at least four," he told the man. "And maybe a couple of mules."

"Sure thing," Luke answered. "How you doin', Chris? Take in any wanted men lately?"

"Three train robbers who murdered some passengers. They were hanged a few days ago in Rawlins."

Luke chuckled. "You're the best."

"I don't know about that. I guess it's more determination than anything else."

Luke shook his head. "You stayin' at Lisa's tonight?"

Chris glanced at Callie. "Well, that's not something to talk about in front of this young lady here."

"Hmm?" Luke walked over and took a closer look at Callie. "Well, I'll be damned. I thought you was a boy. I mean ... I'm sorry, miss. I didn't mean no insult. I just wasn't really lookin', you know? And you wearin' them pants and all—"

"It's all right," Callie answered, wanting to crawl into a hole. "I prefer pants. More comfortable. And me and Mr. Mercy have a lot of riding to do."

"You and Chris?" Luke turned to Chris. "You on another hunt?"

Chris took a cigarette paper from his shirt pocket and opened the small pouch of tobacco tied to his belt. "Well, now, I am, Luke. In fact, I'll let the little lady here describe the men we're looking for. I told her that if anybody had seen them around here, it would be you. The lady here is called Callie Hobbs.

She's hired me to find the men who killed her mother, after raping her. They also stole her best horses.''

Luke squinted as he returned his gaze to Callie. "I see. I'm right sorry, ma'am, for your loss." He motioned for her to follow him. "Come on out back with me, where my horses for rent or sale are kept. You describe the men to me while Chris here looks over the horses. I got a good memory, especially for faces.''

Callie followed him through the stables, which she noticed were swept, and the stalls in it cleaned properly. It was obvious Luke was a man who respected horses. A young boy was forking hay into feeders, and the water troughs were full.

"The only name I heard was Terrence," she told Luke. "He seemed to be kind of the leader. He was a big guy with a deep white scar across his right cheek, really nasty. Somebody must have cut him good in a fight. And he had a deep, ugly laugh.''

They exited the building into a corral where horses ran loose.

"There they are. Take your pick," Luke told Chris. "You lookin' to buy or rent?''

"Depends." Chris reached out and ran his hand over the flanks of a gray-spotted Appaloosa.

Luke turned back to Callie. "Go on, girl.''

Callie hated talking about the incident, but she had no choice. "Well, sir, another one was just a regular-looking man, brown hair, kind of pleasant looks but not really handsome. I can't think of anything special about his looks or dress. I'd know him if I saw him though.''

"Mmm-hmm. Go on.''

"The third man was about as tall as Terrence but a lot skinnier, with a mole on his right cheek and thinning hair. From what was left of his hair, it looked like it was mostly blond, but it was so dirty, it was hard to tell.''

Luke shook his head. "Sorry, but I ain't seen anybody fits the descriptions you give me so far. 'Course the second one you described could fit a lot of men, and as far as the third one goes, Lord knows there ain't many men around here who keeps their hair clean enough to suit a woman. But I'd remember the mole." He scratched at the bristles of hair on his unshaven face. "What about the other two?"

Callie glanced at Chris, who had walked over to lean against a fence post and listen. He quietly smoked his cigarette. She looked back at Luke. "One was built about like Mr. Mercy there, big shoulders and arms but from muscle, not fat. He had little scars on his face, like from fistfights, maybe. His hair was real dark and curly, and his skin was dark. I think he was maybe Mexican. He never . . ." She looked away from them both. "He never joined the others in . . . doing what they did to my poor mother. He just watched . . . and laughed." She blinked back tears. "The fifth one was a skinny little runt of a man, more boy than man, I expect. I think he was maybe only about my age, seventeen or eighteen. He had long blond hair that he wore tied back, and I don't think he was any taller than me. I don't remember any scars or anything. I just remember he had pale blue eyes, and that hair, and how scrawny he was."

She wiped a quick tear. "It was the big one called Terrence, who . . . shot my ma when they were done with her." She shook her head. "No reason, except she could identify them." She felt renewed rage well up in her soul. "But they didn't know *I* saw them, and I *can* identify them! They never knew I was there hiding." She sniffed. "I want every last one of them *dead,* and I hope they suffer first!"

Luke shook his head in sympathy. "Lordy, girl, that's an awful thing to witness. How'd you see all this without them men findin' you?"

"She hid in the wood box," Chris told him. "Her mother told her to stay there no matter what happened."

Luke nodded. "She told you right. It's good you never came out. Your ma went to her peace knowin' you'd be okay." He looked over at Chris. "Sounds like you've got your work cut out for you, Chris. Them five could be scattered in every direction."

Chris kept the cigarette between his lips as he spoke. "Could be. But they also could be the kind that run together in a pack." He drew on the cigarette, then took it from his mouth. "The good part is they don't know Callie. Never saw her. She could walk right up to one of them and he'd never know who she is. That's my ace in the hole. She can identify them for me, and I'll take over from there.''

Luke chuckled. "And Lord have mercy on their souls."

Chris walked out among the horses again, looking over a red mare with black mane and tail.

"I don't expect the Lord will have any mercy for those men," Callie told Luke. "I hope they burn in hell for all eternity!"

"Well, now, I don't blame you there." Luke scratched the back of his neck. It seemed to Callie he was always scratching something. "Wish I could help you, missy, but men of that particular description ain't been around here. Maybe they decided to avoid civilization for a while, after what they did. Lots of horse thieves head straight for the Outlaw Trail to hide, but you're talkin' a lot of territory there."

Callie felt renewed hope. "I figured the same thing, that we might find them somewhere on the trail. That's where we're headed. Mr. Mercy is going to help me find those men."

Luke turned to Chris. "She serious?"

Chris was checking the teeth on a sleek black gelding. "She is."

"You crazy?"

"Could be," Chris answered, throwing down his cigarette stub and stepping it out.

Luke shook his head, turning back to Callie. "Well, girl, you picked the right man for the job, but the Outlaw Trail— that's a lot of land to cover. Sure you've got the spunk for it?"

"She's got the spunk," Chris answered for her. He walked back to Callie and Luke, casting Callie an unusually friendly grin before addressing Luke. "I wouldn't have agreed to help her otherwise."

Callie felt a spark of pride at the words.

"We'll take the Appaloosa gelding and that roan mare over there," Chris said then. "And I like the looks of the black gelding. They all look sturdy, like they wouldn't get easily winded. I guess we'll buy them outright. It will probably be a long trip, too long to just rent them. Besides, we could end up all the way down in Texas. It wouldn't be easy getting them back to you."

"Well, you picked some good ones. Them three are real good stock. I've rode them all myself. They handle easy, real obedient. Got them from a trader come through here just a few weeks ago. I've dealt with him before, so he can be trusted."

"So can you." Chris removed his hat and wiped at perspiration on his forehead with the back of his hand. "If I didn't know you so well, I'd check them over better, ride them first for a few days. But I got Sundance from you, and he's the best horse I've ever owned. When it comes to horseflesh, you definitely know your business, so name your price, Luke. Callie and I have to go and get some supplies."

"Well, the black one there, I'll give him to you for eighty bucks. That's a damn bargain. He's only three years old, and fast as lightnin'. In fact, the breeder named him Night Wind. You're the only one I'd give a deal to like this."

Chris smiled and shook his head. "I happen to believe you on that one, but you're a sharp horse trader, Luke Winston, so don't bullshit me."

Luke let out a high-pitched laugh. "I ain't bullshittin' you, Chris. You're too damn smart for that."

Chris put his hat back on. "How about the other two?"

"Well, the red mare, she's six. Her name's Betsy, and she ain't especially fast, but she's damn strong and has the nicest temperament of any horse I've been around. You can have her for fifty. The Appaloosa gelding, he's called Breeze. Sixty bucks. He'll balk at you once in a while but always comes around. You just have to be firm with him. What about saddles?"

"We have our own. How about a couple of pack mules? I don't want to put our supplies on the horses and tire them out any more than necessary."

"I've got mules. They're in a pasture a little ways from town. Twenty-five each."

"Sold. I'll pay you in the morning when we pick them up. We'll be by around seven A.M. I'll come around later and bring our supplies so you can have them loaded onto the mules for us in the morning."

"Sure enough."

The two men shook hands. "See you later," Chris told Luke.

"Yes, sir." Luke turned to Callie. "Good luck findin' them men, little lady. You just be careful about it."

"Yes, sir, I will. Thank you for the fine horses, and for listening to me describe the men."

"I just wish I could be more help." Luke turned to Chris. "Hey, you have a right pleasant evening, friend."

Chris grinned again. "I'm sure I will."

Callie wondered at the look the two men exchanged. Chris took her arm and led her back through the stables. "Let's go stock up at the Golden Rule. The sooner we get that done, the better. After that, you might as well go straight to the hotel."

Again Callie hurried to keep up. "I ought to pay for one of those horses, Mr. Mercy. So far you haven't let me pay for anything."

"You can pay for one of them after we've been on the trail a while and you decide which one suits you best. I expect it will be the red mare, but certain horses take to certain people, and it's the same the other way around. Right now, though, you can pay for your own supplies."

Callie wondered at the way he could be so aloof and silent one minute, friendly and talkative the next. He started across the street, and she quickly followed. "If I go back to the hotel too early, I won't be able to sleep," she told him.

"There is a little place next to the hotel where you can get a good meal. The lady who runs it is a good cook. Maybe a hot meal will help you sleep. I'll come for you in the morning."

"You still haven't told me where you'll be staying. And who's Lisa? Is *that* who you'll be with? Will she *feed* you, too?" Why did she feel a pang of jealousy? There was no call for it.

"Lisa isn't anybody you'd care to know. And whether or

not I'm staying with her or eating with her is none of your business.''

"Yes it is." Callie hurried to keep up as they headed down the boardwalk to the Golden Rule. "I have to know where to find you."

Chris stopped and turned, looking irritated. "Okay. Lisa serves drinks two blocks down at the Watering Hole Saloon. She also sings and dances. Now are you satisfied?"

Callie felt heat come into her cheeks. "You're gonna sleep there?"

"Yes." He started walking again.

"With *her?*"

"Probably."

"She's a *whore,* isn't she?"

"Whore can mean a lot of things. In a lot of ways she's quite a nice lady."

"Lady?" Callie walked as fast as she could behind him. "The thought of sleeping with a man who's not my husband and who doesn't even *plan* on marrying me makes me want to puke! How can you call somebody like that a lady?"

He stopped and turned again, whisking her into an alley. "Watch what you say. People can hear you, and most men around here know Lisa."

"I'll bet they do!"

Chris put his hands on his hips, a look of obvious irritation on his face. "Look, you haven't been around enough to be judging people. You have a lot of growing up to do first."

"If that's considered growing up, I'll stay just the way I am, thank you."

"Fine. That's your choice. Just don't be so ready to judge other people. You just remember you hired me to do a job, and I intend to do it. I didn't ask for your opinion about me or my friends, and none of it should matter to you. So quit hounding me with all your questions, and quit judging people by their environment or what they might do for a living. While you're with me, your job is strictly to help me find the men

you're after. What I do otherwise is not your business, same
as what you do isn't any of *my* business. Got that?''

Callie felt both angry with herself and embarrassed. She'd
insulted a friend of his. That was stupid. She hardly knew the
man, so why did it matter anyway? He was right about that
part, and if she kept making him angry, he might change his
mind and not help her.

She closed her eyes and sighed. "Yes, sir. I'm . . . I'm sorry
I insulted your woman friend."

"Thank you. Now let's get those supplies."

He turned and walked away, and Callie followed, realizing
when they reached the supply store that Mr. Christian Mercy
was damned efficient. He had a list all ready for the store
clerk—bacon, flour, beans, tobacco, cigarette papers, plenty
of ammunition, blankets, medicines, bandages, peppermints,
coffee, a couple of pans and a coffeepot, matches, gun oil,
saddle wax, towels, a few bags of oats for the horses, soap,
extra boots—size eleven.

"What size boots do you wear?" he asked her.

"Six."

He ordered those too, letting her pick a pair out while he
continued with the list. Dried fruit, baking soda to clean their
teeth with, slickers, extra hats. Again Callie picked out her
own. Creams for Callie. It surprised her that he'd thought of
that. She tried on a long duster, a warm leather jacket with
fleece lining, a woolen scarf, some whiskey—"for washing
wounds," he told her, as though he felt he needed to assure
her it wasn't for drinking.

The list went on. Items were wrapped. Callie gave Chris ten
dollars for her share. The store owner agreed to have the items
taken over to Luke for packing onto the mules. Within an hour
the shopping was finished and they left the store. Luke walked
Callie to the hotel, stopping at the entrance.

"We should be all set. Go on up to your room and clean
up. Get something to eat and get some rest. Stay out of the
streets, understand? I don't want to have to worry about you."

"Yes, sir."

He tipped his hat and walked off. Callie watched after him, feeling suddenly very alone, scared, and anxious. Damned if she didn't feel like crying again. She marched into the hotel and up to her room, thinking how this might be the last night for a long time that she'd get to sleep in a real bed. What disturbed her, and for no good reason, was the fact that Christian Mercy would be sharing his bed with someone else tonight.

The heck with eating. She suddenly had no appetite.

Chapter Ten

Callie found it impossible to sleep. Being in a strange town, staying in a hotel for the first time, the noise in the street below, all combined to prevent her eyelids from closing. Every time she heard men talking and laughing, she couldn't help wondering if one of them was Chris. In the distance she could hear piano music, women laughing. Was one of those women Lisa? Did he care about her, or was what they would end up doing just a plain old animal act with no feelings?

She wished she understood things like that. It made her stomach turn to think that a woman could sleep with men for no reason other than to make a man feel good. That was bad enough. The hardest thing to understand was how men like those who attacked her mother could get pleasure out of taking a woman unwillingly, giving her pain and humiliation. Were all men capable of that? Surely not, or all women would be in constant danger. Then again, if Chris needed a woman like that Lisa to satisfy whatever it was that drove men to do such things, then how safe would she be traveling alone with him for days or weeks, him being unable to get that same pleasure?

She rolled to her side. She hadn't even undressed yet. She

wished she had someone to talk to about these things, about the horror she'd experienced watching those men rape her mother, about her guilt over being too afraid of the same thing happening to her to come out of that wood box, even though there would not have been anything she could do. She stayed there for her mother's own peace, but the guilt of it tore at her heart.

She didn't understand men. She didn't understand sex. She didn't understand her own feelings of guilt and hatred . . . or even this terrible need for revenge. Yes, that was natural, but to go to such means to get it, to give up her pa's beloved ranch, to spend everything she had, travel alone with a bounty hunter she still hardly knew, risking rape or death or being stranded in unknown country . . . what had she gotten herself into?

She sat up, feeling restless. She went to her open window and leaned out, watching two men ride past on horses. A wagon clattered by. Lordy, living in town sure was noisy. Night on the ranch was dead still except for the occasional yip of a coyote. She couldn't help wondering if Chris was still up, wondering what the woman called Lisa looked like. Did she look a little like his wife perhaps? Maybe that was why he was attracted to her.

Curiosity got the better of her. Chris had given strict instructions for her to stay off the streets after dark, but the way she was dressed, if she piled her hair under her hat, who would know that she was a girl? Besides, she could keep to the shadows. Not only did she want to make sure Chris was where he said he'd be, but maybe she could peek through a window and study the men inside the Watering Hole. She just might spot someone who looked familiar. No matter what old Luke said, that didn't mean some of the men she was looking for couldn't possibly have ridden into town that afternoon and didn't go to the stables first. They hardly seemed like the kind who would care about their horses.

She got up, turning up her oil lamp and winding her hair into a knot on top of her head. She pinned it with combs and stuck her hat on her head, then quietly went out. She tiptoed down the stairs, glad to notice the desk clerk was asleep in his chair. Quietly she opened the outer door and left.

Staying close to the wall, Callie walked the full block and a half to the Watering Hole, which she could see across the street from her. Taking a deep breath, she headed across the street, stepping through drying mud and trying as best as she could in the dark to avoid stepping in horse dung. Two men walked toward the tavern from another direction, and she quickly ducked between two horses tied in front. The men stepped through the swinging doors, and Callie moved away from the horses and darted under the hitching post and up the steps. She leaned against the outside wall near the doors.

The piano music from inside was very loud now. A woman began singing a song about someone named Kathleen. Callie moved closer to a window and peeked inside.

"Lordy!" she whispered.

A woman sat on top of the piano, wearing a green, low-cut dress with black feathery trim. The dress came only to her knees so that the whole bottom half of her legs showed. Her blond hair was twisted up on top of her head, and it was decorated with glittery combs and black feathers. She wore black shoes with a high heel and black mesh stockings.

Her singing voice was beautiful, the prettiest Callie had ever heard.

> To that dear home beyond the sea,
> My Kathleen shall again return;
> And when thy old friends welcome thee,
> Thy loving heart will cease to yearn.
> Where laughs the little silver stream,
> Beside your mother's humble cot,
> And brightest rays of sunshine gleam,
> There all your grief will be forgot.

Such pretty words, and sung with such feeling. But when Callie followed the woman's gaze, it went right to a handsome man sitting at a table smack in front of her.

"Christian Mercy!" she muttered. Why on earth did she feel jealous at the way those blue eyes of his moved, his gaze drinking in every inch of the pretty woman? And she was doing the same, looking him over as though he were something delicious. How could a woman flaunt herself that way? And how could she actually *want* a man?

Her lips moved into a sneer of disgust, but her thoughts were quickly interrupted when someone jerked her by the back of her pants and a strong arm came around her, gripping her across the breasts.

"Hey, boy, you gettin' yourself a good look at a pretty woman?" came a gruff voice.

The words were followed by laughter, and whoever held her swung her away from the window.

"Let go of me!" Callie screamed. She began kicking backward, aiming for the man's shinbones.

"Hey! Hey!" the man growled, jerking her to the side. The movement caused his hand to come across her breasts. "Jesus!" he hollered, letting go of her. She started to run, but a strong hand caught her arm and jerked her back, this time locking both his arms tightly around her from behind so her arms were pinned. "It's a girl!" the man declared.

Callie did not have a chance to see the man's face, but now she could see two other men in front of her, standing close, their faces fairly distinguishable by the light filtering out from the tavern.

"*A girl?*" one of them asked, grinning.

"What's under my hand sure says so," the man holding Callie answered with another laugh. He felt her breasts, and Callie kicked and screamed as hard and as loudly as she could. The kicks seemed to have no effect, and her fight caused her hat to come off. Her hair came tumbling down, and a stream of profanities poured out of her mouth.

The three men began hooting and laughing louder, and one of the others took a turn at feeling her breasts. She bent her head down and bit hard, causing the man to yelp like a wounded hound.

"Mr. Mercy!" Callie screamed as the man holding her began carrying her toward an alley. "Mr. Mercy!" She knew she had to yell as loudly as possible to be heard above the piano and singing and the general noise inside the tavern. She wasn't sure Chris heard her until from seemingly nowhere she heard the click of a six-gun being cocked. The gun was right beside her head, the barrel laid against her abductor's cheek.

"Let her go," Chris said calmly.

The man holding her froze in place. "Who the hell are you?"

"Doesn't matter. You've got hold of my little sister, and if you don't let go in three seconds, the back of your brain will be splattered against the next building."

Callie could hear her abductor breathing hard. He released her, and she quickly moved out of the way. "*Kill* him, Mr. Mercy! *Kill* him!"

The other two men ran off, and Chris lowered his gun.

"Sorry, mister," the man who'd grabbed her told Chris.

Chris gently released his gun hammer into place. "Get the hell out of here."

"He assaulted me!" Callie protested. "He did an indecent thing with me, and he was dragging me off—"

"Shut up!" Chris told her, still glaring at the man who'd grabbed her. "Go on. Get going before I change my mind."

The man, who Callie could now see was very stocky and bearded, glanced at her first. "Sorry, ma'am. We was just gonna have some fun, tease you a little. Nothin' more." He turned and walked off into the darkness.

Callie shuddered at the memory of him touching her, something that brought back all the ugliness of her mother's attack. "You should have shot him!" she told Chris.

He shoved his gun back into its holster and walked closer to her. "I should shoot *you* and save myself a lot of headaches! What the hell were you doing here? I told you to stay off the streets!"

"I decided to come down here and have a look inside the tavern, see if there were any men in there who looked familiar."

"There *was* someone familiar in there. *Me!* You sure you weren't just *spying* on me?"

Callie struggled not to cry. "I have a right! I'm *paying* you! Don't forget that!"

Chris leaned down slightly to talk right into her face. "You're paying me to find your mother's killers! That's it! Anything else I do is *my* business! *Your* business is to do exactly what I tell you. If you can't follow orders, we're through, right here and now! You can take the next coach back to Rawlins! You go back to your room and you decide! I'll be there in the morning for your answer!" With that he turned and walked back to the tavern doorway, where the pretty blond woman stood waiting with a grin on her face. She moved her arm around Chris's waist, and he put his arm around her as they both went back inside.

Callie gritted her teeth in anger and jealousy. "Little *sister*, he calls me!" she grumbled. She turned and marched back toward the hotel. "Little *sister!*" She went inside the hotel, slamming the door to wake up the desk clerk. She marched upstairs and into her room, where she promptly broke down into tears. She never felt so miserable and embarrassed and lonely and confused and angry and strangely frustrated in her life.

"I *hate* you, Christian Mercy!" she sobbed.

Chapter Eleven

"*That* was your new client?" Lisa asked Chris.

Chris watched her undress, wishing he could enjoy her in the fullest sense, the way he'd enjoyed Valerie, the kind of enjoyment a man got from the woman he truly loved, the woman he wanted to impregnate because she would be the perfect mother for his sons and daughters.

Daughters . . . God, would this pain ever go away? The heavy weight in his heart seemed to pull a little harder every time he thought of his little Patty-girl, hurting, needing him.

"That's her," he answered Lisa, drinking in her lovely breasts, her round, firm bottom. "She's going to be a pain in the ass, I'm sure."

Lisa laughed lightly, a laugh as pretty as her singing voice. "She looks like she's thirteen or fourteen years old."

"Eighteen."

"Really? You sure she's telling the truth?"

Chris, already naked, rolled onto his back as Lisa took the pins from her hair and let the blond locks fall. "I never considered that."

"Well, you'd better." Lisa came over to the bed and moved

onto it, leaning over him to kiss his cheek. "What if you start getting ideas after traveling alone with her for a while? You don't want to go bedding a kid."

Chris couldn't help his own laughter then. "No worry there. Number one, that freckle-faced little spitfire is the last female who would stir me into anything; and number two, she already told me that if I make any advances she will, as she put it, 'shoot me dead.' "

"Shoot you dead?" Lisa laughed more, and Chris couldn't help joining her. "Is there some other way to shoot someone?" Lisa asked.

"Shoot me *wounded,* maybe."

Lisa laughed harder, but Chris could not deny the slight bit of guilt he felt for the laughter. He knew how much poor Callie was hurting inside, how she'd probably cry if she knew he was talking about her. The worst damned part was a little piece of him did have feelings for her, feelings he couldn't even explain yet. He couldn't decide if they were fatherly, brotherly, friendly, or something else. Good Lord, what if she *wasn't* eighteen? He felt the hole he'd dug for himself getting even deeper, and he pulled Lisa over on top of him. "No more talk about Callie Hobbs," he told her. "I want to concentrate on a *real* woman." He ran his hands along her slender thighs. "And I want to drink in every inch of you."

Her laughter turned to a sly, seductive grin then, and she leaned over, offering him a ripe pink nipple. "Then I'll stay right here, where you can see all of me, while I give you your pleasure, Mr. Mercy." After allowing him a taste of her fruits, she raised herself up and settled on top of him, rocking rhythmically as she took his thoughts to more pleasurable places than bad memories and doubts about helping a crazy kid named Callie Hobbs.

For the next several minutes there was only this pleasure to think about. Might as well get this out of his system. Heaven only knew how long he'd be on the trail with—

No, quit thinking about her. The problem was, he'd always traveled alone before, so he could stop and see women like

Lisa anytime he wanted. He couldn't do that with that doggone kid along, watching his every move, let alone the fact that most of the time he wouldn't dare leave her alone. Callie Hobbs was going to be nothing but a headache the whole time. She'd already gotten herself in trouble, and they hadn't even left yet. He'd had a good urge earlier to turn her over his knee and spank her like a five-year-old who'd disobeyed. But then, he never would do that. He'd never laid a hand on Patty. If she'd lived, she probably would have been spoiled so rotten, she'd be unbearable . . . and he would have loved every minute of spoiling her.

Dammit! Enjoy the moment. It was ridiculous thinking about all these things when the prettiest whore in Wyoming was gyrating on top of him in a way most women wouldn't know how. He thrust himself upward, allowing himself to enjoy her every move, toying with her breasts while she threw back her head and groaned in her own pleasure.

It had been a long time for him, and in minutes it was over. He rolled her over and nestled his face against her neck, smelling her perfumed hair. "Sorry. I'll take longer next time."

She ran her fingers lightly through his chest hairs. "You know I understand. Out here, single men go long and far between . . . but then, so do a lot of married ones." She laughed and moved her hand to run it along his hard-muscled arm. "You sure you weren't thinking about that freckle-faced spitfire, as you call her?"

"Hell no!" He moved down and licked at her nipples, then kissed her belly before moving back up to nuzzle her neck. He moved his lips to hers, tasting her mouth hungrily, then kissing her eyes.

"You're something, Christian Mercy."

"How's that?" He kissed her mouth again.

"Not many men I allow in this bed bother with kissing and affection. It's usually just quick and hard and done. You stay around afterward and treat me like I mean something."

"You *do* mean something."

"Hell, I know better. I know that in your own way you

respect me more than other men do, but I also know I don't mean anything to you emotionally. But you're nice enough to give me some extra time anyway. You, a man who hunts men and sometimes kills them for money. I can tell you used to be a damn nice man.''

He grinned. ''I *am* a damn nice man.'' He kissed her once more before relaxing beside her. ''And I don't hunt those men for the money. I don't kill them for the money, and I don't bring them in and watch them hang for the money. I have other reasons.'' He felt the humor and the relaxation of the moment leave him. ''And none of them has anything to do with money.''

Lisa traced a finger down the center of his chest and circled it around his belly button. ''You've never told me what they are.''

''I've never told *any*body.''

''Well, I know it has something to do with a wife. I take it she's dead.''

There came the pain again, the sudden black wave that still rushed through him at the first thought of that awful night. ''Please don't bring it up, Lisa.''

She sighed, kissing his neck. ''I'm sorry. I had no right.'' She settled into his shoulder, and he stroked her hair away from her face.

''You care, that's all. I appreciate that.''

Lisa rose up on one elbow, resting her head in her hand and looking down at him. ''Honey, I care because I know you're a good man at heart, and I can tell you were once a family man. You're educated, and you're just about the most handsome specie of the male breed I've ever set eyes on. I see you as a terrible waste to society, someone who probably once contributed a whole lot and who now wastes all those looks and education and the love I know you have way down deep inside someplace on chasing after no-good outlaws who aren't worth your time and talents. How long do you intend to keep this up? How long do you intend to keep hating and trying to find a way to get rid of the rage down inside?''

Chris closed his eyes. ''I don't know. Someday I suppose it

will just come to me that it's time to end it and go on. Right now I can't imagine how I would do that."

"So you're going off with Miss Freckle-Face to who knows where for who knows how long to find men whose names you don't know."

"That pretty much says it."

"What did they do?"

"Raped and killed her mother."

Lisa frowned and wilted back down beside him. "Good God," she muttered.

"Yeah."

They both lay there quietly for a moment.

"Seems to me like the two of you have something in common," Lisa finally said.

"What do you mean?"

"You're both carrying a rage inside, looking for some kind of revenge. You think that if you find every man who does wrong and either kill him or watch him hang, you'll feel better about whatever it is that haunts you. And she thinks that if she can find her mother's killers, *she* will feel better. But it doesn't work that way."

Chris turned on his side to face her, running a hand over her back and down over her bare bottom. "How would you know?"

She smiled in a slight sneer. "Because my own father raped me, many times over, when I was growing up. I figured if I shot him, I'd feel better. So I did. And I didn't. I fled Indiana and came here and ended up singing in a saloon and entertaining men upstairs. There aren't a hell of a lot of ways for a woman to make money out here, and marriage is out of the question."

Chris frowned. "Why? You're beautiful and talented."

She smiled sadly. "Well, there you go. We're *both* wasting our looks and talents."

He moved on top of her. "Maybe so. But in your case, you're blaming yourself for something you couldn't help. Your father deserved to die. But you don't deserve to never have a husband and a family."

She ran her hands over his shoulders and moved her arms around his neck. "You're something, Christian Mercy."

"You already said that."

"Want to know something?"

Chris kissed her lips again. "What?"

"Dallas Reams has been after me to marry him for months. He's nice-looking; not a prize, but nice-looking. And he's nothing but a gentleman when he comes here, kind of like you are. He doesn't care about my past, says I deserve to have a nice life. He runs the general store here in Lander. What do you think?"

"I think you should marry him."

"I just don't feel like I'm worthy."

"You're as worthy as a virgin who sits in church every Sunday."

Chris noticed her eyes suddenly tear. "What a nice thing to say."

He shrugged. "It's true. All that matters is what's in your heart. If you're tired of this life and think you can be true to Dallas Reams, then you should marry him. Have yourself some kids. You'd make a good mother."

"Well, listen to you. Here you are, telling me to marry another man, and you're on top of me getting bigger and harder every second."

They both laughed again, and Chris could not resist when she opened herself to him.

"One last time," she said seductively, "in case I'm married the next time you come through town."

"Much obliged," he answered, covering her mouth in another hungry kiss as he moved inside her again. This time he would take longer. It could be his last time for quite a while.

Chapter Twelve

Callie plopped her wide-brimmed hat on her head and tightened the chin strap. She studied herself in the hazy mirror above the dresser, imagining how unfeminine and plain she must look compared to the woman called Lisa. She wore a plain blue shirt tucked into denim pants that hung a little loose on her and were held up by a wide leather belt. Her boots were dusty and faded but comfortable. Her hair was tucked up under her hat again, and she wore leather riding gloves.

Well, that old man at the livery yesterday thought she was a boy at first, and so did those men who grabbed her last night. Who cared? It was better this way anyway, considering where they were headed. She pulled a leather vest on over her shirt. That would help hide her breasts. They were too damn big for her small frame anyway. It embarrassed her. And Lord knew she didn't want Christian Mercy noticing, not that he would, but he just might. And after a while that could give him ideas like those men last night had.

Someone knocked on the door then, and her heart suddenly raced. She told herself she was angry with Christian Mercy because he'd called her his little sister, not because she knew damn well he'd spent the night in Lisa's bed. She wasn't sure how to behave toward him this morning. If she acted angry, he'd think it was because he slept with that woman, and that would make him wonder why she cared. He'd get ideas she had thoughts about him herself, and she damn well didn't! But hell, how could she be nice to him? The thought of trying made her even more angry.

She took a deep breath and opened the door, not even looking at him. "I'm ready," she said, turning around and picking up both her carpetbags.

"My things are at the livery," he told her. "Everything else is packed and ready to go. All we have to do is tie on your bags."

"Good." She marched past him and down the stairs. The front door stood open, so she walked out and down the street toward the stables, not caring to walk beside or behind Christian Mercy. He was the one always walking off ahead of her. Now she'd do the same. He wanted efficiency and timeliness, so he'd get it. She could tell he wasn't right behind her. Fine. He'd probably stopped to drop off her key. She'd left it on the dresser.

She greeted old Luke, noticing their horses and mules were tied out front. Her pa's rifle was in its boot, attached to her saddle, which was on the back of the red mare.

"Got Betsy all ready for you," Luke told her. "Chris will ride Night Wind for starters. Best to let the Appaloosa there get to know you both a little before ridin' him."

Callie mounted Betsy. "You said the Appaloosa's name is Breeze?" she asked.

"Yes, ma'am." Luke turned to Chris, who was just then approaching. "Got everything ready for you, Chris. Mules are all loaded. The little miss is mounted up and waitin'."

Chris made no acknowledgment of Callie. "We all square, then?" he asked Luke.

"Sure are. Always glad to do business with you, Chris. I reckon' Lisa is too."

The old man laughed, and Callie stared straight ahead, pretending not to care.

"You watch out for Lisa, will you, Luke?"

"Always do. She's a nice lady."

"That she is."

Nice! Callie thought. *She's nice all right, nice enough to bring a man up to her bed just to give him his pleasure, whether he loves her or not!* And Christian Mercy was crude enough to do just that.

"You watch out for *your*self, Chris," Luke told him. "And for that nice little lady with you."

"I'll do my best."

In the next moment Chris was beside Callie, handing her a set of reins. "I'll let you take one of the pack mules," he told her. "I'll take the Appaloosa and the other mule."

"Yes, sir." She took the reins without looking at him.

"Don't know when or if I'll see you again, Luke," Chris called back to the old man. "Thanks for your help."

"You're always welcome, my friend."

Callie turned to wave to Luke, feeling she should at least do that much. "Bye, Luke."

"Take care, little girl."

She turned back, understanding the old man's attitude but hating being called "little girl" in front of Christian Mercy, who'd just spent the night with what someone like Luke would probably call a "real" woman.

Chris kicked his horse into a gentle lope, pulling ahead of Callie as he headed northeast. Callie followed, saying nothing, and they rode that way for a good two hours, until the road dwindled into nothing more than a narrow horse trail.

They headed northwest, heading into a deep canyon, where the horses' hooves hitting hard rock echoed through the deep crevasse. The shaded area was blessed relief from the late-morning sun that was already becoming uncomfortably hot.

Callie could hear the sound of trickling water, then soon saw a narrow trail of water filtering down over a wall of sheer red rock, sprouting from some hidden source higher up. Chris drew his horse to a halt.

"We'd better rest the horses," he said. "They can get a drink here, and so can we. That way we preserve the water in our canteens."

Callie reined Betsy to a stop, then dismounted, leading Betsy and the extra mule to the waterfall. Farther up, the water glittered from sunlight, and she thought how pretty it was. A gentle wind made a groaning sound as it moved through the canyon. "It's pretty here," she said almost absently. "Down in here it seems like we've left the rest of the world behind."

Chris removed a glove and leaned forward, cupping his hand and letting the palm fill with water. He splashed it over his face, and Callie noticed only then that he'd also removed his hat. He ran his wet hand through his thick hair before facing her. "You finally talking to me?"

She met his eyes for only a moment, then looked away again, petting Betsy's neck as the horse began slurping at the waterfall. "Who said I *wasn't* talking?"

Chris sighed. "Your silence was somewhat of a hint."

Callie shrugged. "I just didn't have anything to say. You seem like a man bent on timeliness and efficiency, and you did tell me more than once that I talk too much anyway, so I left you alone. I figure you have plenty to think about, figuring where we'll go first and all." She took off her riding gloves and reached out to scoop up some of the water for herself, also splashing it over her face. "Where the heck *are* we going first anyway? You never said."

The horses and mules nuzzled one another out of the way to get a drink. One mule and Betsy turned to nibble at some yellow grass that managed to grow out of cracks in the rock.

"Hole-in-the-Wall," Chris answered. He sat down on a flat rock and took a cigarette from his pocket that he had rolled for himself earlier. He lit it and took a deep drag from it before continuing. "It's becoming an outlaw hangout and is almost impossible for the law to penetrate. It's hard to get to and a good place for lookouts to draw a bead on anybody they don't want there.''

Callie sat down a few feet away. "You think they'll shoot us?''

He shrugged. "Chance we have to take.''

Callie could not help her apprehension. "Lordy, we could get killed before we even get started.''

He smoked quietly a little longer. "Well, it's like this,'' he told her then, studying the cigarette as he rolled it between finger and thumb. "Some of them will know me. Some won't. Those who do won't care that I'm there as long as it isn't them I'm after.'' He glanced over at the horses, then finally looked at her. "These men are a strange breed, Callie. They live by a code all their own. Some aren't all that bad, rustlers mostly. Most respect proper women, even respect whores in their own way.'' He took another long drag from the cigarette.

Callie looked away. "Like you respect that Lisa woman?''

He exhaled smoke as he laughed lightly and shook his head. "I suppose. Something like that.''

She wanted to ask him how on earth he *could* respect a woman like that, but she didn't feel like getting into another yelling match. "What's that got to do with us getting shot?'' she asked. She picked up a little stone and tossed it against the opposite canyon wall.

"What I'm saying is that not all the men we'll come up against are killers, and some might even help us once they know why we're looking for the men we're after. Some will be just as pissed off over what your mother's attackers did as you are . . . and as I am. We won't be in too much trouble at first going in there, even though some might know me. They'll wait to see what it is, or, rather, *who* it is I'm after. Some will even keep it quiet if I ask them to. But you have to let *me* do the talking, and you have to stay put when I tell you to stay put. If I can't trust you to do that, I'm not going any farther, because if I have to worry about what you're doing, I might lose my concentration at a time when it's important I keep it.

Otherwise I could end up with wind blowing through my back and out the front. Understand?''

Callie sighed in resignation, staring at the ground and leaning down to pick up another rock. "Yes, sir."

"Good. I can't lie to most of these men and tell them you're my sister, because they'll know better."

Callie studied the rock, which glittered a pretty pink color. "At least you said sister, not *little* sister."

He took one last drag from the cigarette and threw it down to step it out, grinning. "Is *that* what made you so mad last night?"

She still refused to look at him. She hated him. She liked him. He was nice. He was ornery. He was kind. He was bossy. He respected women like her and her mother, but he slept with whores. He had compassion, but he killed for money. What a strange man he was.

"Mostly, I guess. And those men scared me and made me mad, and then that Lisa woman was watching and smiling, like I was a little kid to be laughed at." She stuck the rock in her vest pocket. "A woman like that has no right laughing at me."

Chris leaned back against a large boulder behind him. "Well, now, you're right. She had no right laughing at you. And I guess I had no right yelling at you, considering the scare you'd just had. That should have been enough to teach you to stay put when I tell you to."

She met his eyes again. Damned if he wasn't so handsome, he made a woman want to change her mind about . . . things. "Thanks for saying that."

He removed his hat again. "Well, we'll be spending a lot of time together. No sense spending it not speaking. Just don't take that as meaning you can jabber the whole time we're together and keep asking questions I'd rather not answer."

Callie found herself smiling. "Yes, sir."

He leaned his head back and closed his eyes. "Get a little rest."

"What about the horses?"

"They'll be all right. They'll stay near the water. Besides, they can't exactly spread out in all directions here, and they're too tired to bother taking off. We'll rest off the noon heat here, have a bite to eat before going on, just some jerked meat and a biscuit or two. No need for a fire, not that there's anything around here to make a fire with anyway.''

Callie moved to sit down in a sandy spot nearby, also leaning back against a rock. ''What about outlaws?''

''What about them?''

''What if some come through here?''

''Lord knows we'll hear them a mile away in this canyon. Don't worry about it. We don't have to stay too alert till we get closer to Hole-in-the-Wall.''

Callie closed her eyes. ''If you say so.''

Nothing more was said for several minutes. Callie opened one eye to see if Chris's were still closed. They were. He was a man of experience in things like this, making her wonder if he was really sleeping or if he was one of those men who could close his eyes for hours and still really be awake.

''Mr. Mercy?'' she said in a near whisper.

His eyes popped open instantly. ''What?''

''Oh, I'm . . . I'm sorry. Never mind.''

Chapter Thirteen

By dusk the canyon through which Callie and Chris rode opened into a wide, grassy valley unlike anything Callie had ever seen. In spite of growing up in a place where big country truly was big country, what she saw now was even bigger, a vast sea of yellow grass, spotted here and there with clumps of trees, framed on either side with forbidding cliffs and mesas that ran as far as the eye could see.

"We'll camp here in the valley," Chris told her. "This place goes on for a lot of miles. It will take us a good five days to get to where we start climbing up to Hole-in-the-Wall. At least it's good grazing land all the way. That's why rustlers like it, plenty of grazing for stolen herds."

Callie followed him down a steep embankment, carefully guiding Betsy along a narrow winding pathway that took much longer than it looked like it would when first venturing onto it. She was beginning to realize that the closest tree she saw was probably two or three miles farther away than it seemed at first. That's the way country like this was; everything stretched out for miles, even though to the naked eye it seemed close.

"How far apart you figure those cliffs are, the ones on the left from the ones on the right?" she asked Chris.

He shook his head. "My guess would be at least twenty miles, maybe more."

"That's what I figure. My ma taught me about miles. Five thousand two hundred and eighty feet. See? I'm not so dumb."

"I never said you were."

"You said I needed more education."

"That's right. There's a big difference between being uneducated and being dumb. You're a smart girl. Anyone can tell that."

For a moment, they literally passed each other on a switchback, Chris several feet below her.

"Going out alone last night, sneaking around looking in windows of a tavern, now, *that* is dumb," Chris added. "Dumb is more a word for when people do stupid things, not for someone who needs a little more education."

Callie felt embarrassed again over last night's happenings. She guided Betsy around the sharp turn and followed behind Chris. "Have *you* ever done anything dumb?"

"Sure. Everybody has."

"What was it?"

"Lots of things, mostly when I was younger," he called back to her.

"Good. Then I'm not the only one."

"Heck no. Everybody does something dumb in their lives, usually lots of things. Most people have said 'if only' many times."

"If only?"

" 'If only I had done this.' 'If only I had *not* done that.' You know . . . if only."

"What's your biggest if only?" she asked.

They rode on in silence for several minutes, and it dawned on Callie that she had gone too far again with her questions. His if only must have something to do with his wife, the one subject he could not, or would not, talk about. She waited, deciding to let him start the talking again.

It took a good half hour to reach the bottom of the cliff, and still Chris had said nothing more. Callie followed him into tall grass, realizing darkness was falling fast, now that the sun began to settle behind one of the cliff walls.

"We'll make a fire tonight," he finally spoke up.

Good, Callie thought. *At least he's talking, so he must not be angry with me for that last question.*

"We'll use the pieces of dead wood we picked up along the way when we were coming out of the canyon," he continued. "Dry pine burns fast though. We'll have to have things ready to cook before we light the fire so we don't waste the heat."

"Yes, sir."

"You up to making coffee and frying a couple of potatoes?" he asked.

"Sure. You make the fire. I'll slice the potatoes into a fry pan and add a little bacon fat. Flavors up the potatoes real good. I did most of the cooking for my folks when they—" The words caught in her throat. "Were alive," she finished.

They headed through high grass toward a spot where a narrow stream cut its way through the now-flat land.

"See why this is such a good place to graze stolen herds?" Chris said. "This is still open, free country. No one has really claimed any of it, and it's too remote to bother, let alone the remaining danger from Indians and now the danger from migrating outlaws."

He halted Night Wind, and the sleek black horse whinnied and tossed its head as though telling Chris it was about time he allowed the horses to rest again.

"Where do the rustlers take their stolen goods?" Callie asked when she rode closer. She reined Betsy to a stop and dismounted.

Chris removed his rifle from its boot, laying it aside, then began unstrapping the belt that held his saddle on Night Wind. "A lot of places—Canada, maybe friends who have a ranch somewhere, in towns farther east, other outlaws, even the army."

Callie followed him in unsaddling Betsy. "Seems like a

waste of time to me. Why not just have your own ranch and do things the legal way?''

Chris dropped his saddle in the grass and removed the saddle blanket from Night Wind. "Too much work for some men. They prefer to get by the easy way—take money and goods from honest folks.''

They spent the next several minutes unloading the mules and spare horse. Callie unpacked the fry pan and some potatoes as well as the coffeepot.

"Might as well take it easy on the horses and mules the first few days," Chris told her. "Break them in a little, let them get used to our voices and the extra exercise." He untied a bundle of hobbling stakes and picked up some rope, leading Night Wind and Breeze closer to the stream.

Callie thought how odd this all was. This would be the first night they would spend alone together, him a near stranger, yet already she felt perfectly safe with him. She hoped that wasn't one of the "dumb" things she'd do in life. She walked over to Betsy, smacking her bottom while she grabbed the bridle to one of the mules, and herded both animals to where Chris was hobbling the other two.

Chris pounded stakes into the ground, then tied Breeze and Night Wind to them. He proceeded to do the same with Betsy and the mule Callie had brought over, while Callie went back for the second mule. She pulled on its bridle and urged it to come with her, but the animal wouldn't budge.

"This one is going to be a problem," she yelled to Chris. She moved around and smacked the beast's behind, but the mule only snorted and twitched its ears.

Chris walked closer, scowling with irritation. He whacked the mule even harder on the rump. "Come on, you stubborn ass!" he scolded. "Get yourself moving!"

Callie began tugging at the mule while Chris whistled and smacked its rump. Still the animal would not budge.

"Come on, Rose, move!" she pleaded.

"You named the *mules?*''

"Sure. Luke said they didn't have any names, and I felt sorry for them."

Chris shook his head. "Well, Rose sure doesn't fit this one. She's more like a damn thorn in the side." He smacked the mule again, then held out his arms as though giving up. "I want some coffee and potatoes, and I don't feel like giving them up for a stubborn mule."

Callie shrugged. "Hobble her right here, then. Maybe a night without water will teach her to mind."

Chris studied her a minute, then suddenly grinned. "Damn good idea. I can't believe I didn't think of that myself."

Callie put her hands on her hips. "See? I'm not always dumb about things."

"Yeah? Well, I already told you I never thought you were dumb. You just—" He stopped talking when Rose suddenly walked briskly toward the area where the other animals were hobbled. He and Callie both stared until she reached the water and began drinking.

Chris turned to Callie then, shaking his head and chuckling. "Now, *there* is the ultimate in stubbornness and independence," he commented. "Reminds me a little of you."

"Me!"

"Sure. Won't do what I say, then does it her own way."

Their gazes held in a way that made Callie feel strangely close to him. She quickly looked away, smiling, realizing he was just teasing her. "You hobble that mule and get a fire going," she ordered. "I'll slice those potatoes and fix some coffee."

She went about doing just that, and it wasn't long before Chris had dug a pit and got a crackling fire going. He laid an iron grate over the hole, and Callie set the coffeepot on it. They both spread out their bedrolls then, and Chris stretched out on his, lying back against his saddle.

"If you need to tend to personal matters, go ahead," he told Callie. "I'll be lying here with my eyes closed."

Callie stirred the potatoes, then reached into her supplies for a roll of the paper folks had come to use for such things. She walked around to a spot where she'd be behind him, thinking how this wasn't so difficult or embarrassing back at the canyon. She could just go around a corner and get behind a rock. But here, lordy, there was nothing but wide open spaces, not a rock or a tree to hide behind. She had to trust Christian Mercy completely not to take a peek when she dropped her britches.

"You just remember what I told you about shooting you dead," she reminded him.

Chris only laughed and raised his hand to wave her off. "Watch out for snakes," he told her.

"Oh, I'll be doing that all right," she answered, "the kind with two legs."

She heard him chuckle as she moved even farther away, quickly taking care of matters, eager to pull her britches back up. Greatly relieved, she marched back to the fire. "Your turn," she announced, handing over the paper.

He opened one eye to look at her. "Number one, I don't feel the need right now," he said. "And number two, men don't need paper, not if all they're doing is watering the grass."

"Watering the—" Callie rolled her eyes and shoved the paper back into the leather saddlebag she'd taken it from. "You can have a crude mouth sometimes, Christian Mercy."

He only grinned, his eyes closed again. "Tell me when the food is ready."

She turned the potatoes again. "Just because I'm a woman doesn't mean I have to serve you like a slave. You can do your share of this anytime you've got a mind to."

"Yes, ma'am, I'll remember that." He breathed deeply. "Smells good."

"Thank you." Callie thought this was at least one way she could show him how grown-up and womanly she could be. "My pa used to say I was the best damn cook there ever was. I've been cooking whole meals since I was ten years old." She was pleased to see his eyebrows arch in surprise. She could tell she'd made an impression.

"That's pretty good," he told her. "I'll let you know if he was right."

She smiled. "Well, it's kind of hard to prove it under these conditions. I can't bake bread or biscuits or a pie. I can't cook fresh vegetables or make a good roast. You'll just have to believe me how good I can cook."

"Oh, I believe you."

She smiled proudly at the words.

"May I say you have a very pretty smile, Callie Hobbs? You should smile more often."

She hadn't expected the compliment. Why did it make her heart kind of flutter? Was he just spoofing her? Maybe laughing at her on the inside? "Do you believe we are safe here, Mr. Mercy?" she asked, suddenly wanting to change the subject.

"No. But from here on we won't be completely safe anywhere, so you might as well get used to it. Just eat and get some rest. I'll keep watch for a while. I'll wake you up later and you can take over. I hope you weren't lying when you said you could use your pa's shotgun."

"I never lie about anything, Mr. Mercy."

"No, I expect not. I don't either. That's probably why we'll argue more than get along. We're both too damn honest."

Callie could not help a light laugh. "Maybe you're right." She let him rest while the potatoes cooked and the coffee finally began to boil. She took a couple of biscuits from her food stash, biscuits she'd baked six days earlier. "We can eat," she told Chris. "The biscuits are getting hard, but they're still good. They were so fresh and soft when I took them out of the oven, but then the Wyoming air gets to them and in no time they turn into rocks. Sorry."

She spooned some potatoes onto a tin plate and plunked a biscuit onto it, then handed it to him with a fork. To her pleasure, Christian Mercy ate heartily. She could tell he liked the food. She ate a little herself but was unable to eat much. Her stomach was too knotted up from her own nervousness over this first day's journey and wondering what lay ahead for them. She poured both of them some coffee into tin cups and sat down on her bedroll. "It sure feels good just to sit on something that doesn't move," she told Chris, picking up her plate and eating a few potatoes.

Chris set his plate aside and yawned, then took a swallow of coffee. "You might as well go ahead and get some rest soon as you clean up. Leave the coffee on. I'll keep drinking it till the fire dies down ... helps keep me awake."

"Okay." Callie ate her biscuit, then carried the fry pan and a rag to the stream, where she scrubbed the pan with sand. She returned to set the pan near the fire, figuring she might have to use it in the morning again. She positioned her father's shotgun beside her bedroll, then crawled under the blankets fully clothed. "Probably best I leave my boots on, isn't it?" she asked Chris.

"Well, sleeping is a lot more comfortable without them, but in situations like this, you never know when you might have to jump and run, so, yes, leave them on."

Callie pulled her blankets up under her chin, resting her head against her saddle. "Gosh, this feels good." She closed her eyes, getting a whiff of cigarette smoke when Chris lit another smoke for himself.

"It's going to be a nice night," he told her. "Clear. It gets cold here at night, even in the hot summer."

It was close to completely dark, and the dwindling fire made a crackling sound. Callie thought how peaceful it was here, thinking how ironic that was, considering the kind of men who rode through these parts. Her eyes popped open again when wolves began howling far off, among the surrounding cliffs and mesas that now were just black lines by the moonlight. She heard Chris sip more coffee, then stand up and walk out into the darkness. Soon she could see only the dim red end of his lit cigarette, and she knew he held his Winchester in one hand.

She felt safe, and she didn't hate him so much just then.

Chapter Fourteen

The day stretched into long hours of riding under the hot sun, too hot even for her to talk. Callie rode Night Wind, and Chris rode Breeze. He didn't seem to have too much trouble handling the horse, but every once in a while Breeze would snort and shake his mane, suddenly shuffling sideways. When Chris gave him a little kick and a stern command to straighten up, the horse would object with a toss of the head but finally obey.

"I can see what Luke meant about this one being ornery sometimes," Chris complained after the latest bout between them. "I don't think you should ride him. I'll ride Betsy tomorrow and you can ride Night Wind again. You're so light that it's not going to hurt any of these horses to carry you two days in a row."

"Maybe the Appaloosa will straighten out when he gets more tired."

"He might. He also might just get ornerier."

Breeze whinnied as though he sensed they were talking about him.

"How much do you weigh anyway?" Chris asked Callie.

They rode beside each other now, the horses ambling through the endless valley at a comfortable walk.

"I have no idea. I've never weighed myself. Pa didn't have a scale."

He looked at her discerningly then, pursing his lips as he calculated her dimensions. "I'd guess you're not much over a hundred pounds." He frowned as he paid attention to the path ahead again. "You really eighteen years old?"

"Of course I am. Why would I lie about something like that?"

"I don't know. Just wondering."

"Why does it matter how old I am?"

"It doesn't . . . not really. I just—" He drew Breeze to a halt before finishing, motioning for her to also stop. Callie obeyed, not sure at first why he'd suddenly stopped, until she followed his gaze to their right. Several men on horses were approaching, a small herd of horses ahead of them. They were still quite far in the distance but close enough that they had most likely seen her and Chris.

"Do you think they're outlaws?" she asked.

"It's a pretty sure bet."

"Should we ride hard? Get farther ahead of them?"

"No. That will just attract their attention and make them think we've got reason to hide from them, or that we're up to something. They might think we're the law. We'll just keep going. If they catch up, they catch up. Maybe we can get some information from them."

Callie felt her heart pound harder. "If we keep going, they'll be behind us."

"I know."

"They could shoot us in the back."

"They could. I'm betting they won't. I told you before, most of these men do live by a certain code of their own. They won't do any shooting unless and until they reach us and find out why we're here."

Callie breathed deeply to calm her nerves and steered Night Wind a little closer to Chris. "Speaking of lawmen, how come you don't just do that for a living? If you're wanting to deal with outlaws and such, why do it as a bounty hunter instead of just wearing a badge?''

"Because when you're a lawman, you answer to someone, which I don't choose to do. You also don't have any choice as to who you chase down. You arrest drunks, card cheaters, men who get in fistfights, things like that. It's not the petty criminal I care about. All I'm after is the worst of them— murderers, especially if they've killed a woman or a child. The higher the bounty, the worse the criminal. They're the ones I'd like to wipe off the face of the earth.''

Callie frowned in thought. "Sounds like you carry a real big hate inside.''

"I do. Just like you.''

"Yeah. I guess I can understand that. Thing is, all I'm after is the men who killed my ma. You're after *all* men who do things like that. I don't suppose you care to explain why yet.''

"I don't.''

Callie sighed, turning to look back at the approaching men. They were getting a little closer and had circled around so that they moved more behind than beside them. "I wonder where those men were last night,'' she commented.

"Probably camped ahead and to the south of us. Could have been in a hollow, down in someplace where we wouldn't have heard them. Sounds are funny out here. The land acts as a barrier. There can be a whole band of Indians camped just on the other side of a rise, and you don't even know it.''

Callie looked ahead again. "Well, that's comforting to know.''

Chris laughed lightly. "I didn't mean to make you worry even more.''

"You're awful calm for knowing there's a whole gang of men behind us.''

"It's going to happen more than once as long as we're on this trail.''

"Will we keep going north after Hole-in-the-Wall?''

"I don't know. I am hoping we can go south. Otherwise

once we reach the Canadian end of the trail, we'll have to double back and cover the same territory on our way south. That's going to take a lot of extra time. I'm hoping to learn something that will tell us which way to go. You just remember one thing, Callie Hobbs, and it's very important.''

''What's that?''

''If you spot one of those men, don't say a damn word. Remember that they don't know anything about you. If you go pointing one out to me the minute you see him, he'll immediately be on the defensive and I've lost my edge. I need to keep him off guard. Understand?''

''Yes, sir. But then he might get away.''

Chris stopped to light a cigarette. ''He won't get away. I promise.''

There was a coldness to the words.

''Tell me something,'' he said. ''Do you think you'll be at peace inside if and when we find all the men and see that they're shot or hanged?''

Callie shrugged. ''I won't know that till it's done.''

He took a deep drag on the cigarette. ''You won't. I've already been through all that. Seeing them dead doesn't change the fact that they killed someone . . . important to you. Some things you just don't ever get over.''

They rode on in silence for a few minutes, and now Callie could hear shouted voices and whistling in the distance behind them. ''Why do you just keep hunting men for bounty, then?''

He took the cigarette from his lips. ''Because it gives me a strange kind of pleasure. Each time I think maybe once I find this one or that one and take him out of society, maybe then I'll be able to forgive and forget and get on with life. That hasn't happened yet.'' He took another draw on the cigarette. ''Damn,'' he muttered.

''What's wrong?''

''I have no idea why I just told you all that. I've never told anybody except one person.''

Callie felt the unexpected jealousy return. ''Lisa?''

He glanced sidelong at her, a smirk of resignation on his face. He said nothing.

"Does she make your toes curl?" Callie asked.

"My toes—" He suddenly burst into laughter. "I forgot I told you about that."

Callie felt relieved. At first she thought he was going to take on one of those angry moods again. She smiled. "You said some man might make my toes curl someday. Can a woman make a *man's* toes curl?"

He laughed more, shaking his head. "I suppose."

"Well? Does Lisa do that to you?"

His smile faded. "Not really. Not in the way I mean."

Callie could hardly believe he was sharing any of these things with her. "Does she love you?"

He kept the cigarette between his lips as he spoke. "In her own way."

Callie felt more alarm when he pulled his rifle from its boot. He handed it to her. "Take this." Then he pulled out his second Winchester, his whole countenance changing. The humorous side was gone. "Remember what I told you," he added.

"I will."

"Don't look back. Just keep riding and keep calm. They'll catch up to us soon."

Callie obeyed, staring straight ahead at the eternally endless horizon as the sounds of horses and squeaking saddles, talk and laughter, whistles and shouts, grew closer.

Chapter Fifteen

Within another twenty minutes Callie and Chris were surrounded by eight men on horseback. Two of them rode on ahead, whistling and shouting at the horses as they spurred the herd on. The other six rode beside Chris and Callie.

"Afternoon," one of them said to Chris. He rode in front of Chris and turned to face him.

"Afternoon," Chris answered, halting his horse. Callie also stopped, Chris's Winchester resting across her lap. She suddenly wished she'd practiced a little with it. So far she hadn't had the chance. The man in front of Chris looked just as she'd expected, unkempt, needing a shave. She guessed him to be not much older than Chris. His black hair hung long and stringy, and the discerning look in his dark eyes when he moved his gaze to her made her uncomfortable.

"You two headed for Hole-in-the-Wall?" the man asked.

"Might be," Chris answered. "That where you're going?"

"Sure enough. Takin' a nice herd of horses on through there and over to Casper."

Chris pushed back his hat, his right hand on his rifle, his finger on the trigger. "That's a damn long way."

The man shrugged. "I figure I'll pick up more on the way."

Chris looked around at the others, some of whom Callie could feel staring at her. "You in the horse-trading business, are you?" Chris asked the apparent leader, turning his attention back to the man.

Several of the men laughed.

"You might say that," their leader answered. "Name's Buck Brooster. How about you?"

"Christian Mercy."

One of the others chuckled. "Christian Mercy! Now, ain't that a hell of a name? You a preacher or somethin'?"

Chris looked his way. "Far from it."

"Hey, I know that name," one of the others said.

Callie looked his way. He was young and skinny. She studied him. No, he wasn't one of them. She began taking a good look at each of the other men, not caring what they thought of it. The skinny one looked over at Buck.

"He's a bounty hunter," he told Buck.

Most of them lost their smiles, and a couple more of them rode closer to Buck to face Chris.

"That true?" Buck asked Chris.

"Might be."

"Who you lookin' for?"

Chris glanced around at all of them. "I'm not even sure. I don't have names, just faces, and the little lady with me is the only one who knows those faces."

Callie kept quiet, just as Chris had instructed.

"What did they do?" the skinny one asked.

"Killed her ma. Down Rawlins way. And they weren't too kind to her before they killed her, if you know what I mean."

There came a moment of silence. Callie glanced at Chris, who continued to carefully scrutinize each man. She suspected he had a talent for being aware of every man's movements.

"Know what you mean," one of the others answered.

Callie didn't see a truly clean-shaven man among them, but that could be just because they had been on the trail a long time. Their attire was typical for riding the trail, but none wore badly soiled clothing. They were simply dusty from riding, as she and Chris were. Chris, however, had shaved at the stream that morning before they left.

"You mind describin' them, little lady?" Buck asked.

The question surprised Callie. She looked at Chris, who nodded his approval. She looked at Buck then. "Well, sir—" She looked around at the others then. "It wasn't none of these men, I can tell you that."

They all looked at each other, some smiling. "Heck no," one of them spoke up. "We'll make off with anybody's horses we can, but we ain't ones to be killin' no woman over it, or doin' anything else to her."

Callie felt a little easier, except for the comment about stealing horses. She and Chris were sitting on a couple of very fine steeds. "One was pretty ordinary-looking," she told them. "But another was real young and skinny, with long blond hair he wore tied back. Another one of them was thin too but older. He had a mole on his right cheek. The fourth one looked Mexican, had big shoulders and arms and black, curly hair. And the one who seemed to be the leader, he's the only one whose name I heard. They called him Terrence, and he was a real big man with an ugly scar across his right cheek."

They all looked at each other again. "Terrence?" Buck asked.

"Yes, sir."

Buck turned his attention to Chris.

"Could be Terrence Stowers. He sure fits the description."

"Do you know where he is?" Callie asked excitedly.

Chris cast her a warning look, and she felt embarrassed. She was supposed to let him ask the questions. Chris turned to Buck. "Have you seen him?"

Buck scratched his chin. "Well, now, that depends. Is there a bounty on him? I could use a few extra bucks myself."

Chris shook his head. "No bounty."

"Aw, come on now," the skinny one spoke up. "You're a bounty hunter. I gotta admit, Christian Mercy is a hell of a name for a bounty hunter, but still and all, that's what you are.

Why would you look for this man if he don't have a bounty on his head?''

Chris raised his rifle so that the butt rested on his thigh and the barrel pointed into the air. ''Not everything a man does has to be for money.''

Some of them chuckled. ''Mister, you and I don't think much alike in that respect,'' one of them said.

Chris took his cigarette from his mouth and smashed it out against his saddle. Callie noticed a black spot on the saddle where he'd put out other cigarettes. ''Maybe so,'' he answered. ''All I'm telling you is that there is no legal bounty on him, mainly because they weren't able to give him a full name. But Callie here is willing to give over her last savings for the man's head. Considering what they did, and what she's been through, I agreed to try to find them. She's along because she's the only one who knows what they look like.'' He faced Buck again. ''Now, how about answering my question? Have you seen this Terrence Stowers?''

Buck looked around at the others before answering. ''Yup. Seen him down in Utah Territory, around Robber's Roost. He was braggin' about gettin' a good price for some fine horses over to Salt Lake City. That was last fall.''

''My horses!'' Callie seethed.

''Maybe so,'' Buck answered. ''He didn't say nothin' about hurtin' no woman, but he knows most of us don't agree with such things. He probably thought it was best he keep quiet about it.''

''Was there anyone with him who fit the other descriptions?'' Chris asked the man.

Buck thought a moment. ''Well, there was a Mexican with him. I didn't see the two skinny ones, but there was one other man with him. Not much of a way to describe him. He was too average-lookin'.''

''That has to be two of the others,'' Callie told Chris. ''Let's go down to that Robber's Roost right now!''

The others laughed, and Chris shook his head. ''It will take weeks to get there," he told her. "Meantime the man will move on someplace else."

"But Buck here *saw* him!"

"Months ago," Chris reminded her. "I told you this wouldn't be easy. Just relax and be quiet."

The others chuckled, and Buck barked at all of them to go on ahead and help keep the herd in line. The men obeyed, some of them tipping their hats to Callie.

"Good luck, ma'am," the skinny one told her.

They all rode off, and Buck turned to Chris. "You're right. Terrence Stowers gets around. God only knows where he is right now. My advice is to go on to Hole-in-the-Wall, rest your horses, ask around some more. Maybe somebody there has seen Stowers or one of the others more recently. Then take your time headin' south, askin' questions all the way."

Chris nodded. "Exactly my plan. Any chance you can convince your men to keep quiet about this? I don't want Stowers finding out by the grapevine that I'm looking for him."

Buck sniffed and wiped at his forehead with his shirtsleeve. "I'll do my best."

"Thanks."

"You folks want to camp with us tonight? Got plenty of food, and you're always safer traveling with extras."

Breeze whinnied and tossed his mane again as though eager to get started. "Well, that depends on who the extras are. Callie and I are sitting on some mighty fine horses. We need them for the long trip ahead. I'd hate to wake up in the morning and find them gone."

Buck laughed. "You son of a bitch!" He laughed more. "I'll make you a deal. You let the little lady there cook for us tonight, and we'll let you keep your horses."

Chris looked at Callie, grinning slyly. "What do you say?"

"I'd say I don't have much choice, considering there's eight of them and two of us."

Buck laughed heartily. "Smart gal! Hey, Mercy, you better keep a good eye on her once you get to Hole-in-the-Wall. She ain't bad-lookin' under that floppy ol' hat and them men's clothes.''

"Well, now I'll make *you* a deal, Buck," Chris told the man.

"What's that?"

"You make sure none of your men tries to take liberties with her, and I won't kill you."

"Me, Hell, I don't have no plans on doin' anything disrespectful.''

"I didn't say you did. I just said if any of your men gets ideas, I'll kill you first. It doesn't matter that there are eight of you."

Buck lost his smile. "Well, now, you drive a hard bargain."

"It's the only way to be sure Callie truly is safe if we camp with you."

The two men glared at each other a moment, but it was Buck who showed resignation in his eyes. "All right. But I assure you, Mercy, there's no worry there. You heard what one of my men said earlier. We don't do things like that."

"Well, now, I understand that. But some men might think there's no harm in getting in a kiss or a feel. Know what I mean?"

Callie looked away in embarrassment.

"I reckon' I do know what you mean," Buck told Chris. "Ain't nobody gonna bring her no harm." He turned his horse. "Come on. Ride with us awhile."

He kicked his horse into a gentle trot.

"Let's go," Chris told Callie.

They rode a little slower, letting Buck ride ahead to talk to his men.

"Would you really shoot him if somebody messed with me?" Callie asked.

"I always keep my promises." He looked over at her, his eyes dropping to her bosom. "Keep that vest buttoned all the way. No sense aggravating the situation."

Callie looked down, forgetting she'd unbuttoned her vest because of the heat. She let go of the reins and began buttoning the vest. She wasn't quite sure why, in spite of her embarrassment, she took pleasure in realizing the man noticed her breasts, and just yesterday he'd told her she had a pretty smile. Buck Brooster had said she wasn't bad-looking, and though Chris was silent, he must agree, or he wouldn't have warned Buck that his men had better not get ideas.

Chapter Sixteen

Callie found Buck's gang of rustlers to be surprisingly courte-
ous and very well supplied. They dug through their stash to
come up with fry pans, a deeper cooking pot, potatoes, salt
pork, onions, turnips, a couple of cans of beans, salt, coffee,
molasses, flour, baking soda, and a large can of corn. They got
a fire started for her and went about unloading their horses and
opening bedrolls.

Chris did Callie's unpacking for her and laid out her bedroll
near his. She began preparing a stew from the potatoes, corn,
onions, turnips, and salt pork, and in one of the fry pans she
cooked some beans with molasses. She mixed flour, water, and
a little baking soda into a dough, which she broke off in pieces,
rolled into drop dumplings, and added to the stew.

While she cooked, the men relaxed and began telling stories,
each man trying to outdo the next in his tales of daredevil,
thievery, bravery, whatever they could think of. Callie suspected they were trying to impress her more than one another,
and they most likely stretched the truth considerably.

She heated some coffee, feeling uneasy when Buck broke
out some whiskey and began passing a bottle around. She had

not led such a sheltered life that she didn't know what whiskey could do to a man. She'd seen drunks in Rawlins, watched her father get drunk once. That was the only time he'd turned mean and hit her mother, who then flat-out told him that if he did so again, she would leave him. Clayton Hobbs never got drunk again and never raised his hand to his wife again.

The men who had attacked her mother had passed around a flask of whiskey, seeming to take more courage, if it could be called that, with each sip they took. Now listening to these men's voices grow louder as they drank brought unwanted memories to mind, and she was eager for the food to be finished. Maybe full bellies would counteract the effects of the whiskey. When Chris refused a drink, she breathed a little easier, knowing he was too smart to sit there and get drunk with a bunch of horse thieves.

"Smells good," Buck told Callie. "Joe over there, he's usually the cook, but what he knows about cooking you could stick in a thimble."

They all laughed, including Joe, and again the whiskey bottle was passed around.

"These aren't the best conditions," Callie apologized. "I'm doing the best I can do, but don't be expecting the greatest meal you ever ate."

"Just watchin' a pretty little gal cook it is feast enough," one of the others said.

"Yeah, and a woman has that special touch," Joe added. "Why is it a man and a woman can cook somethin' exactly the same way and the woman's will taste better?"

They all laughed again. Callie glanced at Chris again. He sat smoking quietly, watching her, saying little. What was that look in his eyes? She saw an odd appreciation there, almost like he . . . admired her.

She tasted the stew, then added more salt and pepper. More than once some of the men had referred to her as a woman. She had no use for this bunch of thieves, but she did appreciate being called a woman in front of Christian Mercy, who apparently had doubted she was even eighteen years old. She still wondered why he'd asked about her age. It was as though eighteen were some kind of magical number, but she wasn't sure what for.

"I'm ready to dig into a dish of whatever you're makin'," one of the men told Callie. "I'm surprised a young thing like you can cook so well, especially out here on the trail. A lot of women wouldn't know how to make do away from a real stove."

Callie seldom looked at any of them when she spoke to them. She thought it best not to make eye contact. "Lived on a ranch all my life," she answered the man. "We never had a real cookstove till just the last couple of years. I'm used to cooking over fires. My pa always said I was a good cook."

"Well, we all hope he was right," the youngest in the group told her.

Callie tasted the stew again, eager herself for it to be done. "Just a few more minutes," she told them.

"Whooee!" one of them shouted before downing more whiskey. Callie cringed at the shout. One of the men who'd attacked her mother had shouted that word. She looked over at the man. No, he wasn't one of them. It was just the word that was familiar.

"You guys remember what a good cook Bertha Tripp was?" Joe asked.

"Who cared about her cookin'?" another put in.

They all shared in more laughter, and Callie felt a flush come to her face. She had a pretty darn good idea Bertha Tripp was a lot like that woman Lisa. When she looked at Chris, he was also grinning.

"You can all eat now," Callie spoke up.

"All right, you guys, pick up a plate and get in line," Buck told them. "Take your turn and don't be rude. Jay, soon as you and Lennie are done, go watch the herd and let Hal and Dennis come on in and eat."

They all lined up with eager grins and empty plates, each making his own remark about how good the food looked and smelled as Callie dipped a heap of stew and then a heap of beans onto each plate. They all politely said their thank yous. Chris was last, and he smiled at her in a way he'd never smiled before, as though he truly thought she was quite the lady, as if she were something more than an uneducated kid.

Callie fixed herself a plate, and while she ate, the others carried on about how good the food was.

"Mister, you got yourself one perfect travelin' partner," one of them told Chris. "Pretty to look at and a good cook to boot. Play your cards right, and she'll—"

"Shut up, Clint," Buck interrupted. "Don't turn a compliment into an insult."

"Huh? Oh, I didn't mean no harm. I just figured . . . hell, Mr. Mercy there, he's a handsome fella, and if they're gonna be travelin' together all the way down the trail, they might as well keep each other warm at night and—"

"She's my client and a very proper woman," Chris said, cutting him off. "And you're looking to get that plate of stew crammed right into your face."

Joe laughed in a teasing cackle, and some of the others chuckled. Clint, a man perhaps a little older than Chris, and who wore his curly brown hair long, glared at Chris.

"I already said I didn't mean no harm," he told Chris. "Hell, I even said you was handsome. Maybe I should mess up that face of yours with my fist."

"You're drunk, Clint," Buck told the man. "Finish your food and put up for the night. You're lettin' the whiskey talk."

Clint glared at Chris a moment longer, then returned to eating. Callie felt uneasy at how quickly men like this could turn from polite to possibly ruthless. There seemed to be a thin line to tread when around them.

"I'm tellin' all of you right now," Buck said. "One insult and you can be on your way. Lay a hand on the little lady and you're dead. Mr. Mercy here has said that if any of you touches her, he'll shoot *me* first. So to keep that from happenin', I'll be watchin' you myself. I don't intend to die because one of you can't think with what's upstairs instead of what's downstairs."

"Ain't none of us gonna insult the lady who just cooked us the best meal we've had in weeks," Joe said.

"Hell no," another man put in.

Callie looked at Buck, who watched all of them carefully. Some of the men took extra helpings, and by the time the two men riding herd came in to eat, their helpings literally wiped out every bit of leftovers. Bellies were full, and to Callie's continued amazement, two of the men even offered to take the pans and plates to the stream and clean them themselves, relieving her of the job.

The men called Jay and Lennie remained out in the darkness to guard the horses, and the rest of them stretched out on bedrolls to smoke and tell a few more stories, more like tall tales as far as Callie was concerned. By the time full darkness fell, most of them were sleeping off their food and whiskey, a couple of them snoring.

Callie left the coffeepot on the fire and moved to her bedroll, which Chris had laid out close to his.

"Very good meal," he told her.

"Thank you."

"Move your bedroll next to mine," he told her in a lowered voice. "I want you right next to me. None of them will try anything with you that close."

The request made Callie feel both reassured and wary. "I guess that's okay," she told him. "Probably a good idea."

He smiled wryly and shook his head. "I think so."

Callie moved her bedroll close. "Will you please watch these men while I go take care of something personal?"

He grinned and lit another cigarette. "Sure."

Callie walked out into the darkness and quickly relieved herself, hardly able to for nervousness over dropping her britches with nine men not far away. She just wished she could overcome the ugly memories of her mother's attack, wished she could learn to trust a little more. She did not like the idea of lying right beside Christian Mercy, but she supposed it was safer than going off away from all of them to sleep.

She finally finished and gladly hiked her underwear and

denim pants back in place. She hurried back and crawled into her bedroll, again leaving her boots on and laying her father's shotgun beside her. Chris finished his cigarette, and by the light of the dimming fire Callie saw him remove his six-guns and lay them between them, along with his rifle. He turned on his side, facing her.

"If you need one of those handguns, use it," he told her.

Callie turned to look at him. "Yes, sir." Their gazes held for a moment, and a quick sensation of wanting Christian Mercy to hold her shot through Callie with such force and surprise that she quickly turned onto her back.

What was that? she wondered. Why did the thought of strong arms around her sound so good? She then realized she'd had absolutely no one to comfort and reassure her that way since the loss of her father. She remembered that in spite of his strict ways, sometimes she just felt better when her father would give her a rare embrace, pat her on the back and tell her everything was okay.

But that was her father, not a man who might get other thoughts if she asked for a reassuring embrace. "Good night, Mr. Mercy," she said, looking up at the stars.

His only answer was a deep sigh.

Chapter Seventeen

It surprised Callie to realize she actually felt safe riding with Buck Brooster and his men. The night had passed with no problems, but she suspected that was not due so much to the fact that the rustlers had respect for a "proper lady" as it was due to the presence of Christian Mercy.

She could not shake the secret thoughts of the previous night and how she'd longed to be held, just for a little while . . . just a hug of reassurance. The Sooners had been supportive, and Betty Sooner had embraced her lightly a few times; but it wasn't the same as her own mother or father hugging her, nor the embrace of someone strong and protective.

How could a man like Christian Mercy understand that? Didn't all men outside of family get ideas if a woman let them embrace her? The last thing she wanted or needed was for the man she'd be traveling alone with getting the idea that she had some kind of womanly interest in him. Even so, she knew damn well that little shadows of desire had passed over her a time or two, feelings that shocked and frightened her . . . feelings that must not be allowed to surface.

All that next day they rode through country unlike anything

she'd set eyes on, through a sweeping valley of yellow grass
surrounded by mesas hundreds of feet high, their red-rock walls
literally intimidating in size and grandeur. Brooster's men rode
mostly ahead of her and Chris, herding their stolen horses,
whistling, calling to them, waving coils of rope, gradually heading toward one of the highest rock walls Callie had seen. It
appeared to be only a day's ride away. But by nightfall she
realized they were only about halfway there. Off to the left the
land rippled upward in a series of hills that had a look of velvet,
while ahead of them and along the right were those rock walls
that seemed to look down on them like mighty gods.

They camped another night, and another day's ride brought
them closer to the same rock wall they'd been aiming for the
day before, yet still they did not reach it. Another day's ride
brought them almost there, and by the fourth day they reached
an area at the base of the rock wall. The land there was peppered
with huge boulders, chunks of rock that over time had broken
away from the walls of the mesas around them and rolled
hundreds, even thousands of feet into the valley. The way they
were scattered about, it made Callie wonder if God had taken
handfuls of boulders and simply thrown them across the valley
like little stones.

In late afternoon Buck rode back to join Chris and Callie,
pointing to the vast wall they'd finally reached. "Hole-in-the-
Wall is just up top of that mesa," he told Callie.

Callie studied the wall with apprehension. "How are we
going to get up there?" she asked.

"Well, honey, where there's a will, there's a way. Me and
my men need a good rest, and so do those horses we've been
herding along with us, so we won't start up till mornin'. Once
we're at the top, you'll see why men like us like it. Up there
you can see for a hundred miles, a good place to watch for the
law in case they're stupid enough to try to come after us. It's
a great place for outlaws to find some peace, and there's good
grass up there for the horses."

Callie squinted as she took another look toward the top.
"Dang long ways," she commented.

Buck laughed. "That it is. Better ride a horse you really trust."

"Which means neither one of us will ride Breeze," Chris said rather absently.

"How come they call it Hole-in-the-Wall?" Callie asked. "I figured it would be some kind of big cutout in the wall itself, not the top."

"Well, it's kind of a cutout we follow goin' up," Buck answered. He sniffed and rubbed at his nose. "I reckon it's really a short way to say a place to hole up on top of the wall. I don't know who come up with the name." Buck tipped his hat and looked at Chris. "We'll make camp at the base of the wall and start up in the mornin'. I reckon we've got a couple more hours of light. That should get us real close." He kicked his horse and rode off.

Callie turned to Chris. "What's it like up there?"

Chris shrugged. "Not much of anything to speak of—just a big, wide mesa and a couple of log cabins."

"You mean there might not even be any others up there?"

"Might not be, but we have to check it out."

Callie sighed with frustration. "This is going to take a really long time, isn't it?"

"Yes, ma'am. We can quit anytime you say."

Callie shook her head. "No. We've been close to two weeks traveling since we left Rawlins. I'm not quitting after coming this far. If we find even *some* of those men, it will be worth it."

"Whatever you say."

Callie caught him looking her over in a rather unsettling way. Damn those blue eyes! If not for what she'd witnessed, she'd be infatuated with the man's looks, like any normal young girl should be. She looked away, reminding herself that he was too old for her. Besides, he probably had some god-awful thing about his own past to get over, something that made him kill for money. Being attracted to a man like that could spell nothing but trouble for a woman's heart.

She kicked her horse into a faster trot, angry with herself for again entertaining such thoughts.

Chris watched the way Callie's small rump bounced in her saddle, finding the sight very distracting. Already he was making one big mistake on this particular job—allowing himself to become emotionally attached. It wasn't that he loved her or anything like that. That was one feeling he would never allow. But Callie Hobbs was a fascinating cross between girl and woman. So often he saw only the kid in her. And then there were times . . .

Like when she slept beside him at night. A couple of times he'd caught himself just lying there, watching her sleep, seeing a little girl, then seeing sweet, full lips that had never been kissed out of passion and thinking about those young, firm breasts that had never been caressed.

He cursed his thoughts and rode up closer. The thoughts she gave him reminded him of the sensual, satisfying relationship he'd had with Val and the beautiful, sweet daughter that relationship had produced . . . his little Patty.

How was he ever going to get over the hurt of losing his family, the awful pain of it? Four years had passed, four years of wandering, chasing outlaws, teaching himself to be damn good with firearms; four years of not caring about a damn thing—man, woman, or animal—four years of feeling completely empty, completely emotionless.

Now comes this freckle-faced woman/child, all alone in this world, just like him. A woman/child with bad memories to overcome, a woman/child filled with hate and revenge . . . just like him. He'd come across a complete stranger who would probably understand everything he was feeling if he would share it with her, and maybe sharing it with her would help her overcome her own horrors. But it hurt too much to talk about it. It was so much easier to keep it all buried so deep that most of the time he could go on with life like it never happened, as long as he didn't allow the hurt to come exploding out of the grave in his soul.

Gunslinging bounty hunters didn't cry. They did not allow feelings of any kind to surface, and there was no use allowing sweet memories to invade daily life. After all, he would never know that kind of life again. He would never see his wife and daughter again, never touch them again, never hold them. He hadn't been there for them when they needed him most, and that was something he would never forgive himself for.

Hatred. That was what kept him going, and he must never allow any other kind of emotion to invade his shattered heart. Trouble was, he hated himself more than he hated any of the men he hunted. He thought that hatred would end if he found his wife's killers, but seeing them die wouldn't bring back Val and Patty, and so the hatred probably wouldn't end there, just as he suspected Callie would find no satisfaction in watching her mother's rapists and killers die.

He should probably tell her that; but hell, he was getting some valuable land out of this. The pay was good, so he'd find them for her and bring them in ... or kill them, whichever way they wanted it. Callie Hobbs could wrangle with her own feelings after that. It wasn't his affair. In the meantime, he could only hope it wouldn't take too long to find them. He could already see that being alone with the woman, possibly for months, was going to be a harder task than hunting the men she was after.

Chapter Eighteen

"Oh, Lord, my God, let me get to the top," Callie murmured, following "Skinny" up the trail leading to Hole-in-the-Wall. The rest of Buck's gang was ahead of Skinny, men interspersed with horses, so that the herd of approximately twenty horses was stretched out in a line of three or four in a row, then a man, then three or four more horses, making them a little easier to manage.

Then came Callie, leading one pack mule. Chris rode behind her, leading the other pack mule and Breeze. All of them knew that any one of the horses, either those ridden or those being herded, could balk at any time and possibly cause one or more men and horses to stumble and fall. If that happened, there would be no getting up. Man and animal would just keep falling and sliding down the terrifyingly steep embankment covered with loose stone, as well as bigger boulders, any of which could come loose and come tumbling down at any moment.

"I've ridden horses all my life," Callie shouted back to Chris. "I've herded cattle, herded horses, walked behind a horse and plow, rode up mountain trails . . . but I've never rode up anything this steep and slippery. I hope Betsy is as surefooted as I think she is.''

''Not much choice. It's the only way up,'' Chris answered. ''By the way, the word is ridden.''

''What?''

''You have *ridden* up mountain trails and have never *ridden* up something this steep—not rode. You said you didn't have much schooling. Just thought I'd give you a quick lesson in proper English to keep your mind off the danger of this climb.''

Callie rolled her eyes. ''Well, it's not working, and when I go rolling all the way to the bottom of this hill or wall or whatever you want to call it, I don't think the good Lord will care about my proper use of words when He greets me. At least I *hope* it's Him who will greet me, and not something with pitchfork and horns.''

Skinny and Chris both laughed.

''I got a feelin' it will be the horns and pitchfork for me,'' Skinny shouted back.

''Better quit talking and concentrate on your horses,'' Chris warned then. ''Talk to them nice and gently. We're headed for an even steeper grade.''

''Lord Almighty!'' Callie whispered as she looked ahead. ''If I didn't *need* to look, I'd close my eyes,'' she said louder.

They all rode on in near silence then, each man, and Callie, watching every foothold, every boulder, every tumble of gravel and dirt. The horses seemed to sense the need to be extra cautious. Suddenly, one of the horses being herded balked and whinnied, stumbling slightly but staying on all fours. That horse was right in front of Joe, and Joe immediately reined his horse to a halt and dismounted, taking the animal by the reins and patting the horse ahead of him on the rump, talking quietly to the animal and urging it to keep going.

It took a few minutes for Callie's heart to stop beating so hard it hurt her chest, and she, too, decided to get down and lead Betsy, choosing to walk up the rest of the way. She looked back at Chris, who remained mounted on Night Wind. The horse had so far proved to be levelheaded and obedient, even today on this steep bank. Breeze had been surprisingly well behaved so far, but then, no one was riding him. It seemed it was only when a human was on his back that he got stubborn.

When they neared the top, she heard Buck calling out to someone, and all down the line men shouted to hold up. She halted Betsy and shaded her eyes to see what was going on. Two men with rifles were guarding what looked like a narrow opening that was probably the last obstacle to reaching the top. It looked like Buck was talking to them.

"Outlaws guarding the place," Chris told her.

Callie's stomach took a flip. More new men—more outlaws. Maybe these weren't as friendly or respectful as Buck and his men. And maybe . . . just maybe . . . she would recognize one of them.

The two guards finally moved out of the way to let Buck through, and the whole procession made the last of the climb, finally reaching the top. They first had to ride through the small "hole" in the wall's top rim where the guards had been. Once through that, the trail opened onto the grassy top of the mesa, the famed Hole-in-the-Wall, where outlaws liked to take their rest.

"Here we are!" Skinny called out. "You can see forever up here. And I mean *forever!* Up here we can fatten up stolen cattle, graze and rebrand stolen horses, then take them down for resale. While we're up here, ain't nobody gonna bother us." He looked back at Callie. "You can see for yourself that that little crack in the wall we came through—hell, a couple of men with Winchesters can stand there and hold off a whole posse of men tryin' to scramble up here. It's pretty much impossible for lawmen to make it up here without bein' seen and stopped, usually with a bullet."

Callie could readily understand what he meant. When they reached the top, she literally gasped at the sight, wondering if she was actually looking at Montana to the north or Colorado to the south. That was how far it seemed she could see. For miles on end in any direction there was nothing but more mountain ranges, and in some places open, flat land stretched out so far, she felt almost like a god up here. "Lordy," she whispered.

"Quite a view, isn't it?" Chris said, dismounting and coming closer.

"Sure is. Almost makes you want to whisper."

"Well, if we don't find the men you're after, you at least have seen a good share of country you never would have seen otherwise."

Callie kept turning in circles to gaze. "I sure never would," she said, feeling almost hypnotized by the view. "Lordy," she repeated. "This is really something."

Chris paused to light a cigarette. "Keep quiet about why we're here," he said, keeping his eyes on the men and horses ahead of them. "I talked to Buck last night, told him to let on that you and I ride with his gang. From what I can tell, there are maybe fifteen or twenty other men up here. If you recognize anybody, don't show it. Understand?"

"It won't be easy, but I'll try."

"Don't just try. Do it."

"Yes, sir."

"And you're my girl. Got that?"

Callie frowned and turned to him. "Your girl?"

Chris rolled his eyes. "Yeah. It's the only way to be pretty sure nobody up here will get ideas about you. They'll figure that if they offend me, they offend Buck's whole gang of outlaws, which wouldn't exactly be healthy for them."

"You mean we're supposed to be *married?*"

Chris took the cigarette from his lips and met her gaze squarely. "No. Women who run with outlaws aren't exactly the type who marry."

Callie's eyes widened. "You mean I'm a—"

"No." He cut her off. "And keep your voice down." He took a deep drag on the cigarette. "Callie, there are some women who are good at heart and who are faithful to their men—who'd follow them to the ends of the earth even if the men don't marry them."

"Why in heck would they do that?"

Chris snickered and shook his head. "Never mind. Just believe me, will you? Being that kind of woman doesn't make you a whore. Men like this will understand and respect the difference. But there will always be some who think you're loose and available. Anybody makes trouble, let me take care of it."

Callie pouted. "Okay, but I don't like anybody thinking like that about me. I'd never go off with a man without a ring on my finger!"

Chris put the cigarette back to his lips. "I don't doubt that for a minute."

He walked off then, leading his horse and the mules. Callie followed him toward a large log building, grabbing her hat when the wind nearly blew it off, a much cooler breeze than down below. Buck had said that up here in the winter the winds were a lot worse, and cold enough to freeze your nose "to where you could snap it right off if you weren't careful." He'd explained that the couple of log buildings had been built mainly as shelter from those winds.

Chris halted Breeze beside the cabin and began unloading some of his gear. "We'll stay the night here, go back down in the morning. Take a good look at new faces before we go. Unload whatever we need for ourselves and stash the rest of our supplies next to the cabin here. If we set up against this wall, we'll be out of the wind. Tether the horses and put some coffee on."

"What are you going to do?"

"I'm going to get you some wood. There's a pile on the other side of the cabin, and I already know it's for sale to men who come up here needing firewood. Then I'm going inside and mix with some of the men. I'll see what I can casually find out on my own. I'll come for you later, and you can go inside and look around. If you happen to see a familiar face, don't say anything to the man. Just wait till I come back and let me know. And don't come running inside for me. I told you I'll be back out, and I will. An outlaw's woman doesn't go searching for him in taverns, and she doesn't go walking alone into taverns full of outlaws. She waits for her man to take her inside.''

Callie shrugged. ''Whatever you say.'' *Her man*? That was an uncomfortable way to have to pretend.

''I just hope we can pull this off,'' he told her, taking his saddle off his horse and dropping it next to the cabin. ''You sure as hell don't look the part. Maybe I should say you're my daughter, or my little sister.''

Now she felt her dander rising. ''I don't look near young enough to be your daughter, Mr. Christian Mercy,'' she answered, yanking at the cinch under Betsy's belly. ''And you don't need to refer to me as a *little* sister!'' She grabbed her own saddle and slammed it to the ground. ''Do you want me to remove this hat and let my hair down? Would that help?''

There was that look again, those blue eyes moving down, then up again. ''Might not hurt. But just let the hair down. Don't go cleaning up and trying to make yourself look too fetching. Then the other men here *will* get other ideas. When you belong to one man, you don't try to look good for any *other* men.''

Did he think she really *could* look fetching? ''All right.'' She took off her floppy hat and tossed it aside, then quickly ripped the combs and pins from her hair, letting the auburn waves fall over her shoulders. ''There. That good enough?''

Damn if she didn't catch something in his look—almost like he was impressed . . . no . . . startled . . . no . . . it was more like . . . like a sudden look of *desire!* Why did that please her?

He nodded with a deep sigh. ''Yeah. That's good enough.'' He looked her over again before turning to walk away, and Callie put a hand to her heart, leaning against the cabin wall.

''Lordy,'' she whispered.

Chapter Nineteen

Callie set the coffeepot on the fire. She started to sit down on her saddle, the only thing handy for a seat, but before she made it all the way down, someone came from around the corner of the cabin. She quickly stood up and turned, squinting against a setting sun that made it impossible to see the face of whoever stood nearby.

She stepped back, taking a quick look around to see if Chris was nearby, but right now most of the men were either inside the cabin or out tending their livestock.

"What do you want, mister?" she asked, reaching behind her to grab hold of the barrel of her father's shotgun that she'd left leaning against the cabin wall. The man made no move for his own six-gun as she brought the shotgun up.

"Heard tell there was a real honest-to-God female out here. Figured I'd come have a look," he answered.

Callie leveled the shotgun at his midsection. "Well, you've had your look, so be on your way."

He didn't budge.

"My man is right inside, and he's got a temper," she warned.

"That so?"

"That's so. And he's right good with a gun."

The man chuckled. "You don't need to be so unfriendly, missy. I just wanted a look, that's all."

"Like I said. You've had it, so get going."

"Well, I would, except I happen to know you're looking for a man with a mole on his right cheek. I'm told this man once ran with a son of a bitch named Terrence Stowers."

Callie lowered the shotgun slightly, excitement beginning to fill her heart. "You know him?"

"I might."

"What do you mean *might?* Do you or don't you?"

"I mean that while your man's inside, I thought if you wanted the information bad enough, you might give me a nice, sweet kiss . . . maybe let me have a feel of your soft parts, you know? Nothin' real bad. Just a feel."

Callie's excitement turned to anger. She raised the shotgun again. "Well, you figured *wrong,* mister! Get the hell away from me!"

He chuckled again. "Well, now, I know you won't shoot me, because then I'd be dead, and you wouldn't have the information you want. Your man inside there, he talked like you wanted to find these men real bad, said as how they'd killed your ma and all, it was real important to you. So I figured that means it's important enough to pay somethin' for the information you want. I just happen to be willing to take somethin' besides money. When a man's been without for a long time, some things become more *important* than money. Know what I mean?"

"I know exactly what you mean, you scummy coward!" Callie noticed the man stiffen, and she pulled back one hammer of the double-barreled gun. "Seems to me like you overestimated what I'd give for the information I need. I suggest you go back and talk to my man about it. He might have a slightly different idea what the information is worth."

The man stood there quietly for a moment, flexing his fingers. "Well, your man is in there drinkin' up a storm and sittin' down to a card game. I don't think he much cares *what's* goin' on out here, if that's what you're worried about. He might not even *mind* if you let some other man have a feel of what's under that shirt to get the information you want.''

''I'm the one who cares, and if you make one move toward me, I'll open your belly, I swear!'' Callie meant every word of it, but even with the shotgun pointed right at him, she was terrified. What the heck was she supposed to do? This man knew something. She couldn't let him get away, but she sure as hell couldn't let him have what he wanted just to tell her what she needed to know. How could she even be sure he knew anything at all?

The man sighed, putting up his hands as though defending himself. ''Okay, lady. You can't blame a man for tryin', can you? I was just testin' you out to see if you really did belong to the man inside. No real harm meant.''

''So *you* say.''

''It's true, ma'am.''

''Then tell me about the man with the mole on his cheek. Where is he?''

The man scratched his chin. ''What else you got to offer? You got any money?''

''That's something to talk to my man about, not me.'' Callie wasn't even sure if she should use Chris's name. Maybe he didn't want some of these men to know it. ''Why don't you step around to where I can see your face better?''

''Not till you tell me how you know for sure that this man killed your ma.''

Callie began to feel suspicions. ''I just know, that's all. And . . . and he wasn't alone. There were others.''

''Others?''

Callie's heart pounded harder. Where was Chris? Was he really inside *drinking?* What the heck should she tell this man? Maybe he knew more than he was letting on. ''You heard me.''

''Where did this happen?''

''What's it to you? All that matters is whether or not you've seen the man who fits the description you heard. You don't need to know anything else, so speak up or go about your business!''

"Well, now, ain't *you* the bossy one?''

"Call it what you like. I think you might as well git, mister. I don't think you know a damn thing!''

Quick as a flash the man grabbed her gun barrel and pushed up, shoving Callie against the wall of the cabin. "I know more than you *think*, missy!'' He sneered. "And I'll take my pay *now!*''

Now Callie could see his face. He was one of them, the one with no distinctive marks! He grasped for a breast, and before Callie could even react, the man jolted away from her. The coffeepot went flying and spilled its contents as the bodies of two men landed in the fire, her attacker's back buried in the hot coals . . . Christian Mercy holding him there. A couple of the bullets in her attacker's gun belt exploded from the heat, and the man jerked and let out bloodcurdling screams as the exploded bullets opened wounds in his already burning back. The screams brought more men running.

Callie leveled her rifle at the other men as Chris yanked her attacker off the coals and landed a hard fist into his face. Blood squirted instantly from a split lip, and the man whirled to the right and landed facedown, his shirt, vest, and the skin on his back still smouldering, while at the same time blood seemed to be everywhere, all from the wounds caused by the exploded bullets.

Quickly Chris yanked the man's six-gun from its holster and tossed it aside before shoving him over onto his back. The man screamed again, letting off a volley of curses from his pain. Callie watched the rest of the men, who included Buck and some of his men. They all stood back, seeming to acknowledge this was between Chris and the man he wrestled.

Chris straddled the man, whipping out his six-gun and holding it against one of the man's ears. "Now, let's hear about your friend, mister! The one with the mole on his cheek! You'll tell me for no pay at all, or I'll fire this gun and you'll be deaf in this ear for life, let alone losing the ear itself! You want the extra pain?''

The man squirmed and screamed more, actually beginning to cry. "Let me up! Let me up! God Almighty, my back! My back!''

Chris cocked his pistol. "Where's the man with the mole on his cheek?'' he growled.

"Ooohhh, my back!'' the man screamed again.

Chris fired, and Callie jumped in surprise. She noticed that even some of the ruffians standing and watching looked surprised. A few of them grimaced as her attacker screamed even louder, putting his hands to the sides of his head and rolling to his knees when Chris got off him. Blood poured through the fingers of his left hand where he was holding his injured ear.

"My God, stop him!'' The man wept. "Somebody stop him!''

Callie waved her shotgun at the rest of them. "Anybody tries to stop him, I'll shoot him myself!''

Chris glanced at her, then leveled his own six-gun at the others. "This is between me and him,'' he said.

Callie noticed his shirt was covered with the other man's blood.

Buck looked around at the others, then pulled out his own gun. "This ain't got nothin' to do with any of you, so leave them be.''

"Jesus!'' one of the others muttered, stepping back farther when Chris kicked the wounded man onto his back again and pressed a booted foot against his throat, cutting off some of his air. Even Callie was surprised at his viciousness, considering what a soft-spoken, calm man he'd been up to now.

"Where's the man with the mole?'' Chris repeated. "Do you want to lose your other ear?''

The man just laid there, weeping, for several seconds. "N-n-no,'' he finally managed to spit out. He screamed again when Chris grasped the front of his shirt and jerked him to a sitting position, then sat down on his legs. "Where is he?'' he repeated.

"R-ranch . . . about . . . thirty miles south of here . . . a little east of Outlaw Trail. Works for . . . Ben Bailey. It's . . . Bailey's ranch.'' He started crying again as blood continued to pour from his wounded ear.

''What's the man's name?'' Chris asked. ''The man with the mole?''

The man literally sobbed. ''Fallon . . . Jim . . . Fallon. Please, mister . . . leave me . . . be.''

He screamed again when Chris shoved him back down, then stood up. He turned to Callie. ''He hurt you?''

At the moment, the look in his eyes frightened even Callie. ''No, sir. Not really. But . . . he's . . . he's one of them. I recognize him.''

Chris just stared at her a moment, then turned back to look down at the man he'd attacked. ''You sure?'' he asked without looking back.

''Yes, sir.''

Chris again clicked back the hammer of his gun. ''Well, my guess is he's dying anyway.''

He pulled the trigger, and Callie jumped again when a hole opened in the man's forehead.

''Lord have mercy,'' one of the others muttered.

Chris looked around at all of them. ''He deserved worse,'' he said. ''Any of you want to argue about it?''

They all backed away. ''Nope,'' one of them answered.

Callie was relieved to see Buck still watching all of them himself, ready with his six-gun. One by one the men walked away.

''I'll get a couple of my men to bury him,'' Buck told Chris.

Chris stared at the body a moment, then slowly replaced his six-gun. He looked at Buck. ''Thanks,'' he told him. ''Fact is, if you could find somebody to get the body out of here and away from Callie's sight, I'd appreciate it.''

Buck replaced his own gun and walked over to the dead man. He grasped his wrists and started dragging. ''No problem,'' he answered. He dragged the body off, and Callie withered against the side of the cabin, sliding down the wall till she sat, her shotgun lying across her lap. "Where in heck were you?" she asked.

"I was right around the corner. The man was at a table, playing cards with me. I noticed a strange look on his face when I asked about a man with a mole on his cheek. He finished his hand and got up and left."

He sighed and turned away, rubbing his eyes.

"I wanted to see what you could get out of him without me around," he continued after a moment. "I didn't expect him to attack you like that." He faced her again, and Callie couldn't quite discern just what she saw in his eyes, a mixture of weariness, terrible rage, and sorrow. "You all right?"

She leaned her head back against the wall. "I'm okay. What about you?"

He shrugged, looking down at his bloody shirt. "I'm not exactly the one who suffered anything physically."

Callie looked him over, suddenly seeing him differently. Surely this ex-teacher was once someone who would never think of doing to any man what he'd done to her attacker. She never expected to see that kind of rage, and she knew it had to come from somewhere deep inside. "I didn't mean physically," she told him. "It bothers you, doesn't it, doing something like that to a man? Even though you know he did something terrible himself?"

He put his hands on his hips, now looking angry again. "You hired me to find these men and bring them in for hanging or kill them, didn't you?"

"Yes, sir."

"Does what I did bother *you?* He helped rape and kill your mother."

She looked at her lap. "I don't know what to think or what to feel."

"You want to quit?"

Callie looked over at the spilled coffee. "Quit asking me that. We've got a lead on at least one of them now. We *have* to keep going." She looked back at him. "If finding them and getting them arrested, or even if we have to kill them, if that means they can't do to somebody else what they did to my mother, then it's worth it. We can't quit yet.''

He nodded. "Just making sure." He looked around. "I think everybody here has a good idea how they'll pay if they give you trouble, so it's probably safe for me to leave for a while."

"Leave?"

"I need to be alone."

It does bother you, she thought. "Sure. I'll clean up around here. Aren't you hungry?"

He smiled almost sadly. "No, ma'am, I am not hungry— not now." He walked over and picked up his bedroll and his own rifle. "I'll see you in the morning. I'll tell Buck to sleep somewhere close enough that if you holler, he can come running." He started to walk away, then stopped. "By the way," he added, "what I did wasn't just to get information or just because of what he did to your mother."

He walked off then, and Callie sat there thinking about his remark. If it wasn't just for those reasons, that left only one other. "Lordy," she said softly. "Was he that angry just because that man tried to hurt *me?*" Why had he bothered to tell her that?

Chapter Twenty

Callie wondered when Chris was going to talk again . . . or eat again. He'd come back early in the morning, drank one cup of coffee, and then announced they would leave as soon as possible. She had time for little more than a trip to the privy behind the cabin, and that was not a pleasant experience, considering mostly men had used it.

The ride down from Hole-in-the-Wall had been as precarious as going up, except that they did not have to worry about all the extra horses this time. Now it was just the two of them. Buck and his gang intended to stay several days at the top and rest up, giving the horses a needed rest also.

Callie figured the main reason Chris was quiet on the way down was that he was concentrating on maneuvering the horses down the dangerous trail; but when they reached flatter country and headed south, he still didn't speak.

Was he brooding over what he'd done to the nameless man he'd killed; or was he brooding over telling her the other reason he'd killed him . . . namely, because the man had attacked her. That was as much as saying he cared. Maybe now he regretted telling her that fact. Maybe he was embarrassed.

Lord knows you can fit what I know about men in the head of a pin, she thought. She'd lived in near seclusion on the family ranch all her life, had never dated other than a few dances with a couple of young men from town at church picnics and such. Since her father died, there had not been any of that. Ranching and farming simply took too much work.

She took a deep breath then and trotted Betsy up beside Chris, keeping her gaze on the land ahead as she spoke. "You going to talk to me sometime today?"

He remained silent as he finished rolling and lighting a cigarette. He took a long drag on it, then let out the smoke in a long sigh. "What do you want to talk about?"

Callie shrugged. "I don't know. Anything would be better than you in one of your moods."

He left the cigarette between his lips. "One of my moods?"

"Yeah. All silent and mad, or whatever you're feeling. Makes me feel lonesome, like I'm out here all by myself."

Another moment of silence lapsed before he spoke again. "You're never by yourself as long as you're with me. Remember that. You thought you were alone yesterday when that man came to talk to you, but you weren't. I was close by." He took another long drag on the cigarette. "I'll always be close by."

Callie thought about the statement, which was spoken as though he meant it in a personal way, not just as business. What was it about the man that continued to make her feel more like a woman and strangely moved? "Well . . . thank you. It's just that the man told me you were inside, drinking up a storm. I still don't know you good enough to know if that was true or not. You don't have a drinking problem, do you? I mean, I've seen drunk men, and it's not a pretty sight."

He took the cigarette from his mouth. "I drink the same as any man, but I'm not a drunk. I can handle my liquor, and I don't drink often. I've never drank so much that I couldn't handle myself, as you saw yesterday."

Callie still could hardly believe how ruthless he'd been. "Yes, sir, I sure did." Betsy whinnied and nodded her head as though agreeing, and they both laughed. That seemed to break Chris Mercy's belligerent mood.

"By the way," Chris added. "You don't know me *well* enough, not good enough."

"What?"

"You describe verbs, like 'know,' with what's called adverbs. 'Good' is an adjective, used to describe an object—like a peach tastes good, or a person is good. But when you describe a verb, you use an adverb. 'Well' is an adverb. So, you don't know me *well* enough, not *good* enough."

"Lordy, I could never remember all of that. What's the difference, as long as a person understands what you're trying to say?"

Chris smiled. "I guess it doesn't really matter unless you're around a bunch of high-nosed scholarly types."

Callie smiled. "Have you ever been around those types?"

His smile faded a little. "Sure. I was even married to one."

Good Lord, he actually mentioned his wife! What was it like being married to Christian Mercy? She imagined he was quite the gentleman then, probably didn't even know how to use a gun. She decided to carefully avoid pressing for more information about the woman, so she resisted the temptation to ask him to tell her more. "You must have been rich back there in Illinois."

He shrugged. "By some standards. Not filthy rich. My folks had money, owned their own business in Chicago. That's how I was able to get a college education. When my folks drowned in a trip overseas, my brother and I inherited everything."

"I'm right sorry about your folks."

"Thank you. They were good people."

They rode on silently for a short way before Callie spoke up again. "So, you have a brother?"

"A couple of years older. He still lives in Chicago—has a wife and kids."

The knowledge made him somehow more human. "Well, since you have money and the education to make a lot more, why do you bother with a dangerous job like hunting down murderers for money?" She immediately regretted the question, felt him tense up.

"You're starting to ask too many questions again."

"Yes, sir, I know. I'm sorry. I have to ask one more thing though."

He sighed, smashing out the cigarette against the black mark on his saddle. "I'll risk it."

"Do you think we can make Ben Bailey's place by tomorrow?"

Chris laughed again. "I was expecting something a lot nosier."

Callie smiled. "I know. I just figured it was time to change the subject before you decided to get mad and stop talking to me again."

He finally looked her way, and she met his gaze, glad to see the anger finally gone from his blue eyes.

"I can't really say how soon. Buck said he knew of the place, and said it was three to four days' ride from Hole-in-the-Wall. We'll aim for the fourth day. We have to be careful not to wear these horses out."

Callie nodded. "What will you do to Jim Fallon if we find him there?"

His smile faded. "I have no idea. Depends on how things go. I didn't exactly plan on doing what I did yesterday. It just kind of happened. When I get that angry, I hardly know what I'm doing."

Callie frowned. "Oh? I sure hope you don't get that mad at me."

He looked at her again with a wry grin. "Then quit asking so many questions."

"Yes, sir."

They rode on silently for a little longer.

"You must know I'd never hurt a woman," he told her then. She nodded. "I know."

"What happened yesterday . . . I never had a temper till the last four years. Not that bad anyway. Sometimes things just happen that send a man over the edge. It's the same as with you. You probably never dreamed a couple of years ago that you'd be out wanting someone's blood like this.''

''No, sir, I sure didn't.''

''When are you going to start calling me Chris instead of sir or Mr. Mercy?''

''I don't know. I suppose the time will come when it feels right, but it still doesn't.''

''Well, somewhere along the line I have found myself calling you Callie.''

''Whatever suits you. Doesn't matter to me how you choose to address me.''

''What's your real name anyway? Callie sounds like it's short for something else.''

''California. Like I said, my pa was headed for California once. He's the one who decided to name me that, said since they never made it there, he'd have a little bit of California with him always. Sounds kind of silly, I know, but Pa could actually be a little sentimental at times.'' She frowned. ''You don't have a kid someplace, do you?''

Total silence. Callie cursed herself, realizing instantly that this was not just a pause in their conversation. She'd hit a very sore spot, and Christian Mercy was not going to say another word. He handed her the lead reins to the two pack mules, then dug his heels into Night Wind's sides and charged off at a gallop.

''Lordy, I'm in trouble now,'' Callie said to herself. Damn! Why didn't she ever know when to stop talking and leave well enough alone? He'd finally changed to a good mood, and then she had to go and get all nosy again. On top of that, her question had gone unanswered, which meant he either had a child somewhere and for some reason had abandoned him or her, or that child was . . . dead . . . and it was too hard for him to talk about it. Maybe the child's death, besides his wife's, had something to do with why he rode as a bounty hunter now. Her curiosity was going to drive her crazy, that was sure.

He rode so far ahead, she could barely see him. All she could do was follow his trail dust for the next two hours, hoping there were no outlaws lurking behind the nearby boulders and craggy rock formations or inside the many cavelike holes she could see in the higher rock walls. Lord knew this country was a good place to hide from the law.

She just kept riding, reminding herself he'd promised he'd never be far away. Finally she spotted him, sitting under the shade of a massive pine tree while Night Wind grazed nearby. Chris sat with his head leaning back against the tree trunk, his hat pulled down over his eyes.

Callie rode closer, deciding she was not going to let him intimidate her. "Should I just keep going, or do I wait here till you're ready to go on?" she asked. "We've got a good five or six hours of daylight yet."

"We'll ride," he answered with a sigh.

Without looking at her, he rose and walked over to Night Wind. He removed his hat and poured some canteen water into it, then let Night Wind drink from it.

"We'll have to take it pretty easy, but we can still get in more miles before nightfall without too much wear on the horses."

Callie was tempted to make a remark to the effect that if he hadn't ridden Night Wind so hard, they wouldn't have to go quite so slowly now. She decided that would probably be the worst thing she could say, so she kept quiet. It sure was hard figuring the man's moods. He let Night Wind drink, then mounted up and headed off at a slow walk.

"I apologize," Callie told him.

"No need. As much as we'll be together, it's only natural to want to know each other better. There are probably things you should know about me, but I can't tell you till I'm *ready* to tell you. Does that make sense?"

"Yes, sir."

"Jesus, will you quit with the sir thing?"

"Yes, sir. I mean . . . all right." Callie sighed with frustration. "It's just that . . . I respect you, that's all."

"Well, it makes me feel like an old man."

"That bothers you?"

"Of *course* it bothers me! Hell, I'm only thirty-two." He let out a snicker. "Of course, I suppose to an eighteen-year-old that *is* old."

Callie shrugged, surprised he was talking at all. "Not especially. It just seems older than it really is because you're so educated."

"Well, quit thinking about it, and quit *talking* about it."

Callie felt her impatience rising. "I'll quit talking about it when you quit reminding me all the time when I say something the wrong way."

He said nothing for a moment, then actually smiled. "You've got me there." He faced her and tipped his hat slightly.

Damn, you're good-looking, she felt like saying.

"We aren't in a classroom," he went on, "and my job isn't to correct your English. My job is to find the men who killed your mother, and I'll by God do it."

Callie smiled in return. "Thank you, Mr. . . . . I mean, Chris."

He nodded. "You're welcome, Callie."

Callie breathed a sigh of relief. He was in a good mood again. Lordy, this was going to be a long, trying journey.

"By the way," he added, "you handled that guy pretty well yesterday. I have a feeling that even if I hadn't stepped in, he would have regretted trying to mess with you."

"He sure would have. I was ready to butt his chin with my head and then ram my rifle barrel into his belly."

He chuckled. "There's a better place to ram a man if you want to render him helpless for a minute or two. A good kick to the groin will usually do it."

Callie felt her face turning red. "That so?"

"Works every time if you aim right and kick hard. While he's down, you jam the end of his nose as hard as you can, break it, or ram it into his brain. Or you can always gouge out his eyes or ram a finger into the soft part of his throat. Any one of those things will buy you time to get the hell away. Or you can always just shoot him, whatever suits you."

Callie shivered. "My gosh, I hope I don't have to find out."

"Just a piece of advice in case you find yourself in that situation again."

"I thought you said you'd always be close by."

"I will, but you never know when we might be up against more than one man. I can do only so much."

Callie nodded. "I'll keep that in mind. And by the way, I could stand to . . . you know . . . stop somewhere for a minute. There's a spot of shade up ahead and some rocks. The horses can all rest a little while I take care of something."

Chris nodded, saying nothing more as they rode to the spot she'd pointed out. Callie dismounted, hurrying behind the rocks to drop her britches and urinate. Just as she started to rise, she heard it . . . right behind her . . . the awful hiss . . . the deadly rattle. She froze in place, but too late. In that one split second she felt the horrible pain of fangs sinking into her skin, just above her right hip.

Chapter
Twenty-one

Chris never heard such a bloodcurdling scream in his life. He grabbed his rifle from its boot and ran toward where Callie had gone to take care of personals. Before he reached the rocks where she'd gone, Callie, still screaming at the top of her lungs, came running toward him, hanging on to her britches.

"I've been bit!" she screamed. "I've been bit! Oh, lordy, I'm gonna die!"

Chris ran past her, keeping his rifle in his left hand and pulling out his Colt revolver. Rounding the rocks, he saw the rattler, one of the biggest he'd ever seen, slithering down from a flat rock to the ground. He quickly aimed and fired, blowing apart its head, then ran back to a still-running Callie. He grabbed her from behind in one arm, and she continued to scream and started to kick him.

"Let go! Let go!"

"If you don't calm down, you *will* die!" he shouted at her, grimacing at the pain of her kicks against his legs as he ran with her toward the shade of a gnarled old pinon pine. He literally threw his rifle aside and forced her down into the grass, but she continued struggling.

"Dammit, calm down!" he yelled at her. "You have to lie still, Callie, or the venom will just travel faster through your blood!"

She finally quit fighting him, but she cried hysterically. "It hurts terrible!" she screamed. "Oh, God! Oh, God, I hate snakes! I hate snakes! What's going to happen to me?"

"You'll feel sick as hell and probably get a fever," Chris told her. "I can help a little by sucking out some of the venom, but you running like that sure as hell didn't help, dammit! Where's the bite?" He pulled a jackknife from his pants pocket.

"My back! Down low! Lordy, what are you going to do with that knife?"

"I have to cut across the fang marks and suck out as much venom as I can."

"No! Lordy, don't go cutting me!"

Chris yanked her up by her shirtfront. "*Listen* to me, god-dammit! If I don't get *some* of that venom out, you *will* die. Now, you'd better cooperate, or I'll *slug* you! You got that?"

She quieted, her body jerking in a sob as she stared at him in wide-eyed terror. "I'm scared," she whimpered, jerking in another sob.

"Of course you are. Hell, I would be too." He noticed her face beginning to flush, and her eyes started rolling back. "You hang on, Callie!" he told her, realizing she was beginning to lose consciousness. Some of the venom was probably already reaching her brain. He had no idea if trying to suck it out would even do any good after all her running and carrying on, but he had to try. Any little he could get rid of might help.

He ran over to his saddlebags and fished out a flask of whiskey, then grabbed his bedroll and ran back to where Callie lay, now just moaning and tossing. He rolled her over and jerked up her shirt, then yanked her britches partway down to see the ugly fang marks. The bite was turning purple.

"Jesus," he mumbled. "Help me do this right."

He'd seen this done once, but he'd never done it himself. He flicked open his jackknife, and taking a deep breath, he cut across the fang marks. Callie let out a mixture of a scream and a groan that tore at his heart. He tossed the knife aside and leaned down, squeezing the flesh and sucking hard, spitting out something bitter that was mixed with her blood. He figured the bitterness must be the venom. Good. He was getting at least some of it.

He repeated the process several more times, then doused the wound with whiskey. By then Callie was lying still . . . already dying, for all he knew. Why did that tear at his heart so? He wiped his mouth and then drank some of the whiskey himself before corking the flask and running over to their supplies, quickly untying ropes and letting things fall.

He opened a small leather satchel in which he knew they'd packed medical supplies, and he took out a roll of cotton strips and ran back to wrap the bleeding wound. He lifted Callie's torso to get underneath so he could wrap the cotton around her midsection a couple of times, then he tied it off.

He quickly opened his bedroll and threw back a blanket, then yanked off Callie's boots and britches. He carried her over to the bedroll and laid her down, removing the rest of her clothes. She would undoubtedly suffer a terrible fever. If the venom didn't kill her, the fever could. He would have to keep her cooled, and that was easier if she wasn't wearing anything. He could keep her bathed with cool, wet rags. He covered her up to the armpits, leaving her arms outside the blanket, then hurried back to Betsy, hastily unsaddling the animal and carrying the saddle back to where Callie lay silent. He set the saddle down near her head, then lifted her head and shoulders and managed to scoot the saddle under her so that her top half would be elevated. Somewhere he'd heard that also helped, something about helping keep down the blood flow to the brain.

He sat down then and took a deep breath, watching her for several seconds, wondering if she was already dead. She sure looked it. Her face now was as white as the clouds in the sky, and her lips looked slightly blue. Her freckled face was dirty from a mixture of dust and tear stains, and just then she did look like a kid.

What if she died? He tried to figure how he'd feel about

that, and he didn't like the answer. He'd long ago decided never to love again, never to care about anything or anyone. Now here was this lonely, lost, poorly educated, scared woman/child who had managed to creep into his heart without even trying. She was so full of life and spit and anger and cockiness that he couldn't begin to imagine lowering her, lifeless, into a grave. Even the mess she was right now, she was still pretty, and it just then dawned on him that he'd been so concerned about her dying that he hadn't even noticed how she looked naked . . . except for a brief sight of those full, firm, virgin breasts.

"Shit," he grumbled, getting up. "You bastard, Mercy! The girl is probably dying."

He left her to make some kind of order out of the things he'd unpacked so recklessly, then unsaddled his horse. He saw no sign of water anywhere and decided to water the horses using canteens. That meant he couldn't give them much, because he'd need some to cool Callie if she developed a fever, which was a sure thing. He cursed the fact that they had not gone as far as he'd planned today. If they had, they would have reached a creek he knew meandered through lower land farther south. There wasn't even good grazing grass around here.

He slung a canteen over his shoulder, led the four horses to the grassiest place he could find, and tethered them there, giving each one some water before going back to set up camp. It worried him, Callie lying there so still. He couldn't even bring himself to go over and make sure she was alive, fearing the worst and for some reason unable to accept it.

With Callie's bedroll, he made up a bed for himself right beside her, using his saddle to lean on. He checked the horses once more, then came back, picking up his rifle from where he'd thrown it, and laying it beside him. It was only then that he realized how hungry he was. He'd not eaten since the incident with Callie's attacker late yesterday, close to twenty-four hours now.

He dug some jerked meat and a can of beans from their gear, using a hooked opener in his jackknife to open the beans. He found a spoon and sat down with a sigh, eating a couple of scoops of beans, then biting off a piece of meat. He set both aside then and stared at Callie, trying to figure out if she was breathing. Finally he noticed the blanket move. Yes, she *was* breathing.

He took a quick swallow of water, deciding not to make a fire for the simple reason he couldn't spare enough water to make coffee, and besides, he wasn't in the mood to heat anything. It would be chilly tonight, like it always was at night in this country, no matter how hot the day; but it wouldn't be so cold that they couldn't get by with just blankets.

He set the canteen aside and got to his knees, leaning over Callie. He brushed some of her thick auburn hair away from her face. "Callie?"

No answer. She didn't even blink or turn her head. He felt for a pulse at her neck and realized it was very weak.

"Shit," he muttered. He patted her cheek. "Callie? Come on, Callie, talk to me."

Still nothing. And a touch to her neck and her cheek told him she was already developing a fever. He closed his eyes, angry with himself for having feelings for her. She was one strong, determined young woman. She'd give any man a run for his money, make any man proud to call her his wife. It was easy to tell she'd be absolutely beautiful with her hair done up right, wearing a pretty dress that fit her right, a little bit of education in manners and . . .

He sat back again with another long sigh, taking out a cigarette paper to roll himself a smoke. It was going to be a long night.

Chapter
Twenty-two

"Callie?"

Callie thought she heard someone calling her, but when she opened her eyes, everything was a blur. At first she couldn't think where she was or who the shadow was leaning over her. It took only seconds to be aware of the pain that wracked every inch of her and the fact that she felt on fire. She tried to talk, but she couldn't. Her throat felt tight, and terror engulfed her when it felt as though she couldn't get any air. She gasped, trying to sit up, and more pain tore through her whole right side, especially her right hip.

"It's all right," someone told her. "Stay calm, Callie."

It was a man's voice. Frantically she struggled for breath, and she sensed the man moving behind her. He put an arm around her shoulders from behind and placed his other hand under her chin, pulling her head back.

"Breathe deeply, honey," he told her. "Come on. Relax and take a nice, deep breath. If you keep your head back, your airway will stay open. The swelling should go down in a few hours and you'll be okay."

Her mouth felt dry as a bone. "Wa-ter," she managed to whisper.

"Keep your head back," the man told her.

She was so hot and in so much pain, she didn't even care who it was, as long as what he did helped her breathe. She felt him move slightly, and as she gained a little more awareness, she realized she was leaning against his chest. He put something wet to her lips.

"Here. I'll squeeze the water from this rag into your mouth. I'm afraid you'll choke if I pour it into your mouth from the canteen."

She felt the water trickle into her mouth, and it felt wonderful, but it was difficult to swallow. Once all the water was squeezed from the rag, he used it to gently bathe perspiration from her face and neck.

"So . . . hot," she groaned.

"I know. You just fight it, Callie. Twenty-four hours from now you'll feel a lot better, I promise. Your throat will be better and the fever will probably break by then. We just have to get you through the night. You've been lying here over four hours and it's just now getting dark. It's a good sign that you're alert again so soon."

She thought a moment, scrambling to make sense of all this while the man continued cooling her face and neck. Slowly her memory returned . . . the familiar voice, the pain . . . snake! A snake bit her! She cried out and tried to sit up. She had to get away! Strong arms came around her, holding her close and tight.

"It's all right, Callie. You'll be all right. I promise. But you have to lie still. And keep your head back."

He moved one hand to her chin again, pulling her head back. Callie fought tears, afraid if she started crying too hard, she wouldn't be able to breathe.

"Chris?" she asked.

"It's me. I'm glad you remembered to start using my first name. That's another good sign."

"Where's . . . the . . . snake?"

"I shot the snake. And I managed to get some of the venom out."

"So . . . hot," she told him.

"I know." A little cool water trickled over her head and down the sides of her face and neck, and she realized he must have poured it over her.

"Don't . . . go . . . away," she said, unable to keep a wrenching sob of terror from moving up through her soul. What was it like to die? She should have looked around better before squatting behind those rocks. Snakes loved to sunbathe on warm rocks.

"I already told you I'll always be close by. Tonight I'll stay right here every minute, until you feel that you can breathe better."

Tears worked their way down her cheeks, and Chris wiped them with the cool rag.

"Don't cry. It will just make things worse."

"Will I . . . die?"

"No. Don't even think about it. You're too damn stubborn and ornery to die, and too damn young."

Callie wanted to believe him. "You really . . . think so?"

"I really think so."

"Don't . . . let go . . . of me."

"I don't intend to."

"If you . . . let go . . . I'll . . . die."

"Well then, I'll hang on real tight."

She wanted to smile but was in too much pain. "I never . . . hurt so bad . . . ever. Can't . . . stand . . . to move."

"Good. That means you'll lie still as I want you to do."

"I'm . . . scared," she repeated.

"Well, so the hell am I. If you die, there's no sense in me looking for the rest of those men, which means I won't get your ranch."

Now she wanted to laugh, but her throat just closed up on her instead. She started gasping for breath, and again he forced her chin back. She gasped for another breath.

"I was only kidding," he told her. "I didn't mean to get such a reaction out of you."

"I . . . know. Just . . . wanted to . . . laugh."

She heard him chuckle. "Want the truth?" he asked.

She rolled her eyes up to look at him, able to see him more clearly now. "What?"

He leaned closer. "I don't want you to die, because I care about you more than you think. How do you like that?"

In spite of her pain, the words brought Callie a tremendous desire to live. She realized Christian Mercy was holding her close, and she didn't even mind. And for him to admit he cared "more than she thought" was really something, considering how hard it must be for him to tell her that. "I'll . . . be damned," she managed to whisper.

"What's that?"

She gasped for another breath, unable to answer. "My head . . . is starting . . . to hurt . . . something . . . awful," she whimpered.

He trickled more water over her head. "I can't do much about that, Callie. It's just going to take time."

Her sight started to go then. She felt the blackness closing in, tried to scream to Chris again not to let go of her but couldn't get the words out.

Chris could see Callie was lapsing into hysteria, probably from the fever. She began gasping harder for breath and fighting him, kicking away her blanket and mumbling something about the heat. He held on tightly to her while at the same time he continued to trickle water over her hair and down over her neck and shoulders. He figured then that as long as she was naked and didn't want the blanket, he'd reach farther down and pour water over her chest and belly, anything to try to keep the fever down. If it lasted too long, she wouldn't make it.

Her strength astonished him, and for the next hour or better the battle was on. Chris was on the brink of figuring some way to literally tie her down, but finally she seemed to lapse into something he couldn't decide was a coma or a deep sleep. After another several minutes he slowly moved back, then grabbed one of the blankets from her bedroll and wadded it up, putting it under her head to cradle her at a slightly better angle and give some softness between her head and neck area and her saddle.

He looked down at his shirt and pants, wet from pouring water over her head and neck, deciding to just leave them on and let them dry that way. He picked up the canteen and bent close to her, pouring more water over her hair and neck, and on down over her breasts and belly, feeling like an ass for taking a moment to study her naked body, yet unable *not* to. Hell, he was afraid to cover her up anyway for fear the fever would get worse again. Night was falling, and the temperature had dropped. If her body was cooling down, he had to let it. He would just have to watch her closely to make sure she didn't start shivering.

A full moon had risen about the same time as the sun disappeared behind distant mountains, and there was still plenty of light to see that she had a damn pretty shape, a small waist and flat belly, slender thighs that led down to pretty calves. His gaze moved back to the dark hair that hid her virgin sweetness, and her breasts were so firm. . . .

He couldn't resist leaning down and kissing her full lips lightly, then turned away. "Lord God," he muttered. He flopped down on his bedroll, deciding to wait a while before he pulled a blanket back over her, just to be sure her fever was heading down. He stretched out and stared up at stars that were becoming more prominent as the sky grew blacker. Yes, this *definitely* was going to be a long night.

Chapter
Twenty-three

Callie awakened to the sounds of birds singing and a horse whinnying. She opened her eyes to see Chris off in the distance, brushing down Breeze. She just lay there, watching him for a while, trying to remember all that had happened. She shivered at the memory of a snakebite, and one movement reminded her where she had gotten bit. Her right hip, just a few inches below the waistline, still ached fiercely when she moved, but she realized that the soreness in the rest of her body was gone.

She swallowed, then thanked God that she could breathe freely and her throat was not sore. She put a hand to her head, which no longer ached, and she could see clearly. She was coherent enough, in fact, to realize she was naked under the blanket that covered her.

She gasped and lifted the blanket to look "Lordy!" Her midsection was wrapped midway down her rear end. *"Lordy!"* she said a little louder. Had Christian Mercy done that? Why in hell did he have to take all her clothes off?

She pulled the blanket completely over her shoulders, realizing she had to pee. How in heck was she going to get up and walk without help, and how could she ask for help with such a thing, especially wearing nothing more than a blanket?

She glanced over at Chris again. He had apparently noticed her stir, and he was walking toward her now.

"Good morning!" he said cheerfully.

Of course he'd be cheerful, Callie thought. *He got to sit staring at my naked body while I had no idea what was going on!* Maybe he had done *more* than that!

"Glad to see you finally waking up. You've been lying there sleeping since late evening day before yesterday." He came closer and knelt beside her. "I was beginning to worry the snake venom had affected your brain and you were in a permanent coma. They say everybody reacts differently to snakebite." He frowned then. "You do *know* me, don't you, Callie?"

She looked away from his handsome face, embarrassed. "Seems to me you must know me a lot better than I know you, Mr. Mercy."

He chuckled. "Ah, you're using my sir-name again. That must mean you're angry about something."

She wanted to cry. "Can't you guess? You said I've been laying here practically two days. How much of that time did you spend looking at me?"

She could feel him smiling without even looking at him. "For one thing, you've been *lying* there two days, not *laying*. And, by gosh, I stared at you the whole time. Prettiest sight I've ever seen. Wish I could have photographed it so I'd have something to carry in my pocket to remind me."

Callie gasped, sitting up now in spite of her pain, and holding the blanket to her throat. "You no-good, dirty-minded, womanizing bastard! A simple snakebite is no good reason to take off a woman's clothes!"

He sobered just slightly. "It is if the woman is dying from fever. And you kicked off the blanket yourself in near hysteria and begged me to hang on to you and not let you die. Are you saying now that you would rather I'd just left you? And it wasn't a *simple* snakebite. That was the biggest rattler I've ever seen. You're damn lucky to be alive, *Miss Hobbs*. And I deserve more for saving your hide than being called names.''

Prettiest sight he'd ever seen? Did he really think she was pretty? She watched him walk away to take what was left of their firewood from the bundle they'd been carrying and bring it over to add to a small fire he already had going, over which a coffeepot hung from a tripod.

"I begged you to hold on to me?"

"You don't remember that?"

She lay back down. "Kind of. I mean, everything is like I dreamed it."

"Oh? Do you dream about me holding you?"

Callie rolled her eyes in exasperation. "Well, more like a nightmare, then."

He laughed again. "Callie, I am just joking with you. And no, I didn't sit and stare at you for the last two days. It just so happens I was very worried you were going to die on me. I did a lot of praying, not that the Lord would listen to me anymore after some of the things I've done." He sobered then, pouring himself some coffee. "Seriously now—how do you feel?"

"I hurt—everywhere—but mostly my right hip. It's sore as hell. I think I remember you saying you were going to cut me with your jackknife."

"I did. I sucked out as much venom as I could. If you hadn't taken off running and been so hard to wrestle down, you would have saved yourself a lot of pain and fever. Worst thing you can do after a snakebite is get up and run."

He'd sucked out the venom? Lordy! Christian Mercy's lips had touched her bare skin—and near her bottom end! How was she going to live this down? "I know I should thank you."

He sat down on his saddle and sipped some coffee. "Well, then, why don't you?"

"I don't know. It's just the thought of you probably getting some kind of pleasure out of this whole thing while I lay there, helpless."

There was a moment of silence before he spoke her name. "Callie. Will you please look at me?"

Cautiously she turned her head to face him. "What?"

"I got no pleasure out of the thought of you dying, all right? It scared the hell out of me, because I've learned to respect you and I like you . . . a lot. You're a strong, sweet young lady who doesn't deserve to die out here in the middle of nowhere."

Callie saw only sincerity in his blue eyes, and now she vaguely remembered him saying he wouldn't let go of her, that he'd hang on real tight. Had he even called her honey? She remembered resting against his chest, his strong arms around her, cool water being trickled over her face, her throat, her . . .

"Lordy!" she whispered more to herself than anyone else. She'd taken comfort in his embrace, felt safe. She looked at him again as he finished his coffee. "You really care?"

He tossed out the coffee at the bottom of his cup. "Of course I do." He set the cup aside. "You ready to eat something now?"

She lay there and thought about it a moment. "I think so. But I have to . . . you know. I have to do what I was doing when the snake bit me. I'm just not sure I can get up and walk."

"Well, then, I'll help you." He came over to where she lay, and as she started to sit up she felt herself being lifted. To her total embarrassment, the blanket hung loosely, so that one hand was under her bare back, his fingers grasping her at the ribs not far from her breast, and his other arm was under her bare legs, his hand grasping her bare thigh! What in the world was this sensation she had at the feel of his strong, rough hands touching her bare skin? It made her feel closer to him . . . in a strangely special way.

She clung for dear life to the blanket so it wouldn't fall away from the front of her. "All you need to do is support me," she protested.

"Better carry you for now. You need to drink something and get some food in your stomach, then rest a little longer before you get up and start walking around. Besides, that could bring back your headache.'' He finally set her on her feet under a low pine.

"I'll go get some paper for you. Use one of these pine branches to hang on to while you kneel down.''

Callie felt she must be turning purple from humiliation. "What if my blanket falls off?''

"Then it falls off. I wouldn't be seeing anything I haven't already seen.''

She felt like crying. "Please don't remind me. And don't look till I tell you.''

He chuckled. "I won't look. You going to be okay?''

"I think so.''

Chris left her, and Callie hurriedly wrapped the blanket completely around herself, then lifted it to relieve herself of pent-up water. She managed to scoot away from the puddle before calling out to Chris. "Bring the paper.''

Chris walked back and handed her a small wad of paper, and she took it sheepishly. "Turn around again.''

Shaking his head, he turned and waited. Callie took care of things and managed to get to her feet, quickly rearranging the blanket so it was wrapped fully around her. "Oh, lordy,'' she said weakly as dizziness overwhelmed her. She felt herself falling, felt strong arms catch her and lift her again.

"Just what I thought,'' Chris muttered.

The dizziness left her as he carried her back to their campsite, but she could not help the tears that came while she was still in his arms.

"What is it?'' Chris asked. "The pain?''

Keeping the blanket wrapped in her fists, she covered her face. "No,'' she wept. "I'm just so . . . embarrassed . . . making so much trouble. I should have looked before I . . . the other day . . . I might have seen the snake. Now I'm just a big burden to you. I promised I wouldn't be. And now . . . how can I look at you again . . . you seeing me like you did!''

She tried to cringe away from him, but he held on tight, and she sensed he was sitting down, maybe on a rock or something, because he continued to hold her in his lap.

"Callie, accidents happen. A snake bit you, and I did what I had to do to save you. In cases like that, a man doesn't sit and ogle the victim and take pleasure out of watching a nice young girl lie dying. Okay? I respect you too much to do something like that. When are you going to learn that not all men are horrible ogres and rapists? You've got to start trusting me. We have a lot ahead of us yet, so quit crying and eat something. You need to get your strength back before we can keep going, and every day we wait, there is a chance our Mr. Jim Fallon will slip away from us."

She wiped her tears on her blanket. "You want to . . . know something?"

"What?"

Feeling dizzy again, Callie let her head fall against his shoulder. She could smell him, a mixture of leather and the lingering scent of shaving cream. So, he'd already shaved that morning while she slept. There came a light scent of perspiration, but it wasn't bad. It was just . . . manly. Why did that comfort her?

"I wouldn't care if you . . . just sat here and held me . . . for a little while. I mean . . . it doesn't mean anything bad. It would just make me feel better . . . that's all. I've been so scared this whole time. I just . . . didn't want to admit it."

She felt him smiling, felt his arms come around her more tightly. Lordy, she didn't want to admit it felt good for *any* man to hold her. She especially didn't want any thoughts of love or desire to move into her bones. Maybe this was all just because she was feeling so sick and helpless right now. She wanted to ask him how she looked compared to a woman like Lisa. How did he feel about her compared to Lisa? Was he thinking about that woman now? Missing her? Why did it hurt more than ever to think he might be?

She wanted to lean back and look into his eyes, but he was too damn close. He might get the wrong idea and try to kiss her or something. Besides, if she looked this close into those blue eyes, *she* might get some wrong ideas. One thing was sure, she was beginning to understand, just a little, some of the reasons why a woman kind of needed a man . . . and how a woman could learn to trust one, even love one . . . even . . . maybe . . . allow one to kiss her . . . maybe even touch her . . . maybe even . . .

No. That was one thing she could never tolerate. That was one thing that terrified her and always would. She supposed maybe she'd never be a wife and mother then, and because of that, she had to get rid of these funny feelings she had for Christian Mercy. He was just a man she'd hired to find her mother's killers. Nothing more.

"I think I can eat something now," she told him. "And if you'll get me my clothes and turn around, I want to get dressed. I don't think it's a good idea, now that I'm better and all, for us to be out here alone with me like this."

She felt him shake slightly as he chuckled. "I thought you were learning to trust me."

Maybe it's myself I don't trust, she thought. "I am," she said aloud. "But, well, you're a man . . . and you've got natural thoughts . . . thoughts I don't want you to be having. So bring me my bag that has my clothes in it."

He sighed, and to Callie's surprise, he kissed her cheek. "Good to see you back to your old feisty self," he told her, picking her up then and carrying her to her bedroll, where he set her down. "Sorry for the kiss—just one of friendship." He gave her a wink and a grin, and Callie felt an unexpected surge of desire rush through her. She hardly knew what to make of it.

"Do you really think about me as a friend?" she asked.

"Sure. We can't but be anything *but* friends by now; at least that's how I *hope* you think of me, even though I'm a dirty-minded bastard."

She smiled and looked down. "Sorry about that. I truly do thank you for trying so hard to save my life."

"No thanks necessary." He walked away to get her carpet-bag, and for the first time in her life she found herself watching a man's bottom, the way he was built. He'd picked her up as though she weighed two pounds. He didn't have his hat on today, and that sandy hair of his was a thick mass of gentle waves that were kind of messy yet not bad-looking. She remembered then his comment about why he'd attacked that man a few days ago. Now he'd saved her life, and he'd actually admitted he cared about her, respected her, and wanted her to think of him as her friend. Did he like her even more than that? Why in the world did she kind of wish he did?

"I'll try hard to be able to leave by tomorrow," she told him. "Sorry I've held things up."

"Couldn't be helped. Just don't push yourself." He brought the bag over to her. "Once we leave, we can be there the morning of the second day. The horses have had plenty of rest, but we're about out of water. I've had to give them water from the canteens, and I used some to keep you cooled down. We've got to reach water by tomorrow before we make camp, so I guess we *will* have to leave by morning. If you absolutely can't do it, I'll have to stow you up someplace and go on ahead to find water; but I don't like the idea of leaving you behind, not in this country. The men in these parts are more dangerous than that rattler you tangled with."

But not you, she thought. *You're different, Chris Mercy.* "Turn around and I'll try to dress myself," she told him. "Start cooking whatever is handy for you. I am actually getting hungry, so I'll eat anything."

He nodded. "I've got just the thing. I'll get out the fry pan." He turned away, and Callie slowly dressed herself, perfectly confident that he wouldn't look . . . and he didn't.

Chapter
Twenty-four

"You sure you can ride?"

Callie limped over to where Betsy stood saddled. "I aim to try. We've wasted enough time."

"Want some help getting up?"

"No." Callie could not quite get over the embarrassment of this whole situation, getting a bit damn close to the fleshiest part of her rear end while squatting to pee, of all things! This man she still felt like she didn't know all that well putting his lips on her to suck out the venom, undressing her, seeing her naked. He'd done and said everything he could to make her feel better about it, but she just couldn't quite get rid of the humiliation of the whole thing. If she just would have looked before she squatted. She sure would from now on, that was sure!

She put her left foot in the stirrup, but pain tore through her right hip when she tried to mount up, and she groaned and laid her head against the saddle. The next thing she knew, strong arms came around her waist and lifted her. Chris set her in the saddle.

"When are you going to learn to ask for and accept help?"

he asked. "You wouldn't even have let me help you after that snakebite if you hadn't been so sick."

Callie grimaced with pain. "I didn't ask you to come out here and nurse me along like a helpless kid. I can fend for myself."

Chris mounted up. "I am perfectly aware of that. You've pulled more than your share so far, so quit worrying what I might think of your abilities. I already told you I liked the way you handled that son of a bitch back at Hole-in-the-Wall. And you ride as well as any man, know everything you need to know about horses, and you've camped out under the stars every night without complaining about a thing. And if I had been the one snakebit, you would have been nursing me along like I've been doing you. So quit trying to prove to me how well you can handle yourself, and quit apologizing for being in pain."

"Yes, sir."

"One more thing."

"Yes, sir?"

"There's a saying in these parts that takes some serious thought."

"What's that?"

He grinned. "Look before you squat."

Callie blushed and looked away. Chris picked up the reins to the packhorse and mules and headed out, riding Breeze today. Still embarrassed, Callie followed, eyeing his broad, firm shoulders, remembering the way he'd held her, seeming to understand her need. What had his wife been like? She still wasn't sure if he had a child, alive *or* dead. She was so full of questions but too afraid to ask them, considering his reaction the other times she'd touched on those subjects.

Riding Betsy only made her hip hurt more, but she followed silently, determined not to do any more complaining. This was the third day since her snakebite, and it was vital they reach water today, tomorrow at the latest. She'd spent most of yesterday sleeping, but once when she woke up she caught Chris reading something called *Shakespeare*. She'd asked him to read some to her, and he read beautifully, unlike the way she'd ever heard anyone read. Neither of her parents were very well schooled, and they had taught her more about numbers than reading, but she thought she could read pretty well until she heard Chris read, using words she never would have been able to pronounce, reading some poems that would have made no sense to her, but the way he read them, she could understand them.

Listening to him read only accented to her just how educated he was, and she tried to picture him wearing a suit, maybe a white ruffled shirt, looking handsome and spiffy in the world he came from, a world that apparently had included money. He must have been quite the gentleman, and she guessed his wife was probably rich and beautiful, a far cry from Miss California Hobbs.

She looked down at her hands, which showed a few calluses, her fingernails ten different lengths and needing a good scrubbing. And there she sat, wearing a boy's denim pants and a boy's shirt and leather vest, her old boots having long ago lost their shine. Her floppy leather hat covered hair that needed washing. She couldn't remember the last time she'd prettied herself up for anything, but now, of a sudden, she wanted to look pretty, fix her hair nice, put on a dress, show Chris Mercy just what a lady she really could be.

Even so, the mess she was, he'd said more than once that she was pretty. Was he just teasing her? Just trying to make her feel better? She watched him light a cigarette, then winced as she urged Betsy into a slightly faster trot to catch up so she could ride beside him.

"Can I ask you something?"

"Not if it's personal."

"I don't think it is."

He glanced at her. "Ask away, then."

"Well, do you think you could teach me to read good as you do?"

He grinned. "As *well* as I do. Remember what I told you

about adverbs and adjectives? You're describing how I read. That's a verb. So you use the word *well* to describe it.''

"Heck, I've never heard words like adverbs and adjectives. My ma just opened a book one day and started teaching me the words. I just kind of memorized what some words look like. Mostly she read to me from the Bible, but she had a couple other books, the kind they use in schools to teach little kids. But I've never heard anything as pretty as what you read yesterday. I mean, I know I already told you all of that, but I can't quit thinking about it, about how nice it would be to be able to read like that.''

"Well, I can teach you a little here and there, depending on how this trip goes. But what you really need is some formal schooling. Maybe when we get back to Rawlins I can look into sending you somewhere in the East. I could pay for it.''

"I'd never let you do that. I'd rather *you* taught me.''

"Well, that would mean staying on in Rawlins, and I doubt I'll do that.''

The thought brought pain to her heart, realizing that once she'd found her mother's killers, Christian Mercy would walk out of her life forever. Suddenly she hated the thought of it.

"I haven't contacted my brother in a long time,'' he went on. "He and his wife don't exactly agree with what I'm doing.'' He sighed. "Anyway, I don't doubt for a minute that they would put you up and help you find a good school where you could learn the basics. Then you could go on to finishing school.''

"Finishing school?''

He took another drag on his cigarette. "It's just a place where refined young ladies of education go to learn proper etiquette.''

"Etiquette?''

He glanced at her, smiling patiently. "Manners. How to dress. How much color to put on your face. When to wear gloves. How to cook, and how to be the perfect hostess. How to greet important people, things like that.''

Callie shrugged. "No need for me to learn things like that

if I'm going to live in a town like Rawlins. I just want to know how to read, that's all. Might help me make money someday, help me get a job, like maybe work for the newspaper in Rawlins, something like that.''

"It always helps to know how to read."

"Well, maybe you could stay on an extra month or so once we get back, just to get me started. I wouldn't really want to go away and live with strangers in a place I don't know anything about.''

He turned and looked her over again in that way he had of making her feel uncomfortable. She felt embarrassed, wondering now if he was picturing her naked.

"What if *I* took you?" he asked her.

"You? Why would you do that?"

He looked straight ahead again. "Just a thought. I could help you get to know people. Get you settled in a school."

"Well, I . . . that's a right nice offer . . . and I'd feel a lot better if you were the one to take me . . . but then you'd leave again, and I'd be there all alone. No, I don't think I'd like that." *Fact is, I don't like the thought of you not being in my life, no matter where I am,* she wanted to say. It hit her again that when this journey was over, that's exactly what *would* happen. Chris Mercy would ride out of her life, never to be seen again. It actually made her want to cry.

"Well, maybe I could stay on a little while," he answered. "We have plenty of time to think about it."

She didn't know quite what to make of his offer. Did it bother him too? The thought of them parting once this was over? "Do you really think I can learn to read good—I mean well?" Callie asked him.

"Sure you can."

They rode without speaking a little while, and Callie thought what a complex man he was. Something had brought him to this place, hunting for wanted men . . . something terrible. "Don't you miss teaching?" she asked.

He took a last drag and crushed out his cigarette. "Sometimes. I might go back to it someday, when the time is right.

I'm just not ready yet. Fact is, I'm getting used to this country. It's pretty out here, and a man is free to do what he wants. A man can start new out here, build on new dreams . . . leave old, broken dreams behind.''

The last words were spoken in such a way that Callie thought her own heart would break. "I'm real sorry, Chris."

He glanced at her. "For what?"

"For your own broken dreams, whatever they were."

He looked straight ahead again. "Yeah, well, so am I."

Was it a good time to ask him what those broken dreams were, or would he just get angry again? Callie didn't get the chance to find out. An arrow sang between the two of them, landing in the trunk of a tall pine ahead. They looked at each other, then looked behind them to see several riders approaching, shouting war whoops.

"Shit!" Chris cursed. "Renegades! Ride hard! We've got to find some cover!" He whipped Breeze into a gallop, keeping a tight hold to the reins of the packhorses.

"Get up! Get up!" Callie screamed to Betsy, slapping the reins against her neck and kicking her sides.

Betsy charged after Chris and the extra horses, but she wasn't as fast as Breeze and Night Wind, and she was trying to hang on to the mules besides. Betsy had trouble keeping up, and Callie was imagining what it would feel like if an arrow slammed into her back.

"Oh, lordy, we're gonna die!" she whimpered. She let go of the packmules and rode Betsy full-out, but the horse just could not keep up. Chris made it to a high rock wall where several boulders had spilled to the ground in front of it, some stacked on top of each other, a good place to take cover. Callie saw him jump off Breeze and lead the horses behind the rocks. Another arrow whizzed past her, so close she could feel the rush of air.

"Chris!" she screamed. She saw something flash in the rocks and had no doubt it was the barrel of Chris's rifle. She heard it fire, and she knew he was trying to cover her until she could get to shelter. Suddenly Betsy tumbled to the ground, and Callie screamed as she rolled off the horse. Pain tore through her still-sore hip at the fall, and now she could hear the war whoops coming closer.

"Run, Callie!" Chris shouted. He fired off another volley of shots.

Callie scrambled over to Betsy and grabbed her shotgun, then got up and tried to run, but it was impossible because of her hip. "Oh, Jesus God in heaven, help me!" she screamed. The next thing she knew, Chris was riding out to her on Breeze.

"Come on!" he yelled when he reached her. "Give me your hand!"

Callie reached up and he grabbed her arm, lifting her in front of him and charging back toward the rocks. Callie ducked her head against his chest and hung on, then thought she felt an odd jolt. They reached the rocks, and Chris quickly lifted her down.

"Get my other rifle out of the supplies and grab the leather pouch of ammunition!" Chris ordered, crouching behind the rocks. "Your shotgun is no good for distance."

He started firing again, and Callie heard someone cry out. Good. He got one of them. She ignored the pain in her hip as she rummaged through the supplies to find the ammunition, then grabbed his spare rifle out of its boot on Night Wind and hurried back to Chris. That was when she noticed a growing bloodstain on the back of his shirt. "Oh, lordy!" she cried out. "You're hurt!"

"Just get over here and keep firing!" Chris ordered. "No time to worry about it now!"

Callie crouched next to him, glancing at him to see the obvious. He was already pale, but he kept firing. She realized then that if Christian Mercy died, her heart would break into a million pieces.

Chapter
Twenty-five

Callie tried to ignore the fact that Chris could be bleeding to death; and poor Betsy lay in the distance, still kicking. It was only then she realized that both mules were down too, poor things. She wouldn't be able to help Chris or put Betsy out of her misery if she and Chris couldn't first deal with their attackers. Before this was over, they might *both* be dead.

She took aim with Chris's Winchester and fired, hitting nothing as far as she could tell. Chris, however, hit two more of the renegades, and the rest, about seven or eight more as far as Callie could quickly count, halted their approach and spread out, taking cover amid surrounding rocks.

Chris fired three more times, hitting two more of them. One of those two got up after falling from his horse and tried to limp to shelter, but Chris took aim and fired again, hitting him square in the back.

"Lordy, you're a good shot!" Callie exclaimed.

Chris handed his rifle to her. "Reload this," he said, watching the surrounding rocks. "Give me the other Winchester. You still have some shots left."

Callie obeyed, opening the chamber of the first rifle and

quickly inserting more cartridges. "I figure about five or six more," she told Chris.

"Once they take cover, it's like twenty," he answered. He closed his eyes and sank to his knees for a moment. "Damn! I should have been more alert, especially out here."

"What do they want?" Callie asked.

He cast her a look that gave her the answer.

"Me?"

"And the horses," he added. "They don't care about mules. That's why they shot them. They just want the supplies they're carrying, plus our saddles and the gear we have with us. They know they will have to kill us to get our guns." He gazed at the surrounding rocks. "It's too damn quiet. You watch ahead." He grimaced and let out a grunt from pain. "I've got to . . . try to get someplace higher . . . pick them off from a better vantage point. They're . . . probably trying to circle around behind us."

He no more than got the words out, when he quickly aimed and fired at a man Callie hadn't even noticed, up high and to their right. The man cried out and fell, his body bouncing on several other rocks before finally landing on one large flat rock with a sickening thud.

"Chris, your back. Your shirt's covered with blood! You can't go climbing around in those rocks!"

"Got . . . no choice," he answered. He removed one of his Colt .45s and handed it to Callie. "If they get closer to you, use this on yourself . . . right against the temple."

"What!"

"It will be a merciful death compared to what they would do . . . if they even bother to let you die."

Swallowing back her terror, Callie took the handgun. "Don't leave me here alone," she begged.

"Use your sense and your guns. You can . . . keep them at bay for a while. And don't forget what I told you . . . about always being close." He gave her a quick grin, but Callie could see the deep pain in his eyes, and he'd gone from a paler look to one that was more like a sickly gray.

"Don't you die on me, Christian Mercy," she told him, her eyes moist with tears.

Now the renegades were shouting back and forth to each other in a language Callie could not understand.

"Tie the horses to that scrub pine!" Chris ordered before darting away. Callie remained crouched behind the rocks until he finally disappeared into a crevasse above her. Fighting an all-consuming terror, she hurriedly grabbed the reins to the remaining three horses and tied them to the stump of a scraggly pine that had managed to somehow sprout from between two boulders. A shot rang out, hitting a boulder to her left and sending pieces of rock flying. Callie ducked her face away, then took her place behind the boulders again, watching ahead, as Chris had told her to do.

"Lordy, what am I going to do if he dies?" she whimpered. She fought hard not to cry. That would only spoil her vision and concentration. She jumped when she heard more gunfire. She had no idea if it was Chris shooting someone . . . or someone shooting Chris. She heard more shouts then. Were they rejoicing? She turned to study the rocks behind her. Nothing.

She screamed Chris's name but got no response. Maybe he just didn't want to let the others know where he was. Maybe he'd already passed out and was bleeding to death. Maybe he was already dead. What if somebody shot him in the belly? She'd always heard that was a terrible way to die.

She caught a movement to her left, then whirled and fired. Her eyes widened when, lo and behold, an Indian fell from a rock higher up, tumbling and rolling until he landed no more than fifteen feet away from her.

"Lordy, I *got* one!" she exclaimed. "Chris! I got one!" she screamed louder. "Only three or four left!" Maybe less if Chris had killed another one moments earlier.

"Who is out there?" someone yelled.

Callie crouched low as the shooting stopped again. Chris made no reply to whoever had asked the question, and she realized then how stupid she'd been to call out to him. Now they knew for certain she was female. "Damn!" she whispered.

"I ask again, who is there? I speak good English. We can talk."

More silence.

"Whoever you are, we want only the horses," the man yelled, his voice echoing against other rocks. "And some of your supplies. Give them to us, and we will let you live."

Callie decided this could go on forever if they didn't find some way to flush them out. She watched the rocks above and still could not see Chris or anyone else. She decided that since they already knew she was female, what was the harm in doing what she could to bring them out into the open? If they wanted her because she was a woman, then they wouldn't shoot her. There were other things they would rather do to her, and although the thought of it made her want to vomit, she decided she had to be brave now. It might be the only way to help Chris. She shoved the pistol into the front of her pants and stood up, raising her rifle in the air.

"It's just me!" she hollered. "You killed my man. Take the horses and get out of here!"

Finally she saw one man raise his head, then a second man emerged from behind another rock.

"Just the horses?" the one who spoke English asked. He came out from behind yet another boulder higher than the first two. Callie could see his wide grin. He was dark, his black hair a tangled mess. He wore white man's clothes, with a red bandanna around his forehead. His rifle in hand, he stepped farther down. "Is that a woman's voice I hear?"

Callie prayed she was doing the right thing . . . and that Chris was still alive up there somewhere . . . and conscious. "You know it is, you filthy murderer!"

Now she heard laughter, and two more men emerged from their hiding places. Callie felt her heart sink. There were more of them than she'd realized.

"She is small but full of fire!" their leader shouted.

He said something in his own tongue, and Callie figured he was repeating the words to the others, who laughed again, this time harder. She looked around. A sixth man rose from hiding several yards to her right.

A sixth man! Lordy! It was hard to count when in a panic. Her guess had been wrong. What if Chris *were* dead ... or passed out! "Oh, God, I'm in trouble now!" she whimpered. She took a deep breath, trying to retain a bold stance. "I said you could have the *horses*," she shouted. "Nothing more!"

"Oh, I think perhaps you have something better to offer," the leader answered, still slowly approaching her. "I think that if you are nice to us, perhaps we will let you live."

Now the rest of them moved closer.

"Perhaps I would *rather* die!" Callie answered, hoping she wouldn't pass out from pure terror.

"Nobody wants to die," the leader answered.

Now he was close enough that Callie could see an ugly white scar across his lips. In fact, he was just plain ugly all over, scar or not. Now they all concentrated their attention strictly on her. That was what she wanted—*if* Chris was still alive. She glanced above them again, sure this time that she saw something move.

"Take off your hat, little girl, so we can see you better," the leader told her.

Callie swallowed, slowly lowering the rifle. "Why don't you come and take it off *yourself!*" She sneered.

"Put down your rifle, and I will do just that," the man answered with a wide grin.

"Not till you promise to take just the horses and weapons ... nothing else," she warned.

The man only laughed. "There are six of us, and you are only one little girl."

"I killed one of your men myself, and I'll kill more if I have to," she told him. She raised her rifle. *"You* will be first."

The man stopped in place, losing his smile. "Please do not make us shoot you," he told her. "It would be such a waste of a pretty girl." He shrugged. "But then, I suppose once you are dead, we could still have some fun with you."

Rape a *dead* woman? Was there no end to the horror men

would commit just to enjoy a woman? She began to lose some of her confidence. If they didn't even care if she was dead first . . .

"Should be a lot more fun if I'm alive, shouldn't it?"

The man grinned again. "Just as I thought. You do not *really* want to die. Just hand over the rifle, little girl. It won't be so bad. There are only six of us." He repeated the words to the others, and they all laughed again. Callie could hardly find her breath.

Suddenly she heard Chris's voice from behind some rocks not far away. "You were right, mister. *Nobody* wants to die, including *you!*"

The voice took all of them by surprise, causing them to turn. Callie knew she had to act fast then. She immediately fired her rifle, catching the leader in the belly. He cried out and fell, but his screams were muffled by an explosion of gunfire, as Chris got off three quick shots, downing three more of the men. Blood splattered and bodies fell as Callie dived between two boulders, realizing then that the two remaining men were concentrated on Chris, heading up the hill after him. She wedged herself between the rocks and took aim, downing one of them when she caught him in the back. The other stopped to look, then turned on her.

That was when Chris fired again, and the top of the man's skull broke apart. He fell forward, and Callie grimaced. She could see the man's brain. She crouched between the rocks again, waiting to see if any of them stirred. Only the leader was still alive, and he lay writhing on the ground, holding his belly.

Callie knew she should feel some remorse for bringing another human being such awful pain, but she felt nothing. After hearing his suggestion as to what he would do with her, she decided he wasn't human at all, so why should she feel bad about shooting him?

Chris half stumbled, half fell down the steep escarpment then, and Callie limped over to him. "Chris! I wasn't even sure if you were still alive! I was just trying to flush them out for you. I knew I had to do something quick, for your sake.''

Holding his rifle in one hand, he put an arm around her shoulders, his breath coming in short pants, perspiration showing on his face. ''Damn smart . . . idea,'' he told her, his voice sounding weak. ''I have to . . . hand it to you, Callie. You're one damn . . . brave girl.''

He managed a grin, and Callie felt proud of herself. Coming from Christian Mercy, she'd just received one great compliment.

''It wasn't so brave,'' she admitted. ''I did it only because I knew you were up there somewhere. I just wanted to get this over with, for your sake.''

''It was . . . brave enough . . . all right.''

Callie grimaced with her own pain as he leaned heavily on her while she helped him over to the horses, still limping herself from her sore hip. ''A fine pair we make, don't we?''

''I guess now *I'm* the one who . . . will hold things up.''

''Hey! Please . . . help me!'' the wounded man begged. He still lay nearby, curled up in agony. ''Kill me! I cannot stand . . . the pain!''

Callie stopped walking.

''Keep going,'' Chris told her.

''But . . . shouldn't we do something? I mean, I'm the one who shot him. I don't really feel sorry for it, but still . . .''

Chris glanced over at the man, who continued to beg that they shoot him. ''After what he threatened . . . to do to you? Let him die slowly.'' Chris sneered. ''We've got to get . . . away from all these bodies. A couple of others might still be alive . . . but they're not worth saving. They sure as hell . . . wouldn't have shown *us* any mercy.''

Torn by her conscience, Callie helped Chris over to Breeze. He managed to get a foot in the stirrup, and Callie gave him a push on his rump to help him mount up. Chris cried out with pain, managing to get into the saddle, and when Callie stepped back, she realized she had blood on her hands. He was bleeding so badly that the blood had run down into the back of his pants and soaked the denim cloth. "Lordy!" she lamented, wiping her hands on her own pants. "You need help bad, Chris!"

"I know. Let's go put poor Betsy out of her misery . . . find a place to . . . make camp."

"Okay. Can you ride?"

"Got no choice."

His voice was getting weaker. Callie hurriedly replaced his rifles, then limped over to Sundance. Grimacing with pain, she managed to climb up onto the horse's back, straddling over the supplies tied there. She picked up the reins to the extra pack-horse and guided both horses out from behind the rocks, Chris following her. They rode out to where poor Betsy lay, now very still.

"Please let her already be dead," Callie prayed. "I don't want to have to shoot her." She thought how strange it was that she was worried about putting a horse out of its misery but didn't care much about the misery the man behind the rocks was suffering.

She slowly slid down from Sundance, then knelt down to check Betsy. "She's already dead."

Chris just nodded. "I . . . thought so. Grab whatever supplies you can from her . . . the mules too."

Callie felt ill from her own pain, but she knew certain things simply had to be done, and quickly. She hurriedly unstrapped the saddle on Betsy, grunting and grimacing as she jerked and yanked at the strap that was caught under the horse's belly, finally managing to get the saddle off the horse's back. Using all her strength, she hoisted the saddle on top of the gear already strapped to Night Wind, then grabbed her blanket, bedroll, canteen, and other supplies from Betsy, quickly tying every-thing onto Sundance. "These poor horses are really loaded up," she told Chris. "And they need water bad."

"Got to keep going . . . maybe an hour south," he told her. "There's a stream there . . . ranch not much farther. Get me . . . to the stream. Take care of . . . this wound. Come morning . . . we have to get to the ranch . . . for help."

Callie ran back to the mules, leading Sundance and Night

Wind. As fast as she could work, she untied supplies and loaded even more weight onto the two horses, hating to burden them so. She had no choice. Out here their supplies were vital.

She walked back to where Chris waited. "I'll climb up with you," she told him. "These other two horses are loaded up awful heavy. Besides, you look like you need something to hang on to."

Chris made no objection.

Grimacing with her own pain, Callie managed to get up on Breeze and scooted back into the saddle. "Hang on," she told Chris, taking hold of the reins.

Chris moved his arms around her, saying nothing. He dropped his head against her shoulder, and feeling the weight of him, Callie knew he was close to passing out completely. "Lordy!" she whispered, taking up the reins to the extra two horses. She had to find that stream before nightfall . . . and before Chris Mercy fell off his horse, in which case she sure as hell wouldn't be able to lift him back onto it.

Chapter
Twenty-six

A full moon was the only thing left to guide her by the time Callie came upon the stream Chris had told her about. By then she could feel Chris's full weight against her, and his hold on her felt limp. She wasn't sure what the heck to do for him once she made camp. Her own hip ached fiercely, and she could tell the area around the bite was swollen. She was in no condition to help someone else, but she had no choice now. Chris was in worse shape than she was.

She didn't have to urge the horses to the water. They hastened their pace on their own until they reached the stream's edge, where they drank eagerly. She moved Chris's arms from around her and managed to slide off the horse. Chris slumped forward, hanging on to Breeze's neck. Borrowing what strength she had left, Callie hurriedly unloaded the packhorses. She spread out a blanket for Chris and carried her saddle over to it for a headrest, grateful for the bright moonlight. To her relief, there was grass along the stream, so she could hobble the horses there and they would have plenty of grass and water for however long it took to get Chris back to riding condition. It also made a decent place for Chris to be able to lie down in comfort.

She walked over to where Breeze stood grazing, hobbling him too, then touched Chris's arm. He'd been so still the last hour or so that she feared the worst, but his skin was still warm. "Chris? Can you hear me? You've got to get down so I can help you."

His only reply was a groan.

"Come on, Chris. I can't handle you alone. You've got to try to get over to the blanket." His hat hung down from his neck, and she moved his head so she could get it off. She tossed it aside and pushed some of his thick hair off his face. "Chris?"

He made no reply.

"Shoot!" Callie took the canteen from Breeze and uncorked it. She reached up and poured what was left in it over Chris's face, then threw the canteen aside when he gasped and raised his head. "Chris?"

"Val?" he answered.

Val? Who was Val? "Yes, it's me," Callie answered, deciding any response was better than none. "Try to get down, Chris. I've got to get you over to the blanket."

"Yeah," he said weakly. Slowly he moved his right leg over the saddle, but just as Callie feared he would, he fell right off the horse. She tried to grab him, but his weight made it impossible, and she cried out with pain from straining to hold on to him at least a little so he didn't hit the ground full force. "Lordy!" she fretted. "I guess this is where you'll have to stay, Chris Mercy."

Yelping an *ow!* with practically every step, Callie pulled up the stake to which Breeze was hobbled and moved the horse farther away, doing the same with Night Wind, who was also a little too close. At least Chris had landed in grass, she thought. She limped over to where she'd fixed his bedroll and brought the blanket over to where he'd landed, opening it beside him. Using all the strength she could muster, she managed to roll him over onto the blanket. Then she used some wood they'd collected since leaving Hole-in-the-Wall and built a fire next to him so she could see better.

He was lying on his stomach now, and she decided to leave

him that way so she could do something about the wound in
his back. She untied her own blanket from her gear and rolled
it up, putting it under his head, then dug some gauze out of
their supplies. Remembering that her mother used to douse cuts
with whiskey, she figured that was all she could do for Chris's
wound. She had no idea if the bullet was still in him, but if it was,
and it hadn't killed him yet, she could only pray it wouldn't. By
now the bleeding must have finally stopped or slowed greatly.
Otherwise he surely would be dead from loss of blood. Maybe
all he needed was to lie still for several hours, get some rest.
Then, if they could reach the ranch for which they were headed,
maybe somebody there knew how to take out bullets.

She told herself to stay calm now and use common sense.
She had to get that wound cleaned up. She brought over a
canteen and a towel, then went over to Breeze and dug through
Chris's saddlebags, where she knew he kept a flask of whiskey.
She'd caught him sipping on it a time or two, and at first that
had worried her, but she had yet to see him drink much or get
drunk from what he did drink, and it dawned on her she really
was learning to trust him.

Actually, she was learning more than that. Much as she was
determined never to care about a man, she cared about Christian
Mercy. She more than cared, and that was probably the dumbest
thing she could allow to happen.

She walked over and filled the canteen with fresh stream
water, making sure to stay upstream from the horses. She came
back to where Chris lay, and grimacing with pain, she knelt
down beside him. Cautiously she folded up his leather vest,
then pulled his red checkered shirt out from his pants, having
trouble at first because of all the blood that had dried and stuck
to his skin as well as making his pants stick to the shirt. She
carefully peeled the shirt up and away from the wound, and
by the light of the fire she could see the ugly hole at his lower
left side, still oozing blood, but very slowly now.

She breathed deeply with relief, then wet the towel and began
washing around the wound as best she could. Chris made no
sound or movement. She uncorked the whiskey bottle then and

poured some of the demon drink, as her mother always called it, into the wound.

She jumped back when Chris let out a cry of agony and started to get up. Quickly Callie capped the whiskey and tossed the bottle aside, leaning over him and pushing on his shoulder. "No, Chris! Don't get up! Don't get up!"

He withered back down.

"Oh, lordy, I hope I'm doing this right," Callie lamented. She grabbed up the gauze and held the end near the wound, then wrapped it over his back. Then she straddled him and forced her left hand under his belly, not an easy task because of his dead weight. She grabbed the roll of gauze and pulled it around under him, back across his back, around under his belly again, repeating the process several times, perspiring from her own pain. She wrapped the wound as firmly as possible before tying it off.

She plunked down beside him, totally exhausted from the trauma of the day. She drank some of the canteen water, then reached over to lazily add some wood to the fire.

Chris groaned. Callie leaned closer to hear, and he again moaned the name Val.

"I'm right here, Chris."

"Need . . . water," he said in a near whisper, his eyes still closed. "So . . . thirsty."

Callie remembered hearing her father once talk about how a bullet wound and/or loss of blood could make a man crave water something fierce. Fighting a terrible need to lie down and sleep herself, she grunted and pushed until she managed to roll Chris over once more so he would be on his back, then slid the rolled-up blanket under his head. She picked up the canteen and moved one arm under his neck, raising him just enough to trickle some canteen water into his mouth. He coughed and groaned.

"It's all right, Chris. You'll be okay. Try to drink a little more water. You lost a lot of blood. My pa once said a man should drink a lot of water if he bleeds a lot. I always remembered that."

He lay panting and groaning, and Callie trickled a little more water into his mouth before he finally quieted again. One other thing she remembered was that a man wounded by a bullet had to be kept warm, something about a shock to the body. Using her last few ounces of energy, she got up and unsaddled Breeze, also removing Chris's gear from the horse. That took care of all the horses for the night. Now she just had to take care of herself and Chris.

She took one of Chris's rifles and grabbed a few more blankets, bringing them over to where he lay. She laid the rifle down beside her, then opened up the two blankets, covering Chris with both of them. Then she crawled in beside him, realizing that an extra body could help provide warmth. She put an arm around him and rested her head against his shoulder, pulling both blankets up around their necks.

"I'm right here, Chris. Don't you die on me now," she said softly in his ear.

His only answer was another groan.

Chapter
Twenty-seven

Callie felt a movement. That and the chirp of a bird woke her, and when she opened her eyes, Chris was lying on his right side, facing her, watching her. There was his face. Right there. So close. What in the world was that she saw in those blue eyes? Admiration? Desire?

She sat up quickly, moving out from under the blanket. "I was trying to keep you extra warm."

He smiled weakly. "I figured that," he answered, his voice strained. He grimaced as he rolled onto his back. "How in hell did we get here?"

"You don't remember?" Callie tucked the blankets around him.

Chris put a hand to his eyes. "The last thing I remember is following you out to Betsy. That's about it." He grunted when he moved his legs. "God, I hurt. And I'm thirsty as hell. Can you bring me some water?"

"I have some right here." Callie reached over and grabbed the canteen. "I gave you some last night, but you kind of choked on it." She uncorked the canteen. "I did everything I could think of. You fell off the horse right here, so I rolled you onto a blanket and I managed to clean the wound a little and pour whiskey on it. I wrapped some gauze around it but probably didn't do a very good job. It was so dark. I had only the light of the fire to work by."

He groaned as he managed to rise up on his right elbow. He took the canteen and gulped down some water. Callie couldn't help her tears then, the horror of yesterday's experience and the fear of Chris dying all mixing together with her weariness and her own pain to bring out her weaker side. The next thing she knew, Chris had put down the canteen and grasped her hand.

"Hey, we'll be all right, Callie."

"I thought sure you'd die . . . for a while there," she told him. "And it would have been all my fault!"

Chris lay his head back down but kept hold of her hand. "Now, why do you think that?"

"Because I'm the reason . . . you're out here," she said. "And I know you're a good man, Christian Mercy . . . in spite of what you do now . . . and all your pretending to not care about anything."

Her squeezed her hand. "Callie."

She wiped her eyes, angry with herself for crying like a baby, then met his gaze.

"I'm out here because I *chose* to be out here," he told her. "We all make our choices in life . . . so we just have to live with the results. No one forced me to do this, okay? If anything more bad happens, it will be my own fault. Nobody else's. Got that?"

She nodded, still sniffling. "How do you feel? I mean . . . besides hurting all over? You sound stronger. Last night you were really in bad shape. You even mumbled somebody else's name—didn't know who I was."

He closed his eyes. "Whose name?" he asked weakly.

She wiped her nose with her shirtsleeve. "Val," she answered cautiously.

He lay there quietly for a while. "Figures," he answered softly.

"Was she . . . your wife?"

He sighed deeply. "We'd better check this wound," he told her, completely changing the subject. "I've got to know if the bullet went through . . . like I think it did, or if it's still in there. Help me . . . get my shirt off."

His shirt off? She'd never seen a man with his shirt off in her whole life. Even the men who'd attacked her mother hadn't taken off their shirts. Her father had never let her see him without a shirt; nor had any of the various men who'd worked at the ranch at different times.

"Help me up," he said, rising on one elbow again.

Callie grasped his right arm and helped him get to his knees.

"Get my shirt . . . and vest off," he told her. "Maybe you can clean the wound better . . . put more whiskey on it. You need to see if there's an exit wound. The bullet must not have hit anything important, or I'd already be a goner. Probably just a flesh wound."

Callie helped him get off his vest. "You ever been wounded before?"

"Oh, yes." He winced. "Took a good one once in my . . . right thigh . . . broke the bone. I was . . . laid up quite a while . . . with that one." He took a deep breath. "In this case . . . I guess I can be glad most vital organs . . . are on the right side . . . and this wound is on the left."

"Yes, sir," Callie answered, feeling nervous as she unbuttoned his shirt, embarrassed at seeing chest hairs when the shirt came open.

"I must have lost a lot of blood," he said then. "I'm as light-headed as a butterfly full of whiskey." He shook his head. "Damn!" He grimaced as Callie pulled the shirt off each arm, and he immediately lay down on his right side again. "How does the gauze look? Any more bleeding?"

Callie looked at his back. "Yes, sir, but not so much." She couldn't help noticing how muscled his arms and shoulders were.

"Cut off the gauze and check the wound. See if you can . . . find an exit wound," he told her. "Use my pocket knife . . .

to cut the gauze. Help me to my knees again so you can unwrap it easier.''

Callie realized she couldn't let her embarrassment stop her. The man needed help. She got him to his knees, then fished into his pants pocket for the knife, feeling oddly stirred so close to him, his chest bare like that, having to reach into his pocket. She kept her eyes averted as she pulled out the knife. Then she carefully sliced through the gauze and unwrapped it. She noticed his stomach was flat and muscled. ''Can you stay on your knees a few more minutes?'' she asked.

''I think so. Do you see an exit wound?''

''I'm not sure, there's so much blood. I've got to clean it up better.'' She dug out a clean washcloth and wet it, then spent the next few minutes washing away more dried blood while Chris used her shoulder to brace himself. ''Looks like a hole right here, under your bottom left rib,'' she told him then. ''Yes, sir, I do believe it is. The bullet went through, thank God.''

''Must have hit a pretty major vein for it to bleed that much,'' he answered. ''I figured the bullet went through, or I'd be in a lot worse shape. Throw some whiskey on the wounds again. The next big thing we have to worry about is infection. If I go a few days with no sign of any, I'll probably be all right.''

Callie reached for the flask of whiskey she'd left nearby and uncorked it.

''Between your wound and mine, I won't have any of that stuff left to drink,'' he told her.

Callie looked up to see him grinning, and she smiled in return. ''I'm glad to see you smile, Chris,'' she told him.

''How about you? How's that snakebite?''

She wiped her eyes. ''Still sore as hell, but I'll make it. You ready for this?''

''Ready as I'll ever be.''

Callie doused both sides of the wound, and Chris growled in pain, gritting his teeth and stiffening. Callie picked up the gauze and wrapped clean bandages around the wounds, doing a neater job this time.

"Now . . . help me to my feet. I've got personal business to take care of."

"Chris, you can't get up and walk."

"Sure I can. This isn't anything you would want to help me with, believe me."

Feeling her face turning crimson, Callie rose and helped him to his feet. He leaned on her until they had walked far enough away for him to do what he had to do. She left him leaning against a pine tree, and she went back to rekindle the fire and start some coffee. She decided some bacon and potatoes just might help. He needed to eat and rest today, get more strength back before they went on to the ranch. Heaven only knew what they would find there. They would both need to be a lot stronger than they were at the moment.

"Help me do this, mama," she said as she put some wood on the few embers left of the fire. "I don't want those men to ever do to somebody else what they did to you." She looked up. "And if you have any connections up there," she continued in a whisper, "tell Him to watch over Chris Mercy for me. Don't let anything happen to him. Right now I'd just die myself if he got himself killed for me."

She stuck the wood on the fire and cautiously glanced back to see him walking toward her. Quickly she got up and hurried over to help support him as he came back to the blanket. He lowered himself with a grimace and a groan, then lay down on his right side again.

"I'll make you something to eat, and some hot coffee will help too," Callie told him. She let him rest while she cooked, then fixed him a tin plate full of bacon and potatoes.

"I can't eat much," he told her.

"Well, neither can I, so we'll share this," she told him with a supportive smile. "I'll feed you if you're not too proud."

He grinned. "I accept your offer. Pour me some coffee. I can handle that myself."

Callie obeyed, and he took a sip before she held up a fork with a piece of bacon and a piece of potato on it. He opened his mouth and she gave it to him, thinking how personal it seemed to feed him. There was just something special about it . . . and something provocative. She noticed how full and nicely etched his lips were, and even with a few days' growth of beard, he was good-looking.

She took a bite of her own then, not even minding using the same fork as Chris. She held up another bite for him. "Thank you for being so good at what you do," she told him. "I'd be done for if you weren't such a good shot."

He swallowed his food. "And we'd probably still be up there dodging bullets if you hadn't come up with the idea to stand up and draw their attention," he answered before accepting another bite.

Callie smiled bashfully. "Well, heck, I had to do *some*thing." She fed him more and ate more herself. "Chris?"

"Hmm?"

"Do you think that man we left there is dead by now?"

He nodded as he swallowed. "Bet on it."

She handed out another bite, but he waved her off. "No more. I've got to rest." He lay back down. "Look in my saddlebags. There's a silver cigarette case in there with some pre-rolled cigarettes. Get one out for me, will you? And bring a match to light it for me."

Callie obeyed, again feeling a strange sense of satisfaction as she held a match to the end of the cigarette while he drew on it. She liked waiting on him, liked pleasing him. He pulled on the cigarette, then exhaled with a deep sigh. "Her name is . . . was . . . Valerie," he said, surprising her with the statement. "She was my wife."

Callie could hardly believe her ears. He was finally telling her about his wife! She just sat there and listened, afraid one word out of her mouth would shut him up again. She hadn't asked one question. This was his own offering, and she was not about to do anything to spoil it. She was too damn curious.

"We were married in Chicago as soon as I graduated from college. I was twenty-four, she was nineteen. One year later we had a little girl." He paused, swallowing. "We named her Patricia. I always called her my Patty. She even would say that when someone asked what her name was. She would say 'My

Patty.' " He smiled, but Callie caught a quiver to his bottom lip. He took a deep breath and cleared his throat. "She had blond hair . . . a mass of curls. She had big blue eyes . . . and dimples that would melt Satan's heart. She came to mean everything to us, because when Val had her, there were . . . problems. The doctor told us Patty most likely was the only child we would ever have." He sniffed and cleared his throat yet again. "Not that we didn't try for more, but I guess he was right. Over the next three years Val conceived only once, and she lost that one."

Callie couldn't help feeling a little uncomfortable at the personal connotation of the remark . . . a man and woman in Chicago mating . . . trying to have a child. The way he'd put it, the tone of his voice, made it sound beautiful, and she felt embarrassed at feeling as though she was in that bedroom with them, watching them make love.

"As much as I loved Val," he continued, "there was nothing on this earth I loved more than that little girl." He swallowed. "Val was only twenty-three, and Patty only three . . . when they both died . . . a very senseless death."

He smoked quietly for a while, and Callie just sat and waited, watching a morning breeze ruffle his hair.

He sighed again before continuing. "I'd been teaching at high-school level after we married, then decided I wanted a master's degree so I could teach at college level. We moved to New England so I could go to Harvard. We both had plenty of money . . . both came from good families. We had a beautiful brick home, ran with the best of them . . . and I was a cocky son of a bitch, high I.Q., getting my master's, and all that bullshit. I thought teaching at college level would make me even more accomplished and admired . . . thought maybe I'd even end up dean of a university someday. I probably would have, in fact, if it hadn't been for what happened . . . something that made me realize that money, education, social importance, intelligence—none of those things matter. It's only the people we love who matter."

He swallowed, taking a last drag on the cigarette, then throwing it into the fire. Callie could feel the seething anger in his soul.

"I came home from a late-night session with one of my professors, feeling important and cocky because he was so impressed with some of my teaching theories. The door was slightly open and when I walked in the house, I saw it had been ransacked, valuable items stolen. I ran upstairs to find Val—raped and murdered."

He stopped, and Callie knew how hard it had to be for him to go on. She remained quiet in spite of the horror of the picture he painted.

"I, uh ..." His voice choked a little. "I ran to Patty's room." He sniffed. "That was the worst part. A grown woman is bad enough. But to kill ... a helpless ... beautiful little girl."

It took him several minutes to continue. Callie heard him sniff and take several deep breaths.

So goddamn senseless," he said in a gruff voice. "Worst of all, they never found who did it. I was so sick with grief and rage, I felt like someone had cut me open and torn my guts out. I needed ... wanted ... some kind of revenge. But back East you go to jail if you seek your own justice." He sniffed again and took a deep breath. "I decided that if they couldn't find the men who committed such an unspeakable act, I would at least try to find other killers and rapists ... bring them to justice or kill them myself. Out here it's easier. Out here men understand the law of the hangman's rope ... or law at the end of a gun."

He drank down more coffee before going on.

"So, here I am. After the funeral I never went back to that house, never finished my master's. I was like a madman, lived in a hotel, hounded the police, did some investigating of my own, but all to no avail. Finally I took enough money out of my little fortune to live on ... and I left. I had to get away from there. I bought what I would need to wander on the back of a horse ... taught myself how to shoot ... started collecting wanted posters ... and now I'm out here on the Outlaw Trail with you . . . looking for men who did to your mother what they did to Val, men who would have done the same to you if they'd known you were in that wood box.''

Callie could not help the lump that rose in her throat in pity for what had happened to him. Her chest shook in a sob as she spoke. "I don't know . . . what to say, Chris. I'm so . . . awful sorry for what happened to you. How can God let things like that happen?''

He picked up the silver case and took out yet another cigarette. "I need another light," he told her.

Callie took a burning stick from the fire and held it to the end of the cigarette, seeing his eyes were red and watery. He took a deep drag.

"There is another force at work on this earth, Callie, a dark force that hates good people, happy people, close families. It likes to try to destroy them . . . and it uses men whose hearts can easily be infested with that same evil to accomplish what it wants. All I can do to stop that evil is to stop those men. The only trouble is . . . no matter how many men I kill or bring in, the hurt and frustration inside never go away. I don't know if I'll ever be able to lead a normal life again. I just take a day at a time, an arrest at a time, a killing at a time . . . and figure I'll know when it's time to stop and get back to living again.''

Callie wiped her tears. "Thank you for explaining it all to me. It had to be awful hard. But maybe . . . maybe it's good to talk about it sometimes. Pa once said that if a person keeps his troubles all bottled up inside, they're bound to fester there and turn to poison that will eat him up till he's dead. A handsome, intelligent man like you shouldn't let that happen.''

He leaned his head back and drew on the cigarette again. "Maybe not. But watching the men who killed your mother hang will also help. I tell myself that every man I kill or bring in could be the one who . . . did that to my wife and daughter. I just can't seem to stop. Not yet.''

Callie nodded. "One thing is sure, I can understand how you must feel. I'll never forget what I saw either. At least in my case I know who did it, so if we find them all, I'll know for sure it's finished. That's the one thing you haven't been able to find ... a way to finish the hate."

Their gazes held, and Callie wished she could read the look in his eyes. "I never thought of it that way, Callie, a way to finish the hate. One thing you should know is ... I've never told another soul that story ... not since I left New England. My brother knows because of the telegrams and letters I sent him; but I never even stopped off to see him on my way out here. I just got on a train and headed west. You're the first person I've opened up to."

Callie felt a warmth move through her. "That makes me feel right special. And if it helps, just a little, then I'm glad."

"Yeah ... well ... I guess we're even now. I saved you. You saved me. We saved each other back there against the renegades." He looked at her again. "I guess that makes us pretty good friends, doesn't it?"

Callie smiled. "I guess so. Does that mean you won't get mad at me so easy from now on?"

He grinned and took hold of her hand again. "I'm not guaran teeing anything."

Callie looked down at his strong hand, thinking how small hers looked in comparison. Just the gesture of taking her hand, for the second time in the past few minutes, and telling her about his wife and daughter ... that all had to mean an awful lot coming from a man like Christian Mercy. She wasn't quite sure what to think of it, or what to think of the way her heart was pounding at the mere touch of his thumb gently rubbing the back of her hand. And, lordy! There he sat, half naked!

She drew her hand away, suddenly needing an excuse to distance herself from him. "I'd better tend the horses."

"Callie," he said as soon as she rose.

She met his eyes, and they were still misty.

"Thanks for listening," he said in all sincerity.

She nodded. "I'm touched that you told me." She left him to check on the horses. *Lordy, I think I love you, Chris Mercy.* She couldn't even think about saying it aloud. Besides, maybe it wasn't love at all. Maybe she just felt sorry for him.

Chapter
Twenty-eight

Callie followed Chris through the ranch gates, thinking how he was now more like the Christain Mercy she'd first met. He'd gotten much stronger again over the last couple of days and also more distant. She couldn't help wondering if he regretted sharing his personal tragedy with her. Was the softness he'd shown just due to his pain and weariness? She had a feeling this return to a cool, unattached attitude was more from fear of caring again than anything else; and maybe that was good, considering the fact that she was scared to death herself to care about a man.

And yet she hadn't been able to stop thinking about the way he'd held her hand, the fierce temptation she'd had to kiss him that morning she woke up to see him watching her. For that one little moment she had literally been lying in his arms. And before that, when it was she who needed help, he'd been so caring and understanding . . . and so concerned that she might die. Had it just brought up bad memories for him? Or did he really care for her in more than just a friendly way and would truly miss her and mourn for her if she died?

He was so hard to figure, she didn't know what to say to

him or when to say it. She refused to say anything about some of the feelings she was beginning to have for him for fear she would make a complete fool of herself. After all, the fact remained he was a lot older, a *whole* lot more educated, used to a far different social life than she'd ever known or could ever lead herself. Besides that, the man still mourned his wife and daughter. He likely was nowhere ready to love another woman.

Love. Lordy, was she really thinking about such a thing?

They had spent the last two days just lying around, resting themselves and the horses, both they and the animals needing to get some strength back. Callie told herself to be satisfied with the fact that they were both going to be all right. They just needed a few more days to get rid of the aching soreness of their wounds.

One good thing was she fully trusted him now. She'd bathed in the creek with no fear that he'd look or try anything inappropriate. Chris had bathed and changed out of his bloody denim pants, and Callie had scrubbed them with lye soap. It felt good to be clean. She'd even washed her hair, and today she wore it tied at the back of her neck, letting it hang down her back. She wore her split suede riding skirt, tired of wearing boys' pants. She'd put on a clean white shirt and a suede vest, and Chris wore clean denim pants and a blue calico shirt that seemed to match his eyes. He wore a brown leather vest and was clean shaven.

Callie couldn't help a secret satisfaction at the way he'd looked at her once she cleaned up and changed. She looked more like the woman she was now, and she had to admit, down deep inside, she didn't mind showing that woman to Christian Mercy. She couldn't tell just how impressed he was, since he was back to pretending he didn't see her as anything but the woman who'd hired him to find her mother's killers. He was bent on finishing what they'd started out to do . . . and so was she. There was no sense in letting other feelings get in the way.

Their search brought them to the Double B Ranch, on a path that with any luck would lead them straight to Jim Fallon. Callie shivered at the thought of seeing the man again, especially that big, ugly mole on his right cheek. That was one man she could pick out easily, one man's face that was hard to forget.

She began looking around the minute they spotted the main ranch house from a good mile off. "I wonder if he'll be there," she said to Chris, riding up beside him.

"The best thing we can do first is get to know the owner. Ranchers and their hands tend to be protective of their own. We can't just ride in there and accuse Fallon and call him out—if he's even there. We need to talk to Ben Bailey first."

They rode a little farther.

"I just realized I don't even know the date or what day of the week it is," Callie said.

"Doesn't matter much. I'm guessing it's at least mid- to late June. We've been on the trail a good three to four weeks."

The knowledge made Callie understand a little better how she could feel so attached to Chris. Three to four weeks was a long time to travel alone with someone, especially considering what they had already been through together. No wonder she felt so close to him.

Two men came riding out toward them then, and Chris motioned for Callie to stop as he reined up on Breeze, waiting for the men to get closer. "If you see Fallon, don't say a word," he warned.

"Yes, sir." Callie actually felt relieved when neither man was the ugly Jim Fallon. Both were crusty-looking cowboys wearing worn leather chaps, dusty boots, and stained hats. And both needed a shave.

"State your business," one of them said to Chris. He tipped his hat to Callie.

"We're here to see the owner, Ben Bailey," Chris answered.

"Reason?" the other asked.

"That's between him and me."

"This is outlaw country, mister," the first man stated. "We can't let you walk into Mr. Bailey's house without knowin' why."

Chris sighed, nodding toward Callie. "Does this pretty little lady look like an outlaw?"

Both men grinned a little. "Well, out here you just never know," one of them answered. Then he nodded to Callie. "No insult meant, ma'am."

"I understand," Callie answered.

"You can have our weapons if that makes you feel any better," Chris told them. "We just need to talk to Mr. Bailey for a few minutes. And we need to buy a couple of horses. Does he have any to sell?"

The second man nodded. "Got plenty. Hand over your guns and come on in. You'll get your weapons back when Mr. Bailey says you can have them."

Chris and Callie handed over rifles, shotgun, and handguns, then followed the two men up to the main house, a tidy but weathered-looking frame home. The boards of the porch that wrapped around the entire home were warped from years of rain and sun, and two windows were each missing a shutter. Some sorry-looking rose bushes decorated the sides of the front steps, their pitifully few blooms bringing at least some color to what was otherwise only hues of drab gray and brown.

A big-bellied, aging man stepped outside to greet them, and a gray-haired woman with a plain, weathered and tanned face moved into the doorway behind him.

"These two say they need to talk to you, Mr. Bailey," one of the hands told him. "And they're lookin' to buy a couple of horses. We've got their weapons."

Bailey looked at Callie and grinned. "Well, this one here sure doesn't look dangerous. Come on in, both of you." He looked at one of the men who'd brought them in. "Bill, take care of their horses, will you? See that they're watered, and give them a few oats."

"Yes, sir."

"Sure appreciate it," Chris told him. "These horses have been through a good deal. Lost one a few days north of here when renegades shot it down." He and Callie both dismounted gingerly, and limped slightly as they came up the steps.

"Renegades!" Bailey said. "You two are lucky to be alive."

"And they're limping. Were you wounded?" the woman asked as she took hold of Callie's arm.

"I was snakebit a couple of days before that," Callie told her. "And my friend here, he took a bullet in the side when the renegades attacked us. I'm afraid we're both still a little down under, ma'am."

"Oh, you poor thing! Come on in. Coffee's on, and I just baked a couple of pies."

"Lordy, that sounds good," Callie told her, following her into the house.

The Baileys, who were refreshingly friendly and hospitable, brought them into the kitchen and set them down to the table. The gray-haired woman, Mrs. Bailey, brought out coffee, then cut each of them a piece of apple pie.

"Ma'am, this is the best coffee I've had since we left Rawlins," Callie told her. "I don't even know how long ago that was. I've lost track of time."

"Rawlins! Well, you *are* a long way from home," Mrs. Bailey answered. "Are you two married? Brother and sister?"

Callie glanced at Chris, realizing she wouldn't mind at all if she could call him her husband . . . except for the intimacy that involved. He'd sure be one fine man to have around— handsome, strong, protective, able, smart, good inside, gentle.

You've got to stop having these thoughts, she told herself.

"Actually, we're just acquaintances," Chris told Bailey. "You're nice people, so I'll be honest about why we're here. My name is Christian Mercy, and before you go out of your way any more than you already have, you should know I'm a bounty hunter."

Bailey frowned, and his wife lost her smile. "Goodness me!" she said, putting a hand to her chest. "You sure don't *look* like a bounty hunter."

Chris couldn't help a slight grin. "Well, ma'am, I don't know what you think a bounty hunter is supposed to look like, but I assure you, I have good reason to do what I do. And it isn't always for the money. For personal reasons, I'm just out to get rid of the kind of men who keep the West lawless . . . the *worst* kind . . . the kind who—''

He hesitated, and Callie figured he was weighing his words, not wanting to offend Mrs. Bailey.

''—abuse women in the worst way,'' he said, ''and who murder innocent people for no good reason.''

''Oh, my!'' Mrs. Bailey sank into a chair.

''So what brought you to the Double B?'' Bailey asked.

Chris glanced at Callie before answering. He still hadn't eaten any of his pie. ''I'll let Miss Hobbs here explain,'' he answered. He drank more coffee.

Callie turned her attention to the Baileys. ''I'm Callie Hobbs,'' she told them. ''I hired Mr. Mercy here to find five men who abused my mother something awful. It was about a year ago. Then they killed her and made off with most of our cattle and horses. My mother and I were running a small ranch and farm alone, after my pa died a year earlier. The law never found the men who did it, but I can identify every one of them; so I decided to go find them myself. We found one of them up by Hole-in-the-Wall, and he told us another one is working here on your ranch.''

Chris swallowed a piece of pie. ''I don't think you want the man around, Mr. Bailey,'' he added. ''Especially not around this house when you aren't here.''

''Oh, my!'' Mrs. Bailey repeated, putting a hand to her mouth. ''Who is it?''

''The man who told us he was here said his name is Jim Fallon,'' Chris answered. ''He has a big mole on his left cheek.''

Bailey closed his eyes and sighed. ''Fallon.'' He nodded. ''Yes, he does work here. He's a pretty good hand.'' He looked at Chris. ''If what you're saying is true, I sure don't want him around, but I won't hand him over unless Miss Hobbs here makes sure he's the man you're after.'' He looked at Callie. ''How can you be so sure? If you can identify them, you must have been right there. Why didn't they kill you too?''

Callie looked down at her coffee cup. ''I was hiding . . . in the wood box. There was a space between the slats, and I . . .

saw. When they attacked us, my ma told me to get into the box and not come out, no matter what." Her eyes teared. "When I saw . . . what they were doing . . . I was too terrified to come out . . . and now I feel so guilty, I can't hardly stand it. The only way I can make up for it is to find those men and make sure they can't ever do that to anybody else."

A tear slipped down her cheek, and Mrs. Bailey reached over and took hold of her hand. "You did the right thing, Callie," she told her. "Your mother wanted to protect you. She'd never blame you for not coming out of that wood box to help her, because it wouldn't have done any good. She would just have had to watch them do the same thing to you, and she'd have gone to her death with that horror. She wanted you to live, honey, that's all. You satisfied her wishes. I would have wanted the same for my daughter. She's gone right now, going to a special school in Denver. Susan is a beautiful young lady, and I would gladly die for her. That's what your mother did, you know. She died for you, and there is no responsibility for that on your part."

Bailey leaned forward, resting his elbows on the table. "I'll tell the boys outside to ride out and bring Fallon in. Trouble is, what the heck are you going to do with him? You're a long way from the law, Mr. Mercy, and you've got this young lady with you. You intend to drag Fallon along to the closest jail and risk him somehow getting loose and doing you in? That would leave Miss Hobbs here alone with him, in the middle of nowhere."

Chris nodded. "I've been thinking about that. I'm not the kind of bounty hunter who shoots a man in the back just for the money. And by the way, Miss Hobbs isn't paying me cash for this. She's offered her ranch. I'm not sure I'll accept. I may end up doing this for nothing, the crime is so heinous. And I've come to like and respect Miss Hobbs a great deal. Doesn't seem right taking anything for this."

Callie, surprised, glanced at him, her heart warmed at the words. He'd not mentioned any such thing to her. This was the first she'd heard of him possibly taking nothing. "You deserve whatever I've offered," she insisted. "I won't let you do this for nothing."

Chris met her eyes. "We'll talk about that when the job is done. Right now we have to decide what to do about Fallon." He turned to Ben Bailey. "I'll drag Fallon along with us by the heels if that's what I have to do. I don't much care how he comes with us or if he lives through it, if you know what I mean."

The two men shared a look of understanding. "I *do* know what you mean. Could be something my men can take care of, if you know what *I* mean. Out here we live by a code of our own. A man can cuss and smoke and gamble and drink and fight and tell dirty jokes. He can even shoot another man if need be, but he can't abuse a good woman and he can't steal what belongs to another man. And he sure as heck can't murder innocent people. There's no judge or jury out here but each other." The man rose. "Tell you what I'll do, Mercy. I'm sure you two could use a couple good nights' sleep in real beds. You both look to me like you'd better rest a few more days before you go on to wherever you're headed."

"On down the Outlaw Trail," Chris told him. "I have a pretty good guess that's where we'll find most or all of them. The law won't touch this area, so this is where they're safest."

Bailey nodded, then turned to his wife. "Mother, do you mind if these two spend a couple of days here, take honest-to-God baths in honest-to-God hot water, sleep in honest-to-God beds instead of on the ground? Eat some honest-to-God home-cooked foods?"

"I don't mind at all," the woman answered, still holding Callie's hand. "It will be nice having another woman around for a couple of days. I miss our Susan so much." She squeezed Callie's hand again and gave her a reassuring look. The woman made Callie realize how much she missed her mother.

"Well, then, Mr. Mercy," Bailey said, turning back to Chris, "I'll have my men go get Jim Fallon and bring him back here. I won't tell them why. No sense setting them against Fallon until we know for sure. We'll let Callie here have a look at him, and then we'll let my men decide what to do about it. Might end up saving you some trouble.''

Chris rose, wincing with pain as he did so. ''I can't thank you enough, Mr. Bailey. We have a lot of riding ahead of us, a lot of searching yet. One thing I *would* like to do is see if we can get anything out of Fallon as to where we might find the rest of them.''

Bailey shrugged. ''We can try. By the way, what happened to the first man you found up at Hole-in-the-Wall?''

Chris glanced at Callie again. ''Let's just say he resisted arrest.'' He looked back at Bailey. ''And now he's dead.''

Bailey nodded. ''You and Miss Hobbs finish that pie. It's too good to waste. I'll have my men unload your gear, and the wife here will show you up to a couple of bedrooms where you can get some deserved sleep. You'd better let her have a look at your wound while you're at it. The wife here is pretty good at patching up cuts and bruises, broken bones and bullet wounds. No doctors out in places like this.''

Both men grinned, and Chris put out his hand. ''You're an oasis in the desert,'' he told Bailey, shaking his hand.

Bailey chuckled. ''Only people who live out here understand the needs in these parts,'' he said. ''My wife and I have been through a lot ourselves, settling here. But at least out here a man can claim as much land as he wants, most of it damn good grazing land. You mark my words, this place will be worth thousands someday, maybe even millions. Who knows? I've got two sons, one working here and one off East at college. They stand to inherit a lot someday, and they all make me damn proud. They are a chip off the old block and intend to keep running the Double B after I'm gone. Wish you could meet the one here, but he's off riding fences, probably a day or two away.''

Chris smiled. ''You're a lucky man to have such a nice family,'' he answered.

Callie knew he was aching for his own lost family.

''How about a smoke?'' Bailey asked Chris. ''Come out on

the porch with me. I just want to get a few more facts straight before I send my men after Fallon.''

Chris turned to Mrs. Bailey. "Save that pie," he said. "I'll be back to finish it.''

He walked out with Mr. Bailey, and Callie turned to Mrs. Bailey. "We sure do appreciate your hospitality," she told the woman. "Things have been real hard for us so far. I thought sure Chris was going to die when he took that bullet. He came close to bleeding to death. We've been kind of a sorry pair the last few days, me still sore from the snakebite and him weak from losing so much blood. A rest here in a real bed will really help.''

"Well, I'm glad for the company," the woman answered. "Out here you go long between visits from outsiders, even longer when it comes to seeing another female. A woman gets real lonely.''

"I'll bet.''

Mrs. Bailey sighed. "Christian Mercy. That certainly is an unusual name for a bounty hunter.''

"Yes, ma'am. And he's a real unusual man, real educated, had money and social standing back East. He even taught school and was getting his master's degree. He left it all when his wife and little girl were murdered and they never found the killers. That's what drives him.'' She gasped. "Oh! Please don't tell him I told you that. He doesn't like talking about it. He told me about it in a rare moment of weakness. He wouldn't like me telling it to others.''

Mrs. Bailey nodded. "I won't say a word.'' The woman rose and walked to her wood-burning stove, picking up the coffeepot. She brought it over to pour some more. "It won't take our men long to go and get Mr. Fallon. He's out helping build a new fence not that far away. You'd better beef up your stamina with a little more strong coffee before you have to look at that man again. Such a thing can't be easy, you poor child.''

Callie swallowed. "No, ma'am, it sure won't be.'' She took a deep breath and drank more of the hot coffee, definitely not looking forward to setting eyes on Jim Fallon again.

Chapter
Twenty-nine

Callie sat in a rocker on the porch, waiting to get a look at Jim Fallon. Mrs. Bailey sat beside her, and Chris stood leaning against a porch post, smoking quietly . . . waiting. She knew how tense he became in moments like this. She could feel it. Bailey had given him back his guns, and Chris took one of them out of its holster to check the cartridge.

What went through his mind at times like this? Probably the horrible visions of finding his beautiful young wife, his precious little girl . . . How did a man ever get over something like that? Maybe he never did, and maybe he could never love again because of it.

Lordy, what was happening to her? Lately she saw him in a whole different way, the manliness of him; the fine, muscled build; the cut of his firm jawline; those blue eyes that had a way of disturbing a woman; those full lips; that straight, handsome nose; that thick, wavy hair. She'd begun watching the way he moved, with the sureness of a man who knew what he was about. She admired his strength, his courage, the way he handled his weapons, the way he sat a horse, the way he cared about being clean and shaved, the way he seemed to know what to do no matter what the situation.

Damned if she didn't like everything about him. All of a sudden she couldn't imagine him *not* being a part of her life now. What the heck was she going to do when this was over and they had no more reason to be together? She felt safe with him. He had a way of making her feel like everything would always be okay. When he was around she felt . . . complete? She couldn't think of another word to describe it. He was the only man she would even begin to trust to do what it was men did to women they loved. The thought still scared the hell out of her, but something about Chris . . . she knew he'd understand. He wouldn't hurt a woman if his life depended on it. He'd be so sweet and gentle.

What a stupid thought! He'd never think about her that way. And she'd hardly known him long enough to be having such thoughts and feelings. It was just that now that she knew the truth about his past, watching him, knowing the torture he suffered in his mind and heart, it made her ache for him. It made her want to hold him and tell him everything would be all right . . . that she could love him the way Valerie had loved him . . . she could give him more children, a reason to live and love again. He was too fine a man to be wasting his life and his talents like this . . . wasting the ability to love and be loved.

Men were coming now, and she shook away the thoughts she knew were nonsense. Her heart pounded harder as the riders came closer. Ben Bailey walked toward them from the stables where he'd gone to check on a pregnant mare. The original two men who'd greeted them approached with two other ranch hands. When they reached the house, the sight of one of them brought a sudden lurch to the pit of Callie's stomach. He took off his hat and nodded to her, grinning at her with that same ugly grin she'd seen on his face when he was raping her mother. It took only one look at that ugly mole to know he was the man she was after.

Chris glanced at her then, and she nodded, then got up and ran into the house, unable to look at the man again.

"You ugly bastard, you scared that pretty little girl right off!" one of the ranch hands said.

Callie stood against the wall just inside the front door. She could hear all of them laugh at the remark.

"What is it you want, boss?" a man asked when the laughter calmed.

Callie recognized the gruff voice. It sent shivers down her spine.

"Your name Jim Fallon?" Chris asked.

"Sure is. Who wants to know?"

There came a pause. "I do. So does the young girl who just went inside. Her name is Callie Hobbs. You know the name?"

"Nope."

Another pause. "Well, maybe you didn't bother to stop and ask her mother what her name was before you raped and murdered her."

Callie turned then and peeked through the lace curtain at a window beside the door.

"Go on inside, Clara," Ben Bailey told his wife.

Mrs. Bailey got up and went in, and Callie could see Jim Fallon staring at Chris. "What are you talkin' about?" Fallon asked Chris. "And who the hell are you?"

"My name is Christian Mercy," Chris answered. "Do you know *that* name?"

Fallon stiffened and moved his hand toward his gun. In a surprisingly swift move, Chris had his own handgun drawn, cocked, and aimed at Fallon before the man could even think about pulling his own gun. Fallon froze in place, and seeing that he was contemplating running, one of the ranch hands grabbed his horse's bridle. The other took Fallon's gun from its holster. The three ranch hands lost their smiles, looking confused.

"It's all right, boys," Ben assured them. "Let this man finish his business."

"You're a goddamn bounty hunter," Fallon sneered.

"That's right. You just sit there while I refresh your memory. Maybe you'll understand then why I'm looking for you. Callie's mother's name was Ellie Hobbs. She and her daughter ran a ranch and farm all on their own, over by Rawlins. You remember being in that area a year or so ago?"

Fallon just swallowed. "Who's to prove it?"

"You and four other men attacked their ranch, took turns raping Ellie Hobbs, then murdered her. You were running with a man by the name of Terrence Stowers. Remember him?"

"What the hell?" one of the ranch hands muttered.

"Wait a minute!" Fallon protested.

"Might go easier on you if you tell me where Stowers is now," Chris told him.

"I don't know no Terrence Stowers," Fallon claimed. "How do you know *any* of us was involved in what you're talkin' about?"

"Because Callie Hobbs saw the whole thing."

"She *couldn't* have! There wasn't nobody there but—" The man stopped, realizing he'd just implicated himself.

Chris walked down one step, his gun still on Fallon. "Callie was hiding in the wood box, while you and the others shared whiskey and took turns with her mother."

"Oh, God in heaven!" Mrs. Bailey fretted, running off to the kitchen.

Fallon looked around. "She . . . she *wanted* it!" he protested. "It *wasn't* rape. She invited us in."

"Liar!" Callie screamed, charging out the door. "You filthy liar!"

Chris grabbed her around the middle before she could reach Fallon to beat on him.

"You all raped her! You took turns with her and then you *killed* her! You stole all our money and our horses and cattle! You ugly, filthy *bastard!*"

"Get inside!" Chris growled at her.

She wilted slightly, and he let go of her.

"Go on. We'll take care of this."

Sobbing with rage, she jerked away from him. "*Shoot* him Chris! Shoot him right here and now!" she screamed, tears streaming down her face.

"Go inside!" Chris snapped.

Callie stood there with fists clenched. Fallon grinned at her. "I sure am sorry we didn't know you were in that wood box, honey," he said, an obviously deliberate attempt to upset her more. "I expect you would have been a whole lot more fun than your ma."

The man to his right, who still held Fallon's pistol, suddenly whacked Fallon across the face with his own gun, sending Fallon sprawling. Instantly the three ranch hands jumped on the man and began beating him. Bailey finally broke them up and ordered them to take Fallon to the main barn and tie him to a post.

"Mr. Mercy here needs to ask him a few questions," he told his men. "Then we'll hold court and decide what to do with him."

The men dragged a kicking, struggling Fallon off, and Chris turned to Callie. "Go on inside like I told you," he said. "You don't need to have anything to do with this."

"I *want* to," she sobbed, furious at what the man had said about her mother. "I want to cut off that ugly thing between his legs and feed it to the *hogs!*"

Chris and Ben looked at each other, and Ben actually chuckled. "That's a picture," he said.

To Callie's surprise, Chris grinned and shook his head. Bailey walked off toward the barn, and Chris turned to Callie.

"I don't doubt Fallon deserves whatever you'd like to do to him." He holstered his gun. "But first I want to see if I can get anything out of him that might help us find the other three. It will be worth the time we might save. All right?"

Callie sniffed and wiped her eyes. "If you're going to shoot him or hang him, I want to *watch!*" she declared. "You promise you'll come and get me, Christian Mercy!"

He reached out and took her face between his hands, wiping

her tears with his thumbs, then leaned forward and kissed her forehead. "I promise."

He turned and walked away, and all the rage left Callie with that kiss, the touch of his hands on her face. The gesture astonished her. She watched him walk toward the barn.

"Damn," she whispered. "I *do* love you, Mr. Mercy."

Chapter Thirty

Callie stood at the bedroom window, watching the barn, where she could see only a very dim light from a lantern. Chris was out there . . . alone. What was going through his mind? He'd told Ben Bailey she should stay at the house and get some sleep, said he needed to be alone for a while.

Was he drinking? Had the events of the day just brought back too many memories?

She sat down on the window seat and leaned out the open window, resting her arms on the sill. Earlier in the day, more of Bailey's ranch hands had been brought to the barn for a "trial." Bailey had held his own form of court, with him as the judge. All present voted that Fallon should be hung; and so he was, from a support beam inside the barn.

Callie had been allowed to watch, as she'd insisted on doing. It was an ugly sight, a slow, fitting death for the likes of Fallon. Frontier justice had been served, and now Fallon lay buried far out in a field, with no marker for his grave. It was as though he'd never existed, and that was fine with Callie.

It had not even been necessary to try to beat information out of the man, since he'd bragged to one of Bailey's men that one of his "best friends," Terrence Stowers, now ran a saloon at a place called Hanksville in Southeast Utah, a few miles south of the notorious Robber's Roost, another outlaw hangout. Two other "friends" by the names of Luis Hidalgo and one just called Penny helped with the business. Callie had a pretty good idea they were the last three men she was after.

So, Hanksville had to be their next stop, but she knew from talking to Ben and Clara Bailey that it was a good two hundred miles away, maybe more. Time was of the essence, since men like Terrence Stowers didn't usually stay put for long. Bailey had advised they ride to Cheyenne, accompanied by some of his men, who were herding some cattle there, then take the Denver & Rio Grande south to Pueblo, then the Western Denver & Rio Grande to Greene River, which was about fifty miles north of Hanksville, via more country that would take them right along the Outlaw Trail again, through Robber's Roost.

It was going to be a very long train ride, preceded by a back-breaking cattle drive, followed by another journey through dangerous country. Callie's one consolation was that meant she'd be spending a lot more time with Chris Mercy, although from now on and for several weeks they would not be alone.

Maybe that was best. It wasn't that she didn't trust Chris. It was her own feelings she didn't trust lately, and the last thing she wanted to do was make a fool of herself.

The thought of women like Lisa brought a truly burning jealousy to her soul. Once this was over, would Chris just leave her off in Rawlins and go back to that whore, just to relieve whatever it was men had to relieve themselves of? Lordy, how could she let him walk out of her life like that? He could go away and be killed on his next job. Or he could find some nice woman he would fall in love with and marry . . . and take to his bed.

She could hardly stand the thought. Nor could she stand wondering why he was out in that barn alone when he could be in here sleeping in a good, comfortable bed. She leaned farther out, noticing the only sounds were the whinny of a horse here and there, the lowing of cattle, and a hooting owl.

Far off in the distance she could hear coyotes yipping. The moon was still plenty bright, and she could see a ranch hand riding slowly around the corral area, keeping watch. She knew two more men were farther out, watching some cattle. One of them was singing softly, as men often did when trying to keep cattle calm. The air was still and cool, a beautiful night. Chris shouldn't be sitting out there alone in that barn with his awful memories.

She got up. It was going to look bad, but she didn't care. She was going out there to try to talk Chris into coming into the house. She should be with him. Maybe he needed someone to talk to. She walked to the bed and picked up her flannel robe. She hadn't worn this cotton nightgown since she left Rawlins, not even that night she spent in the hotel ... that night Chris slept with Lisa.

She pulled on her robe and walked with bare feet out the door and down the wooden stairs to the parlor. The house was so quiet, she could hear Ben Bailey snoring in a downstairs bedroom. That was good. They wouldn't know what she was doing. She decided to go out the back door, her bare feet making no sound on the floor as she walked through the house. If she kept to the shadows, the men outside wouldn't know she was going to the barn. They all thought she was upstairs sleeping. Her reputation wouldn't suffer, but she didn't really care if it did. Chris was more important than her reputation.

Once outside, she kept to the darkest areas as she made her way across ground soft from being churned up by the constant beating of horse and cattle hooves.

She reached the barn door, and taking a deep breath, she peeked inside. Chris sat leaning against the support post under the very beam from which Jim Fallon was hung earlier. A piece of rope still dangled from the beam. Callie shivered at the memory, then ducked inside. Chris caught the movement, and in a split second his six-gun was drawn and aimed. She gasped and stepped back, only then noticing he held a bottle of whiskey in his other hand.

"It's just me!" she called in a loud whisper.

He leaned against the post again, putting back the gun. "Get out of here. I could have shot you."

"Why don't you come inside, Chris? You need some real sleep, in a real bed."

"Leave me alone." He drank down some of the whiskey. "You shouldn't be out here, dammit. Get back in the house, where you belong."

Callie folded her arms in front of her and walked closer. "I will not. I belong out here with you. Something is bothering you bad, probably your memories. I came out to tell you that if you need somebody to talk to—"

"I *don't!*" he snarled. "And it isn't *memories* that bother me right now!"

His anger startled her.

He looked up at her almost scathingly. "It's *you* that's bothering me, all right? *You!* So get the hell out of here!"

Callie frowned. *"Me?* What are you talking about? What did I do to make you so mad at me again?"

He snickered and looked away. "My God, you're so goddamn stupid sometimes."

Callie felt like crying at the remark. "Chris, please don't be like this. I thought we were at least friends now."

He looked back at her, his blue eyes looking bloodshot. He looked her up and down, his gaze seeming to drink in every inch of her. *"Friends?"* He slowly stood up. "You come walking out here in the middle of the night, barefoot, your hair all brushed out long and beautiful, wearing a loose nightgown and robe with probably nothing underneath; you see me sitting here drinking and feeling sorry for myself, and you want to talk about being *friends?"*

Callie blinked back tears and backed away a little. "Y-Yes. What's wrong with that?"

He laughed and took another swallow of whiskey. He leaned against the support post before continuing. "You don't have the slightest idea how beautiful you are, do you?"

Callie's heart raced with confusion. He really *did* think she was beautiful, or was that just whiskey talk? Was he angry?

Laughing at her? Did he hate her? Love her? "Me? Heck no, I'm not beautiful. I've never even *tried* to be beautiful, or even much cared if I was."

He stepped a little closer. "You don't *have* to try, Callie. It shines through you, from those freckles on your nose all the way down that pretty little body to your small feet. It comes out in your brown eyes, in the way you talk, the way you smile. Mostly it comes through in your unabashed innocence, and in your bravery, your feistiness, your strength."

He took another swallow, and Callie looked away, astounded by his admission, flattered, confused . . . totally in love. "Well, I reckon I should be flattered. I don't know what to say, Chris."

He laughed again. "You *reckon* you should be flattered? That's some of the *worst* English I've ever heard, but when it comes out of your mouth, it's . . . I don't know . . . cute. Yeah, that's the word. *Cute!*"

Callie looked at him with a scowl. "You're insulting me, Christian Mercy! I don't like you this way! You've been drinking, and by God, I don't think that you really think I'm beautiful at all! That's *whiskey* talk! You're fighting something inside, and you're just trying to cover for it. I came out here with good intentions, but to *hell* with you!"

She turned to go, but he grabbed her arm, tossing the whiskey aside. He jerked her around. "Good intentions?" He grasped her arms and yanked her close, wrapping strong arms around her so she could barely move. "You and I both know the real reason you came out here, and it wasn't just to *talk!*"

He met her mouth before she could turn away, parting her lips in a long, demanding kiss, moving one hand over her bottom, pressing his fingers between her legs from behind. Callie finally managed to turn her face away, and he moved his lips to her neck, her throat, moved a hand around to fondle her breasts. Callie pushed at him.

"Stop it! This isn't you, Chris. You're drunk and you're fighting the *truth.*"

"Am I?" he said huskily. He clamped a strong hand under her jaw. "And what truth is that, Callie? Is it the fact that no man has ever kissed your pretty lips, or touched your pretty breasts, or made a *real* woman out of you?''

Callie managed to get one hand free, and with all the strength she could muster, she punched him with her fist, slamming it into his left cheek. Startled, he let go of her and she stepped back. "And I thought you were *different!*" she said, fighting tears. She started to hit him again, but he caught her wrist.

"I *am* different! I just don't want you to see it. I want you to *hate* me, Callie Hobbs. Understand? I want you to hate me because that makes it easier for me *not* to love *you!* But it doesn't much matter how I fight it. It's happening, and I can't stop it . . . and that scares the *piss* out of me!" He gave her a light shove. "Are you satisfied now? *There's* your truth! I love you, and I've got no right ever loving again. I should have been *home* the night Val and my Patty died! I should have been *home,* but I was out feeding my own intelligence ego, my own self-righteous belief that I was the smartest goddamn young man on the face of the earth! I was too damn *dumb* to know what was really important in life! I found that out too late, and I don't deserve to ever know that kind of happiness again!"

He remained turned away, leaning against the support post.

"Go on back to the house," he said quietly then.

Callie stood there undecided, truly hating him, truly loving him, truly aching for him but wanting to hit him over the head with a shovel. "You *are* dumb, Chris Mercy, too dumb to see a chance to be happy again, to have more children, to love and to *be* loved. If you're willing to throw all that away, then all your schooling didn't teach you a damn thing! Hell, *I'm* smarter than you are, and I've never spent more than two years in a real school my whole life!"

She turned to walk out.

"Callie, wait!"

Callie froze in place, not sure what to expect. She felt him come closer, wondered if she should scream when he put his hands in her hair while she stood with her back to him. He ran his fingers down through her hair.

"You're absolutely right," he said, sounding calmer now.

"I'm the dumbest son of a bitch who ever walked." He put his hands on her shoulders. "But there is something you have to understand."

Callie remained turned away. "What's that?"

He sighed deeply. "It's . . . hard. I mean, I had a family once, and I lost it. It's hard to let yourself love again after something like that."

" 'Course it is. You didn't have to tell me that."

"It's not just that. You're sweet and innocent and damn young."

"I'm as much a woman as that stupid Lisa."

He pressed her shoulders. "That's what I mean about you. You have no idea what a statement like that does to a man who's fighting the very strong desire to find out just how much of a woman you are. You tempt a man without even trying, just by being yourself."

"I don't mind tempting you, Chris Mercy. I *love* you, plain and simple. I don't even want to finish this trip for fear something will happen to you. I'm not sure I could go on living if it did."

"We *have* to finish this trip for our own closure, our own sanity. You know we do. And for as long as that takes, I need that time to decide whether I should be a part of your life or get out of it all together."

Callie turned. "I don't want you to ever leave me, Chris. You're the only man I've ever had feelings like this about, the only man I could stand to . . . let touch me. But not the way you just touched me a minute ago. That wasn't you."

He put his hands to the sides of her face again. "If I touched you the right way, we just might end up doing something neither of us is ready for yet. So go on back to the house. *Please* go on back to the house. If you love me, you'll do what I ask."

Callie could not help her tears. She grasped his wrists, thinking how strong they were. "Promise me you'll think real hard on the fact that I love you?" she asked.

"I've *been* thinking about it already. You didn't have to say it. I knew. And you don't have to try to make me love you by coming out here and offering yourself like some kind of sacrifice. All you have to do is just be you, and the real you is scared to death of being with a man that way. If and when something like that happens, we'll know when it's right, and it sure as hell won't be in a barn with a drunk man. A girl like you doesn't deserve to have it be that way. So just do me a big favor and *go away!*"

Callie sniffed. "Not till you kiss me nice. I don't want to remember that last kiss. It hurt."

He sighed, bending his head and resting his forehead against the top of her head. "Jesus," he whispered. "I'm so sorry, Callie."

"I know. It's okay."

"No, it isn't." He gently kissed her forehead, her eyes, her nose ... her mouth ... the most sweet, delicious kiss she'd ever known. It lingered, and Callie felt like she was melting into him. He enveloped her fully into his arms then, crushing her against his strong, broad chest. Here was where she felt safe. Here was where she felt loved. Here was something that made her feel whole.

This time she didn't want to pull away. It was Chris who pulled away, but one hand lingered near her breast, and he moved a thumb along its fleshy side. "Go on back," he told her. "I swear I've never been so tested in my entire life." He let go of her and stepped back.

Callie touched her lips. "Thank you for the kiss. That's one I don't mind remembering." The last thing she wanted to do was leave, but she knew he was right. She didn't want it to be this way any more than he did. Chris Mercy had a lot of things to think about, a lot of bad memories to get over.

She turned and ran out, hurrying back to the house, sneaking in the back door and up the stairs. Softly closing the bedroom door, she ran to the bed and fell facefirst onto it, breaking into tears that came from a mixture of terrible need and desire, as well as frustration at not knowing how to behave around a man as experienced as Christian Mercy.

What if he decided he wasn't right for her after all? He could ride right out of her life tomorrow, and there wasn't a thing she could do about it. This new revelation of his feelings would only make things more strained between them now, until he made up his mind what to do about it. What made it worse was having to be around him every day, look at him every day, want him every day but not be able to act on her feelings until she knew he was ready to accept her love. She curled into the pillow, wishing it were Christian Mercy lying next to her.

Chapter
Thirty-one

Callie washed and dressed, looking in the mirror to make sure her eyes weren't baggy from not enough sleep and too much crying. They didn't look nearly as bad as she felt, and now her stomach churned at the thought of facing Chris today, wondering how he would behave toward her.

She left her hair brushed out long, pulling the sides back with combs. Chris seemed to really like her hair left loose. She wished she could wash off her freckles, but then, he seemed to like those too. It was just that her only real sign of maturity was her breasts. She crossed her arms over them, wondering if Chris would remember touching them last night ... and if he would remember how hard she'd clobbered him.

Maybe she should just have let him do what he wanted to do, but she'd be damned if any man would have her that way, even Christian Mercy. Besides, he knew damn well he'd done wrong, and she hoped he would be properly embarrassed this morning.

Trouble was, *she* was the one who was embarrassed. Chris had been right when he'd called her stupid about men; but he'd also said she could attract a man without even trying. She studied herself in the mirror, and for the life of her, she couldn't understand how that could be. He hadn't even seen her in a dress except for that first day they met, and that was just a plain old calico day dress that hung too big on her.

Of course . . . he *had* seen her naked. Lordy! The man sure had a way of leaving a woman in a bad position, embarrassed, in debt to him, dependent on him for her safety.

She adjusted her riding skirt and made sure her shirt was clean, then pulled on her suede vest. She went downstairs to help Mrs. Bailey prepare breakfast, finding the woman busy taking warm biscuits out of the oven.

"Oh, my, it's getting warm already!" Mrs. Bailey told her after greeting her with a smile. She grabbed a towel to wipe perspiration from her forehead after she set down the biscuits.

"Let me help you, ma'am," Callie told her. "I'm a good cook, and you shouldn't have to do extra just because of me and Chris."

"Oh, it's a privilege. I truly enjoy the company. I'm not so sure, though, that Mr. Mercy will be down for breakfast."

"He's upstairs?"

"Yes, he finally came in last night. Three sheets to the wind, I might add. He won't be feeling very good today, I can tell you that. I've seen it before. Mr. Bailey himself tips the bottle a little too much sometimes. It's just the way men are."

"It is?"

The woman chuckled as she set a fry pan on the stove, then grabbed some wood from a pile nearby. "You're young," she told Callie. "You'll learn." She lifted the skirt of her dress to use as a hot pad and lifted a burner plate by the handle, shoving in the extra wood to make it hotter. She replaced the plate and set the fry pan on it, then took a can from a shelf above the stove. "Honey, men are stubborn, stupid little boys sometimes. A woman can't hardly live with them, can't live without them neither, especially in places like this." She nodded toward a cupboard. "Get some plates down and set the table if you want something to do. I'll fry some pork. Just slaughtered a hog the other day, so I've got plenty."

Callie took down some plates. "I agree about the stubborn, stupid part," she told the woman. "Mr. Mercy is stubborn as a mule and stupid as a stump about what really matters in life. I mean, he's smart. Real, real smart. Graduated from college with honors. But he just wastes it now, wandering around killing men for money, afraid to let himself care about anybody."

Clara Bailey removed a towel that covered the open can and spooned a little grease out of it, dropping it into the fry pan. "I'll make a few potatoes too," she said. "They're already peeled."

"You're going to too much trouble."

"I don't mind. I'd be doing it anyway for Mr. Bailey. He likes a big breakfast." She hesitated, then turned. "Your Mr. Mercy must drink to forget."

Callie set out the plates and went back to get some coffee cups. "Is that why men drink? Mostly to forget?"

Clara began slicing some potatoes into the fry pan. "Some. Not really to forget but more to dull the pain of it. Then again, a good share of them drink for the pure pleasure of getting drunk and acting like idiots. Don't ask me why, considering how they feel the next morning."

Callie smiled at the woman's humor, some of the weight lifting from her heart.

Clara picked up another potato. "Was he pretty drunk already when you went to the barn last night?"

Callie lowered the cups she'd taken from the cupboard, feeling her face turning red. "How did you know?"

"Honey, there isn't much I miss around here. In country like this, you learn to pay attention to every unusual sound, and there's one floorboard at the bottom of the steps that creaks just a certain way when someone steps on it. You okay? I heard you crying when you came back. He didn't offend you, did he?"

Callie thought about Chris's first forceful kiss, the way he'd fondled her breasts and threatened to do a lot more. But the kiss that followed, the admissions he'd made . . . "No," she answered. "I didn't go out there to . . . I mean, nothing bad or improper happened. I'm not that kind, and neither is Mr. Mercy. I was just worried about him being out there all alone with whiskey and bad memories. I think that hanging just kind of triggered something in him. He was more angry than anything else.''

"Mmm-hmm. Drinking can make a man happy as a lark or mean as a skunk.''

That's sure, Callie thought. She walked to the table and set down the cups. "Can I ask you something personal, ma'am?''

"Go right ahead,'' the woman answered, still swiftly slicing the potatoes into the pan.

"How do you know . . . when you're in love?''

Clara stopped her work, and the potatoes in the pan began to slowly sizzle. "Well, I guess it's when you can hardly stand the thought of being away from him, and when you get all excited when he's around, and you have a great admiration for the way he looks and the way he carries himself.'' She finished slicing the last potato as she spoke. "I have to say, any woman can appreciate Mr. Mercy's looks.'' She laughed lightly. "He is one fine specimen of man. You sweet on him?''

Callie spotted some silverware in a basket on the cupboard. She walked over and picked out some knives and forks. "Yes, ma'am, I guess I am, but we have to travel together and we're still not completely sure what we feel. He said some things last night that I'm afraid was just whiskey talk.''

"Well, generally you can figure whiskey will force a man to tell the truth he'd never tell when he's sober.''

"Really?''

"Oh, yes. They always deny it the next day, but the whiskey will trip them up every time.'' She faced Callie again. "You sure he didn't get out of line last night? He's got a swell bruise on his left cheekbone.''

"He does?'' Callie put a hand to her mouth. "Oh, my goodness!'' She reddened again. "Well, ma'am, I know him pretty good. I mean, he did try to get a little too romantic. I set him straight.''

Clara laughed loudly. "I guess you did! Knowing that, and

hearing what you said yesterday about what to do with that Jim Fallon, you are quite something, Miss Callie Hobbs.'' She shook her head. ''Quite something.''

Callie giggled. ''I take it that's a compliment.''

''It sure is! No man is going to get the best of you, is he?''

''No, ma'am. Fact is, I told him when we started out on this trip that if he tried anything funny, I'd shoot him dead.''

Clara laughed some more as she turned the potatoes and Callie set out the silverware. Clara sobered then when she turned around again. ''You watch yourself, Callie. You might be able to handle a man physically, but a man can be a perfect gentleman and still break your heart. There's no way to protect yourself from that.''

Callie felt her chest tighten, thinking about how she'd ached last night for her pillow to be Chris Mercy. ''Yes, ma'am, I'm learning that too.''

Clara took the lid off a small pork barrel and used a fork to dig a slab of ham out of the lard. She set it on a cutting board on the cupboard and sliced it, laying it in a pan. ''Would you go out to the henhouse and gather some eggs for me?'' she asked Callie. ''There's a basket right there by the door. It will be just the four of us. The ranch hands do their own cooking in the bunkhouse, and our son stayed out at the line shack last night.''

''Yes, ma'am.'' Callie picked up the basket and walked out. It was a pretty morning. When she glanced at the barn, she had to almost wonder if last night was just a dream. Had Chris really said all those things? Did he really love her?

She sighed as she headed for the chicken coop. So what if he did? He was bound to fight it tooth and nail, might even be stupid enough to turn away from all of it and leave. She wouldn't put it past him, but the thought of it made her stomach hurt so that she wondered how she was going to get any food down. It would be rude not to eat decent, with all the trouble Clara Bailey was going to.

The chicken coop was some distance away. Callie figured that was so it wouldn't smell bad by the house. Lord knew, chickens sure could stink sometimes. But fresh eggs made for a darn good breakfast. She walked out to the coop and went inside, shooing away some of the hens and then investigating their nests.

"Well now, I expect Mr. Rooster has been right busy," she commented, picking out several still-warm eggs. She grinned at the thought, but then sobered again, thinking how silly she was to think for the past year or so that she could go her whole life without a man. Even female animals needed a male to continue the circle of life. Growing up on a ranch, she'd seen plenty of animals mate. Still, the thought of doing the same thing, even with Chris Mercy, was pretty intimidating. That was pretty intimate stuff. And how in hell could it not hurt? Then again there were women like Lisa, who didn't seem to mind it at all. And women had been having babies since the beginning of time. There sure as heck was only one way for that to happen, and deep down inside she did want to have babies someday. It would be especially nice to have Chris's babies. It would be good for him to have more children, to ease the ache in his heart for his little Patty.

She finished picking through the eggs, filling the basket with fourteen of them. Mr. Bailey looked like the kind of man who ate plenty big meals. She headed back out, and as she approached the front porch she saw a man standing there, leaning against a post and smoking.

Lordy! It was Chris.

Chapter Thirty-two

Callie hesitated. What the heck was she supposed to say this morning? One thing was sure. She had to be firm. She was not going to crumble and cry in front of him; nor would she gush over him. He'd told her to leave last night, said he had a lot of things to think about. Maybe he was even thinking about telling her everything he'd said last night was a lie.

Fine. He could cover up all he wanted, but Christian Mercy loved her. The whiskey made him tell it straight, and she would hang on to that no matter what he did when he was sober. It would just be damn hard to pretend it didn't matter if he tried to back down from the truth.

He was watching her, and something about the way he looked at her made her feel stark naked. Lordy, this was going to be hard! She marched closer, secretly happy that he looked like he felt like hell. His hair stuck up every which way, and he needed a shave. His eyes were bloodshot, and he carried a towel, soap, and razor in his hand.

"Morning," she said to him, remaining unemotional.

He nodded. "Morning."

His gaze moved over her in a way that made her want to hide her breasts.

"You look real nice this morning."

Callie told herself not to let those blue eyes undo her. She moved past him up the steps, then turned. "And *you* look like something a pack of dogs dragged around all night. Maybe you should put a raw steak on that bruise on your cheek."

He cast her a sidelong glance, half grinning. "Maybe I will." He walked off, and Callie watched him a moment. Lordy, they had so much to talk about. And she had no idea how to bring it all up, or if he even *wanted* it brought up.

She walked inside, catching Mrs. Bailey walking from the direction of the doorway.

"He's going to wash up and shave at the bunkhouse," Mrs. Bailey told her. "Did he have much to say?"

"No, ma'am."

"I didn't think he would. He's got some thinking to do, so my advice is not to press him about anything."

Callie carried the basket of eggs over near the stove. "I thank you for all your advice, ma'am."

"Well, I saw something there between you two when you first arrived. Young love is always a joy for old people like us to watch."

"Hmmph!" Callie grumbled. "I'm not so sure you could call it love . . . yet. So far there hasn't been anything much romantic about it."

Clara chuckled. "Honey, men have no idea what the word *romance* means. They have a whole different way of looking at such things than a woman." She set out another fry pan. "Come on over here and cook some of those eggs. Ben likes his over real easy."

"Yes, ma'am." Callie turned to helping finish breakfast. When all was ready, she went outside and clanged the dinner bell that hung at the corner of the porch. Moments later, Ben Bailey came walking from the barn, and Callie couldn't help but be amused by the sight. He was bowlegged as a frog, probably from spending more time on the back of a horse than

on his own two feet. She glanced toward the bunkhouse . . .
no sign of Chris.

She went back inside, and when Ben arrived, they all sat
down to the homemade wooden table. Mrs. Bailey prayed.
Callie thought what nice folks they were, putting them up this
way, Mrs. Bailey being so easy to talk to. Ben's men had even
taken care of Jim Fallon, saving more danger to Chris. Still,
they had a long way to go, and three more men to find.

Clara passed the biscuits, and by the time Chris came back
to the house, they were all half done eating. He nodded to
Clara.

"I apologize, Mrs. Bailey, for being late."

"Never you mind. Many's the time Mr. Bailey has had a
little problem getting up on time due to too much spirits."

Ben guffawed as he stabbed at more ham, eating as though
it were his last meal. Callie figured he probably always ate that
way, which explained his big stomach.

"Yes, sir, I don't know of a man yet who didn't relax with
a bottle of whiskey once in a while," he answered.

Callie glanced at Chris as he sat down, and her appetite left
her. Now that he was shaved and cleaned up, she was reminded
of how handsome he was. He even smelled good. She felt kind
of bad now about the bruise on his cheek, then chastised herself
for caring. He deserved a fist in the face after the way he'd
come after her like she was a dang whore. Trouble was, for
the last couple of years, that was the kind of woman he was
used to.

She looked back down at her plate. Lordy, how could she
compare to women like that? She forced herself to finish her
food, just to be mannerly, while the men talked about ranching,
and how Ben and Clara came to be here, having fled the South
years earlier, when they saw trouble coming.

Chris ate and visited as though Callie were not even there,
and a vague premonition of impending heartache began to creep
into her blood. Chris discussed buying one or two horses, and
the two men discussed ranching, something Chris had never
tried.

"Well, for an educated easterner, you've adapted well out here," Ben told Chris.

Chris shrugged. "I like it out here. I like the climate, the mountains." He poked at a piece of ham, sobering. "And the fact that a man can deal his own justice."

"Well, if a man deserves to die, he *ought* to die," Ben answered. "Out here it's still each man for himself, and land-owners are kind of masters of their domain. You do what you have to do to protect your own."

Chris nodded, swallowing the ham.

"There *is* still a great need for one thing out here," Clara spoke up. "It's just as important as having law and order."

Chris glanced at her. "What's that?"

"Teachers," she answered, a look of wise suggestion in her eyes. "More people to come here and educate our children so we don't have to send them far away for such things."

Ben waved her off, and Chris glanced at Callie, looking slightly irritated. Clara had made it apparent that Callie had told her Chris once taught school.

"Mother, you put too much emphasis on education," Ben was telling his wife. "Our sons can read and write and know enough arithmetic to figure how many cattle we have and how much we should get for them. Only reason you sent Susan off to that school in Denver is so she can learn how to dress fancy and do things she'll never need to know out here."

"I want her to have a good life, maybe meet and marry someone in Denver and live real nice," Clara answered. "And I think the boys *should* have a better education, regular schooling. And so should *their* children. Whether we like it or not, the whole West will slowly get more and more populated and settled, and the time will come when our grandchildren will need a good education to understand how to manage their ranches and do their banking and such. Isn't that right, Mr. Mercy?"

Chris leaned back in his chair with a sigh. "Yes, ma'am, I don't doubt you're right."

"Well, you think about that. Educated men like you could

do wonders making the West more civilized. Surely you don't intend to spend the rest of your life hunting killers. It's a waste of a good mind. Someday you'll have to settle and go back to what you're meant to do. That's my advice, son, for what it's worth.''

Chris grinned patiently. "Well, ma'am, I thank you, but right now I'm not ready for a settled life. I had that once, and I lost it.''

"Mother, you've got to stop puttin' your nose in where it don't belong,'' Ben told Clara. He shook his head. "Women. Always wantin' things like schools and churches and all that.''

Chris just smiled obligingly, but Callie knew damn well Clara was right, and that *Chris* knew she was right. A man like him could be of great benefit out here.

Ben changed the subject back to horses, and Callie could tell Chris was relieved. They finished eating, and Ben invited Chris outside for a smoke. The men walked out, but Chris took a minute to finish his coffee, then excused himself from the table, thanking Clara for the good breakfast.

"Callie cooked some of it herself,'' the woman answered. "She's a right good cook, that girl.'' She smiled and winked, then turned away to clean up some pans. Chris turned to Callie before going out.

"We have to talk,'' he told her.

"Yes, sir, we sure do,'' she answered.

"Come on outside after you help Mrs. Bailey clean up.''

Callie nodded, her heart pounding. What the heck was he going to tell her? She couldn't tell if he was still angry with her for coming out to the barn last night or not. He was so damned unpredictable.

She helped with the dishes while Clara babbled on about making jelly and how much she enjoyed her twice-a-year trips to Medicine Bow.

"Only chance I get to wear a nice hat and see what the latest fashions are,'' she told Callie. "My, I sure would like to see you all gussied up. You sure would make one pretty bit of temptation for Mr. Mercy.''

Callie wondered what she would think if she knew Chris had already seen her naked. "I don't know," she answered. "Do you really think I'm pretty?"

Clara glanced at her and chuckled. "My goodness, girl, don't you own a mirror? You're as pretty as a daisy wakin' up to greet the sun. And don't you think your Mr. Mercy doesn't know it."

Callie put away the last plate. "He's not *my* Mr. Mercy," she answered. "He might never be."

"Well, you have to think more positive than that, child. Go on out there and find him now. I heard him say he wanted to talk to you."

Callie removed the apron Clara had given her to wear, then straightened herself and took a deep breath, walking to the screen door to see Chris standing at the corral fence, looking over some horses. She wished her heart wouldn't pound so hard that it almost hurt.

Chris glanced back when the screen door slammed as Callie came out onto the porch. Callie saw him light a cigarette. Was he nervous too? He remained turned away and said nothing at first when she reached him. She climbed up onto the fence railing, facing the inside of the corral. Instead of meeting her gaze, Chris braced his arms on the top railing and watched the horses as he spoke.

"If we buy two horses from this bunch, which ones would you pick?" he asked her.

Callie watched the horses for a few quiet seconds. "Maybe that there buckskin with the black mane and tail and black feet. He looks strong and proud." *Like you,* she thought. She watched them a moment longer. "And the paint. She's kind of small, but she looks spirited."

He smoked quietly for a moment. "Like you?" he commented.

She smiled, not quite sure if she should take that as a compliment or not. "If you think so."

He inhaled, releasing the smoke as he spoke. "Well, for

someone so small, you do pack quite a punch. No one would argue that you're spirited.''

"I didn't mean to set a bruise on you. I just meant to let you know I'm not like that Lisa woman.''

He grinned and chuckled softly. "Lord forbid I should think that.''

Callie felt a little better but still wasn't sure what to expect from him. "You mad at me?''

He shook his head. "No.'' He still had not faced her.

"Does it hurt?''

"The bruise?''

"What the heck else do you *think* I'm talking about?''

He chuckled again. "Never mind.''

Callie took a deep breath for courage. "Did you mean everything you said last night?''

He studied the cigarette he held between his fingers for several tense seconds. "You're the one who told me your pa said whiskey makes a man speak the truth.''

Callie wanted to jump down from the fence and hug him. She fought an urge to cry from sheer joy, but she warned herself to choose her words carefully. "Well then, what do we do now?''

He turned around, this time leaning backward against the fence and looking toward the house. He still had not met her gaze. He smoked for a few more quiet seconds, then stepped out the cigarette.

"We'll be leaving here tomorrow with a crew of men who are taking cattle down to Medicine Bow, so we don't have to worry about traveling alone together.''

Callie swung around so she'd face the same direction as he. "Why is that a worry?''

He rubbed his eyes, then ran a hand through his thick hair. "You know damn well why. What's been going on is most likely the result of two lonely people who don't really know *what* the hell they want, and traveling together makes you begin to depend on each other and have feelings you can't really be sure of. We can't act on those feelings until this thing is over and we get back to a normal life.''

Callie's joy began to dwindle. "It just so happens I *am* sure of *my* feelings. If you're doubting yours, it's because you don't want to admit to them. You're just scared to love again, Chris Mercy, and I can't really blame you for that. And if you really aren't sure how you feel, you just ask yourself if, when this is over, you'll be able to drop me off in Rawlins and ride out of my life, never to see me again. Maybe you think I'm too young, but I'm not. I know one girl only fifteen years old who married a forty-year-old man, and they're happy as lovebirds. Got two kids now. So I don't want to hear age as an excuse. And I know I'm uneducated, but you said yourself that I'm smart, so you could teach me anything you think I should know. And if you want to know the truth, that last kiss you gave me last night . . . the nice one . . . it made my toes curl. So there. No sense beating around the bush about any of it. I've laid it flat-out, and I'm not ashamed to admit that if you'd been nicer to me last night and not so mean . . . well then . . . might be we'd have been out in that barn all night. I just won't tolerate meanness.''

Chris burst into a solid chuckle and walked a few feet away, putting his hands on his hips and shaking his head, laughing some more before finally turning to face her. "I've never known a woman who could speak her mind the way you do,'' he told her, still grinning the handsome grin that woke the woman in her.

He walked closer then, bracing both hands against the railing on either side of her and looking up at her, his grin fading as he spoke. "Callie Hobbs, you are beautiful and sweet and innocent, and a prize catch for any man, and that's why I don't intend to touch you again until I know, down deep in my guts, that I'm ready to let go of the hellfire that rages down inside me, the memories that make me drink like I did last night and do stupid things like I did last night. I called you out here to apologize for that, and to ask you not to force the issue of you and me. We have three more men to find and bring in . . . or kill . . . whichever way it happens. Until then, that hellfire is going to keep burning. After that . . .'' He sighed. ''I don't know. I'm not sure I even have a right to *be* happy again.'' He turned around, leaning against the fence again. ''I'll never forgive myself for being gone that night. If I had been there, I might have been able to stop it.''

''And I'll never forgive myself for staying in that wood box,'' Callie told him. ''Some things in life just . . . *are* . . . and there's no trying to figure it out, and no going back. You just have to accept them and tell yourself God had some kind of plan for those He took from us . . . and that He has plans for us too. Maybe He's the one who brought you to Rawlins so I could hire you . . . and so we'd come to love each other . . . on account of maybe each of us is what the other one needs. Does that make sense?''

He nodded slowly. ''Some.''

Callie climbed down from the fence. ''Then you think on it.'' She faced him, looking up into his blue eyes. ''I won't embarrass myself or you by carrying on like some lovestruck cow the next few weeks. I'll try to give you room to think, Chris Mercy, so's if and when you know what it is you really want, you can tell me in your own good time. If you decide to go your own way when we get back to Rawlins, it'll hurt like somebody pulling my belly right out of me bare-handed, but I'll just watch you go.'' She couldn't stop the tears that filled her eyes then. ''Because I love you enough to *let* you go.''

She turned away and walked toward the house, refusing to break down and cry in front of him. She could only pray she'd said the right things. Maybe he expected her to throw herself at him and beg him to never leave her. Damned if she'd make a fool of herself like that. She'd said her piece, and that was that. And she'd gone out to that barn last night of her own accord. The next move was up to Chris Mercy.

Chapter
Thirty-three

Chris wondered just how long he could keep the promise to himself not to touch Callie Hobbs until after finding those last three men. He could not forget the feel of her breasts, the fetching innocence of her kiss, the smell of her hair, the firm roundness of her bottom. Every part of him wanted her. He hadn't ached this way for a woman since . . .

Val had also been an innocent, so beautiful, so trusting. It was that realization that always brought his temptation to claim Callie for himself to a grinding halt. Val had trusted him, and in his mind he'd failed that trust. His little Patty had trusted her daddy, but he wasn't there for her when she needed him most.

What if he failed Callie that way? He'd have to turn his pistol on himself if that happened. He'd been tempted more than once after burying Val and Patty. How many times had he gotten drunk those first few months? How many times had he stuck the barrel of a handgun into his mouth, or pressed it against his temple? But always something had stopped him . . . that little tiny thread of hope that lingered down deep inside . . . the hope that somehow, something would happen to make him want to live again.

Maybe that something was Callie Hobbs. For some reason, that scared him, let alone the fact that he felt guilty for daring to believe he could be happy again while Val and Patty lay in their graves. They were the ones who deserved to live and be happy, not him. And if he let himself love Callie, he just might end up destroying another innocent life.

He was glad as hell for the fact that they now traveled to Medicine Bow with seven men and Ben Bailey himself. That made it easier not to think about Callie, and it prevented him from doing things he'd promised her and himself he wouldn't do until this was over.

They'd been on the trail nearly five weeks now. The days were spent herding cattle and eating dust, and they were long days that left a man too weary at night to think romantic thoughts.

Tonight it was Callie who'd offered to take a turn keeping the cattle calm after dark. He lay on his bedroll, listening to her sweet voice as she sang softly, the most common way to assure steers that everything was all right. For some reason, soft singing by the cowboys at night kept cattle from spooking.

Damn her. That was part of what he loved about her. The kid was so able at things most women either didn't know a thing about or felt they were too feminine or too "proper" to take part in. For the past week, Callie Hobbs had shown she could manage cattle as well as any cowhand. She could cook over an open fire, sleep on the hard ground without complaining, and wasn't too bad with a firearm. She was brave and cocky, and he smiled every time he thought about the way she had of speaking her mind. She was honest and good-hearted, a good cook and damn pretty. He wanted to own every part of her, kiss every part of her, taste every part of her, claim every part of her.

Over and over again he argued with himself how wrong that would be. He couldn't trust his own emotions yet, and she was right about one thing—they couldn't be more different as far as background and education. Those things didn't really have to matter though. He doubted he would ever go back to where he came from and live that life again. He was attached to this land, no matter what he decided to do with his life; and Callie *was* this land, different, exciting, rugged, bold, daring, tough, challenging—none of the things he once thought he'd want or love about a woman. And there was still a soft side to her, just waiting to be taught how to please a man . . . and he couldn't stand the thought of anyone else doing the teaching.

Damned if he wouldn't have to give in to his need of her just to be able to get a decent night's sleep. He could see that his promise to stay away from her as much as possible until they found Terrence Stowers and the other two men was not going to be easy to keep. After an hour or so of staring at the stars, he finally felt truly sleepy. He closed his eyes, listening to the peaceful sound of cattle lowing and the stirring sound of Callie singing. He thought how nice and cool the night had become, a northeast wind relieving the men from the day's blazing heat. He worried a little about Callie. The heat had been hard on all of them, and now she had to stay awake half the night. . . .

All thoughts left him as he allowed weariness to take over, but sometime later he was jarred awake by a crack of thunder. He had no idea how long he'd dozed when he awoke to mass confusion . . . more thunder . . . a rumbling sound.

He bolted upright, grabbing his six-gun from its holster, which he'd left lying beside him. A lightning bolt split the sky, and the earth literally shook with another boom of thunder, that sound mixed with the rumble of stampeding cattle. At the same time, the sky opened up with a torrent of rain.

Callie!

"Stampede!" someone yelled.

Now everyone was up and heading for the area where their horses were tethered. There was no time to saddle up. Chris joined the other men in jumping onto the bare backs of the first horses they could grab that still had bridles on them. The sky lit up with lightning again, and Chris could see the cattle were thundering off to his right. He and the other men rode after them, firing guns and shouting, trying to slow the stampede and doing what they could to keep some of the cattle together. The pouring rain and vibrating thunder made the job even more difficult, and thoughts of Callie lying somewhere under the deathly crush of cattle hooves ripped through Chris's heart.

"Callie!" he shouted.

He heard a scream and headed in that direction, yelling Callie's name again at the top of his lungs. The sky lit up again, and he spotted the paint Callie had been riding that night, one of the horses they'd bought from Ben. Just then the horse slipped in mud created instantly by the downpour. Chris saw it go down, and Callie fell off with a scream. He charged his horse to the site as part of the herd thundered closer. Callie was desperately trying to get her foot out from under her horse, who lay kicking in the mud.

Chris jumped down from his own horse and grabbed Callie under the arms, kicking at the calico mare until he was able to yank Callie's foot out from under it. By then there was no time to run, and his own horse had bolted away. Without hesitation, he shot the calico in the head to stop its kicking, then shoved Callie down against the horse's belly and threw himself on top of her.

"We're gonna die!" Callie screamed.

"Just stay down," Chris yelled in her ear as he hovered over her. "The horse might protect us. They'll jump over it!"

He covered her as best he could as the terrifying sound of thundering hooves almost instantly beat the earth all around them. Chris grunted when a hoof crashed into his back.

"Chris! Oh, God!"

"Stay still!" Chris ordered, pressing closer against the calico's belly and literally pressing Callie farther into the mud. Another hoof slammed into his right calf, and he dug his fingers into Callie's shoulder.

Finally the thundering vanished into the distance, and they lay there together in the mud, more rain soaking both of them. Chris clung tightly to Callie for a moment, almost afraid to move for fear he'd discover something was broken. When he finally relaxed a little, he moved his leg to discover it was sore as hell, but as far as he could tell, it was intact. He rose slightly on his elbows, wincing with the pain in his lower back, glad the clobbering hoof had landed on the right side and not on the wound in his left side. He looked down at Callie, noticing when lightning glared again that her hair was wet and stuck to her freckled face. She was looking up at him, her big brown eyes full of questions and terror.

"Chris, are you all right?"

"I think so."

Their gazes held for a few quiet seconds.

"You saved my life," Callie told him then. "Those cattle could have trampled you to death."

He sighed and rested his forehead against hers. "You didn't really think I'd ride off and let them turn you into part of the mud, did you?"

"I don't know. There wasn't much time to think about anything." Their faces remained close together. "You're a fast-thinking man, Mr. Mercy."

Her lips were so close.

"And you're a brave little lady, Miss Hobbs." He couldn't resist the need to kiss her then, in spite of the pain of his bruises. He covered her mouth with his own, and she responded to the kiss, moving her arms to wrap them around his neck. The kiss grew deeper . . . and deeper, until he literally groaned with the want of her. That quick moment when he thought he might end up watching her die told him all he needed to know.

"I love you, Callie," he told her, leaving her mouth to whisper the words in her ear. "I'd die for you."

"Chris," she answered in a husky whisper. "I love you too! You know I do. I'd die for you too. It makes me so happy to hear you say those words."

He found her mouth again, searching deeply, wanting to devour her. They heard voices then. Men were coming. He left her mouth again, kissing her eyes. "I have to get up. Are you hurt?"

"I don't even know for sure. You sure you're not?"

"I won't know till I get up and walk around."

"I don't want you to get up."

"I'd just as soon stay right here myself, believe me. You have no idea how hard this is." He saw her grin by the light of more lightning.

"I'm so happy, I could cry," she told him. "But you gotta get up anyway. Your gun is poking my thigh something awful."

His *gun?* He'd thrown it aside when he tackled her to the ground. He stifled the urge to laugh. She literally had no idea what was poking her thigh, nor could she possibly understand the pain it was causing him at the moment. He was glad it was dark.

He raised himself off her, realizing he'd done it now. There was no going back. He'd admitted his love for her yet again, while stone sober. He'd broken every promise he'd made to her and to himself and let this thing go too far too soon. He stood up and reached down to help her up.

"Lordy! My ankle!" she cried out.

Chris's right calf ached fiercely, but he picked her up and carried her through the mud to the chuck wagon, which now lay on its side. "We're going to find a damn mess in the morning," he told her.

Callie threw her arms around his shoulders, kissing his cheek, his neck. "I don't care! If this is what it took to make you say again how much you love me, then it doesn't matter."

Chris smiled, kneeling down to set her on the ground. "Not in front of the men," he told her. "We'll talk later. Right now we need to help Bailey clean up this mess and tomorrow we have to dry everything out and go round up the cattle. And I want to have a look at your ankle."

"Chris! That you?"

Chris recognized Ben Bailey's voice. "Yes, sir. It's Callie and I both."

"Thank God! Jeff Harper, the man helping Callie keep watch, is dead. I was afraid we'd find Callie the same way!"

"Chris shoved me down against my horse and laid over me," Callie told Ben before Chris could reply. "He saved my life! But I'm afraid we had to shoot the calico, Mr. Bailey. She slipped and fell and was hurt. We had to use her to shield ourselves."

"Well, there's not much we can do now till first light," Bailey answered. When the sky lit up again, Chris could see the man wore a yellow slicker. "Either of you two hurt?"

"Callie's horse landed on her foot," Chris answered. "Her ankle hurts pretty bad. I took a couple of hits, one in the back and one on my right thigh. I expect I'll have some pretty good bruises, but I don't think anything is broken."

"Good. Bill was hurt by a cattle horn. Sam's gonna find a lantern and light it so he can pour some whiskey in the wound and wrap it. Should be enough light for you to take a look at Callie's ankle. If you rummage through the chuck wagon, you should be able to find a few dry blankets up in the front part. Wrap her up in one. Yourself too. With those wet clothes on, you'll take a chill in this wind. I managed to grab my slicker just in time, so I'm dry." He turned his horse. "I'm going out to see if I can find a few of the cattle. One thing is sure. We'll have our work cut out for us tomorrow, so try to get what rest you can. If we manage to round up the cattle, we should be able to make Medicine Bow in about three days. Then we can hole up in the hotel and sleep in nice dry beds."

The man rode off, and someone finally lit a lantern. The rain had already let up, and men milled around, lamenting about the storm, their soaked clothes, the lost cattle, and the death of one of their own. Chris touched Callie's arm. "I'll find some blankets and try to find another lantern. Maybe I can locate our supplies and dig out some dry clothes for both of us."

Callie grasped his hand. "Thank you, Chris, for what you did, and for . . . for what you said."

He couldn't help smiling at how childlike and vulnerable she could be sometimes in spite of her tough, bold attitude. "Just be patient with me, Callie. I still have a lot of things to sort out."

"Yes, sir, I can be as patient as a coyote waiting for a mouse to come out of its hole."

Chris grinned as he stood up to go get the blankets. One of the other men called out to him then. "Hey, Chris, that remark the boss said about a hotel room . . . I know a better place to stay in Medicine Bow, and there is something there you can take to bed with you to keep you *extra* warm!"

Some of the other men laughed.

"A lot more welcome after a trail drive than just a lonely hotel room," one of the others put in.

"Shut up, you guys," someone else put in. "There's a lady present. Besides, this is no time for joking. Poor Jeff is layin' out there dead. We've got to have a buryin' come mornin'."

Everyone sobered, and when Chris started for the chuck wagon, Callie grabbed hold of his pant leg. "Chris!"

He knelt down close to her again. "What is it?"

"You won't . . . I mean . . . you wouldn't go to that place they were just talking about once we get to Medicine Bow, would you?"

He leaned closer. "No," he said softly. "Just don't let the men hear you say things like that. I'm just supposed to be the man you hired, remember? I don't want anybody thinking less of you. You're too good for that."

"Promise me you won't go there," she whispered.

He grasped her hand. "I promise." He rose again and walked to the chuck wagon to see what he could find in the wreckage. For one quick, blinding moment he stopped at the memory of hearing Callie's scream, again visited by the nightmare of wondering if Val or Patty had even been given the *chance* to scream the night they died. Even if they had, he would not have heard them. He wasn't there.

The sick feeling at the thought of it, the way he'd found them, again brought pain to his guts. What the hell had he done, telling Callie he loved her, giving her all that hope? What right did he have doing this, loving again, letting someone love him back? He walked around to the front of the chuck wagon and crawled inside to look for blankets. When he found one, he put his face into it and wept.

Chapter
Thirty-four

The first three days after the stampede, Callie spent most of her time sitting in the chuck wagon with her left leg propped up because of a painful, swollen ankle. Chris spent that time riding far and wide with several of the other men, in search of scattered cattle. Callie had a feeling he purposely volunteered for the job to stay away from her, but that was okay.

He loved her! That was all that mattered. She knew it before he said it, but he'd never said it the way he did the night of the stampede. And now she knew that she loved him more than she'd even realized. She'd never been touched so gently in her life as when he'd pulled off her boots and dressed her ankle later that night, after the men tied ropes to the chuck wagon and got it back upright. She'd changed inside the wagon and slept in it the rest of the night, and she'd never slept better. She was so full of contentment and joy. Now she knew exactly what love was, and what it meant to have her toes curl.

Chris had not said another word about love since then, nor had he even come close to talk to her. She tried not to let it worry her. After all, he'd asked her to be patient, and there was no doubt in her mind he'd been sincere that night. He just didn't want the other men to think there was anything like that between them, and he still had things to think about, memories to deal with. She trusted that what they shared was strong enough now that he wouldn't let those memories get in the way and stop him from being happy again.

After those three days she was able to ride again. Four more days led them to Medicine Bow, and Callie rode in with the rest of the men, helping guide the cattle into the holding pens designated by the owner of the railway corrals. Most of what was left of the day by then was spent counting cattle and dickering with the buyer there, who represented a slaughter-house in Chicago, that big city to the east, one of those places familiar to Chris.

Did he miss that city life? Would she fit in in a place like that? Hardly. Chris talked to the man awhile himself, and Callie's exuberance at how much he loved her began to dwindle just a little when she reminded herself how different they were. Did men say and feel things when they were alone out in the kind of wild country they'd just come from . . . things they no longer felt once they reached civilization again? No, Chris wouldn't go back on the things he'd said that night. They just had to get settled in someplace, decide when they'd leave on the Union Pacific for Salt Lake City, talk about how much they loved each other and what they would do after . . .

Lordy! She didn't want him to go after those last three men now. What if he got hurt? Or was *killed!* She couldn't go on living if that happened. There was so much to talk about. She waited with the packhorses, watched some of the cowhands go up to Chris, talking and laughing. They pointed up the street, and when Callie looked in that direction, she saw more SALOON signs than anything else. She knew the men were filling Chris in on which saloons had the best whiskey, the best gaming tables . . . the best women . . . the kind who slept with men for money.

Chris had promised he wouldn't go see any women like that, but the way he carried on with the cowhands! Would he change his mind? Women like that didn't ask for love or commitment.

They just showed a man a good time. That was one thing she didn't know how to do.

It was already dusk when Chris left the rest of them and walked over to his horse. He rode up to where Callie waited. "Let's go get you a room," he told her.

Her heart fell a little. He didn't say anything about getting himself a room. Where did *he* intend to stay? What about that kiss the night of the stampede, his words of undying love? She was afraid to ask anything about it or about what he intended to do that night. When he asked her to be patient, he hadn't said for how long, or just what degree of patience she would need.

She followed him to the hotel, thinking what a crazy mess this trip had turned into. How strange that she'd fallen in love with the stranger who had brought three murderers to Rawlins for hanging; the man with an ornery attitude; the man who killed men or brought them in to hang . . . for money. She'd almost forgotten that Christian Mercy was a bounty hunter; almost forgotten how savage he could be when pushed into it; almost forgotten how angry he made her sometimes.

Was he going to do that again? Was he planning to again become the cold, distant man afraid to love? She swallowed before speaking. "We need to talk about what we'll do next," she told him. "Are you going to find out when the next train comes through here headed for Salt Lake City?"

"We'll do that tomorrow."

We. Well, that was a start. "Fine. How's your back and your leg?"

"The leg is bruised pretty bad. I expect my back is too, but I can't see it." They rode up in front of the hotel, and Chris dismounted. He came over to help her down from her horse because of her sore ankle, and Callie felt a surge of desire at the feel of his strong hands around her waist. He didn't lower her all the way to the ground at first. Instead, he held her so that her face was even with his. "Don't ask, Callie. We'll get you a room and you'll go there without asking me a damn thing."

She frowned as he lowered her. What the heck did he mean? She wanted to scream at him that if he had a need, she'd gladly fill it, even if she wasn't ready for that. She'd manage it if it meant he wouldn't go to one of those loose women at the saloons. He wouldn't really do that, would he? He'd *promised* he wouldn't! But he'd had time to think about it, and there was that damn stubborn side of him that still didn't want to care.

She limped inside with him, and he ordered a room for her, asking that a tin tub be taken up to her room, and paying extra for someone to fill it with hot water for her so she could take a bath. He helped her up to her room then, looking around to make sure it was decent. The room was small, but the bed looked comfortable, and there was a dresser and a washstand, and rugs on the floor and a coat rack in the corner.

"I'll go get your things," he told her.

Don't ask, she reminded herself; but she wanted to scream the question at him. *Where are you staying tonight?*

He returned with her carpetbags. "I'll go put up the horses and make sure our supplies are stored safely," he told her. "You take a nice hot bath and relax. Enjoy a good night's sleep in a real bed again. After tomorrow we'll be riding a train for at least two days, which won't be the most comfortable trip. Still, it will be a hell of a lot better than that stagecoach ride up from Rawlins."

Callie sat down on the bed. "Yes, sir, it surely will be," she answered. "When should I expect you . . . in the morning?"

He just stared at her a moment. "Let's just say you won't know when to expect me. Just get some sleep and don't worry about what time you wake up."

Why! Was he going to lounge around in bed tomorrow morning with some painted lady? She looked away. "Fine." Lordy, he was unpredictable and hard to figure. How could so much joy and contentment turn to such aching frustration?

"Callie?"

She met his gaze again, still unable to read him.

"I love you. I wasn't lying about that."

Hope cast a little light on her heart. *Don't ask,* she warned herself. "I love you too, Chris Mercy. I love you high and wide as the mountains."

He grinned a little. "Get some rest." He turned. "And keep this door locked."

He closed the door, and Callie could hear him going down the stairs. She wanted to beg him to stay, wanted to demand that he tell her where he was staying. But he'd said not to ask, and so she didn't. Seemed like every time she'd blabbed at him before when he was in one of these moods, she'd made him mad, and that was the last thing she wanted to do now. Still, she wasn't going to let him keep trouncing on her this way. If he intended to go to the saloons . . .

Anger filled her aching soul, and she got up and limped over to a window, looking down into the street. Chris untied the horses and led them up the street toward the LIVERY sign. Beyond that was a bathhouse. He'd probably go there and get himself all handsome and cleaned up and smelling good for some whore. Her heart ached so, she thought it might burst, and tears filled her eyes.

"I love you, Chris Mercy, but sometimes I *hate* you!"

Frustrated, she angrily unpacked her bags and dug out her cotton nightgown, the one she'd worn that night out to the barn. Someone knocked on the door, and she opened it a crack to see a Chinese woman standing outside with a kettle of hot water. Two men stood behind her, holding a copper tub. Callie stepped aside and let them in, and the woman poured the hot water into the tub. As she left, a second Chinese woman did the same, the two women taking turns until there was enough water in the tub for Callie to bathe.

The women left her some towels and went out, and Callie locked the door and undressed. She got into the tub and lay back, wondering what Chris really thought of her naked body . . . longing to let him look at her that way again. Would she have the courage? Could she ever let him do that one thing that still terrified her?

It might never happen. He'd said he loved her. He didn't say he wanted to spend the rest of his life with her, have babies with her. A man could probably love a woman and still leave her. They were strange creatures. She might never understand them and wasn't sure anymore if she even wanted to understand. Why did they have to be so complicated?

With a scowl, she finished washing. She'd been a damn fool, that's what! Chris Mercy was not going to keep doing this to her! She got out of the tub and dried off, then put on some powder that her mother once used. She liked the smell of it. She pulled on her nightgown, then pulled the combs and pins from her hair, which she'd kept wound up under her hat again that day. She wished she had a second washtub just for her hair, and someone to pour water over it to rinse it. Since she didn't have those things, she decided she could only brush out the tangles and trail dust. She spent the next few minutes doing just that, tugging her brush through her thick tresses until all the tangles were out. She continued brushing then, until her long auburn locks shone.

She walked over to the dresser and looked at herself in the mirror above it, listening to the tinkling of piano music coming from a nearby tavern, the laughter of a woman, men shouting and laughing. The sounds reminded her of that night she'd peeked through the window to see Chris watching Lisa sing. Was he doing the same thing now with some other lady of the night?

"Chris," she whispered, looking herself over. She didn't much compare with those fancy women. Maybe he'd decided she was still too much of a kid to act on his love for her. She walked over to the bed and turned down the lantern there until it was just a dim light, then went to the window and leaned out, listening, trying to hear his voice, his laugh.

Someone knocked on her door then, scaring her a little. This town was full of wild cowhands. She went to the door, hoping it was just the Chinese women coming to take the water out of her tub. "Who is it?" she asked.

"It's me. Chris."

Callie felt like her heart had leapt right up into her throat.

She unlocked the door and opened it, just staring at him at first. "You here . . . to talk?" she asked cautiously.

"I'm here to do a lot more than that," he answered. He opened the door farther and swept her up into his arms, then kicked the door shut. "And I'm sober," he added. He carried her to the bed.

Chapter
Thirty-five

Chris yanked the covers back and moved onto the bed with Callie, pinning her down with his body weight.

"Wait!" Callie could hardly believe this. "What—what are you doing?"

He kissed her nose. "I am doing exactly what you want me to do."

"You are? I mean, how do you know what I want?"

He grinned. "Callie, are you going to fight this?"

She watched those blue eyes. He actually looked happy. "I smell whiskey on your breath."

"Two shots. That's all. Not enough to be drunk, but just enough to be honest with you."

"Honest?"

"I love you, and I want you, Callie Hobbs."

"Really?"

He kissed her eyes. "I love you enough that I don't want to hurt you. So I considered going to one of the saloons in town where there are women who will do this for a couple of bucks. Figured that way I didn't have to risk truly committing to you. God knows if I make a woman of you, I can't turn around and leave you, not a woman like you." He kissed her lips lightly. "But then I figured, what the hell? If I go to one of those women, I'll hurt you anyway. Besides that, you're the only woman I want."

"I am?"

"Yes, ma'am." He stroked her hair back and kissed her forehead. "Don't move." He sat up and pulled off his boots and socks. "By the way, I've had a bath and I shaved." He unbuttoned his shirt and pulled it off.

"Are you going to undress?" she asked, wide-eyed.

"That's the best way."

"Oh, my goodness!"

He stood up and removed his gun belt, then the belt to his denim pants. Callie noticed a scabbed hole surrounded by lingering inflammation under his left rib cage, from the bullet wound during the renegade attack. When he turned around, she saw a black bruise on his back from the stampede. Both wounds were suffered from him trying to save her neck.

He started unbuttoning his pants then, and she turned to her side. "I can't watch," she said.

She heard him chuckle, heard him removing the rest of his clothes, felt him climb in bed and pull up the covers. "Turn the lamp out," she said, curling into a ball.

"No. I want to see you, and I want you to see me." He leaned over her, kissing her cheek as he enveloped her into his arms. "Callie? Do you love me?"

"Yes, sir."

He laughed, pulling her over onto her back and pinning her under him again. "You want to know something?"

Callie kept her gaze fixed on his face, afraid to look anyplace else. "What?"

"This right here is why I love you. You're cute, you're innocent, you're sweet, you're good, and most of all, you make me laugh. You're so damned honest and forthright, you make me happy. I haven't been this happy in years, and until I met you, I hardly ever smiled, let alone laugh. Don't ever change, Callie."

She swallowed, still rather astounded at this change in him. "I'm just me. I *can't* change."

"Good." He kissed her, a lingering, deep kiss that brought fire to her blood. He moved his lips to her neck, and she stared at the ceiling.

"You sure you want this?"

He burst into a chuckle. "Callie, *I* am supposed to be asking *you* that."

"Oh."

"Do you want this?"

She studied his handsome face. "You're too handsome for me, and too refined and educated."

He shook his head, still grinning. "You are something, Callie Hobbs."

"Well, it's true."

"Maybe I think you're too pretty and sweet for me. So there. We're even."

"But you aren't just handsome. You're beautiful."

"Men aren't supposed to be beautiful."

"You are. I mean, you're perfect—your beautiful blue eyes, your face, your build, your nice hair, your nice teeth, your strong arms, the way you handle yourself . . ."

He cut her off with another kiss, reaching down to move her nightgown upward. "Do you intend to talk all the way through this?" he asked, moving his lips to her throat.

"I don't know. I'm nervous as hell. I mean, heck, I don't know a dang thing. How can I possibly please you?"

"You don't *have* to know anything. And what pleases me is the fact that you *don't* know anything."

The nightgown moved higher.

"What about you?" she asked. "Was your first time with somebody experienced?"

"Definitely. I was fifteen."

"Really? Who was she?"

He put his head down beside her and laughed into the pillow. "Callie, it doesn't *matter* now. Besides, you don't ask a man something like that."

"You don't?"

"It's just understood that men usually experiment at a young age with willing women. End of story."

"Why can't women also experiment first?"

He rolled off her and onto his back, still chuckling. "Some do, but not the proper ones."

Callie closed her eyes, refusing to look at his nakedness. "I just . . . I don't want to disappoint you."

He turned on his side, moving a hand down to rest it on her bare thigh. "Believe me, that is impossible."

"Well, it's just that . . . I *want* to please you."

"You have nothing to worry about. And you're still talking too much." He pushed her gown up to her waist, gently caressing her belly. She drew her legs up and curled into a ball against him, still refusing to look at anything but his face.

"I always talk a lot when I'm scared," she told him.

"What are you scared of? Me?"

"No. I don't know what it's like."

"You want an honest answer?"

"Yes, sir."

He moved a hand over her bare bottom, then to her belly again, and around between her thighs, sliding his hand upward so that his thumb rested against her most private place. "The truth is, sweet Callie, that the first time hurts like hell." He kissed her gently. "That's just the way it is, but then you heal, and after that it gets better." Another kiss. "And better." Another kiss. "And better, until making love is all you want to do." Another kiss. "Every night." Another kiss. "Every morning."

She gasped when he moved his fingers into her, and whatever he was doing, it made her want him to touch her more. His kisses lingered and grew deeper, his tongue searching her mouth while his fingers searched a part of her that for a time she thought she would never let any man touch. She felt on fire with the want of him, and suddenly she had no more control over herself. Christian Mercy became the master of her body, and she relaxed under his kisses and caresses, returning his kisses now, wanting him so bad, it hurt.

She ran her hands over his muscled arms, wrapped them around his strong shoulders. For several minutes she allowed him to touch and explore, and then came a surprising pulsation deep inside that made her cry out his name and kiss him wildly. She actually let him slide her nightgown all the way off, and he maneuvered himself between her legs, bending down to taste her breasts.

Callie arched up to him, wanting him to taste her, aching to please him. He licked at her breasts as though literally hungry for them, then moved his lips to her neck and whispered her name as he moved his hands under her bottom. It was then she felt it, his hardness pressing against her thigh. For a moment flashes of something ugly pervaded her mind, and she gasped and froze.

"Callie, look at me."

"I can't! I can't!" She kept her arms wrapped tightly around his neck. "I'm too scared! It's too ugly!"

"Let go, Callie. Open your eyes and look at me." He reached up and grasped her wrists, pulling her arms away. She opened her eyes to meet his gaze.

"Do you trust me?"

"Yes, sir."

"Do you love me?"

"Yes, sir."

"We're making love, Callie. It isn't something terrible and ugly. It's something natural and beautiful. That's all you have to remember."

A tear slipped down the side of her face. "Okay."

He smiled softly. "I love you, Callie Hobbs. All we have to do now is get the hard part over with so we can enjoy that love. And all *you* have to do is remember it's me doing this, Chris Mercy, the man you love and who loves you."

"Yes, sir." Callie felt his hand move down to guide himself. She squeezed her eyes shut and gasped when he entered her with one hard thrust. The size of him and the pain of it astonished her.

It was worse than she'd figured. She kept her eyes closed and her fists clenched as he moved into her over and over with rhythmic thrusts until she felt something pulsate inside her. He relaxed then, moving to her side and pulling her into his arms. Only then did it truly dawn on her that she was lying naked against an equally naked Chris Mercy.

She buried her face against his chest, and she couldn't help the tears.

"I'm sorry, Callie. I tried not to let it last too long."

"No. Don't be sorry. I'm just crying because I'm happy. You're my first man, and the only one I'll ever, ever, ever love like this."

He kissed her hair. "I intend to be your *only* man. Fact is, I checked around for a preacher before I came up here, but there isn't one in town."

Callie wiped at tears and moved back slightly to look at him. "You did?"

He pushed some of her damp hair away from her face. "You didn't think I'd do this to you without intending to marry you, did you?"

"I guess not. I mean, I hoped for that, but I wasn't sure you were ready."

He smiled softly. "I'm ready. I just thought maybe we'd wait until we reach Rawlins. You have friends there. It would be nicer for you to get married there. Is that all right with you?"

"Oh, yes, sir! I can't hardly believe you really want me to be your wife. I surely can't hold a candle to—" She stopped herself when she saw the slight change in his eyes. "I'm sorry! I didn't mean to bring that up."

He kissed her gently. "It's all right. That's what you do to me, Callie. You're the only person with whom I've been able to talk about it. That's part of the reason I love you. You're good for me. You bring out a side of me that I've kept buried for a long time."

"Will we live on my ranch in Rawlins, then?"

He sighed and pulled her closer again. "I'm not sure yet. I

have some thoughts on that, but I don't want to make any decisions until after we do what we have to do in Hanksville.''

Hanksville! She'd practically forgotten about that. "It's okay, Chris. We don't have to go there. I love you too much now to risk you getting hurt or killed.''

He stroked her hair. "We *do* have to go there, Callie. You need an end to the nightmare . . . and so do I. I just have this feeling that if we can find those men and bring them in, it will bring an end to the past for both of us.''

She kissed his chest, wishing she could talk him out of it, but she knew him well enough by then to see that was useless. "I'd die if anything happened to you, Christian Mercy.''

He moved back a little, bracing her face in his hands. "Nothing is going to happen. For now let's just enjoy the rest of the night, and maybe we'll just lie here all day tomorrow too.''

She smiled through tears. "I'd like that.''

He kissed her hungrily again, caressing her breasts, running a thumb over one nipple in a way that made her want him all over again, in spite of the pain. He moved his mouth to kiss and lick at her shoulder.

"Chris?''

"What?''

"I want to do it again. I mean, I want to do it over and over till it doesn't hurt anymore. We might as well get to the fun part quick as we can. Do you mind?''

He rose up on his elbows, meeting her gaze. "Do I *mind?*'' He burst into another chuckle and moved on top of her again. "Glad to oblige you, ma'am.''

Another deep kiss made her more relaxed again, and already she could feel his hardness against her belly. He gently moved inside her again, and although things still burned there, it wasn't as bad this time. It was a strangely sweet, pleasant kind of hurt. She found herself arching up to greet him as their kiss grew deeper. Already she could tell Chris had been right about this. It just got better and better.

Chapter Thirty-six

Callie hated leaving Medicine Bow. She would not forget this place for the rest of her life. Here was where she became a woman. Here was where Christian Mercy proposed to her. Granted, his method was rather unconventional, but she didn't mind. For two days they didn't leave that hotel room except to go eat.

She'd finally got up the courage to look at a naked man, and Chris Mercy was certainly a "splendid specimen." That was what her father used to call his best stallions. When she told that to Chris, he'd laughed again. She loved his laugh, loved being able to *make* him laugh.

She just wished things could stay like this forever, but they both knew that sooner or later they had to leave that room and get back to business. Then, finally, they could go home to Rawlins. She could hardly wait to call Chris Mercy her husband. He'd told her that in their hearts they were already married, but it would be so nice when it was real, a ring on her finger, the name of Mrs. Christian Mercy to go by.

She waited while Chris saw to it that the horses were loaded up: Breeze, Night Wind, Sundance, and Blackfoot, the buckskin with the black feet they'd bought from Ben Bailey. Poor Betsy had died trying her hardest to get Callie to safety; and Racer, the calico mare bought from Ben, had given her life to save Callie and Chris. They had left behind dead horses and dead men. Now there were three left still to find. She could only hope Chris would not be added to that number.

Chris loaded up all their gear and supplies, then came toward her carrying just the carpetbag they would keep with them for the times the train stopped long enough for people going the farthest to clean up a little. Callie drew a deep breath at the sight of him, all man, all handsome, and all hers. He wore no guns now, but soon he would have to again. Once they left Salt Lake City, they would head back into outlaw country.

"You ready?" he asked, leaning down to kiss her cheek.

"As ready as I'll ever be."

"We'll be okay, Callie."

She fought tears as she turned to board the train. She wanted to go back to that hotel room and make love again. She wouldn't mind at all making love every night and every morning. Now she understood how mating could be so pleasurable, and why women were always having babies. She sure would love to give Chris another child, a little baby for him to love and hold and be a father to again, a child who would help ease the hurt of losing his Patty.

They waited for a woman and a little girl to get on board ahead of them, and the little girl looked up at Chris and smiled, her blue eyes dancing with curiosity.

"Hi!" she said. "I'm Amanda." Blond hair stuck out from under her hat.

Chris smiled. "Well, now, Amanda is a *very* pretty name."

"Amanda, you shouldn't talk to strangers," her mother chided, herding the girl onto the train car. Callie looked up at Chris. "It's hard for you to look at little girls, isn't it?"

He sighed. "Let's just get on."

Callie went up the steps and walked down the aisle, choosing a seat next to a window. Chris took the aisle seat beside her as Callie opened the window. "It's going to be a hot one," she told Chris.

"You open that window, you might as well be prepared to be covered with soot by the time we make Bitter Creek. That's where we'll stop for the night." Chris settled into his seat with a deep sigh.

"Better covered with soot than sweating to death," Callie answered. She opened the neck of her shirt. Today she'd worn her split riding skirt again, the only "presentable" clothing she'd brought along. She hadn't packed even one dress. She wore only a clean white shirt, leaving off her vest because of the heat, and she wished she'd had a chance to clean her boots better. She smiled at the reason she hadn't had much time for preparing to leave. She'd spent most of that time in bed with Christian Mercy, and it sure was time *well* spent. She felt vigorous and excited, eager now to end this journey and get to living as Chris's wife.

"You realize, of course, that we'll be going right through Rawlins," Chris told her then.

She looked at him. "I never thought about that. We've bygosh traveled in a big circle, haven't we? Will we stop there?"

"Probably, just long enough to release passengers and take more on. We won't have time to hop off and find a preacher."

She leaned her head against his arm. "I don't want to do it that quick anyway. I want it to be nice. And I want what we have to do next to be over and done with." She frowned. "Do you realize you've never even seen me done up nice and wearing a pretty dress?"

He grinned, patting the hand she rested on his arm. "When this is over, I want you to buy the prettiest dress in town for getting married in. In fact, I want you to buy a whole new wardrobe."

"I don't want you to spend too much money."

He grinned. "Money is not an issue. Don't worry about it. In fact, I've figured out what we're going to do when we settle in Rawlins."

Callie turned in her seat to face him. "What?"

He leaned over and kissed her forehead. "We'll sell your ranch, and I intend to build you the biggest, prettiest house in Rawlins. Then I will build a school and start teaching."

"You will? Chris, that's wonderful! But it will take more than what I'd get from that run-down farm to do all that."

He squeezed her hand, laughing lightly. "Callie, I have money, more than enough, so quit worrying about it."

"Well, I'm *used* to worrying about money."

"And now you can stop. And by the way, there is something else I want to do before we do any of that. Once we're married, I want to take you to Illinois to meet my family."

She gasped. "You *do?* Oh, Chris, I'd be so nervous! What if they don't like me?"

"They can't help but like you."

"But I won't know how to act around people like that."

"What kind of people do you think they are?"

Callie waited while a conductor came by to take their tickets. The train whistle blew, and she heard the hiss of steam being released from the huge locomotive pulling them.

"They're *rich,*" she finished.

He rested his head against the back of the seat. "Not *that* rich."

"Rich is rich, and it's something I've never been."

"Well, when you marry me, you'll *be* rich then, so you won't be any different from them."

"Christian Mercy, you know what I mean!"

He squeezed her hand. "Don't worry about it. I will have married you. That certainly makes you good enough for my family, who, I might add, are just like me. They don't look down on people, so relax. And let me finish what I was telling you."

"Yes, sir. What else is there?"

He sobered, giving her no reply right away. Then he let go of her hand and took a cigarette from his vest pocket, along with a match. He struck the match and lit the cigarette, throwing the match out the window. He leaned back and smoked quietly as the train got under way.

Callie looked out the window as they left the station, again feeling sad at leaving Medicine Bow . . . and that hotel room where she'd found so much happiness. She turned to Chris then, concerned at his change of mood. "What's wrong, Chris?"

"There is one last thing I want to do after we visit my family. We'll make a honeymoon out of the whole trip, by the way, stop in Chicago. We'll go on a shopping spree for furniture for the house and clothes for you. And I'll show you around the city, take you to fine restaurants, the theater. You'll see a lot of things you've never seen before. I can't wait to watch how you react, hear what you have to say. I have no doubt you will keep me laughing through the whole trip."

"Well, I hope I *do* keep you laughing. I love your laugh, and I'm glad I've been able to make you happy again."

Chris turned to face her. "There's something more though, Callie."

There came that look again, the one of deep tragedy.

"I want to take you to New England . . . to Val's and Patty's graves," he finished.

Callie lost her own smile. "Oh, my! Do you think you *should* go there?"

"I have to. I've never been back since they were buried. I owe it to them. And it will be like . . . I don't know . . . introducing you to them . . . a way of telling them I'm okay." His eyes misted. "A last good-bye, I guess. Leaving the past, coming back here with you to start a new future, something like that."

She kissed his cheek. "If you're sure you need to do it. Actually, I think it would be good for me too. Help me understand you even better."

He put the cigarette between his lips and leaned down to open the carpetbag, fishing for something inside. He retrieved a lacy-looking metal picture frame. "When we were packing this bag for our overnight stays, I stuck this in it. I've never gone anywhere without it." He handed her the picture, and Callie drew in her breath when she looked at it. There, in a fading, brownish-hued photograph, was a handsome family . . . Chris, wearing a very expensive-looking suit . . . a woman sitting beside him, dressed in the finest dress Callie had ever seen . . . and the prettiest little girl . . .

"Oh, Chris," she said softly. "Your wife . . . she's *beautiful!* And your little girl . . ." The hair on the child in the picture was a mass of blond curls, and joy shone in her eyes. Her smile showed two deep dimples. The picture radiated a happy family. To imagine finding the woman and child in the picture raped and beaten and murdered . . . no wonder Chris had gone on a rampage of hunting down murderers and rapists. "Dear Lord," she muttered.

Chris drew deeply on his cigarette. "Yeah. I guess I should have shown that to you sooner."

"I've never seen a prettier woman, *or* child." Tears came to Callie's eyes. "It isn't fair what happened to them."

He sighed, quickly wiping at his own eyes. "Yeah, well, a lot of things in life aren't fair. It isn't fair what happened to your mother either." He took the picture, rubbing a thumb over it gently before putting it back. "I'd like to keep it on a mantel in the house we build if you don't mind."

"Of course I don't mind."

"Well, we'll have pictures taken of us too, and our children."

She smiled through tears. "I hope I can give you a whole bunch of kids," she answered. "I certainly won't mind the trying."

He smiled through tears, wiping his eyes once more. "See what I mean about you? You have a way of lifting me out of sorrow, Callie Hobbs." He leaned over and kissed her lightly. "I swear, with one remark you could pull me right out of the pits of hell if you had to." He leaned back again. "And I agree. The trying is the best part."

Callie felt a surge of desire, wondering how she was going to stand not being able to make love for the next two or three days while they traveled. She rested her head on his shoulder again, noticing that in the seat ahead of them on the left side of the aisle, little Amanda peeked around the edge of her seat, smiling at Chris again. Chris smiled and winked, and she giggled and ducked back. Then she peeked around again, this time waving. Chris waved back, and she broke into another giggle.

"Amanda!" Callie heard the girl's mother scold. "Sit still and quit bothering people."

"She's no bother, ma'am," Chris said. "If she gets to be a handful, she can come sit with us awhile. I had a little girl of my own once. I know how full of energy they can be."

The little girl peeked around again. "Where *is* your little girl, mister?"

Callie glanced at Chris, who reached across her to put out his cigarette in an ashtray built into the side of the train car.

"Is she with you?" Amanda asked.

Chris cleared his throat. "No, honey, she's not. She went to heaven to become an angel."

"An *angel?*" The child's eyes widened, and her mother looked back over her seat then, embarrassment on her face.

"I'm so sorry. She doesn't know any better."

"It's all right," Chris told her. "It's a natural question."

"Can *I* be an angel, Mommy?" the girl asked.

"You are *already* an angel," her mother answered. "Some angels live here on earth, and others live in heaven."

"Oh." Amanda turned to look at Chris again. "What's your little girl's name?"

"Patty."

Callie knew this had to be painful for Chris, but he continued to oblige the little girl's curiosity.

"Do you get to see her sometimes?"

Chris closed his eyes and sighed. "I see her in a picture. You want to see it?"

The girl whirled around. "Can I, Mommy?"

The woman looked back at Chris again. "I'm really sorry for this. My daughter fears no one, loves everybody, and is always asking questions."

Chris pushed his hat back a little. "I really don't mind. I miss my own daughter. She can come back here for a minute if it's all right with you."

The woman sighed. "All right, I guess." She leaned down

to the child. "You be a good girl, and don't be bothering those nice people too much."

"I won't!" Amanda jumped up and hurried over to Chris, nearly falling when the train car lurched sideways. Chris caught her, and the child giggled again when he whisked her up onto his lap. He leaned over to get the picture out of the carpetbag, and the little girl kissed his cheek.

"Well!" Chris exclaimed. "What a nice treat!"

The little girl laughed. "You're a nice man, and you're silly."

"I'm silly? Why do you say that?"

She just giggled more. "I don't know. You're just silly, silly, silly!"

"And you are a little clown," Chris answered, tickling her belly. She screamed and laughed again, then Chris held up the picture for her. "There. That's my little girl."

The child took on a serious look, puckering her lips as she studied the picture. "Is that lady her mommy?"

"Yes, she is."

"Is she an angel too?"

"She is. She went to heaven to be with our little girl."

"Why don't *you* go there?"

Chris laughed lightly. "Well, honey, when God is ready for me to go, then I'll go. Until then, I can't get in."

"Oh. I hope you get to go someday."

"Well, so do I."

Amanda turned to Callie. "And you too. Then you can all see each other again. I'll go there too, and I'll call you silly." She smiled, showing a row of tiny white teeth and deep dimples.

Chris laughed lightly, touching one of her blond curls. "You want to ride here on my lap for a while?"

"Can I?"

"If your mother doesn't mind."

She jumped down to go ask her mother, then ran back to climb onto his lap. "Mommy says it's okay as long as I'm good."

"Well, now, I can't believe you've ever been bad," Chris answered. "And your mommy is right. You *are* a little angel."

The child giggled again and gave Chris another kiss on the cheek. Callie's heart ached for him, and already it was easy to see what a great father he'd be . . . and surely once was.

After the train rumbled along the tracks for about an hour, the rocking of the car caused little Amanda to fall asleep, curled up against Chris's chest. Chris leaned his head back and closed his eyes, and Callie gently took the picture he still held in his hand and placed it back in the bag. When she looked back at Chris, a tear slipped out of one of his closed eyes. She laid her head on his arm and took hold of his hand. He gripped hers tightly.

Chapter
Thirty-seven

Callie wanted to suggest that she and Chris just get off the train in Rawlins and stay there; but Christian Mercy was on a mission. She knew without asking that holding little Amanda on his lap that first couple of hours only made Chris more determined. He'd sat stroking the child's soft little cheek while she slept; and when Amanda woke up and went to sit with her mother again, Chris just sat with his head back and his eyes closed, hardly speaking.

Mother and child rose to disembark at Bitter Creek, and Amanda ran back to Chris first to give him a kiss good-bye. Chris held her an extra few seconds, telling her to be a good girl. She turned to wave and smile again before getting off with her mother. Chris stayed inside while Callie left the train to use a privy behind the station. When she returned, she found Chris sitting with his head in his hands.

"You okay?"

"Sure," he answered, getting up to let her sit down. "I'm going to go check on the horses."

Callie saw the agony in his eyes when he looked at her, and she ached to do something to take away the painful memories.

She realized all she could do was love him, and maybe be the bright star in the dark recesses of his mind.

Once the train was under way again, they stayed on it all the way to Salt Lake City, riding through the night and into the next day. Callie's legs ached when they finally got off to stay in Salt Lake City the second night. Horses and supplies were unloaded and put up for the night at the depot, and the train went on without them. They would catch yet another train the following day for Green River, and then they would begin their ride to Hanksville.

The thought brought a sick feeling to Callie's stomach, and she decided to make the best of this one night of comfort she would enjoy with Chris before things got rough and dangerous again. Chris at least made that part easy, ordering a carriage to take them to the loveliest hotel Callie had ever seen. Their room was large and carpeted, the window tall and dressed with velvet curtains, "just a hint" of the kind of places where they would stay in Chicago, Chris told her. He ordered a bathtub be brought up and filled for Callie, then grabbed some clothes from their carpetbag and left without explanation, telling her to relax and bathe and just wait for him.

Curiosity consumed Callie, but she did as she was told, and sliding into hot, soapy water never felt so good. She washed her hair, and caressed her body with sweet-smelling soap, eager to share her newfound womanliness all over again with Chris. The thought of where they were going suddenly made lovemaking something more important than just desire and sexual fulfillment. Tonight it would be mating of the souls, after his sharing that picture with her, and knowing the dangers they would soon risk.

She toweled herself off and splashed on some lilac water, then pulled on her robe and ran a comb through her tangled hair until it hung smooth and wet. The hot air would dry it soon enough.

She walked to the window to watch and wait. So far Salt Lake City was the biggest town she'd ever visited, and by the pale light of dusk she watched carriages and wagons move up and down the bricked street. She'd heard stories about this place. Everyone had certainly been friendly enough, and supposedly Mormon men took several wives.

"That's sure not for me," she murmured, just then spotting a man in a black hat herding four women and several children across the street. "I'm not sharing Christian Mercy with *any* woman! He ever tries anything like that, I'll give him and her *both* what for, and drag my husband home by the ear!"

She decided that her handsome future husband would take some watching. It wasn't that she didn't trust him. It was other *women* she didn't trust. And if some of the fancy women back East who maybe knew him pretty good ever tried flirting with him, she'd clobber them, even if that *wasn't* good etiquette! Considering Chris had slept with that Lisa woman, and probably with others like her . . . and since Mormon men proved that some men just weren't happy with just one woman . . .

Lordy, Chris would never do something like that, would he? He loved her dearly. He'd told her so. But where the heck was he? She waited and watched for nearly an hour. Dusk was falling when she finally spotted him stepping across the street carrying a basket as well as a large package wrapped in brown paper. She could see that he had changed clothes. She smiled with relief that he was finally returning, and with a package! Was it something for her? She hurried to the door and waited, flinging it open when he knocked.

"Where did you go?" she asked. "I was getting worried."

He grinned, walking over to the bed and telling her to close the door. "I picked up some food so we could eat right here. Now we don't have to leave the room for the rest of the night." He set the basket on a nightstand and threw the package on the bed.

"Oh, Chris, what a good idea!" Callie hurried over to the bed. "What else did you bring?" She looked him over, clean-shaven, wearing a new blue shirt that matched his eyes, his hair trimmed. He wore a new cowhide vest over the shirt as well. "You look wonderful!"

He leaned over and kissed her. "And you look and *smell*

wonderful." He began unwrapping the package. "I bought you a couple of dresses to wear home after this is over, and new lace-up boots. Have you ever worn shoes or boots with a higher heel?"

"No!" Callie lifted the dresses. "Chris, they're beautiful! I feel like it's Christmas!" She stood up and held one in front of her. "Chris, it's a Dolly Varden dress!"

He laughed. "There, see? You *do* know fashion."

"Not really, but the few times I'd go to town I would look through a catalogue at our only clothing store and just dream. It's kind of like a Polonaise dress, but prettier. Oh, my gosh!"

She ran to look at the dress in a full-length mirror attached to a stand near the room's dresser. "How did you know what size to get?"

"I've seen you naked, remember? I had a pretty good idea. But you still should try them on to be sure before we leave here. It isn't easy finding such small sizes."

Callie blushed, holding out the chintz skirt and imagining herself wearing it. It was a beautiful mint-green color, the bodice and overskirt made of white silk, with the same mint-green color in the bordering ruffle and velvet appliquéd flowers that decorated the bodice, which was short in front and gathered into a cluster of ruffles at the back.

"Chris, you have such good taste!"

He smiled rather sadly then. "I had a good teacher. My wife was the one with good taste. She loved the best and wore the best, but there wasn't an uppety bone in her body. Val was a very generous and loving person."

Callie lost her smile, thinking how she couldn't compare to the woman she'd seen in the picture. "I guess I have a lot to learn about how to dress and all."

Chris lit a cigarette. "You'll learn. And out here it's not so important. At any rate, this stuff needs pressing. We can have that taken care of whenever you're ready to wear them. And you need hats. You will be beautiful in hats. We'll shop for those in Chicago. You also need proper underwear for dresses like that. That was one thing I was not about to shop for.

Besides, you need to try on things like that for yourself, although I wouldn't mind watching."

He smiled and winked as he drew on his cigarette.

Callie reddened and just shook her head. "I'm not sophisticated enough for dresses like this, Chris."

"Quit worrying about it. Come and look at this other dress."

She walked over to pick up the second dress, a lovely yellow gauzy cotton material with a ruffled bib.

"I figured both colors would look nice with your auburn hair," he told her.

"Chris, this was so thoughtful!"

"Just wait till we get to Chicago. This is just the beginning."

She laughed and laid the dress aside to look at the black leather dress boots, her eyes widening at their elegant style. The toe was narrow, and the heel was high. The high ankle part of the boot was made of black lace.

"Lordy, I've never worn anything like this. I'll probably fall over in them and embarrass you half to death."

Chris chuckled, tossing everything to the floor and pulling her farther onto the bed. "Stay right there." He removed his boots and socks, then his vest and shirt. "I remembered the size boots you wear from when you bought an extra pair back in Lander," he said as he continued to undress. "And by the way, I got you something else. I had to guess on it too, but I think I probably came pretty close."

"What is it?" Callie could hardly stand the wondering. He finished undressing, and Callie found herself watching, drinking in his masculinity. The scar on his right thigh and the one on his left side where that bullet had exited reminded her of the dangerous life he'd been leading . . . and the dangers still ahead. He picked up his vest from the floor and reached into its pocket, taking out a small box. He sat down on the bed then, pulling a sheet over his bottom half as he held out the box.

"This."

Callie eagerly took the box and opened it, losing her smile at what was inside, a beautiful gold wedding band, and another ring, one with . . . "Real diamonds?" she asked.

"Real diamonds. We are officially engaged, Callie Hobbs. You can wear the diamond ring, and once we're married, I'll put the wedding band on your finger and you will be my wife, if you're willing."

Her eyes teared. "If I'm *willing?* Oh, Chris, you know I am! I've never seen such a beautiful ring in my life!"

"I figured there had to be a goldsmith somewhere in this town. Took me a while to find him, but he had a pretty good display of rings. Probably needed plenty for all his wives."

Callie laughed and handed him the box. "Put it on me!"

He removed the engagement ring. "I've had plenty of chances to figure the size of your ring finger when you slept," he told her. "It's just about the size of the tip of my little finger, actually a little smaller."

The remark told Callie he'd been thinking about this quite a while. With his own strong hand he took hold of Callie's hand and slipped the ring onto her finger. It fit well, and Callie wiggled her finger, watching the diamonds sparkle. "Oh, Chris, I don't know what to say."

"You don't have to say anything. It's all in your eyes."

She sniffed, then leaned forward and threw her arms around his neck. "I love you so much! I want so much to make you happy forever."

Chris gently pushed her back on the bed. "You will, Callie. I have no doubt about it."

He met her mouth in a hungry kiss, moving a hand inside her robe and opening it, caressing her bare skin in gentle strokes that brought all her desires alive. "We'll eat afterward," he told her softly.

Callie had no objections. Fire rushed through her at the feel of his lips as they left her mouth. He kissed and licked his way over her throat, down to her breasts, relishing each one as though it were a succulent fruit, while his fingers explored secret places that belonged only to Christian Mercy. Callie was surprised at how easily she had come to be able to allow this, to share herself, body and soul, with a man. All inhibitions left her around Christian Mercy. Once he began working his magic, he became master of her entire being, and she was so full of love, she thought she might burst.

He moved down to kiss her belly, her thighs, and that part of her he owned now.

"Chris . . ." She curled up, and he moved his kisses back up her body to her neck, moving on top of her.

"There is plenty of time for you to learn all the ways there are to take pleasure in this," he told her.

"Lordy, Chris, you mean there's more?"

Chris chuckled softly, meeting her mouth again in a deep, hungry kiss. She felt as though she were melting into him, as she opened herself to him, aching to feel him inside her again. In the next moment, she languished in the glory of his rhythmic thrusts, ecstatic at being able to please him this way. He had a way of rubbing against her that brought forth a desire so intense that in moments she was groaning his name in an almost painful climax that left her breathless.

He moved his hands under her hips then, his kisses hot and searching as he thrust himself deeper, and in an even wilder rhythm. Callie still could hardly believe this was real, that Christian Mercy wanted her this way, that he'd just put an engagement ring on her finger. She dug her fingers into the hard muscle of his upper arms, when finally she felt his life surging into her, and, oh, how she prayed it would take hold! How she prayed she would give him a pretty little girl like Amanda.

He kissed her again, then kissed her eyes, back to her lips. "I love you, Callie."

She kissed him back, studying the blue eyes, the handsome face. "I've never been so happy in my whole life."

He smiled softly. "And, little lady, we are going to wash, eat, and do this again." He kissed her softly. "And again." He kissed her again. "I intend to get my fill of you before we leave here tomorrow. Making love on the hard ground isn't quite this convenient."

"I'd make love with you on a hard rock at the North Pole if that's all we had," she answered.

Chris pulled her close and laughed. "Now, that's a picture!" He rolled onto his back and pulled her on top of him, reaching up to caress her breasts. "And you're a picture right now, a beautiful picture, perfect form, that pretty hair all tumbled over your shoulders."

Callie stretched out on top of him, laying her head on his chest. "I wish tomorrow would never come," she told him.

He gently stroked her hair. "We can't stop it, Callie, and we can't turn back, not just because this is something we have to do, but because those men are very likely to find out someday that we were looking for them. Word gets around among the outlaw world, and a good many of them know all about Christian Mercy the bounty hunter. Those men could decide to turn the tables and come looking for *us*. I don't want to have to always worry about that."

Callie had never thought of it that way. "Then I guess we *don't* have a choice," she answered.

He wrapped strong arms around her. "Let's not talk about it anymore tonight." He rolled her onto her back again. "And by the way, I'm not that hungry yet."

Callie already felt the hardness returning to that part of him that was so gloriously pure man. "Neither am I."

"It's just sandwiches anyway," he said. "They'll keep." He smothered her with yet another deep, ravishing kiss, and the sweet lovemaking started all over again.

Chapter
Thirty-eight

A long day's train ride through sprawling canyons and what seemed pure desolation, broken at times by spots of yellow aspen, brought Callie and Chris to Green River after dark. Callie kept having to take deep breaths to stay calm. Circumstances were so different now. When they first left Rawlins, Christian Mercy was just a hired bounty hunter, and her own heart was so lonely and so full of hate that she didn't much care what happened to him or even to herself.

How long ago was that? A good six or eight weeks. It surely was at least July now. The burning hot weather told her so. Now the thought of Chris being hurt, maybe killed, made her feel downright sick. She wished they could have met some other way, or that she could talk him out of this. Finding those men wasn't so important to her anymore, not if it meant losing Chris. But she knew he could not totally settle again until this hell was finished. Leaving those men alive and letting them get away with what they had done would always be at the backs of their minds, a little raw, gnawing thing that would keep them from the total peace and happiness they wanted together.

She helped Chris unload their things, leaving most of the supplies at the depot to be watched, then turning the travel-weary horses out in the railroad corral so they could stretch their legs. Breeze humored them by flopping down in the sand and wiggling on his back, kicking his legs and whinnying as though realizing he was finally off that railroad car for good, or at least for a while. He got back up and shook the dirt from his mane and body, then pranced around the corral as though eager to get going.

"We'll be off soon enough, boy," Chris said.

Too soon for me, Callie thought.

Chris picked up their bag. "We'll get an early start tomorrow," he told her. He put an arm around her. "I know the man who owns the livery here. Mind sleeping in a clean stall if he has one? It's too late to try to get a room, and that way we can leave right at sunup."

"Whatever you say," Callie answered.

Chris led her along the boardwalk with his arm still around her. "Ol' Pete will likely have something cooking on the stove in his shack behind the livery. And he has a pump where we can clean up a little in the morning and a privy farther out back. No comparison to the nice hotel we left this morning, but we don't have time for those things now."

Callie walked with him to the livery, and the man named Pete, a large-muscled man with a bald head and a rather intimidating appearance, was pleasant enough as he greeted Chris with a handshake.

"Well, I see you're still alive," he told Chris.

"I do my best to stay that way," Chris answered. He introduced Callie. "She's hired me for something," he told Pete, "and we . . . uh . . . took a liking to each other, you might say. Soon as this is over, we're getting married."

Pete grinned and shook Chris's hand again. "I'll be damned! Christian Mercy getting married. If that don't beat all! It's about time you settled down, Chris."

"That's the way I see it."

Pete shook Callie's hand, and Callie feared he would break

it, his hand was so huge and solid, his grip so tight. "Congratulations, little lady! You must be right something to land the likes of this guy. First time I've ever seen him come through here smiling."

Callie moved an arm around Chris's waist. "He *needs* to smile more."

"I agree with that. Come on over here."

They followed the man to a stall filled with fresh, untouched hay. "Cleaned out this one and another one just this morning," Pete told them. "This ought to make a good bed for the night. Straw's nice and thick. No worry about touching the actual floor of the stall." He leaned close to Chris. "You ... uh ... *sharing* the stall?"

Chris laughed lightly. "Yes, we are."

Pete chuckled, putting a finger to his lips. "Your secret. Say, I've got some damn good smoked pork ribs still hangin' over an open fire out back, basted in the best tomato sauce you ever tasted. You two hungry? Sarah Jane brought me some homemade bread today, and real butter."

"Sounds good," Chris told him. "How is Sarah Jane doing?"

Pete rubbed his chin, hesitating as he glanced at Callie. "Well, good as ever—plenty busy, if you know what I mean, now that the railroad comes through here."

Chris laughed, keeping his arm around Callie. "Got some clean blankets?"

"Sure do. I'll get them and you two can fix yourselves up here, then come on out back and get somethin' to eat. Got some good whiskey too."

"Not too much for me," Chris told him. "Like I said, we're leaving out early. I don't want to start the trip with a hangover."

"Where you goin'?"

Chris sobered. "Hanksville."

Pete rubbed the back of his neck. "Hell, Chris, that's right through outlaw country."

"I am well aware of that."

"You think it's safe for the little lady?"

"No. But we've already been through a lot, and believe me, she can handle herself. Frankly, I hope she never gets too pissed at *me*."

Pete guffawed, slapping Chris on the shoulder. "I'll get the blankets." He walked out, and Callie looked up at Chris.

"Who is Sarah Jane?"

He gave her a teasing grin. "A very nice lady." He turned to spread out the hay better in the stall.

"Oh? *How* nice?"

Chris chuckled. *"Very* nice."

Callie put her hands on her hips. "You don't think about ladies like that anymore, do you? I mean, seemed like you really liked that Lisa woman."

Chris came back to her and pulled her close. "Quit calling her 'that Lisa woman.' Lisa would like you a lot. So would Sarah Jane. They would completely understand what you mean to me, and they wouldn't even think of trying to interfere. And no, I don't *think* about them . . . not in the way you mean. I think about them only as a concerned friend. Lisa is the one who helped me after that leg wound. I might have died if she hadn't been there, so you have no need to hate her . . . and no need to worry that I would give a second thought to availing her or anyone like her of their . . . uh . . . services. I have *you*, Callie Hobbs. I don't need anything more."

"I'd *clobber* any woman who even *thought* about touching you."

Chris hugged her tightly and whirled her around. "Callie, I have absolutely no doubt about that." He laughed, kissing her as he set her on her feet. "The thought of it scares the hell out of me."

Callie laughed at herself then. "You *should* be scared. You belong to *me*, Christian Mercy, and don't you ever forget it."

Pete brought the blankets then, and they hung them over the side of the stall, then left to eat some of Pete's smoked ribs. Callie decided they were the best ribs she'd ever tasted. After Chris smoked and downed a shot of whiskey, they both returned to the stable and fell onto the blanket in the stall, rubbing at full stomachs.

"Oh, my gosh, I don't think I could get back up if I *had* to," Callie said, tossing her hat aside.

Chris literally groaned, rubbing his stomach. "You aren't the only one. We'd better enjoy it. Starting tomorrow, we won't be eating anything very fancy. Half the time we won't even be able to cook because we won't want a fire that might attract attention."

Callie sighed deeply. "Do you have a plan, Chris? I don't know what to expect when we get to Hanksville."

"I'm afraid I don't either. That's the hell of it. All we can do is go there and see if Terrence Stowers and the other two are still there, then decide what the hell to do about it. I prefer to take them to Rawlins for hanging, for your sake. We might even be able to get them hanged right there in Hanksville, considering what they did. Even most outlaws won't put up with something like that. You already learned that from the way Buck and his men behaved. They were decent enough, and if Stowers had been anyplace close, they would have gone to find him and would have done him in. The important thing is for you to follow my direction, just like you did before."

They both lay on their backs, looking up at the wooden rafters of the stable. Callie grasped his hand. "It didn't matter before, you know? Now it matters."

He squeezed her hand. "I know. Whatever happens, I don't want you putting yourself in danger like you did to flush out those renegades. Understand?"

"I'll do whatever I have to do to protect you."

"It's supposed to be the other way around."

"I don't care. We'll do this together, Christian Mercy. Promise me. Don't do something stupid, like stepping in front of me to take a bullet or something."

"Oh, I'm supposed to let *you* do that?"

She shrugged. "You know what I mean."

He turned on his side, resting a hand on her stomach. "That's the problem. I *do* know what you mean, and the last thing I need is to lose you now, Callie. That *would* be the end of me. Maybe I should leave you here and go on alone.''

Callie gasped and sat up. ''Don't you *dare!* Besides, I'm the only one who can identify them.''

''I have names now, remember? And I sure as hell have a pretty good idea what they look like. A scar like Stowers has can't be hard to miss.''

''Chris Mercy, if you take off without me, I'll *follow* you, and that means I would be out there in outlaw country alone, tracking you. Is that what you want?''

''No,'' he sighed. ''I just thought I'd take a chance on suggesting you stay here. I knew you would never stand for it, but I had to give it a try.''

''Well, you can just *forget* about it.'' Callie pulled off her boots. ''Now let's get some sleep and let our stomachs settle.''

He laughed lightly and turned on his back again. ''Yes, ma'am.''

They both lay there quietly for a few minutes.

''I *can't* sleep,'' Callie finally spoke up. ''I'm too nervous.''

''We have to try,'' Chris told her.

Callie closed her eyes, fighting images of Chris being shot down right in front of her. She decided to think about things that made her happy, and she concentrated on early last night, when Chris gave her the beautiful ring she wore now. It was all still so unreal.

When she finally heard Chris's breathing turn to a rhythmic light snore, she turned on her side. God knew he'd need as much rest as he could get before they reached Hanksville. She finally dozed off herself, but somewhere deep in the night she felt herself being turned over, felt warm kisses, woke up to her denim pants and her drawers being pulled off. The lamp in the stable had gone out, and there was only dim moonlight that filtered in through an open stall next to them by which to see her handsome lover's gentle blue eyes.

''Once more, Callie,'' Chris whispered. ''Just in case it's the last time.''

"It won't be," she answered in a near whimper. "It *can't* be."

"Then we won't let it be."

He entered her softly, slowly, both of them with their shirts still on; and it was just as sweet and beautiful as if they were stretched out comfortably in a nice bed with satin sheets. They didn't need all that. All they needed was each other, and the love they shared.

Intense passion swept through Callie as again she reminded herself this truly *could* be the last time they did this.

No! God wouldn't let that happen. Surely He wouldn't. Chris deserved love and happiness now. She arched up to him in sweet abandon, wanting every inch of him, aching to please him, to show him how much she loved him. They moved in blissful rhythm, each taking and giving at the same time. Each time they did this, Callie discovered new pleasure. It was never the same, yet always fulfilling, exciting, and the most pleasurable thing she'd ever experienced.

She cried out with ecstasy when he again brought forth the deep pulsating that caused her to dig her fingers into his shoulders and accept his surging thrusts with intense desire. He groaned her name as his life surged into her, and afterward he continued to kiss her, over and over, clinging tightly to her.

"I can't lose you," he told her. "I'm sorry, Callie. I'm sorry, but I can't stop myself. I have to find those men."

"It's okay," she soothed, gently running her fingers through his hair. "I understand all of it, and it's the same for me."

He sighed, resting his face next to hers. "I just didn't expect things to turn out like this. I didn't expect to get so involved with the person I'm supposed to be working for. I sure as hell didn't expect to fall in love."

She leaned up and kissed him. "Neither did I. But now I believe this was all meant to be. And you have more healing to do than I do, Chris. It's such an awful, awful thing you found. There can't be anything worse than something like that happening to a little child, and to be your own." She traced her fingers over his lips. "I love you so much. Don't ever be sorry for anything. Even if this turns out bad, you've made me happier than I ever thought I could be. And I sure never dreamed I'd end up with a man like you loving the likes of me. You've helped heal my bad memories, and I want to help heal yours. I know part of that means finding those men, so we'll do it. With God's help, we'll do it.''

He moved away from her, pulling a blanket back over both of them. ''Sorry I woke you up like that.''

''Heck, you can wake me up anytime if it's to make love, and especially if it keeps you away from women like Lisa.''

Again her honesty made him laugh, and they fell back to sleep in each other's arms.

Chapter
Thirty-nine

"Oh, lordy, Chris."

They rode only a few miles south of Green River before coming upon the most rugged, unforgiving-looking country Callie had seen yet. It was a maze of red-rock canyons, their high walls topped by flat, rocky mesas, and, at the bottom, pure desert, hard, parched flats where only sparce scrub brush grew.

Chris shifted in his saddle and took a moment to light a cigarette. "It's hard country, Callie," he told her after taking a deep drag on the smoke. "And you'd better keep a good lookout this time for snakes. That's about the only form of life out here. That's why I stocked up on more potatoes and canned goods before we left. We might find a rabbit or two, but otherwise there's not much for food."

Callie shook her head. "It looks . . . violent."

"Like the men who occupy it."

Callie swallowed, studying dark ridges where high canyon walls blocked the sun, a maze of gullies and gulches, spiraling rocks, and from what she could see, not a drop of water in sight.

"What happens when our canteens run dry?"

"Well, believe it or not, there *is* water out there, natural springs. You just have to know where to look for them. Men who hide out here know where they are. Most others don't. That's why the law doesn't like to trail a man into this country. I know of a couple who came in here, never to return. Most think they probably just got lost and died of thirst and exposure."

"Do *you* know where the springs are?"

He took another drag on the cigarette. "Enough of them to keep us alive."

Callie rolled her eyes. "Healthy alive? Or just *barely* alive?"

Chris laughed. "Would I bring you here if I thought you'd die of thirst?"

Callie adjusted her hat to keep the sun out of her eyes. "I reckon not."

"Now, *there* is a word you have to stop using."

"What?"

"Reckon. The way you use it, it's just slang."

"What's slang?"

Chris laughed again. "Never mind. You ready to ride through these canyonlands?"

Callie sighed. "I guess I have no choice." She studied the savage land before her a moment longer. Other than a splatter of sage and junipers as far as the eye could see, everything else was red. Red soil, red rocks, red canyon walls, so much red that even the sky seemed to take on a red hue. "One thing for sure, I've seen a lot of country on this trip." She looked at Chris. "We sure have traveled a long way together, haven't we?"

Chris nodded. "Sure have. It's been a pleasure, Miss Hobbs."

"Same here, Mr. Mercy."

Chris smiled sadly. "Let's get started. If we're lucky, we can make thirty miles in one day. We just might make it to Hanksville by tomorrow night. Depends on how things go. Then, if we're *real* lucky, we'll find the men we want still there, which means we won't have to go into Robber's Roost.

That's a tricky journey, through the worst of those canyons. If something happened to me, you'd never find your way out.''

He started down a steep, rocky escarpment into land that just seemed to drop down from where they'd been for no reason at all. Callie likened it to riding down into hell and leaving the rest of the world behind. The July heat was only going to make things more unbearable. Chris rode on Blackfoot and led Night Wind behind him; Callie rode Breeze today, leading Sundance.

''What's Robber's Roost like?'' Callie asked.

''Well, getting there isn't easy,'' Chris called back to her, ''but once you're there, it's just a huge, open, flat area where there are actually a couple of ranches and a fairly large log building where men can get whiskey and food. A couple of the women who live there are actually married to outlaws.''

''I can't imagine living way out there like that. They must get awful lonely.''

''I'm sure they do.'' Once he reached the bottom, Chris slowed his horse so Callie could catch up. ''At any rate, it's a good place to graze cattle stolen in Nevada or Utah; then they take them on east and sell them in the mining camps of Colorado.''

''Seems to me like an awful hard way to make money. Why can't they just have their own ranches and live life the normal way?''

Chris shrugged. ''It's just the way some men are. They aren't made to settle anywhere. Some are brought up that way and don't know any better.''

''Well, I'm glad *you're* the settling kind.''

Chris took a last drag on his cigarette. ''Well, all the roaming around I've done the last few years, I can sometimes understand why some men never settle. But I'm tired of it, Callie. I've discovered that all the running doesn't change anything that happened. The memories go with you wherever you are.''

''Yes, sir, they do.''

Chris sighed as he crushed out his cigarette. ''From here on we'd better not talk too much. It uses energy, and the more you open your mouth, the faster it will dry out.''

"Well then, I'm in trouble, that's sure."

Chris laughed hard at the remark. "You'll learn not to talk so much when you realize your life depends on it. The other reason is that in some places along these canyons your voice echoes incredibly far. We don't need to be letting the likes of the men who lurk in these places know that we're here. Those canyons are filled with caves and places where men hole up. Some are even makeshift saloons, believe it or not."

Callie shook her head in wonder at the unusual capabilities and inventiveness of men running from the law. She kept quiet then, riding alongside Chris for mile upon mile of sun and sand, stopping only when Chris signaled they should stop and water the horses with their canteens.

Late in the day Chris led her into a deep crevasse between two high walls, where to Callie's surprise water bubbled out of the ground, feeding a stream of water that did not trail very far before drying up. They refilled their canteens at the natural spring, then let the horses drink from it. All the while Chris motioned for Callie not to speak, so she kept quiet about how exciting it was to find the little spring of water in the midst of such desolation. She was so hot, she wondered if the sun was actually frying her, and she made sure to keep her hat low to shield its light and help keep from getting more freckles.

They kept going then until it was too dark to see, sometimes dismounting and walking to relieve the horses of their weight, then changing horses so that Blackfoot would carry Callie's lighter weight for a while. By the time they stopped to sleep, Callie was glad they had made love the night before. She was so weary, it was out of the question tonight.

They tethered the horses, spread out their bedrolls, and ate just a little—raw potatoes and beans out of a can, drinking only water. Then they both collapsed on their bedrolls, speaking only a little, and in whispers, before they both became lost in much-needed sleep.

The next day brought more of the same—endless riding toward an endless horizon, sometimes forced to weave through canyons, where Chris led Callie to yet another spring. Callie knelt down and splashed some of the cold water on her face, relishing the temporary relief. She removed her hat and splashed more through her hair, then cupped her hands and took a long drink. When she rose, Chris grasped her arm and leaned close.

"Don't look around," he told her softly, "but someone is watching us."

Callie's chest tightened. "How do you know?" she whispered.

"I saw something flash in the cliffs in front of us, probably a rifle barrel. Act natural."

Callie turned around to check the horses. *Act natural?* How was she supposed to do that? She was shaking like a leaf. She led Breeze to the spring and let him drink. Chris brought Blackfoot around for the same, maneuvering the horse so he could stand next to Callie and between the horses.

"What the heck should we do?" Callie whispered.

"Water the horses and ride out. Whoever is up there, he's probably keeping watch for someone else. If we don't make any trouble, they might leave us alone. Then again, they might be eyeing our horses and supplies."

"And they might shoot us!" Callie squeaked.

Chris put a finger to her lips. "We'll walk the horses out, keeping on this side of them so they are between us and whoever is up there. Soon as we reach the open flats, mount up, then ride like hell. We'll put some distance between us and them and hope they don't bother to follow."

"They?"

"You can bet there is more than one. Once we start riding, bend over low so we're not an easy target. Most men won't shoot a good horse."

"Oh, that's nice to know," Callie answered sarcastically.

They let the other two horses drink, then began leading them out of the canyon, the sound of their hooves striking rock echoing loudly. Callie's heart beat so hard, she had trouble finding her breath. They finally made the open land, then casually mounted up.

"Let's go!" Chris said then. Riding Breeze, he whipped the

horse into a full-out gallop. Callie rode Night Wind today, and it was a good thing. He had the wind and the power to keep up, but both of them were slowed a little by Blackfoot and Sundance, who weren't quite the runners their two counterparts were. Still, Callie felt they were making damn good time, and when she looked behind her, she saw only a cloud of red dust left by their own horses.

They rode as far and for as long as Chris guessed the horses could manage, then Chris headed for a spill of rocks ahead of them. They both charged behind the rocks and dismounted, and Callie yanked her shotgun from its boot while Chris pulled out both his Winchesters. He handed one to her. "We'll wait behind these rocks to see if anyone follows," he told her. Both crouched and waited, holding the reins to the panting, lathered horses, listening, watching. Finally they heard the sound of approaching horses.

"Shit!" Chris swore. "Stay low! I'm going up in the rocks above for a better angle."

"Chris!" Callie turned to see him heading for higher ground. She cocked the spare Winchester and leveled it, supporting the barrel on top of a rock and waiting until four men appeared. She knew they could see the horses. The rock formation was not big enough to hide them. She was herself well protected by the rocks, but having to keep her rifle ready meant they could see her head.

All four men stopped. They wore long denim dusters and were well outfitted with weapons.

"Afternoon, kid," one of them said.

"State your intentions," Callie answered the man who had spoken. "If they aren't proper, I'll blow your head off!"

The man, who was tall and young, looked at the rider next to him, and both men laughed. The first man turned back to Callie. "Well, that's about as unhospitable a greeting as I've ever heard," he told her.

"That's as friendly as I intend to get. Why are you following us?"

The man looked around at the rocks above. "Speaking of us, where's the man who was with you?"

"None of your business. Be on your way and we'll be on ours. We aren't here to cause any trouble."

The man leaned forward slightly. "You *female?*"

"Yes, sir. Now get going!"

The man pushed his hat back slightly. Callie quickly glanced at the other three men, two of them middle-aged, the other young like the first. They all were dusty and needed a shave, but that was to be expected in country like this. She was covered with red dust herself. The men in front of her were otherwise dressed pretty decently; but their array of weapons told her they were accustomed to violence.

The first man leaned on his saddle horn. "Well, now, the man with you wouldn't be the law, would he?"

"No, sir, he wouldn't."

"You *runnin'* from the law?"

Callie wasn't sure how to answer. "Might be."

"Well, then, you don't have to be afraid of us. You're out here for the same reason we are. This is outlaw country, and anybody on that side of the law is welcome."

"Well, sir, the very fact that this is outlaw country is why I'm holding this rifle on you. Don't make me use it. You're awful young."

All four of them laughed. "You really know how to use that thing?" one of them asked.

"Good enough to open a hole in your belly," Callie answered. "I've heard that's a real hard way to die. Fact is, my friend and I left a man to die that way, a long way north of here, up by Hole-in-the-Wall. You ever been there?"

They looked at each other, appearing a little astonished. "Sure have," the first man answered.

One of the others lit a thin cigar. "Where you headed?"

"None of your business," Callie answered. "Just like it's none of mine where all of you are going. Just be on your way."

The first man shook his head. "I don't know, ma'am. That's

mighty fine-looking horseflesh you have there. Interested in selling those horses?''

"And *walk* out of here? Why don't you be honest and just say it out. You want our horses and supplies. Well, you can't have them, so get going!''

The young man just grinned. "Well, ma'am, I'll tell you what. I don't think you're that good of an aim. I bet that if I moved real fast, you'd miss. And if your man is up in those rocks above, well, it's damn hard for a man with a rifle higher up to hit moving targets. Besides that, there are four of us and two of you. I expect we could—''

Callie fired before he could finish. A bloody hole opened in his upper chest, and he immediately flew backward. The horses of the other three men reared and whirled. Callie tried to fire again, but the rifle jammed. She heard three shots then, cracking loudly in the thin air. Each of the other three men went down with each shot.

Callie slowly stood up. The first man had been wrong about having trouble hitting men from above. He didn't know that the man above was Christian Mercy.

The air still rang with the sound of the three shots as Chris jumped and dodged his way down out of the rocks above, running to Callie. "You all right?'' he asked frantically.

"Heck, yes! They never got off a shot.'' She set her rifle aside and hugged him around the middle. "That was some shooting, Chris. Dead on! One. Two. Three.''

He kissed her hair. "I figured you of all people could keep them talking.''

Callie grinned, breathing a sigh of relief. "Do you think that's all of them?''

"We have to hope so.''

Callie closed her eyes and hugged him tighter. "The Winchester jammed, but I wasn't scared, Chris. I knew your aim would be right. You're the best.''

He gently pulled away from her and took hold of the horses' reins. "Let's get away from here. We'll have to walk a ways. The horses are done in, so we won't make Hanksville tonight.

We'll camp somewhere away from here and ride in in the morning. That's probably best anyway. We'll be fresh and rested.''

"What about these men? The horses?"

"Their horses will find their way, smell out water. We can't arrive in Hanksville with their horses or any of their possessions. That way, when their bodies are found, no one will know who did it. They probably have friends in Hanksville. It wouldn't be good for those friends to know we're the ones who did them in. Let them wonder.''

Callie shivered with delayed reaction to what had just happened. She stared at the dead bodies sprawled on the red earth, then hurried to catch up. "Lay close to me tonight, Chris. I want to touch you all night and know you're okay." She took the reins to Blackfoot and walked along beside him.

He stopped to shove his Winchester into its boot. "Let's just hope the men we're looking for are still in Hanksville, so we can finish this once and for all.''

Callie had to walk faster to keep up.

"I'll clean that Winchester tonight and figure out why it jammed,'' Chris told her. "I want you to have it on hand tomorrow. And I'll give you an extra handgun again, just like when we went to Hole-in-the-Wall.''

"I almost wish Buck and his bunch were with us again.''

"Well, they aren't. It's just us, Callie. I wouldn't worry a bit if it was just me, but I worry about a stray bullet hitting you, if it comes to shooting. If I had to take on half the town, I could do it. Hell, I've been up against some pretty poor odds before, but I never had to worry about the woman I love being in the middle of it all. That changes things.''

"I've proven I can handle myself, Chris. I won't get in the way. Heck, it might end up you'd need me anyway.''

He stopped and looked at her. "I *do* need you, but not that way. That's just the problem. I fell in love with the woman who hired me, and now look at the fix I'm in.''

Callie studied his dusty face, streaked from sweat. "You're a hell of a man, Christian Mercy. You'll do just fine.''

He grinned, shaking his head. "Let's get the hell out of here, find a place to settle for the night where we won't be noticed. The horses need to be rubbed down, and we need some rest. We have a big day ahead of us tomorrow."

Callie swallowed back her dread. "Lordy, we sure do."

Chapter Forty

Callie thought how odd the sky looked as she and Chris headed for Hanksville. Behind them and to the west were black clouds, great bolts of lightning cutting through them. It was an almost mystic sight, for it was obvious a violent storm was going on, yet there was no sound. To the south, the direction in which they rode, the Henry Mountains were brightly lit with sunshine, and to the east the sky was pink, casting an eerie glow on the maze of hundreds of miles of rock and canyon beyond which, somewhere out there, lay Robber's Roost.

It was as though they were in the midst of peace and tranquillity, while all around them was violence. Four men lay dead north of them. Outlaws dwelled in caves and other hiding places east of them. An intense storm surrounded them. And to the south lay Hanksville . . . and its own threat of violence. But right here was only silence, except for the scuffle of their horses' hooves.

Chris did not want to exert the horses that day in any way, not merely because of their hard run late yesterday, but because they just might have to be ready to run hard again. He didn't want them winded and tired before they reached Hanksville.

The town was in sight now, and Callie breathed deeply for courage. Chris's extra Winchester rested in her rifle boot. Guns were loaded, as were ammunition belts. Chris had given her an extra belt he owned, and she wore it over her shoulder because it was too big to buckle tightly around her hips. In its holster was the extra six-gun Chris wanted her to have. She felt like they were going to war . . . and maybe they were.

She thought about those pretty dresses Chris had bought her. Would she ever get to wear them? They had fit so nicely when she'd tried them on, and she'd daydreamed about the kinds of hats she should wear with them, how she would look in them with her hair all done up fancy and some color in her cheeks and on her lips, maybe some pretty little diamond earrings decorating her ears. She'd never be as elegant as the woman in that picture Chris carried, but she sure as heck would try.

It helped to think about things like that because it helped keep her from thinking too much about Hanksville . . . and Terrence Stowers . . . seeing his face again . . . that ugly scar. What a contrast Chris was to men like that, so fine to look at, so respectful, so gentle.

She was a woman now, a full-out, flat-out woman, as able to meet Christian Mercy's needs as any woman, even the ones like Lisa. But it wasn't just her sexual awakening that made her a woman. It was the things she'd learned on this journey, the places she'd been, the way she'd learned she could be strong and brave and that she could handle herself against dangerous odds better than she thought. She was a far cry from the half-child she still was when she first left Rawlins, on her way now to becoming Mrs. Christian Mercy, the wife of a man of money and education, a man who would take her to wonderful places and teach her wonderful things.

But first . . . Hanksville. Her thoughts had drifted so much that she hardly realized until just then how close they were, only a few hundred yards now.

"We know Stowers supposedly runs a saloon here," Chris told her. "I don't doubt there is more than one in Hanksville, like any other town out here. We'll just have to go into every one of them until we find him. Be alert. Heaven only knows how many new friends he has here besides the two men you know of.'' He faced her. "You okay?"

Callie took another deep breath. "Couldn't be better."

Chris cast her a sympathetic smile, then stopped to light a cigarette before kicking Night Wind into motion again. "Let's go."

Callie urged Breeze into a faster lope to catch up, and within minutes they were riding down the main street of Hanksville, which was more of a dirt path than a street, an assortment of wooden buildings and hitching posts on either side of the street. The town was much like any other small town out west, a livery, a blacksmith, a dry goods store, no church, several saloons. Men of questionable nature hung out on the boardwalks, watching them. Some wore long dusters, some wore regular shirts and vests, some even wore suits. All wore guns, and hats pulled down far enough that it was difficult to see their faces.

They passed a sign that said just BANK. A bank? In a town habitated mostly by outlaws? She supposed outlaws needed a place to put their money same as anybody else, but it sure seemed strange. A dark-haired, dark-eyed man stood in front of the "bank," wearing a suit and looking quite spiffy. How strange, she thought. She was even more surprised to see a woman walk across the street leading a little boy by the hand. Apparently there were a few plain folk who lived here.

Chris stopped in front of a building with a sign that simply read SALOON. She wondered if anybody named their businesses here. Everything just said what it was. LIVERY, MERCHANDISE, HOTEL. Maybe no one lived long enough here to name anything. Businesses probably changed hands every few months due to death.

Now she could hear thunder. The storm was coming closer. Chris dismounted and tied Night Wind. Callie followed suit, tying Breeze to the same hitching post. They tied the packhorses then, and Callie followed Chris's movements when he pulled his Winchester from its boot. She took out the second rifle and walked up the steps with Chris, who nodded to a big-bellied man who stood just outside the swinging doors to the saloon. "Morning."

The man nodded. "Closer to noon."

"I suppose so," Chris answered. "You live around here?"

The man nodded. "I run a delivery service for the outlying ranchers. Even make runs up to Robber's Roost."

"You mind telling me who owns this saloon?"

The man looked him over. "Who wants to know?"

"I'd rather not say."

The man shrugged. "You the law?"

"No."

The man glanced inside. "Jeremy Webster is the current overseer."

Chris looked across the street at a building that read TAVERN. *Another nameless business,* Callie thought.

"How about that tavern over there? Do you know who owns it?"

"Who exactly are you lookin' for?" the stranger asked.

"Just tell me who owns it, if you know."

"You don't look to me like you have any good intentions for whoever your lookin' for, mister."

"I don't. He's a rapist and a murderer, preys on helpless women. I'll tolerate a horse thief or a cattle rustler, even a bank robber. And I'll warrant you don't mind those things either. But I don't tolerate men who rape and murder good women, and I'll bet you don't either."

The man shifted and cleared his throat. "The man who runs that tavern across the street is a big guy, ugly as sin, if you'll pardon my sayin' so. Got a big white scar down the side of his face. Calls himself Terrence."

Callie sucked in her breath. He was there! "Let's go!" she told Chris. He grabbed her arm before she could get away. "You stay right here." He looked back at the man he'd been talking to. "Is there a Mexican who hangs around with Terrence? And a younger man, real skinny, blond hair? Calls himself Penny."

The man took a thin cigar from his vest pocket. "You got a match?"

Chris took a match from his own shirt pocket and struck it against the building, lighting the man's cigar for him. The man puffed it a moment before finally answering Chris's question. "I could get myself in a lot of trouble giving you that information. You have to understand, I have to deal with these men. They trust me, and because I run supplies up to Robber's Roost, they don't mess with me or try to rob me, and they trust me in turn not to divulge names."

"Is that where the other two are? Robber's Roost?"

The man shifted again, taking another look around as though worried he was being watched. Callie stepped forward.

"Mister, we're talking about men who took turns raping my *mother!*" she told him, keeping her voice down. "A widow, and a good, hardworking woman. Then they murdered her and stole our horses and cattle! These are the kind of men even other *outlaws* won't tolerate!"

The man sighed and glanced inside the saloon again before answering. "All right. Penny generally sleeps at a whorehouse up the street. He always sleeps in, so he's probably still there. The stucco building up that way to your right. The Mexican calls himself Luis. He helps Terrence run the tavern. But he's not needed this early, so he's likely to also be at Grace's place."

Chris nodded. "Thanks." He turned.

"Hey," the man spoke up.

Chris faced him again.

"If you're not the law, then who are you?"

"It doesn't matter." He turned away again, taking Callie's arm and leading her across the street. "Stay outside," he told her.

"I have to *see* him! I have to be sure."

Chris sighed. "Just look, then. If it's him, give a nod and leave the rest to me."

"Chris—"

"*Promise* me!"

Callie shrugged. "All right."

Chris kept hold of her arm as they crossed the street, stepping around horse dung to get to the other side. The thunder was growing louder now, and Callie felt a few raindrops. Chris stopped in front of the tavern doors. "Remember what I told you."

"Yes, sir."

Their gazes held. "We lucked out finding him still here," Chris told her, "so let's get this over with."

Callie nodded, and taking a deep breath, she followed Chris inside. They scanned the room to see two men sitting at a table, smoking and drinking whiskey, one of them playing solitaire. They both looked up and stared, probably surprised to see new faces, let alone the fact that she and Chris were heavily armed. Chris led her up to the bar, and just then a man who had been doing something underneath the bar rose up.

Callie felt instant rage and a sudden plunging pain in her heart. After all this time and all her searching, she had finally found the main culprit in her mother's attack. She would never forget that nasty scar across his right cheek.

Chapter
Forty-one

"Help you?" Stowers asked, his gaze scanning Callie's bosom before looking at Chris. "What's your choice, mister?"

Chris looked at Callie. She nodded and backed away. In barely the blink of an eye, Chris's revolver was pulled and aimed at Stowers. "My choice is to take you to the nearest jail in Utah and have you manacled and sent up to Rawlins, Wyoming, to hang," he answered. "Or I can kill you now. Makes no difference to me. Which way would you prefer to die?"

Terrence's eyes widened. "What the hell are you talkin' about, mister?"

There was that deep voice Callie remembered. "He's talking about you raping and murdering my *mother!*" she answered. She cocked her rifle and leveled it at the man. "This man's a bounty hunter, and I've paid him to bring you in so's I can watch you *hang!* And I hope you die *slow.* I want to watch your face turn purple and see your feet kicking!"

Terrence stood still. "I don't know what you're talking about." He started to move a hand under the bar.

"Keep your hands where I can see them!" Chris ordered.

"Come on out from behind that bar. And I hope you have your walking boots on, because you have quite a journey ahead of you."

"The hell I do!" Terrence answered. He dived behind the bar, and at the same time Callie noticed movement at the table where the two men sat. She whirled to see one of them had a gun pulled. She fired just as Terrence appeared at the end of the bar with a shotgun in his hand.

Everything happened in a matter of two seconds. Callie's shot missed. Chris fired at Terrence, then whirled and shot the man at the table. At virtually the same time, Terrence's shotgun went off as the man crumpled to the floor. Stray pellets from the wildly fired shotgun splattered into Chris's right hip and the back of his thigh. Stumbling slightly, Chris turned and fired a second shot into Terrence, who, although wounded, was trying to rise and shoot at him again. Chris's bullet slammed into the man's face, opening a hole in his left cheek. He slumped forward and landed in an awkward position, blood quickly forming a pool under his face.

"Chris, you're hurt!"

The second man at the table charged out the door.

"Stay here!" Chris ordered Callie, running out after him.

"Chris!" Callie was not about to obey such an order. Chris was hurt. She ran out after him, knowing he would head toward the stucco whorehouse. The man who had run out of the saloon was headed that way himself. He ducked into an alley, but Chris, obviously favoring his right side but still running, kept to the main boardwalk.

"Oh, God, Chris," Callie whimpered as she followed.

Chris reached the stucco house and Callie was close behind. She could hear women screaming inside, and someone fired a shot out the front window at Chris, who ducked and jumped down from the boardwalk on the other side of the building.

"Oh, lordy!" Callie exclaimed. "Chris!" she shouted. "I'll go around back!"

"No, Callie!" he yelled back at her.

Callie refused to listen. Apparently the man in the saloon

had managed to get there and warn Penny and Luis, who just might escape out the back door. She cocked the Winchester again and charged around behind the whorehouse to see a skinny blond man climbing out a back window, apparently thinking the only person he had to worry about was Chris, out front.

Callie knew it had to be Penny climbing out the window. She raised her rifle and fired, hitting him across the top of his shoulder. Penny cried out and raised a pistol. Callie quickly fired again, this time hitting a piece of the stucco above his head. She ducked and rolled as he fired two shots back at her. She felt a sharp sting at her left calf, and she dodged behind the thick trunk of an old pine tree behind the house. She looked around to see the wounded Penny fall the rest of the way out of the window, then get up and start to run. She raised her rifle to shoot at him again, but someone else fired first, and Penny cried out and fell sideways, then collapsed.

"Chris," Callie muttered. At least he was still alive. She stepped out from behind the tree trunk. "Chris!" she called. No answer. "Oh, God! Oh, God!" she whimpered. She heard shouts from inside the house, then more screaming, more gunfire. The Mexican was the only one left. Chris must have gone inside after him. What about the man who'd run out of the tavern? He must be inside too!

Callie ran to the back door, pounding on it. No one opened it. She heard crashing sounds inside. She ran to the window where Penny had exited and she climbed inside, falling onto a bed. A wide-eyed red-haired woman stood naked in a corner.

"You stay right there!" Callie ordered, pointing her rifle at her as she got off the bed. The woman shivered and nodded. Callie ran into the main room then, where Chris and a powerfully built Mexican man were involved in a vicious fistfight. The man who had run to warn Penny and the Mexican lay dead against the wall. Callie had no idea how Chris lost his guns, but one woman stood nearby, holding his handguns, her lip bleeding; and another, who had a cut on her face, held Chris's Winchester.

Both women were so engrossed in the fight that they didn't even notice Callie. The one holding Chris's six-guns was screaming at the Mexican to "beat the hell out of him," referring to Chris. The other woman lamented at all the damage inside the house. It looked to Callie as though everything breakable was broken, and she watched with horror as Chris and the Mexican went crashing through the front door and on outside.

Chris was wounded! The Mexican was strong and mean. Frantic, Callie walked up behind the two women and laid her rifle against the back of the one holding Chris's two six-guns. "I don't have time to fool around, ladies," she told them. "That's my man out there looking to die, and I'm not gonna let it happen, so put those guns down and step outside."

The one with the six-guns turned a painted face to look at her. "Who the hell are you?"

"Name's Callie Hobbs, and that Mexican out there raped and murdered my ma. Is that the kind of trash women like you try to protect?"

The two women looked at each other, then back at Callie.

"You sure about that?" the second woman asked.

"Sure as I am that if you don't stay out of this, I'll pull this trigger," Callie answered the one she still held her rifle on. "If you happen to live, you'll sure as hell never walk again, let alone entertain men."

The woman dropped the pistols. "Hell, honey, we didn't know what was going on. All we knew is your man came charging in here like a wild man after Luis. Luis didn't have a gun, so he jumped him from behind. We managed to grab his guns and the fight was on."

Callie nudged the rifle harder. "Go on outside where I can keep an eye on *both* of you!" she ordered.

"All right! All right!" the first woman answered, grimacing at the sight of the dead man still lying against the wall as they went out. Thunder and lightning crashed all around them, and rain came down in torrents. It was as though nature had let loose its anger in an effort to match Chris's own anger as he and the Mexican wrestled wildly in an already-muddy street.

A few men gathered to watch the fight, and Callie felt sick at the sight of Chris's bloodied face. The Mexican was no better off, but Callie could not imagine how Chris could fight at all, with his right side full of shotgun pellets, enough that he had to be bleeding badly. She knew it had to be pure, burning rage that fed his energies. In spite of his wounded hip, he managed to land a hard kick to the Mexican's groin. The man buckled over. Chris reared back a hard fist then and smashed it into the Mexican's nose. Callie winced at the splintering sound, and the Mexican flew backward, his nose literally flattened and bleeding profusely. He started to rise, then wilted back to the ground, completely out.

Callie eyed the rest of the men, while a panting, bleeding Chris stumbled toward her. "Anybody tries anything, he's dead," Callie warned the rest of the men. "That Mexican raped and killed my ma, along with the one called Penny and with Terrence Stowers. We came here to make them *pay!* There's nobody else here we came to mess with, so go on about your business!"

A couple of them actually tipped their hats. "No quarrel, ma'am," one of them said. "We've got no use for men who would do something like that. We'll see that they're buried."

"There's a dead man inside too, and you'll find Terrence and one more down at Terrence's tavern," Callie added. "And one in back of the house. Penny."

A couple of them chuckled and shook their heads, heading into the house to drag out the dead man. Another walked up to Luis, bending over to feel for a pulse.

"Luis is dead too," he announced. "I don't doubt that blow sent a bone into his brain."

"Callie?" Chris panted her name as he stumbled toward her.

"I'm right here, Chris." Callie dropped the rifle and hurried to him. He grabbed her tight against himself.

"Callie, are you . . . all right?"

"I'm okay. Just a nick on my leg. Nothing big. But you're hurt bad, Chris!"

"I'll be . . . all right."

"Bring him inside," one of the prostitutes told Callie. "We've treated all kinds of wounds, from bullets to knives. We'll fix him up for you, honey."

Callie figured she didn't have much choice. Chris needed help—and fast. Both the prostitutes came to her aid, each taking a side to support Chris back into the house, while Callie picked up her rifle and hurried behind them, collecting Chris's six-guns and rifle from the floor once she got inside. The prostitutes helped Chris into one of the bedrooms, straightening the blankets and letting him lie back on the bed.

"Heat some water," one told the other. "I'll get some gauze and some towels. And find the laudanum, Brenda." The woman turned to Callie, putting an arm around her. "Don't worry, honey. He's young and strong. He'll be fine after a few days."

Callie leaned over Chris, who called her name again. "I'm right here, Chris," she answered, her eyes tearing. "It's done. We got them all. It's done, Chris. We can go home now."

He opened his eyes, and her heart ached at the sight of him. Her handsome Chris was a bloody, bruised, cut mess, but there was something in his eyes that made it all worth it, a look of peace.

"It's over," he told her. "It's all . . . out of me."

Callie leaned down and kissed his cheek. "I know, Chris. It's out of me too. We're gonna be okay, you and me."

His eyes rolled back, and he slipped into unconsciousness for several minutes. Callie helped the other two women strip off his wet clothes, and through it all he muttered Callie's name several times. Callie had to smile. This time he didn't call for Val. He called for her.

Chapter
Forty-two

Wearing an alpaca-lined, deep green velvet hooded cape over her elegant taffeta day dress, Callie shivered against the brisk, New England autumn wind as she knelt down to lay a large bouquet of flowers on Valery Mercy's grave. She felt almost guilty for being lucky enough to now share the man who was once this woman's husband. Her and Chris's trip to this very somber place had been, by contrast, the most exciting time of her life, filled with fine dining, live theater entertainment, shopping at exclusive stores, and traveling throughout the East in an elegant private train car, a far cry from the kind of traveling they'd shared in their search for Terrence Stowers.

Christian Mercy was wealthier than she'd even realized when she married him, but it sure as heck wasn't the money that mattered. She thought how she would have married him even if he were a pauper, for it was the man himself she loved, everything about him. And now she loved his family too.

Chris's older brother, Joseph, was just as handsome as Chris, and his wife was gracious and accepting. Mary spent many hours with Callie, explaining the rules of dress and etiquette for her new social standing, both women laughing at how silly some of those rules were.

Joe and his family had at once made Callie feel welcome and comfortable, and they and their three children, ranging in age from seven years to twelve, had all been caring enough to accompany Chris to this place, realizing how hard this would be for him. The brothers' reunion after so many years, knowing the horror Chris had been through, had been touching indeed, and after closing themselves off in Joe's study for several hours, Chris had emerged looking like a man much more at peace.

Joe and Mary Mercy lived in a virtual mansion on Lake Michigan near Chicago, Joe now the president of a steel mill. But like Chris, he was down to earth and seemed totally unaffected by his wealth. Callie felt warmed by the fact that Joe seemed to enjoy her still rather unrefined attitude, and when she made his brother laugh, Callie could see pride and love in Chris's eyes.

But for the moment there was no laughing. There was only this quiet moment at a grave that bore the name Valery Mercy, and beside it a stone reading Patricia Mercy, under that, "My Patty."

Chris stared at the graves, and Callie thought how utterly handsome he looked wearing a silk suit and woolen overcoat, such a far cry from the Chris who wore six-guns and leather vests and dusty boots.

One thing Chris had refused to do when they came here was go back to the home he'd shared with his first family, the home where all the horror had taken place. He had no idea what had happened to it or its contents, figured the state had probably taken it over by then. Maybe it was just sitting and going to ruin. It didn't matter. He could never step foot in it again.

Soon they would go home to Rawlins and build a new home, the fanciest house in Wyoming, Callie thought, at least by the way Chris described what he wanted to build for her. It all seemed so unreal, but the graves before them were very real. She laid another bouquet of flowers on Patty's grave, then rose, grasping Chris's hand.

He took a deep breath and swallowed before speaking. "I . . . uh . . . haven't been back here since they were buried," he told her. "I didn't want to admit they were really gone. Fact is, I left right after prayers. I didn't want to see my little Patty's coffin being . . . lowered into the ground . . . all that sweetness . . . that bright smile . . ."

His voice broke, and Callie moved an arm around him. Joe stood on the other side of him and moved an arm around Chris's shoulders.

"What you have to realize, Chris, is that your little girl has been with you every day since she lost her life," Joe told him. "How in heck do you think you survived everything, especially all the times you've been shot at? You have a little angel watching over you, and she's perfectly happy where she is."

Chris wiped at silent tears and sniffed. "I told another little girl that once . . . just a little girl who rode a train with us and . . . uh . . . took a liking to me. I told her I had a little girl too . . . and that she was an angel now."

"You know she is, Chris," Callie told him.

He turned and folded her into his arms. "She was so little," he whispered. She felt him tremble, and her hood fell back as he wept into her hair. Joe and Mary and their children, who Callie thought were remarkably well mannered, surrounded them, also embracing Chris, and it was several minutes before they were all able to let go. Chris pulled a linen handkerchief from a pocket inside his overcoat and wiped his eyes, then pulled Callie in front of him, facing the graves. He moved his arms around her.

"Thanks for coming here."

"I'm *glad* we came, Chris. You made the right decision. You've come full circle, and now you can go on with something new. They would understand."

He sighed deeply and they stood there several more minutes before finally turning away from the graves.

"Let's go home," Chris said, his voice strained. He put an arm around Callie, the other around Joe's shoulders. "I expect you and the family to come to Rawlins sometime," he told his brother. "You can take the train all the way out, so you have no excuses."

"We will definitely do that. Let us know when your home is finished, and we will all come out and see it," Joe answered. "Besides, it will be fun getting a look at the Wild West. Some of the stories you have told sound like the dime novels we read here in the East about what things are like out there. And the Outlaw Trail—you two sure have some memories to share."

"I can't believe how brave you are," Mary told Callie. "Riding through wild country like that on horseback, wearing pants, shooting at outlaws!"

Callie smiled as they all climbed into the fancy three-seater carriage Joe had rented for them. "I had Chris with me," she answered. "A woman can't be much safer than that. You ought to see how fast he can whip out a gun and give a man what for. I reckon . . . I mean . . . I expect he's as good as there is. Fact is, most outlaws must shake in their boots when they hear Christian Mercy is looking for them."

Joe and Mary laughed, and Chris just shook his head. He sat down facing Callie, and they were off. After a few minutes Callie looked at Mary questioningly. Should she tell Chris the good news? Mary nodded.

"Now would be a good time, Callie," Mary told her.

Chris frowned. "What's she talking about?" he asked his wife.

Callie reddened a little and looked back at Mary. "You sure it's okay to tell him in front of everybody?"

"Definitely," Mary replied.

Callie took a deep breath and faced Chris. "Okay." She reached out and took his hands. "I know this is true, because Mary and I talked about it, and she knows . . . and she took me to see her doctor back in Chicago before we left."

"Her doctor? You okay?" Chris asked.

"I'm *more* than okay, Mr. Mercy. I am carrying a child . . . *your* child."

Callie waited for his reaction. At first he showed quiet surprise, and then a look of absolute worship came into those blue eyes. "You're *really* sure?"

"Yes, sir. I hope it's a little girl. I'd like to give you another little girl, Chris. I mean, I want to give you sons too, but I'd be right happy if the first one was a girl. I'm so excited! A *baby*, Chris! You be sure to build plenty of bedrooms in that house we're building, because we'll need all of them. And I—"

"Callie!" he interrupted.

She frowned. "What?"

"I swear to God I never knew anybody who could talk so much during the most important moments of her life."

Everybody laughed, and Callie thought about that first time they'd made love. *Are you going to talk all the way through this?* Chris had asked. Her eyes teared with happiness. "It's mostly when I'm scared or nervous," she explained. "I mean, heck, I've never had a baby before!"

Chris laughed more, leaning across to kiss her cheek and to whisper in her ear. "It's kind of like that first time you make love—hurts like hell, but it's damn well worth it."

Callie laughed, glancing over his shoulder then at the gravesite. She drew in her breath but quickly covered her surprise, not wanting to upset Chris. He kissed her cheek again, and she smiled at him, deciding not to tell him what she'd just seen. She could swear that for one quick moment she saw a little girl standing by that grave, smiling and waving. She looked again, but the little girl was gone.

> *Across the gateway of my heart*
> *I wrote, "No thoroughfare,"*
> *But love came laughing by, and cried,*
> *"I enter everywhere."*

> —Herbert Shipman

Please turn the page
for an exciting preview of
Mystic Visions—another exciting story by Rosanne Bittner,
an April 2000 hardcover release from Forge Publishing.

Chapter One

The Month of Making Fat
June, 1836

Emerging from swirling clouds, warriors rode out of the sky toward Buffalo Dreamer. Their bodies glimmered a ghostly white. Coup feathers and quilled ornaments decorated their hair. Colorful quills adorned quivers, lance covers, leggings, moccasins, and armbands. Each man wore a bone hairpipe breastplate tied to his otherwise naked chest. Some wore bear-claw necklaces. Their faces were painted black, making the whites of their eyes seem to glow an eerie white.

Buffalo Dreamer watched, astounded, afraid. Buffalo-hide war shields hung at the sides of the warriors' painted horses, the shields decorated with hand-drawn pictures of personal spirit guides: eagles, horses, wolves, bears, birds, beavers, suns, stars, lightning bolts.

As they charged forward in thundering glory, the riders' long, black hair trailed in the wind. Eagles circled above them like sentinels. The hooves of galloping warhorses rumbled like thunder, but even though the warriors' mouths were open as though shouting war cries, they made no sound.

Buffalo Dreamer tried to run, but she could not move. Sod sprayed in all directions as panting steeds charged past her, determination on the faces of the riders, who stared straight ahead as though they did not see her. Now she could see they were Lakota, but men of another Nation rode with them. Shihenna, those the white man called Cheyenne.

Suddenly the terrain changed, and Buffalo Dreamer found herself standing on a ridge, looking down at many white men wearing blue coats. More Lakota and Cheyenne rode out of the sky, until they numbered in the thousands. The fierce warriors surrounded the men in blue coats, circling, killing, until the white men were pounded into the earth and disappeared in a pool of blood. The warriors rode back into the clouds, carrying scalps and sabers, their eyes gleaming with victory. Many now wore the blue coats, taken from the bodies of the dead white men.

The clouds swirled around and engulfed them, then fell to the ground and took the form of a white buffalo. The sacred beast stared at Buffalo Dreamer, its eyes bright red. Red tears of blood trickled down the white hairs of its face.

"Beginning of the end," it said. "When next I appear to you, I will die. Eat of my heart, and keep my robe with you always for protection. And beware of the men in blue coats."

Buffalo Dreamer awoke with a gasp and sat up. Taking a moment to gather her thoughts, she was almost startled to find herself in her own tepee. Big Little Boy, her two-year-old son, still slept quietly beside her.

After hearing the thundering hooves of the warriors' horses, everything seemed too quiet, and Buffalo Dreamer found it difficult to remove herself from the very real dream she'd just experienced. She shivered, for her dreams carried great significance. Though only nineteen summers in age, she was considered a holy woman by the Lakota. In her medicine bag she carried the hairs of her spirit guide, the white buffalo. Among all living Lakota, she alone had seen and touched the sacred beast.

She pulled a wolfskin shawl around her naked body and looked at her husband, who slept soundly beside her. Because Rising Eagle was a man of vision and possessed great spiritual power, she knew she must tell him about her dream. She watched him quietly for a moment longer, hating to disturb him. In sleep he appeared just a common man, peaceful, calm. Awake, no man could match him in strength and bravery, in hunting and raiding. He'd even fought the great humpbacked bear to win her hand in marriage, for her father had demanded the hide of a grizzly as part of the price for marrying her. Rising Eagle still bore scars on his throat, chest, and back from his struggle with the fearsome beast.

Other scars spoke of Rising Eagle's prowess, a deep scar on his left calf from a battle with Crow warriors; a narrow white scar ran from above his left eye, over his nose, and across his right cheek, making him appear fierce and intimidating. He had sacrificed his flesh more than once at the annual Sun Dance. And twice *Wakan-Tanka*'s messenger, the Feathered One, had spoken to Rising Eagle in a vision, making Rising Eagle a highly honored man among the Lakota, one whose prayers were heard beyond the highest clouds. No other Lakota man had ever seen or spoken with the Feathered One; and so, at twenty-eight summers, Rising Eagle already claimed the status of *naca*, a very important leader among the Oglala and the entire Lakota Nation. Red hands painted on the rumps of Rising Eagle's most prized horses depicted his many wounds suffered at the hands of the enemy. Black hands represented the number of enemy warriors killed.

Buffalo Dreamer touched his shoulder. "Rising Eagle," she whispered.

He started awake, frowning at being disturbed. "What is wrong?"

"I had a dream," Buffalo Dreamer said softly. She still

expected to hear the thundering of horses' hooves go charging through the Oglala camp. "I saw the blue coats again."

Rising Eagle rubbed his eyes as he sat up to face her, concern in his eyes. "Tell me."

Buffalo Dreamer explained what she saw in her dream. "It is surely an omen. When you saw the Feathered One in your vision at Medicine Mountain, he warned us of the *wasicus*. I think it is those who wear the blue coats we must fear the most, more than any enemy we have now."

Rising Eagle lay back down. "You said that in the dream the warriors destroyed those who wore the blue coats. Surely that is a sign that there is nothing to fear from them."

Buffalo Dreamer pulled her knees up and wrapped her arms around them. "But this time the sacred white also appeared, and it told me to beware of men in blue coats. When the warriors disappeared into the clouds, it said, 'Beginning of the end.' You know that this is not the first time I have dreamed about the men in blue coats."

Rising Eagle reached up and teasingly yanked at her hair. "Lie down, woman. I enjoy lying beside you in the early hours, when the camp is still quiet."

Buffalo Dreamer obeyed. "There is more." She told her husband about the words of the white buffalo, that when she saw it again, she must eat of its heart.

Rising Eagle breathed a long sigh, then turned on his side and ran a hand over her nakedness. "I will speak with Runs With The Deer about your dream. My uncle is wise in his old age. We must decide what to do about the men in blue coats when finally we see them in life."

Buffalo Dreamer traced her fingers along his firm jawline. "When I have a dream that frightens me, it is good to wake up to the safety of your strong arms. I know that with you by my side, nothing can harm me, not even the blue coats." She watched the love sparkle in his handsome dark eyes. A vision had led him to her, a man she'd never before set eyes on. Now she loved him beyond her own life.

"I would die for you, and for my sons," he said softly.

Buffalo Dreamer smiled. He said "sons," not son. He counted Never Sleeps, their adopted son, the same as Big Little Boy, even though Never Sleeps bore no blood relationship to them.

"Never Sleeps might as well belong to my mother," she replied. "Since she agreed to care for him while I still nursed Big Little Boy, she came to love him like her own son, the son she was never able to bear."

Rising Eagle grinned. "Never Sleeps has been good for Tall Woman, and also for your father. Every man wants a son. Since Never Sleeps has no uncle to teach him the warrior way, I asked Looking Horse to train him."

Buffalo Dreamer drew in her breath with joy. "I know my father will be happy and honored to lead our son to manhood. And my mother will also be happy."

Rising Eagle moved on top of her, laughing lightly. "Looking Horse often jokes that Never Sleeps is in his tepee so often that he cannot enjoy your mother's company at night. Often she takes Never Sleeps to bed with her so the child can sleep close to her." He leaned down and licked her neck. "There is, however, nothing between you and me right now, Buffalo Dreamer. I wish to enjoy *you* this moment."

He moved his mouth to lick and taste her lips, and Buffalo Dreamer tasted his in return. They did not know what to call this touching of lips and tongues, but they had discovered once, during lovemaking, that it was very pleasant. It usually led to the exploring of more secret places. She had only recently stopped nursing Big Little Boy, and so they had renewed their lovemaking only a few days before. Passions still ran high.

Rising Eagle caressed her breasts, her belly, and private places that had always belonged only to him. She breathed deeply with the want of him, enjoyed the scent of him. Soon she felt the pleasant, erotic pulse that made her ache to be filled with this man who first taught her the glory and pleasure of mating.

"I need you, my husband."

Rising Eagle mounted her, grasping her hips and thrusting his most virile self into her with movements that made her groan with pleasure. For the moment, Buffalo Dreamer forgot about her strange dream. All that mattered was the ecstasy of mating with this most honored warrior. For many months after first marrying him, she'd refused his advances. Now all she could think about was the pleasure she'd missed by being so stubborn.

They moved in sweet rhythm, and Rising Eagle rose to his knees, moving even deeper and faster, the look of a conquering warrior in his eyes. Finally Buffalo Dreamer felt a rush of life pour into her, and Rising Eagle groaned in his own pleasure. He held himself deep inside her a moment before pulling away and lying down next to her again.

The morning sun began to brighten the inside of the tepee then, and they lay there a moment longer, each lost in his and her own thoughts, until a small voice broke the early morning quiet.

"*Ate.*"

Buffalo Dreamer turned at her son's call to his father. Big Little Boy was awake and watching them. She thought how the boy truly fit his name. The husky child walked sooner than others his age, and he was a bundle of energy, always ready for mischief. Once he ran into the nearby river and was caught by Buffalo Dreamer just in time before he surely would have drowned. All the Oglala took great joy in his antics, everyone agreeing that Big Little Boy was definitely his father's son when it came to fearing nothing.

Rising Eagle sat up and gave Big Little Boy a frown in mock scolding. "You are awake too soon, my son."

A naked Big Little Boy giggled and jumped up. He ran out, and Rising Eagle shook his head. "It is a good thing the weather has warmed." He reached for his breechcloth and rose, tying it on. "I will catch him for you this time. You can stay here and dress. I will wash myself in the river."

He ducked out of the tepee, and Buffalo Dreamer lay still,

feeling pleasantly happy, until suddenly a flash of apprehension moved through her. She sat up, whispering Big Little Boy's name, deciding to hurriedly wash and dress. Perhaps it was just a reaction to her still vivid dream, but something felt very wrong.

Chapter Two

Rising Eagle chased Big Little Boy into tall grass beyond the camp, where he caught the child urinating.

"You must do this farther away from camp," Rising Eagle scolded. He leaned down to grab his son, teasingly allowing Big Little Boy to scamper off again. The boy laughed with glee, and Rising Eagle smiled at the child's excitement in thinking he could outrun his father. He shook his head and took his time following, allowing his son to play his game of tag. After all, it was not too soon for the boy to begin practicing hiding from the enemy.

Rising Eagle stopped to also urinate, then casually traced the pathway of trampled, broken spring grass left by Big Little Boy.

"So!" he shouted. "You think you can hide from me!" He heard another giggle. He noticed the pathway led toward thicker brush and trees that bordered the river, and he felt a sudden alarm. Later in the summer the river near where they were camped would be shallow and sandy, but heavy spring rains, mixed with snowmelt from the mountains far to the west, had caused it to swell far beyond its banks.

"My son!" he shouted. "You know you are not to go near the river! You will cut your feet running into the tangle of brush there, and you must not go into the water!"

Somewhere deep in the heavier brush he heard more laughter, then a light shriek. It sounded like a normal child's shout of excitement, yet something about it made him wary.

"Big Little Boy!" he yelled, but there came no reply. He did, however, hear a loud splashing sound. He began running, ignoring the sticks and stones that gouged his own bare feet. He reached the north riverbank, but Big Little Boy was now-where in sight. Again he called for him. He heard voices behind him then and realized his shouts of alarm had disturbed the rest of the camp. He ran alongside the riverbank, desperately searching the rushing water. He saw nothing, but as he ran farther, he spotted a lance stuck in the ground on the opposite bank.

A new dread charged through him when he looked down to see fresh hoofprints in the soft sand along the riverbank. No Oglala horses had grazed in this area since making camp, and none were in sight now. He looked across the river at the lance, then hurriedly waded into the chilly water. Worry obliterated all sensation of cold.

My son! he thought. *Not my only true son!* He swam toward the opposite bank, still hearing voices somewhere behind him. He heard Buffalo Dreamer scream her son's name.

Fighting the strong current, he headed toward where the lance was stuck in the ground. The rushing water slammed him against a boulder, literally knocking the breath out of him. He clung to the cold, slippery rock until his breath returned, then struggled to the opposite bank. He crawled out and onto the sandy ground, where he saw moccasin prints. Staying low, he studied them closely, and he knew from their shape that the prints did not belong to the Oglala, nor any other Sioux band.

After scanning the immediate area, he rose and walked over to the lance. He yanked it from the ground and studied the beaded edge of the buffalo hide wrapped around the upper half. The Oglala had only recently begun trading for the white man's colorful beads. No Lakota man yet decorated his lance with beads but only with quills. One other tribe, however, now traded frequently with the *wasicu,* and he knew the design of his most hated enemy.

"Pawnee!" he growled. The surrounding trampled grass was an obvious sign that several men had been hiding there. A deep rage began to swell in his soul.

"Rising Eagle!" Buffalo Dreamer shouted from the opposite bank. "Where is our son?"

Rising Eagle's gaze fell upon a wide pathway left by many horses. He turned to see the look of terror on Buffalo Dreamer's face, and it made his heart ache. He held up the enemy's lance.

"Pawnee!" he shouted. "They have taken our son!"

AUTHOR'S NOTE

I hope you enjoyed *Love's Bounty*. For information about the many other books I have written about America's Old West, send an SASE to me at P.O. Box 1044, Coloma, Michigan 49038, or check out my Web site at www.parrett.net/~bittner. Happy reading!

Rosanne Bittner